Praise for Ali Vali

One More Chance

"This was an amazing book by Vali…complex and multi-layered (both characters and plot)."— *Danielle Kimerer, Librarian (Nevins Memorial Library, Massachusetts)*

Face the Music

"This is a typical Ali Vali romance with strong characters, a beautiful setting (Nashville, Tennessee), and an enemies-to-lovers style tale. The two main characters are beautiful, strong-willed, and easy to fall in love with. The romance between them is steamy, and so are the sex scenes."—*Rainbow Reflections*

The Inheritance

"I love a good story that makes me laugh and cry, and this one did that a lot for me. I would step back into this world any time."—*Kat Adams, Bookseller (QBD Books, Australia)*

Double-Crossed

"[T]here aren't too many lesfic books like *Double-Crossed* and it is refreshing to see an author like Vali continue to churn out books like these. Excellent crime thriller."—*Colleen Corgel, Librarian, Queens Borough Public Library*

"For all of us die-hard Ali Vali / Cain Casey fans, this is the beginning of a great new series…There is violence in this book, and lots of killing, but there is also romance, love, and the beginning of a great new reading adventure. I can't wait to read more of this intriguing story." —*Rainbow Reflections*

Stormy

Stormy Seas "is one book that adven
Reflections

Answering .

Answering the Call "is a brilliant cop-and-killer story…The crime story is tight and the love story is fantastic."—*Best Lesbian Erotica*

Lammy Finalist *Calling the Dead*

"So many writers set stories in New Orleans, but Ali Vali's mystery novels have the authenticity that only a real Big Easy resident could bring. Set six months after Hurricane Katrina has devastated the city, a lesbian detective is still battling demons when a body turns up behind one of the city's famous eateries. What follows makes for a classic lesbian murder yarn."—*Curve Magazine*

Beauty and the Boss

"The story gripped me from the first page…Vali's writing style is lovely—it's clean, sharp, no wasted words, and it flows beautifully as a result. Highly recommended!"—*Rainbow Book Reviews*

Balance of Forces: Toujours Ici

"A stunning addition to the vampire legend, *Balance of Forces: Toujour Ici* is one that stands apart from the rest."—*Bibliophilic Book Blog*

Beneath the Waves

"The premise…was brilliantly constructed…skillfully written and the imagination that went into it was fantastic…A wonderful passionate love story with a great mystery."—*Inked Rainbow Reads*

Second Season

"The issues are realistic and center around the universal factors of love, jealousy, betrayal, and doing the right thing and are constantly woven into the fabric of the story. We rated this well written social commentary through the use of fiction our max five hearts."—*Heartland Reviews*

Carly's Sound

"*Carly's Sound* is a great romance, with some wonderfully hot sex, but it is more than that. It is also the tale of a woman rising from the ashes of grief and finding new love and a new life. Vali has surrounded Julia and Poppy with a cast of great supporting characters, making this an extremely satisfying read."—*Just About Write*

Praise for the Cain Casey Saga

The Devil's Due

"A Night Owl Reviews Top Pick: Cain Casey is the kind of person you aspire to be even though some consider her a criminal. She's loyal, very protective of those she loves, honorable, big on preserving her family legacy and loves her family greatly. *The Devil's Due* is a book I highly recommend and well worth the wait we all suffered through. I cannot wait for the next book in the series to come out."
—*Night Owl Reviews*

The Devil Be Damned

"Ali Vali excels at creating strong, romantic characters along with her fast-paced, sophisticated plots. Her setting, New Orleans, provides just the right blend of immigrants from Mexico, South America, and Cuba, along with a city steeped in traditions."—*Just About Write*

Deal with the Devil

"Ali Vali has given her fans another thick, rich thriller…*Deal With the Devil* has wonderful love stories, great sex, and an ample supply of humor. It is an exciting, page-turning read that leaves her readers eagerly awaiting the next book in the series."—*Just About Write*

The Devil Unleashed

"Fast-paced action scenes, intriguing character revelations, and a refreshing approach to the romance thriller genre all make for an enjoyable reading experience in the Big Easy…*The Devil Unleashed* is an engrossing reading experience."—*Midwest Book Review*

The Devil Inside

"*The Devil Inside* is the first of what promises to be a very exciting series…While telling an exciting story that grips the reader, Vali has also fully fleshed out her heroes and villains. *The Devil Inside* is that rarity: a fascinating crime novel which includes a tender love story and leaves the reader with a cliffhanger ending."—*MegaScene*

By the Author

Carly's Sound

Second Season

Love Match

The Dragon Tree Legacy

The Romance Vote

Hell Fire Club in Girls with Guns

Beneath the Waves

Beauty and the Boss

Blue Skies

Stormy Seas

The Inheritance

Face the Music

On the Rocks in Still Not Over You

One More Chance

A Woman to Treasure

Call Series

Calling the Dead

Answering the Call

Forces Series

Balance of Forces: Toujours Ici

Battle of Forces: Sera Toujours

Force of Fire: Toujours a Vous

Vegas Nights

Double-Crossed

The Cain Casey Saga

The Devil Inside	The Devil's Orchard
The Devil Unleashed	The Devil's Due
Deal with the Devil	Heart of the Devil
The Devil Be Damned	The Devil Incarnate

Visit us at www.boldstrokesbooks.com

A Woman
to Treasure

by
Ali Vali

2021

A WOMAN TO TREASURE

ISBN 13: 978-1-63555-890-6

This Trade Paperback Original Is Published By
Bold Strokes Books, Inc.
P.O. Box 249
Valley Falls, NY 12185

First Edition: May 2021

CREDITS
Editors: Victoria Villaseñor and Stacia Seaman
Production Design: Stacia Seaman
Cover Design by Tammy Seidick

Acknowledgments

One of my best childhood memories was being at home during the summer with my brother. Every afternoon we'd sit and watch "The Big Movie." It was a local channel's lineup of movies that had theme weeks. The pirate/treasure hunts were at the top of our list of favorites, so thank you, Radclyffe, for the opportunity to create my own adventure stories. Thank you, Sandy, for another great title idea and for all you do. Thanks to the BSB team for your support and hard work.

Thank you to my awesome editors, Victoria Villasenor and Stacia Seaman. Vic, thank you for dragging me along until I see the light. You and Stacia have taught me so much and I appreciate both of you. Tammy Seidick, thank you for this awesome cover—I love it.

Thank you to my first readers Lenore Beniot, Cris Perez-Soria, and Kim Rieff. Your comments, questions, and commentary really make me consider every possibility, and that's always a good thing.

A huge thank you to every reader. You guys send the best emails, so every word is written with you in mind.

Last year was interesting as well as challenging for all of us. Hopefully, everyone had as wonderful a quarantine partner as I did. C, thank you for keeping us both sane and laughing. We can add this to our adventures. Hopefully there are plenty more to come that do not include a pandemic. Verdad!

For C
and
The adventurous soul in all of us

CHAPTER ONE

Lot number twenty-six—a collection of scrolls recovered from the grave of a young girl. These are believed to be on ram's skin and are a form of a childhood diary of the young girl they were buried with." The auctioneer pointed to the rolled skins tied with leather strips. "The paleography and carbon dating put them at about 1300 AD."

Levi Montbard sat on the end of the fourth row in the famous Drouot auction house in Paris and tapped her numbered paddle on the side of her thigh. This was the lot she'd come for, although her grandfather Cristobal had already made quite a few purchases. He had a good eye for what would sell in Montbard Antiquities and Rare Books back home in New Orleans, but the scrolls were for her private collection.

"We'll start the bidding at five thousand euros," the man said as he smoothed down his tie. Levi lifted her paddle as her grandfather perused the rest of the catalog for the day's auction. There was a back-and-forth between Levi and an older man in the front, but he wasn't willing to go over thirty-eight thousand. "Sold to number forty-two. The next item…"

She and her grandfather stood, their mission accomplished.

"Lunch?" her grandfather asked.

"Are you sure you don't want to stay?" She flipped through the catalog and pointed to the last lot. "A Kelmscott Chaucer doesn't come up often. It's in poor condition, but if it goes for a good price it'll be a good investment."

"You've seen it already?" Her grandfather laughed. "Of course you have. Who's the beautiful woman working in the back who's willing to give up the house secrets for time with you?"

"I'm not revealing any of my sources. Come on and I'll buy you a crepe and a latte." Levi slowed her gait, not because her grandfather was feeble but because he was six inches shorter. "We'll be back in plenty of time."

"Do you know anything else about the scrolls you bought?" Cristobal Montbard was the head of their family, and he'd instilled in his only son and then his only grandchild the family's love of history. The Montbard family wasn't in the antiquities business simply for profit but to share with those who loved the past as much as they did and to provide the treasures that would fuel people's imaginations.

"They were found outside Jerusalem in an unmarked grave in what the archaeologists describe as a peasant burial site. The grave held a young girl, and the code the scrolls was written in was declared childhood nonsense." They sat at an outdoor café and she ordered for them in French. "They most probably are, but it's good practice at breaking codes. They'll make a good wall hanging for someone if they turn out to be nothing."

"How hard could the code have been that the auction house didn't attempt to crack it?"

"You know the auction houses, as well as the people putting the items up for sale, are all about profit." She dropped two sugar cubes in the espresso the pretty waitress delivered and smiled at her grandfather. "Why spend good money translating a simple exchange between children?"

"But you don't think that's all it is?"

"Think of the time period and where they were found. No one, much less a child, would've wasted scrolls on foolish childish musings. Parchment was too valuable back then, and it wasn't as if they could reuse it. The site held plenty of other graves with museum quality pieces, so I was lucky this one fell through the cracks. It doesn't happen often when it's state archaeologists, but it happens. The pieces they let go of will fund the rest of the dig they're on."

"No wonder the girls can't leave you alone when you're using words like *musings*." Her grandfather's teasing was a constant, but she loved it.

Levi was close to her parents, but her grandparents, Cristobal and Diana, were two of her favorite people in her life. Her mother's parents were also important to her, but they lived in London and she didn't see them as often. While her grandfather Cristobal enjoyed his books, cigars, and whiskey, her grandfather Percy had summited Everest twice and had a professor at Oxford. It was an intimidating family to be a part of when you considered the list of accomplishments on both sides, but they'd given her an adventurous heart.

"Believe me, there's a lot more than my grasp of the English language that makes that true." She loved the way her grandfather laughed. "I have a gut feeling there's something hidden in that code, and I'm going to find it. It was good luck they weren't highly advertised."

"Ms. Montbard." A man in Levi's periphery said her name in a cultured English accent.

She wasn't concerned since her grandfather didn't appear alarmed or worried. Whoever this guy was, she wasn't going to give him the satisfaction of turning around. She'd been taught an honor code all her life, and the first lesson was that to get respect you had to give it. This guy was clearly playing a game to get her attention instead of politely coming to the table.

"Ms. Montbard," the guy repeated. He was standing next to the table now, acting like she was supposed to curtsy. "Are you hard of hearing?"

"Not at all." She rested her chin on her palm and didn't invite him to sit. "Is there something I can do for you?" She tapped her index finger against her cheek and waited him out.

The man stared at her and appeared to be trying to control himself. He wore a beautifully cut suit and nice Italian dress shoes. On his lapel she saw a simple pin of a circle with a cross. The vertical line of the cross was at the center of the gold circle, but the horizontal was closer to the top. Opus Dei.

"I've come to offer you a deal you shouldn't turn down." He sat without an invitation, and the waitress placed another espresso before him without asking.

"My name is Baggio Brutos, and my employer would like to pay you fifty thousand euros for the scrolls you just purchased. You're making a profit already."

"Thank you, but I'm not interested in selling."

"Sixty thousand is my final offer."

"Do you promise?"

Brutos appeared confused. "Promise what?"

"That it's your last offer." Her grandfather was the only one who laughed at her joke. "If it is, my answer is no, and my grandfather and I can go back to our coffee while you walk away."

"Name your price and I'll talk to my client."

"Mr. Brutos, you had the opportunity to buy this morning at

the auction, but that window has closed. Your desperation makes me think selling would be a mistake even if I was tempted to do so." She nonchalantly texted her contact Claudette at the auction house and asked her to take care of her purchases in accordance with plan C. Brutos was still sitting and staring when she finished.

"Here's my card." Brutos stood and placed it next to her cup, tapping it loudly with his knuckles. "Call me when you change your mind. I know how to find you."

"That sounds so ominous," she said, maintaining eye contact.

They watched Brutos walk away with a slight limp. Men like that who acted as if they lived in a bubble where nothing or no one could hurt them made Levi want to make them bleed. Her phone buzzed—she needed to make a reservation for dinner to thank Claudette for the errand she'd run for her.

"That was interesting," her grandfather said. "Did you have Claudette mail my stuff too? I'd hate to lose my finds to that asshole if he tries anything."

"We're both probably acting paranoid, but of course." She finished her coffee and dropped some money on the table. "Let's go get your book so I can deliver you to your room. Mail errands require dinner."

"Do you have any idea what's going on?"

"Opus Dei are unpredictable when it comes to antiquities. They're not as powerful as they once were, but their searches have more to do with burying history than bringing it to light." They entered the auction house and she picked the same seats even though there was more of a crowd now. "The Mother Church wants a certain perception put out. Anything that changes or questions the carefully crafted message is stifled."

Cristobal raised his paddle when the bidding started on the book he wanted. "And you think childish musings are a danger to the church?"

"I have sixty thousand reasons to think it's something else. No one offers that much for something worthless. I think my instincts were spot-on."

"The bid is eighteen hundred," the auctioneers said. "Do I hear two thousand?"

Cristobal raised his paddle. "You know what we've always taught you."

"Life's simply the next adventure, and that's true, but this is more like a mystery."

"Then get to it. I'm curious as to what you'll find. Men like Brutos are the real plague of humanity. Zealots seldom learn anything from history."

"I'm curious myself, and I promise not to share it with Brutos once I find it."

❖

"Are you listening to me?" Zara Hassani sat on her sister's desk and tapped her heels on the side.

"I haven't decided yet. It's been almost a year since I've had any time off, and I was looking forward to the summer. Sometimes doing nothing is the way to go." Yasmine deleted every email and sent a message to everyone in her class that there'd be no extensions or assignments for extra credit. "Remind me in the future to stick to women's studies. These history courses for freshmen are a nightmare."

"Doing nothing for three months is the real nightmare, and you know they all fall in love with you in that class. They spend their college career pining over you once they've gotten a taste." Zara poked her in the ribs with her foot, making her laugh.

"Why are you here again?"

"To talk you into taking this offer. You know all you're going to be doing here is ditching Mama's attempts to marry you off." Zara poked harder. "A trip to the States would relieve both of us of all that nagging."

"I don't remember inviting you along, *if* I do decide to go." She laughed when Zara pouted. "Okay, I'll think about it. Now get out of here so I can get back to work."

Yasmine was an oddity in her family, not because she was able to support herself, was highly educated, and wasn't afraid to stand up for herself but because she had no interest in marrying. Her job at the University of Marrakech wasn't something she'd willingly give up in order to please a man, and she had yet to find a man who'd willingly step aside and let his wife shine.

She pulled her hair into a ponytail and grabbed her briefcase. Her last class of the day was her favorite, a great group of young women who wanted to learn what their role in modern Morocco could be. The sight of her boss walking quickly toward her made her want to hide behind a tree, but he'd already seen her.

"Professor Hassani," Emir Rami said. The formality had started when Yasmine had turned him down for a date. It'd taken six times, but her lack of interest had finally penetrated his testosterone-soaked brain. "Tulane would like an answer by tomorrow if at all possible. They'll be disappointed if you turn it down, but I'm willing to send someone else."

"I'll give them a call. Thank you, and if there's nothing else, I'm late for class."

"Your mother invited me to dinner tomorrow night. I look forward to seeing you there. We have so much to talk about."

He gave her the creeps, with his graying hair and hard eyes, but her mother was trying to pave the way to a marriage. "I hope you have a wonderful time, but I have an engagement planned." Never mind that it was watching the next season of the show she was binging on.

"That's disappointing."

"On so many levels." Yasmine stepped around him and lost her smile. "Excuse me. As I said, I'm late."

The classroom was empty when she arrived, and she stared at her watch. She wasn't so late that her entire class would've left. Any confusion disappeared when she saw who was sitting in the first row of her lecture hall. Nabil Talbi was the head of Morocco's Foreign Intelligence. Before she took the position with the university, she'd worked for him.

"Did you scare off my students?"

Nabil was still a handsome man, but the scar that marred his left cheek gave people pause. "They took some convincing, but I was nice about it."

"You do remember I don't work for you anymore?" She put all her stuff down and stared at him. "Did you miss me?"

"From the moment you decided on this boring existence instead of the work you did for me." Nabil's smile widened, and it made her laugh. "It's never too late to change your mind. You should remember that."

"The time I spent with you was special, but this is what I love doing."

"Please, I have people kissing my butt all day long." Nabil put his hands up. "You're the only person in my life who has never done that—don't change now. I'd never take you away from these kids. My nephew is in your beginning history class, and he raves about you."

"Now who's kissing butt?" She moved to sit by him and kissed both his cheeks. "You seldom leave the palace in Rabat. Seeing you here means you either did miss me, or you need something."

"We intercepted three messages from Algeria that require your special talents." Nabil and his staff spent most of their days chasing down terrorist threats that came from less stable areas. Their leader, King Driss VI, had done plenty to bring women into prominence, and he also quelled and dismissed anyone who tried to seed terrorism within their borders.

"Are you sure? There have to be plenty of people at your disposal who could do this." Yasmine loved her country, but like her mother, the government had specific ideas on the life she should be leading. Once she gave in, it was a slippery slope to being sucked in completely.

"You trusted me once, Yasmine. What's changed?" Nabil's tone became serious, but his expression radiated kindness.

"My sister reminded me today of people's expectations for my life," she said, shrugging. "The expectations of *others*, and they'll push until I either give in or have to give up on relationships altogether."

"My expectations for you are to stay here. How will I find the next Yasmine Hassani to make my job easier unless you're in the classroom molding young minds into something extraordinary?" His smile was warm, and she believed his words. Nabil's world didn't have room for flights of romanticism and empty flattery. "Until I find this wonderful person, I'll come by and ask for favors. In honor of our friendship I'll try not to overburden you."

"Do I need to come in or can I take this with me?"

Most of the terrorists working around them spoke in code. One of the cells must've read about the code talkers of World War II, Navajo tribe members in the US Marine Corps who transmitted messages. The language was so unique to the Navajo people the codes were never broken. Now the modern-day bad guys were using old tribal dialects to do the same thing. That had been her specialty when she'd worked for Nabil. History buffs were good at old tribal dialects, and with some government training, had become good at breaking codes.

"Consider it homework you can do on your way to America. It's not high priority, but I want something in place to decipher these should this become a recurring issue." Nabil handed her the folder and jump drive sitting next to him. "Sometimes we must walk in the past to understand our future."

"And sometimes our past should be left buried." She accepted the items and squeezed his hand. "I'll call you as soon as I have something. I'm not even going to ask how you know about my invitation to the US."

"Good, that'll save me from a stern lecture." Nabil laughed as he slapped his hands together. "Go, take your sister, and enjoy the food. You could use a few pounds. While you're gone, perhaps your mother will find a new interest besides trying to marry you to the imbecile you work for now."

"Get out before you sound any more like my sister." She kissed his cheeks again and put the files he'd brought in her bag. Her students started to come back, meaning they'd been released by Nabil's people. "Let's get started."

Those words held meaning for more than the lecture. Her mother not only wanted her married but believed in signs. Yasmine had no idea what Nabil's appearance meant, and she wasn't looking forward to finding out if it pushed her in the direction her mother wanted her to walk in. She was a grown woman, but in their culture, she'd never truly be an adult until she had a husband and children. That was the way of their world, and it was her mother's job to make sure she conformed. Failure would not only shame her family name, but her mother would bear the burden as well. No matter what Yasmine wanted, she couldn't do that to her.

❖

Ransley Hastings let his mind wander as he stared unseeing out the window of his study. Most would consider it a dreary day, but he loved the rain—had from the time he was a boy. Rainy days meant staying inside with his grandfather and hearing the stories of their family's rich history.

His grandfather loved to say they were educated and enlightened men forced to bear a world full of philistines. Their family had been central to the forming of what people now knew as Opus Dei, but in reality it had started way before then. Their Catholic faith had a difficult history, but like all Hastings men, he was committed to the cause.

"What makes you so sure this is of any value to us?" Baggio asked Ransley. Baggio had flown back to London to get him to authorize more money. "From your report, this isn't worth our time."

"I haven't finished my research, and I might be wrong about the historical significance. It's where they were found that gives me pause."

"You should've mentioned this earlier. I would've been more insistent, sire." Baggio only used the title Ransley preferred when he wanted something.

Despite their long history, the Hastings family had never achieved a title of any consequence. But in the order, he was a lord like his ancestors before him. "We need this, so do whatever you have to in order for the Montbard woman to see reason. If not, go back and see if you can get this some other way that won't require a large bank draft."

"Yes, sire. I'll keep you informed and head back in a few hours. What you're asking will require more than just me, however. I trust that's acceptable?"

"Get it done." Ransley was having Cardinal Richard Chadwick for tea and perhaps dinner, and didn't need any distractions. Ransley had found a true partner in Richard, and they'd enjoyed each other's company from the time Richard had entered the seminary. Richard's rise within the Church was due to the Hastings family's influence, and he had never forgotten it. They shared the same worldview, which made it easier to achieve Ransley's ultimate goals. The Church had to give up on the liberalism that had started to take root, especially under the current pope.

"Cardinal Chadwick, sir," the maid said after a brief knock.

"Richard, so good to see you. How was Spain?"

"Relaxing and reflective." Richard embraced him before they headed for the sunroom. It was a perfect place to enjoy the weather. "Sometimes you have to get away from the phones and other distractions to remember our purpose."

"You were missed, my friend." Ransley waited for the maid to finish laying out the tea service before continuing. He personally poured Richard's cup as the door closed, leaving them alone. "Did you have a chance to have your meeting?"

"We were able to use the Samos monastery." Richard nodded as he took a sip of his tea. "It's out of the way enough to serve our purposes. The cardinals who attended were receptive to the message and to our plans."

"The world needs us now more than ever." News sources were becoming a burden as the world spiraled more out of control without the right spiritual guidance. "It's time for a spiritual rebirth, and to put the Church back into the hands of men who know how to rule it. Once we've achieved that, the world will follow and fall to their knees."

"All this talk of equality, women's place in history, and the minorities' place as our equals has to be done away with. That is God's will and our duty to carry out."

Ransley was reminded of his father when Richard spoke passionately like this. Their charter wasn't simply to reestablish

Christian ideals in society but to assure that it was men like them who had the loudest voices and the most power. "The Illuminati had the right idea when they infiltrated world governments. But their maneuverings have led us to the hell we're living in now in this new world order."

"A new world order is nothing more than a modern-day Sodom and Gomorrah. Like our Lord commanded, the deceivers, sodomites, and unclean must be driven from the temple." Richard crossed himself and finished by kissing his fist. "Now is the time to say if you're not fully committed."

"I'm in until death. With everything happening in the world today, it's time to start using the people we've worked to elect to start driving our message home—our time is now. There will be a new world order, all right, and those who don't conform will suffer."

Richard stood and poured them a stiffer drink. "To the future and the men who will rule."

"Amen."

Chapter Two

This dinner is delicious," Claudette said in her beautiful French accent. She was an assistant director at Drouot's and worked with Levi whenever she was in town.

Levi held up a spoonful of the dessert she'd ordered for them to share. The bistro was one of Levi's favorites, and it'd been a few years since she'd visited. "Thank you for agreeing to join me. Dinner is always better with a beautiful woman."

"You are sweet." Claudette accepted the last bite. "And you know I'll take care of you even without all this."

Claudette was memorably beautiful, so much so that she came to mind before any offerings the auction house had. "You say that every time, but you'll eventually have to accept that I'm telling you the truth. I look forward to these dinners as much as whatever treasures are up for grabs."

"Is it the dinners or what comes after?" Claudette ran her foot up Levi's leg, and her smile made Levi want to kiss her. "Do you know what I look forward to?"

"The great dinner conversation?" Levi motioned for the check.

"You do have great skill in that area, but no." Claudette went up the outside of Levi's trouser leg until she pressed her foot into Levi's crotch.

"The after-dinner walks, then." The waiter dropped off the small leather folio and walked away as Levi took a deep breath. Claudette had really pressed down with her foot, and she was ready to get out of here.

"You love teasing, but not tonight." Claudette scratched the tablecloth with her fingernail as Levi counted out the right amount of cash. She wasn't interested in waiting for a credit card receipt, and Claudette seemed grateful.

They didn't have to wait long for a cab, and the valet smiled when she handed him a good tip for holding a large umbrella over them while they walked to the car. A storm had rolled in during dinner, and the streets were starting to flood.

"We're closer to the hotel, if you don't mind." The traffic was terrible thanks to the bad weather, but Levi put all that aside when Claudette grabbed her by her jacket lapels and kissed her. This wasn't their first time together, and she loved the way Claudette claimed everything she wanted.

"Do you feel adventurous, lover?" Claudette bit her bottom lip before sucking it in.

"My life is all about adventure." They were still about five blocks from the Ritz, and they'd be soaked by the time they arrived, but making a run for it beat sitting in this cab. She paid the driver and took Claudette's hand.

They were dripping by the time they went through the revolving doors. It didn't take long for Claudette's dress to drop with a plop on the bathroom floor. Seeing her naked made Levi take a breath and mentally remind herself to go slow. Passion should never be rushed, and women like Claudette deserved her time and attention.

"Do you have any idea what I'd like to do to you?" Claudette moved across the room like a predator with prey in its sights. "You don't come into town very often, and I shouldn't want you this much, but I can't help it."

Levi glanced down when Claudette unbuckled her belt and opened her pants. "You do make me regret I don't come to town more often." She widened her stance when Claudette dropped to her knees, taking Levi's pants with her.

"You are perfect." Claudette ran her hands up the back of Levi's legs until she reached her ass. Levi took an awkward step forward when Claudette pulled her closer.

The laughter at her own clumsiness stopped when Claudette put her mouth on her. All the buildup at the restaurant was working against her. "Son of a bitch," she said louder than she meant to. It didn't help when Claudette sucked as if she was trying to drain the life out of her.

"Are you going to give me what I want?" Claudette kissed Levi's sex, and Levi put her hand on the back of Claudette's neck.

Levi blinked and glanced down when nothing happened. She wasn't finished, but Claudette simply waited. There really wasn't anything better and more beautiful than a curvy feminine woman who had the ability to get whatever she wanted from you. Right now, Claudette's pleasure took precedence over hers.

"Whatever you want, as many times as you want." She helped Claudette to her feet and lifted her up until her legs wrapped around her waist.

She left the glare of the bathroom and sat on the bed. The way Claudette kissed her as she ground herself into her abdomen was driving her crazy. Levi could taste herself on Claudette's lips and it made her ravenous for more of Claudette's attention, but she could be patient.

The way Claudette was breathing made her lean back and enjoy the flush on Claudette's skin. She stared at Claudette's hard nipples, prompting Claudette to hold one breast and pull Levi's head forward. "Suck me," Claudette demanded.

She followed the order as she slapped Claudette's ass hard enough to make her moan. The sting made Claudette grind harder into her and pull her hair. She slapped her again, which seemed to make Claudette lose control.

"Show me what you want, or I'll stop." She squeezed Claudette's ass and waited. This part was always the same; Claudette started off dominant and took what she wanted, but all she desired was to be dominated herself. Levi wasn't totally into pain, but Claudette was hard to say no to. "Show me or I'm going to stop."

"Here, chéri." Claudette went up on her knees, reached down, and opened her sex. "I want you right here."

Levi pinched Claudette's clit and Claudette moaned loud enough for Levi to feel the vibration in her chest. She entered Claudette fast and hard with three strokes and smiled when the moans turned into a yell. Claudette held on to Levi's shoulders as her body stiffened and Levi pulled out and entered her one more time. It was all Claudette needed to come and fall limply against her, so Levi moved to lie back and cover them both with the comforter.

"Let me," Claudette said.

Levi caught her hand and kissed her forehead. "Give yourself a moment. I'm not going anywhere, and neither are you."

The way Claudette laid her head on Levi's chest as she ran her fingers along her side made Levi close her eyes and concentrate on the touch. Her life revolved around the past, and she loved the way all those found stories fueled her imagination, but the present had its perks.

"What are you thinking so hard about?" Claudette let her hand move farther down, and Levi didn't stop her this time.

"For once I'm not thinking about anything. You managed to empty my head." She put one hand behind her head and looked at Claudette, who moved to kneel between her legs.

"Is that a good thing?" She cupped her own breasts and smiled down at her.

"It's a very good thing." She stared as Claudette's nipples hardened. She wouldn't mind putting off her own pleasure to touch Claudette again.

"Ah," Claudette said, leaning forward a little. "I can see the wheels turning in here." She tapped Levi's forehead. "But you're going to be a good boy and keep those beautiful hands to yourself."

Levi took advantage of Claudette's nearness and bit down gently on her nipple. Claudette's intake of breath made Levi's clit double in hardness, and she couldn't wait anymore. She put her hand on Claudette's head and pushed her down. She was throbbing to the point of pain and needed Claudette to release the pressure.

"Can I help you with something?" Claudette sounded amused. "You certainly know how to flatter a girl."

"Do I need to spank you again?"

Claudette laughed and stuck her tongue out at her. "Don't tempt me into stopping, or you might damage something."

Before Levi could complain, Claudette lowered her head and moved her tongue from the base of Levi's clit to the top. She was so turned on that she had to concentrate not to come like a firecracker with way too short a fuse. Claudette was relentless, though. She switched from moving her tongue over her clit to sucking, and Levi tightened the muscles in her thighs and her grip on the back of Claudette's head.

"Son of a bitch." She was having trouble forming words but couldn't help the curse when her orgasm started. "Fuck," was all she could manage when Claudette entered her. She had to push Claudette's mouth away from her sex once she came, then she moaned when Claudette straddled her face. Claudette was wet and ready again, so Levi squeezed her ass and gave her what she wanted.

Claudette lay back down and curled up next to Levi just as her cell phone rang. "Whoever that is, they have good timing."

"Believe me, lover, I would've ignored it had it been a minute sooner." Claudette rolled off her and reached for her phone. "Oui."

Levi yawned as Claudette sat up and listened to whoever had called. Considering it was almost two in the morning, it couldn't be good news. Claudette tapped the phone against her palm when she finished.

"Everything okay?"

"It was work."

Levi glanced at the clock. "Are there emergency auctions in the middle of the night you've never told me about?"

"No, someone tripped the alarm. The code they used on the door was from my department, and they're checking with everyone. It's a good thing I have such a good alibi."

"Was anything taken?"

"They don't know yet, but it couldn't be much. The police arrived in six minutes." Claudette lay back down, and Levi ran her hand from her shoulder down to her ass.

"I can testify that all your break-ins tonight were totally consensual."

Claudette laughed and kissed the palm of Levi's other hand. "It's been a while since this happened, and it's foolish to try and beat that security system. Management installed it four months ago after plenty of research. Supposedly it's the best in the world."

"We'll be in town until tomorrow afternoon if you need me to talk to anyone." There was plenty on her schedule in the coming month. She mentally reviewed each appointment. It would be nice to be home, and with any luck her team had made progress on the assignment she'd left them.

"It's because of you and your family that I'm on the management team, which is why I got the call. I doubt they think I'm breaking in. You do owe me breakfast, so don't run off."

"After tonight I owe you more than that. Go to sleep and tomorrow we'll eat in bed."

"In more ways than one, lover," Claudette said.

Levi laughed. "I'm looking forward to all the meanings behind that statement."

❖

The flight to the States landed in New York first, and Levi made sure they had a long enough layover to run one more important errand. She and her grandfather checked their luggage and took a car to a small coin shop in New Jersey. The owner, Charles, had tracked down some of the collectibles their clients were interested in, but Levi was more interested in the other service he provided when necessary.

They were buzzed in and Charles stepped out from behind the display cases, hugging her and then her grandfather. "Levi, Cristobal, it's so good to see you."

"Thank you, Charles. It's been too long. Thank you for signing for our deliveries." Levi followed Charles to the stockroom and smiled when she saw the three boxes Claudette had put together and shipped express for them.

"You two were about an hour behind the delivery service, so good timing." The boxes had the name of the coin shop and, with Claudette's help, hadn't been held up in customs.

Levi used the letter opener on the desk and opened the box labeled number two. In the middle of the books her grandfather had purchased was a small velvet bag. These hadn't been in the auction, but a quick shopping trip with Claudette before the auction began had brought her to a place similar to this one.

"We'll pay the usual fee, but these are for you." She handed the bag over and smiled as Charles bounced slightly with what could only be excitement. "Near mint condition from 1200 or so. I purchased a lot of twenty as your bonus."

The coins Charles spilled on the desk were Templar silver coins stamped with the distinctive cross on one side and two knights riding one horse on the other. Templar coins weren't exactly rare, but finding them in a condition where you could see every detail was.

"Levi, you shouldn't have, but oh my God." Charles put on gloves and picked one up reverently. "Oh my God, thank you."

"They belong with you. I knew no one else would love them as much."

"You didn't have a problem with the shipment?" Cristobal asked, taking out the two rarest books.

"Were you expecting trouble? They came in as usual with no hassle." Charles was enthralled with his gift, which gave Levi time to open the first box and remove the leather bag Claudette had placed the scrolls in.

"We had a strange encounter in Paris, but all that's behind us now," Cristobal said.

"Your boxes are heading out in thirty minutes, so you'll have them by tomorrow. I'll call if anything comes up." Charles showed them out to the waiting car.

The security line at the airport was short, which gave them time to grab a sandwich and coffee before boarding. Another three hours and they'd be home. Levi loved traveling, but her own bed was also welcome after weeks away. She'd spent three weeks in South America slogging through dense rain forests before her week in Paris. The search for the tomb they'd uncovered through extensive research had paid off.

Levi was happiest in the dirt but had willingly attended the black-tie affair when they'd donated the major pieces to Peru's National Museum. Her family had gotten exclusive rights to the inventory the Peruvian government had been willing to part with, and that alone would cover the expense of the dig as well as make them a hefty profit. There'd been plenty of interest when her mother had put out the press release, but they'd done similar digs where all the artifacts went to the museums in the countries where they'd been found. It was the right thing to do.

After a month away, though, she was looking forward to office hours and hunting for the next treasure. "I'm sorry, what?" She'd only heard the last of what her grandfather had said.

"I said, good job, kid." Her grandfather sat back and held his drink up to her. "I'm proud of you. When it comes to field work, you're better than me and your father."

She tapped her glass to his and enjoyed the compliment. "Thanks, and you owe me some veal piccata this coming week."

"You know I love cooking for you." Cristobal smiled at the woman who refilled their coffees. "Are you home for a while? Your parents won't ever complain, but they miss you."

"I left Pia working on something before I left, but even if it pans out, it'll keep me close to home. It might turn out to be total fiction." She added sugar to her cup and stirred. There was only a need for milk with Louisiana-strength coffee. "If it isn't a complete fantasy, then some treasures are still close to home."

"Good. I'll keep up the research on my end for the next major auctions."

"You should think about bringing Gran. I'm sure a romantic trip to Paris or London is something she'd jump at." Their flight was announced, and she picked up their bags while her grandfather paid the bill.

"When you get married, kid, you need to plan romance all the time, not just trips. That is a good idea, though."

The weather was perfect and they got back to New Orleans forty minutes ahead of schedule. They shared a car back and she sat with her grandmother for an hour before walking across the street to her home. The Montbard home in the French Quarter had been in their family as long as the Quarter had existed. Her grandparents lived there now, and her parents lived next door in what was once the carriage house for the servants of another large house on the block. That location and the place Levi lived were purchased in the early 1900s.

She flicked her lights on in the foyer and saw the neat piles of mail on the antique table that was older than the house. Her assistant, Pia Adler, was the most efficient person she'd ever come across and had to be responsible for the blatant display of OCD.

"You should've called. I would've made dinner." Pia sat behind the library desk in the study with Levi's checkbook open. Levi trusted Pia with everything, whether she was out of town or not.

"If I'd done that, I couldn't take you out." She dropped her briefcase and carry-on by the door and walked over to kiss Pia's cheeks.

"You've been gone forever, so I know going out isn't on your list of wishes tonight." Pia pinched Levi's lips together and smiled. "Don't try lying, it's unbecoming."

"How about takeout from Irene's and we open a bottle of wine? The cases arrived, didn't they?" She opened the wall safe and dropped her remaining cash and her passport inside, along with the inventory invoices for what was coming from Peru. Another bag of Templar coins she'd purchased went in as well.

"There's one breathing in the kitchen, and George should be here in fifteen minutes with our delivery." Pia placed the large binder back in the desk drawer and took her hand. Levi didn't mind being dragged to her kitchen. "Did you have fun?"

"My grandfather is always fun. South America was hot as the sun, but survivable. The additions to our inventory were worth the heat rash." She accepted a glass from Pia and followed directions to sit at the long farmer's table. Three places were already set. "Did you get anywhere with the book I left you?"

"I had a whole month," Pia said, sounding somewhat offended. "Of course I did. The location doesn't make sense, though, so don't get too excited."

"The weird locations are the ones that usually get us somewhere. Give me the details." The knock that echoed through the house from the heavy bronze knocker shaped like an anchor made her put her hand up. "Hold on. I'll get that."

George stood with two bags and the big smile he was seldom without, and it brightened when he saw her. He worked for them as a jack-of-all-trades and never minded running errands like this even when she'd told him he was free to decline. Every time, he'd nod and then offer to do something not in his job description.

"Levi!" He hugged her even with the bags in his arms.

George was in his late fiftiesbut had an intellectual disability, so they were all protective of him. His mother had been their bookkeeper for years, and at her death Levi's parents had become responsible for him. George lived in Levi's guest cottage and he treated her like a little sister.

"Hey, George." She kissed his cheek and hugged him back. "You okay?"

"I missed you, and I told Miss Pia I could ride my bike okay. See?" He held up the bags as proof of the independence his bike gave him.

"She worries because she loves you, we all do, but you did a great job. Come in and eat. Pia always orders a lot." Levi took one of the bags so she could hold his hand as they walked to the back of the house.

"Did she order peanut butter and strawberries?"

There was a sandwich and a glass of milk at the table when they entered, and Pia winked at her. George was a creature of habit who only liked to eat three things on a rotating basis. He started his days with two scrambled eggs, followed by a plain hamburger for lunch and a peanut butter with strawberry jam sandwich for his nightly meal. All three meals had to be served with a glass of milk.

"Would I forget you?" Pia asked as George hugged her. "Sit and talk to Levi while I get all this ready."

She had fun telling them about the ruins and the large number of snakes that seemed to protect them. George appeared to hang on every word, and Pia was right there with him. Both of them smiled when she dug out two gifts from her carry-on and handed them over.

George was thrilled with the two books about pirates she'd found, and Pia kissed her for the pearl and diamond brooch she'd bought at auction. Pia wore a light sweater every day no matter how hot or cold it was, and always with one of her numerous brooches.

"It's beautiful." Pia took off the jade one she wore and replaced it with the new one. "Thank you."

"I couldn't resist." She yawned, unable to help it, and George excused himself. He left through the back, and Levi helped Pia clean up. "It's late. You should stay."

"Are you sure?" Pia wasn't with anyone, and she knew Levi wasn't in the mindset to settle down anytime soon. It was a perfect arrangement. "You're not tired?"

"There's always tomorrow, but you need to be here for me to do anything about it."

They stood in the moonlight of her bedroom and undressed each other before Levi kissed her. This relationship, or whatever it was, had been initiated by Pia, and Pia was hard to resist. Levi had tried somewhat at first because she didn't want to lose a good friend if the sex ever got in the way, but Pia had argued they were two adults who knew better.

The exhaustion of travel melted away at the sight of Pia's naked body. Levi turned her around so Pia's back was to her front, cupped Pia's breasts, and got closer. Pia dropped her head back and gazed up at her. They didn't do this often enough for Levi to know everything about Pia, but she recognized the expression. Naked desire was hard to miss.

"You've lost weight, but you're still perfect." Pia reached up and grabbed a fistful of hair at the back of Levi's head.

"I'm far from perfect, but I *am* in the perfect place right now." Levi brought her hands down slowly, wanting to enjoy the feel of Pia's skin as she made her way to the hot wetness she knew was there.

Women really were God's gift, and she never took moments like this for granted. Commitment to only one was a long way off, and the lack of happily ever after didn't take away from intimate experiences. She loved and respected women, and she absolutely loved making them feel good. Sex wasn't ever just sex, and the best thing about it was how every experience was different.

"Are you going to make me beg?" Pia rocked her hips back and forth, chasing Levi's fingers as she pulled her hair harder.

Levi bit gently on Pia's neck as she moved her hand more firmly between Pia's legs. They both stopped when her fingers reached Pia's clit. "You're so wet." It was stating the obvious, but it deserved mentioning. To get a woman this turned on made her want to beat her chest a little, but she wasn't quite that egotistical.

"It's been so long." Pia sounded winded, and she squeezed Levi's wrist to the point of pain. "You know what dating is like these days."

"Do you want me to swipe right, baby?" She moved her fingers and smiled at the loud moan Pia let out. It ricocheted through her chest, and she didn't want to keep Pia waiting for another moment. She turned her around and held her when Pia moved to wrap her legs around her.

"Stay up here with me," Pia said when Levi went to move down once they were on the bed.

Levi held Pia against her as she entered her with two fingers and stroked to the rhythm Pia set. "Oh, oh…oh." Pia closed her eyes. "Ah, fuck," she said loudly when she stopped moving and came. She rested her head on Levi's shoulder as she caught her breath. "Why can't I find someone like you who wants to marry me?"

The question made Levi chuckle. Though she was still young, all Pia wanted was the wedding, the kids, and someone who turned her on to share it all with. That she hadn't found that person in all her dating experiences frustrated her, but Pia also wasn't one to settle. Until the right butch with nesting tendencies came along, she was fine with the occasional dinner with the happy ending Levi provided.

Levi had never had those desires. The example of successful relationships she had in her parents and grandparents meant when she picked, it would be forever. Her family never pressured her—that she did herself—and right now this was all she wanted. Gratification without having to play house.

"They're out there, and whoever it is will be loads better than me."

Pia moved to lie on top of her and rested her chin on Levi's chest. "Don't knock yourself. Except for the fact you aren't the one," Pia made air quotes, "you're pretty awesome."

"It'll be a sad day when you do find your match." She raised her head and kissed the tip of Pia's nose.

"You're good at flattery, Levi Montbard, and since most women suck, I hope you don't mind providing stud services. It keeps me sane."

She laughed, knowing there wasn't any worry of misunderstanding that could come between them. Pia was a special woman. It wouldn't take much longer for someone to realize that, and then their time together at work would have to do.

"Go to sleep and we'll talk about your sanity in the morning."

Pia moved off her but kissed her again. "Are you sure you want to go to sleep now?"

"You're sexy as hell, but if I yawn in the middle of a good time I'll never forgive myself. I'm exhausted." She held Pia and relaxed at the way Pia ran her fingers along her abdomen in a circle. The last thing on her mind before she fell asleep was the scrolls. There had to be something there, but they'd have to wait. She'd continue the chase for as long as she had life left in her.

CHAPTER THREE

Yasmine moved her head from side to side to try and work out the pain from keeping her head down over the file Nabil had given her. She had another five hours to New York, and Zara was sleeping. Being able to fall unconscious as soon as the plane was wheels up was a talent Yasmine didn't possess. Zara looked cute with the bit of drool at the corner of her mouth.

The only blessing of a ten-hour flight was the first-class ticket Tulane had provided, and she'd paid Zara's fare so they could enjoy the entire trip together. There weren't that many people in their section, which meant no line at the restroom. She stood and stretched before making her way to the front.

"Can I get you anything, Dr. Hassani?" The attendant had been by her seat every thirty minutes asking the same question. It gave her the impression he was interested in more than serving her a drink. Before she fell asleep Zara had teased her about it.

"No, thank you." She was polite but standoffish. It didn't dent his enthusiasm. "Excuse me."

He still didn't move. "I have three days in New York. Where would you like to have dinner?"

"Blanchard's."

"I've never heard of it."

"It's in New Orleans, and you're the last person I'd like to go with." She pushed him aside and stepped into the restroom. "And I don't want to see you again during this flight or at any other time. Some women might find this strong come-on flattering, but I'm not one of them."

The female attendant smiled at her and handed her a cup of tea when she came out. "I'll be by later with your meal, but let me know if you need anything. I promise I won't be a nuisance."

They landed and were through customs in plenty of time to make their connecting flight a few hours later. The heat when they stepped out of the New Orleans airport reminded her of home. Hot temperatures had never bothered her, but the humidity made her glad she'd packed cool clothing.

"We have time for a walk through the French Quarter before dinner," Zara said.

Yasmine allowed herself to be pulled toward the car that the university had sent. By Moroccan standards New Orleans was a new blip in history, but from what she'd read, it was very different from the rest of the country. The driver gave them a brief rundown of the city and what she needed to do to get a ride to campus.

The man carried their bags inside the townhome they were being provided and pointed out everything they'd need. They changed and headed out to see all the sights Zara had put on her list. An hour later they stopped for a drink and some cool air.

"Live a little, as the Americans say," Zara said, tapping the drink menu. "I promise I didn't pack Mama in my bag. I won't tell anyone if you have a drink."

"Give me a day before you start corrupting me." She laughed but ordered a white wine, not yet ready to try the hurricane Zara had ordered.

"Is there any way we can stay longer than the two weeks you signed up for?" Zara sucked on the straw and hummed in apparent pleasure. "This place is wonderful."

"You only have two years left on your master's degree. Why don't you take a gap year before you go on to your doctorate?" She took a sip of her wine and kept her eyes on Zara. Sometimes her expression was the only way to know what she was thinking. "Or is that not in your plans any longer?"

"I'd rather work through it and finish, but I do dream every so often of finishing somewhere else." Zara's head was down, and Yasmine understood every emotion she was feeling.

"In my class I try to teach the history of women in our world, but the real lesson is how we fit into a world that hasn't quite caught up to us." She reached over and covered Zara's hand with hers. "What you need to learn is to be happy and tune out the objections of others. If finishing somewhere else will make you happy, then do it."

"It's kind of hard to tune Mama out."

"Mama has her own life, and she has no right to live yours. Decide what it is you want, and I'll help you get it."

"If I tell them I want to study abroad, they'll cut me off."

"I have enough money, so that won't be a problem. The only problem you have now is walking a straight line after you finish that drink."

They laughed together as they kept walking toward Canal Street. Their driver had said Canal was the dividing line between the Quarter and the Uptown and Garden District neighborhoods. The street they were on was lined with restaurants and antique stores. One in particular caught Yasmine's attention not because of the larger space, but because of the merchandise on display.

"Let's go inside," she said, and Zara nodded.

"Welcome," a handsome older man said as they stopped at the display being set up. "Is there something I can show you?"

"These pieces are beautiful." Yasmine couldn't place the year, but the Inca artifacts were authentic, of that she was certain. "It's hard to find something like this outside a museum."

"There have been plenty of pirates in the Montbard family tree, but trafficking illegal antiquities was never one of our sins." The older gentleman seemed to have a wonderful sense of humor. "My granddaughter found and retrieved what you see here, and the best finds are still in Peru, heading for their museum. Are you a collector?"

"More of an admirer. Are you a Montbard?"

He cocked his head and smiled. "Cristobal Renaud Montbard at your service." He held his hand out.

"I'm Yasmine Hassani, and this is my sister, Zara." She took his hand and returned his smile. "Considering you're surrounded by history every day, you must know the history of your name. I can't imagine it's common here."

"Ah…*Dr.* Hassani." Cristobal bent at the waist and kissed her hand before repeating the move on Zara. "Ms. Hassani, it's so wonderful to meet you both."

"Is guessing a talent of yours?" she asked. She liked him right off, and that didn't happen often.

"I'm on the committee that chooses our visiting professors. Your reputation in the classroom made you my top candidate. With any luck you'll accept our invitation for the fall semester once you get a taste of the city."

"Let's not get too far ahead in our planning, but meeting you makes it easy to see why your distant relative became a Temple Grand Master." She followed Cristobal to the next room of the store.

The space was smaller but the Templar pieces he had were phenomenal. She was surprised to find such a jewel outside of Europe. Most people loved Templar lore, but not too many actually knew much about them. From the displays around her, that wasn't the case here. The Montbard family understood the importance of the past.

"If you don't have plans, I'd love for you and Zara to join me and my wife for dinner tonight." He invited them to sit as he turned the dial on a wall safe. From her vantage point she could see there were quite a few trays inside when he opened the door. "If you do have plans, we can schedule for another night."

"We'd love to, but are you sure it won't be an imposition?" Yasmine glanced at her watch. "It's late."

"My wife loves to entertain. It won't be a problem." He sat across from her with three trays. "And even though you teach another section of history, I know your Templar expertise isn't rivaled by many."

She stared at the trays and found it hard to keep up with the conversation. The collection of Templar crosses and coins was unbelievable. "Are these leads?" The tray closest to her had ten, which appeared as if they'd been worn on a leather thong or small chain. Making jewelry and religious icons out of lead was quite commonplace in years past, but they were hard to find now.

Cristobal handed her a pair of gloves, picked up one of the crosses, and handed it to her. "The Templars were financially independent, but most of the members were a brotherhood who took their vows to their faith seriously. Lead was easy to carve, and they were talented at that."

"They fought against my people for decades." The crosses varied from lead to gold, but none of them were too ornate. "They had better marketing, though," she said and laughed. "The mystique of who they were still fascinates the world. Even good Muslim girls like me."

"It's their secrets," Zara said as she ran her finger along the silver coins. "Secretive groups good at keeping secrets invite curiosity."

"That's true, and it's a pleasure to share these with fellow enthusiasts. I doubt we're enthusiasts for the same reasons, but you can still appreciate the history." Cristobal took off his cotton gloves and placed them on the table. "We can talk about it over dinner tonight."

"All we need is an address and the time."

"You're a half block from the house, so I'll come walk you over at seven thirty if that's agreeable. We don't offer it often, but the townhome you're in belongs to my family."

"That would be wonderful. It seems like fate that we found you." Yasmine placed the cross she'd been examining back and removed her gloves. "Though perhaps it was you who found us."

"My father was a big believer in fate. He always said there were no coincidences, and at times I think he was right."

"You don't believe in fate?" Zara asked.

"I believe in living, and helping fate along whenever possible." Cristobal sounded like he got most of his philosophy out of fortune cookies, but it was sweet nonetheless.

"If you're responsible for us being here, then thank you." She took his hand and on impulse leaned in and kissed his cheek. "All of us could use a helping hand."

❖

Levi read the report Pia had compiled as she sat at the bar off the lobby at the Piquant. It was a long walk from her place, but she enjoyed the solitude in the crowd. New Orleans was always full of strangers and friends, but when you needed some downtime there was always an empty barstool with great bartenders.

"What can I get you?" The young woman placed a coaster in front of her.

"An old fashioned, please."

"Are you an attorney?" The woman worked as she asked her questions.

"God forbid," Pia said as she joined her. "Could you make another one of those, please?"

"How'd it go?" Their next search would take place on private land, so they'd need permission as well as a contract on how to handle anything they found. "This sounds even crazier after my fifth read."

"You're the one who found the book. That means your insanity can be cured by taking up golf and giving up reading." Pia lifted her glass and handed it to her. "But I know you too well. The books are your keys to the past."

"But Choupick, Louisiana? It's got plenty of swamps and it's circled in bayous. That's a lot of dark water, gators, and fish. I doubt there's going to be treasure to find."

One of the things she'd been lucky about in her career was finding the kind of books that led somewhere. The kinds of books written in the best codes of their time. They weren't widely distributed but were more like journals than historic tomes. She'd collected them at first as a way to glimpse the daily lives of people in the past. And then she'd found a journal of a family who had fled during the French Revolution. Their treasure and history had been swallowed by the time they'd died on the guillotine.

"I didn't believe it either, but the journal was definitely from 1450 AD. We authenticated the origins and did the carbon dating. You know all that, but it's who wrote it that should convince you."

"You know I don't need much convincing, and with all the paperwork done I'm willing to start tomorrow." She flipped through the pages again. It'd taken her four months to work out the key that would unlock the code.

"Your grandfather called and asked you to dinner. There's some people he wants you to meet."

"I love him, but not tonight."

"You call him and tell him that. He always thinks I don't try hard enough when you say no."

Levi excused herself to do just that. Dinner with the visiting professor sounded good, but all she wanted was a quiet night. "I'm heading out in the morning, Papa. Even if I'm gone longer than I expect to be, I'll come back and host another dinner."

"Don't forget to call us and keep everyone updated. Pia showed me the report. I'm not sure about this one. As much as I'd like to believe it, I think it's a little too far-fetched."

She laughed and sat outside in the open courtyard where guests enjoyed breakfast and lunch. The space at the center of the building had such an old feeling, it made her believe she was no longer in the United States. All of Poppy Valente's properties gave you a sense of calm.

"Aren't you the one who tells me not to discount even the fanciful? That's where most hidden things are found." She smiled when the door opened and a tall woman stepped out with two drinks. "Have fun tonight and pass along my regrets."

"Welcome home, world traveler, but it sounds like you won't be here for much longer." Poppy handed her a fresh drink and then sat. "We need to set a date so you can tell me about all your latest adventures."

"Cut the crap." She tapped her glass against Poppy's. "You've had your share of exotic adventures, but I suppose marriage and kids have curbed your adventurous side. How are Julia and all the offspring?"

"Marriage hasn't made me dull," Poppy said, sounding offended. "Julia is fine, the kids are great, and Elizabeth is engaged." Poppy had started her business with her first partner Carly and now owned a number of resorts around the world. Carly had passed away after a battle with breast cancer, but her youngest daughter Elizabeth had stayed with Poppy and now ran the day-to-day operations of the whole business. That left Poppy time to spend with her two younger children and her new wife, Julia.

"Make sure I get an invitation to that—you throw an awesome party. I'd love dinner one night. It's been way too long." She and Poppy had grown up together and had been good friends since grade school. The happy, easygoing guitar player she'd known forever had disappeared when Carly passed away, and it'd been painful to watch. "I even miss the kids."

"They'd love to see you, and I'm holding you to it."

"Give me a couple of weeks and it's a date. I've got work out of town, but it's close by. It'll beat South America and Paris, which is where I've been for the last month. Peru will give you a whole new experience when it comes to heat."

"My motto is to stick to the beach. And you must've dragged some business over with you. We've had some guests check in from Paris today." Poppy glanced at her phone when it chimed softly.

Levi nodded, surprised Poppy mentioned anything about a guest. The Piquant was a favorite of people who valued their privacy. "I went with Papa to an auction, so it was all work this time." She smiled when she noticed Julia Valente walk out, with Pia following behind. Poppy's beautiful wife seemed as if she'd found the answer to happiness, always projecting joy. "Finally, the better half of this relationship." Levi stood and hugged Julia after kissing both her cheeks.

"You'd better butter me up. Tallulah has dug up the yard in search of treasure after your gift of a field kit." Julia laughed, but Levi knew how much she loved her flowers. Valente Resorts had a new head of landscape design, and she was good at it.

"Think of all that great imagination she's developing."

"That's all you got?" Julia asked. "It's a good thing we like you so much."

"You're on thin ice, buddy," Poppy said. "If you two are free, how about dinner here?"

"We'd love to," Pia answered before Levi found an excuse.

"We would." They headed to the restaurant and the Valente private table. The place was full, but a majority of the diners were locals since this wasn't your typical hotel restaurant.

The two sisters who ran the kitchens came out and offered to feed them—it was something you didn't turn down. When Levi stood to hug them before they headed back to their chef duties, the men five tables down caught her attention—one guy in particular. The odds against seeing Baggio Brutos in New Orleans were too high to waste time calculating.

"You okay?" Poppy asked.

Levi sat slowly and nodded. "I thought I saw someone I recognized." Brutos wasn't facing their table, but there was no way he didn't see her when they walked in.

"Is it someone who's given you a problem?" Julia asked. "Your expression isn't a sign of happiness."

"He's not a friend, but not a problem either." She wasn't ready to talk about the scrolls. "Excuse me a moment, please." She didn't want to text at the table, so she stood at the entrance to the kitchen and sent her grandfather a quick note.

"Do you need me to do something or get you anything?" Poppy asked when she returned.

"A filet with a loaded potato." She tried lightening the mood as everyone asked questions about the Peruvian dig. "Julia, you should drop by the gallery. If you have any indoor space, there are a few pieces that would blend in well with the right landscaping."

"Ooh, I'd love to."

"My luck is turning around if I'll get to see you more than once."

❖

Baggio stared at the man Ransley had insisted on enlisting for this job and listened to him brag. There hadn't been a situation this guy hadn't found himself in and handled like a black ops commando and a ninja rolled into one. It was an effort to keep his attention on the moron and not glance at the table Levi Montbard shared with the three other women.

The way the other tall woman held the blonde's hand disgusted him in a way that made him crave his rosary beads. How could they not see their souls were in danger for eternity? No amount of pleasure was worth that.

"Why couldn't you handle this yourself?"

Baggio had to think what the star of the table's name was. "Donnie, you weren't my idea. Any job the cardinal asks you to do should be considered a privilege. Apparently, however, unless it's worthy of a Tom Cruise movie, it's beneath you."

Donnie Nelton glared at him, which was almost laughable. "I know my job, so there's no reason to be condescending. Why don't you order dessert, and my partner and I will take care of this. It's what we're here to do since you couldn't close the deal."

His appetite left along with Donnie. These scrolls Ransley wanted to retrieve should've been handled with a large check, but now he was wasting time on all of this instead of what he wanted to be working on. The information they'd found in modern Turkey was the gasoline that could burn the church down around them, and they needed his expertise to bury it.

"Do you have it?" Ransley asked when Baggio answered his call.

"Your warrior is headed into battle now. He seems competent enough, so I'd like to come back and start on what was turned over to us." He waved off the waiter after signing the credit card slip.

"Once this is done you can head into the Vatican vaults and lose yourself in the stacks. Call me once you hear anything."

"Yes, sir." He crumpled his napkin and tossed it on the table.

He left for his room to wait for Donnie to call, but he really wanted to stay and watch Levi Montbard until she was done with dinner. Levi hadn't been intimidated by him at all, and from what he'd read about her, she seldom was no matter the situation. She'd walked into places that would terrify the average person and had walked away with things no one knew still existed. They were alike in that regard. Both of them found lost things, but for totally different reasons.

"I'll need an eight o'clock wakeup call, please." The hotel was accommodating enough that he could almost convince himself he was in old England.

He stripped, wanting to shower to wash away all the filth he'd witnessed during dinner. Though he wanted to ignore his ringing cell, he couldn't. The sooner they finished, the sooner he could go home to Rome. "Brutos."

"You need to leave the hotel now." Donnie sounded winded as well as panicked.

It was no time to smile, but he couldn't help it. The asshole actually sounded scared. "Why would I do that?"

"My partner's dead." Donnie spoke fast and seemed to be panting.

"He had his ID and passport on him, and you rented our rooms. It's not going to take long for the police to get there, and you don't want to be dragged in for questioning."

"What the hell happened?" He stood naked in the cold air, mentally deciding what he could leave behind.

"The security system wasn't engaged, and the back door was easy to pick. We started our search with a safe in the office. It was the logical choice until some weird guy screamed and ordered us to put our hands up. Rene reached for his knife and died as he threw it." There was loud music coming from Donnie's end as well as shouting.

"Take a cab to the airport and I'll meet you there." He put his slacks back on and packed his briefcase first. That was all he cared about.

"We can't go to the airport yet. I'll get us a car, and we'll move until things calm down."

The phone went dead, making Baggio curse. Ransley had only himself to blame if the scrolls turned out to be something of importance. If someone died because of whatever the scrolls told, there was no easy path to them now. He'd underestimated Montbard, and that wasn't a mistake they could afford to repeat.

Donnie's plan sounded good in the heat of the moment, but he took a breath with his hand on the doorknob. There was nothing that could make him run. He made a call. "Your man got his associate killed. Tell me what all this is about, or I walk and go back to the stacks you like to tease me about. I didn't give up my calling for you to keep me in the dark."

"It didn't take much convincing for you to give up the collar, so try selling that to someone who's not familiar with your tailoring bill." Ransley never liked being confronted about anything, but Baggio wasn't backing down.

"Good luck with Donnie and his ego, then. I figure he'll fold like cheap lawn furniture if he's caught. When I talked to him he sounded like it wouldn't take much to rattle him apart." He hung up and took his time packing everything in the room. His days at the pulpit were sacrificed to the mission of Opus Dei, but he wasn't going to take any abuse.

The phone rang and he hesitated before picking it up. "Yes."

"You need to find Donnie and come back to London. Once you get here I'll share everything I know with you. We can't afford to leave any loose ends, and Donnie would be one."

"If you're lying to me—"

"You have my word as a gentleman. This is too important not to finish, and I need you. The scrolls are out of reach for now, but they could unlock something that needs to stay in the dark. Call me when you have a flight."

Baggio took a deep breath and called Donnie. "Meet me downstairs and be ready to travel. Make sure you pack—we're leaving tonight."

"We can't go to the airport. What about that don't you understand?"

"We're leaving tonight. Your opportunity to work without supervision is over." That was all he could do to throw Donnie a lifeline. He either did as he was told or he lost more than his job. "I need you alive long enough to tell me what happened. After that it might be time to cut you out."

Chapter Four

L evi bounced her leg in the car Poppy had provided. George's frantic call had made her and Pia run out of the Piquant. George killing someone seemed like a joke at first, but his hysteria on the phone convinced her that he thought that's what had happened. The only thing that allowed her to maintain her control was hearing that her parents were there with him.

"Dad," she called out to her father, who stood on the street talking to two men. "What the hell is going on?"

"Take a breath, Levi, and let me finish up here." Renaud Montbard was a tall man with thick dark hair and the brightest green eyes in the world. Every time Levi looked at him it gave her a sense of belonging. She resembled him in almost everything, but her father was calmer than she was no matter the situation. It was hard to imagine him being outwardly angry, since his smile was a fixture.

"I don't recognize him, but he did have a mask on. According to George, there were two of them, and the door was locked." He appeared to study the detective's phone screen. "They must have broken in."

"How can you be sure the door was locked?" the other, shorter detective asked. "There wasn't any sign of forced entry."

"George lives in a guest cottage in my yard." Levi didn't care for where this was going. "He takes care of the place for me and works for my family. He also forgets to lock up after himself, so I installed knobs that automatically lock once the door is closed. George wouldn't have messed with that."

"What exactly was he doing in your house?"

"He's invited to come and go as he pleases. If there's a dead guy in there with a mask on, he was *not* invited." She accepted the phone from her father and looked at the picture. "I don't know this guy, but he was having dinner with Baggio Brutos at the Piquant tonight. There was another guy at the table, and he and this guy left together."

"Who's Baggio Brutos?" the short detective asked.

"He tried to buy something from me in Paris a couple of days ago. I turned him down, so I guess this was his counteroffer." She glanced through the door but saw only police inside. "If that's all, I'd like to see about my friend and mother."

"What was it he wanted?" the other guy asked.

"Some scrolls I purchased at auction. Brutos was interested, but he had his chance when they were up for sale. If it's important to the case, then start at the Piquant and ask him. Who the other two men are isn't something I can tell you." She handed the phone back and returned the detective's handshake. "Please know that George is harmless, regardless of what happened here tonight. He must've been truly scared to use lethal force."

"We're not charging him. This is clearly a case of self-defense. He's being treated for a knife wound. George said the man threw it at him as he asked him to put his hands up." The detective stepped aside to let her in the house.

"Thank you. George is more than just an employee."

She found George and her mother in the study along with two EMTs. The body, thankfully, had been taken away. George's shirt was off, and he had a large bandage on his upper left chest near his arm. If the guy's aim had been more to the right, they'd have lost him. She smiled when George spotted her and started crying.

"I'm sorry." George was as upset as when he'd first called her.

"You don't need to be sorry, buddy. You didn't do anything wrong." She held his hand and sat next to him. "Are you okay?"

"He's going to need to go to the hospital," the EMT said. "That blade went in a good ways."

"We'll take him," her mother said. "It might be easier."

"I'll go with you, Madelena," Pia said as she entered. "Renaud and Levi can meet us when they're done here and lock the place up again. We can treat George to chocolate milk and beignets when he's done."

"Really?" George suddenly acted as if the trauma hadn't happened.

"You bet. Let me go get something of Levi's for you to wear and we'll go." Pia took Levi's hand and led her upstairs. "Where are the scrolls? They might come back, and we can't take the chance they'll be stolen."

"They didn't need to waste time with the safe. They're in the nightstand. I was going to start on them on my downtime in the next couple of weeks." Levi and Pia went up to her bedroom and checked. She liked the nightstand, a type of apothecary table with numerous drawers that was good at keeping numerous books as well as her laptop close when she sat up in bed.

"Are they there?" Pia asked.

"It's always the simplest place that people never look." She took out the four scrolls still in the leather satchel Claudette had purchased for her. "That's what people who were good at code in the past understood."

"What do you mean?" Pia stood next to her and placed her hand on Levi's forearm.

"Human nature is to make things complicated when it's anything but. When something is basic, it's seldom easy to believe. The best codes are hidden within layered inscriptions. This code started in the top drawer of my nightstand and not the high-security safe downstairs."

"What would've happened if the idiots who broke in were simplistic thinkers?" Pia gazed up at her and smiled in a way that meant she wanted to laugh.

"They'd both be alive, but they went for cloak and dagger, aka complicated."

"You make no sense sometimes, but oddly you're right. Why would someone break into your house for these?" Pia shook her arm gently. "From the description of where they were found and what they are, they're not worth dying over."

"Something about them is wrong. The guy I mentioned out there approached me, and at first I figured it was because he missed the auction."

"You don't think that now?"

"The Opus Dei pin he wears is what makes me curious, but it also pisses me off. Brutos was willing to hurt someone I love to get these."

"To play devil's advocate, they might not have known George was here."

"Breaking in means you need to consider that. Let me take care of these before we go." She pointed to the closet. "Get something for George and I'll meet you downstairs."

She walked out and knelt in the middle of the hallway. The guys who'd broken in were trained to find safes or hiding areas that were in rooms. Hallways were conduits to places where things were hidden. The lead-lined space in the floor held some of the things she'd loved for most of her life, but there was plenty of room for the bag.

"Ready?" She went back for Pia and grabbed a sweater for herself.

George relaxed as her mother drove them to the emergency room, and Levi sat with him holding his hand. She was the only one he wanted with him, and she'd complied. Her mind was reeling, so she tried to stare at the buildings they were passing. It was a good way to reboot her brain. Right now, her priority was George, but work was the only way to prevent this from happening again. She'd have to decipher what was on those scrolls and make it public. A secret out in the open was no longer worth hurting anyone over.

It took six stitches and George going home with Madelena to assure him he'd be okay. They'd kept their promise and taken him for beignets before they all said good night, which seemed to make him feel better. Her grandparents were waiting for Levi when she walked into her house, and her grandmother hugged Pia before pinching Levi's cheeks.

"You missed a good time, my love. All the excitement made us cut our night short, but you're going to like our new professor." Her grandparents had met in college, and her grandmother would still be taking classes if she had the time. "I'm not sure if she knows exactly what to make of us, but I'm sure you'll bring her around."

"She does have some interesting opinions on one of our favorite subjects." Her grandfather's smile appeared mischievous, and that wasn't good news for her blood pressure.

"What's that?" The day felt like it had lasted fifty hours, and Levi fought not to yawn while she asked.

"The Templars aren't her favorite, but she's knowledgeable as heck. She'd be hard to beat in a debate."

"And you know how much your grandfather loves to debate," her grandmother said. "What happened to George is horrible, but it kept our night from becoming more heated."

"So, your crush crash-landed, huh?" Levi asked her grandfather. He'd talked all about Dr. Hassani, speaking her praises over many a meal.

"I think the good doctor loves a debate as much as your grand-father." Her grandmother laughed as she poured them all a brandy. "Now, tell us what happened. This is a first when it comes to someone trying to steal from us."

"Pia and I were having dinner at the Piquant, and we saw Baggio Brutos with two men. George killed one of them after the man threw a knife into his chest."

"Cristobal told me about Brutos. It's not a wild guess that he's responsible for this." Her grandmother ran their business from behind the scenes, while her grandfather loved the client relations part. They worked well together, and their communication was wonderful. It wasn't unusual for Levi to get numerous text messages and calls from her family on a daily basis.

"Dad sent the police in the right direction, so we'll see. I'm thinking of putting off leaving until we know more."

"Don't do that," her grandmother said. "Between your parents and us we'll take care of business. You need to go and see if the impossible is possible."

"I don't feel right leaving while George is hurt." She sipped the brandy that was a staple in all three houses and glanced at Pia as something occurred to her. Things in her house magically appeared, or, more accurately, never ran out. There was always liquor in the decanters, toilet paper on the rolls, and clean underwear in her drawers. She hadn't stepped foot in a grocery store in so long she couldn't remember, and she had no idea how to run the washing machine. All the comforts were because of wonderful Pia, and she had to remember to do something nice in return.

"We'll take care of George." Pia sat next to her. "Once he's up to it, I'll drive him out myself. He'll love watching you work."

"I'll try and make it as fast as I can manage." There was no stopping the yawn that slipped out, and her grandmother stood.

"Get some sleep and stop by in the morning for breakfast. I've missed you and making the pancakes you love."

The house was quiet once Levi locked the front door. There was no echo of the excitement from earlier other than the blood on the rug in her office and the memory of the lifeless body. Pia sensed her mood and put her arms around Levi's waist. The comfort made her sigh and lower her shoulders a little.

"It's not your fault. Stop beating yourself up." Pia spoke softly as she put her hands behind Levi's head. "George did the right thing, and he's going to be okay."

"We were lucky, but have the alarm guys come in and recheck that there's no holes in security at all our places."

"You want to go to bed?"

"Only if you join me. I don't want you driving home alone right now."

They headed upstairs, and the feel of Pia's skin pressed against her relaxed her into closing her eyes and evening her breathing. "Tomorrow we start again."

❖

Yasmine studied the street from her bedroom window, glad to see everything was quiet. That her hosts' employee shot some man dead wasn't something she could wrap her head around, but that's what had ended their night. There was crime everywhere in the world, she wasn't naïve to that, but this was shocking.

"Get away from the window and come over here." Zara handed her a cup of mint tea and sat on her bed. "If anyone's going to kill you, it's going to be Cristobal with a sword through the chest. He owns enough of them."

"Thanks for that vivid description."

"Calling the Templars jackals of the devil was certainly a new way of thanking someone for a lovely meal. It's like you forgot their last name. Montbard isn't common, so you know where their family roots might lead." Zara crossed her legs and waved her over. "Are you nervous about tomorrow?"

"A little, but more excited than scared. Thank you for talking me into this." She kissed Zara's cheek and joined her.

"That's what annoying little sisters are for. Cristobal offered to give me a tour, but I'll come with you if you need me to."

"Go and have fun. If anyone knows the city, it's him. We'll meet up after and have dinner somewhere. I'm headed out early, so sleep in and call if you need anything." She went back to the work Nabil had given her. At midnight she gave up and went to sleep. New adventures were better enjoyed with enough rest.

The same driver who had picked them up from the airport was waiting for her in the morning, and he gave her directions to her temporary office when he dropped her off. She'd toured the Tulane campus virtually, but the grounds were beautiful. Large oak trees set off the old buildings as well as outdoor artwork, and she enjoyed her stroll along the wide sidewalks. Every student appeared to be wearing shorts and a T-shirt, which was more casual than what she was used to. The heat and humidity made the clothes a good choice, though.

Her office was bigger than the one back home. The wood-paneled walls gave it an old sophisticated feel, and the book-lined shelves made her fall in love. She wanted to linger here for more time than she'd signed up for. She sat in the leather chair and slipped her shoes off, liking the silkiness of the Persian rug under her feet. Her view was of a large quad that was also tree lined. The grassy open area was probably a favorite hangout.

"Enough daydreaming." She was there to give several special lectures in women's studies, and Cristobal had said the large theater classroom would be filled to capacity with all the students who'd signed up. The summer session had three visiting professors, each there for a two-week stint. She was the first.

The door opened and startled her, and she pressed her hand to her chest. "Don't you knock at this university?"

The woman seemed surprised to see her, and she cocked her eyebrow. "What are you doing in here?" The woman was as blunt as she was accusatory.

"Is there something I can do for you?" She stood, feeling foolish when she realized she was still barefoot.

"You can tell me why you're in my grandfather's office." The woman stepped in and closed the door, as if trying to keep her trapped inside. "Well?"

"This is where they put me. If it's someone else's office it's not my mistake, so I'd appreciate you not being so hostile. My key fit." She put her fists on her hips and glared, but there was something about the woman that seemed familiar. The pictures on the walls clued her into why that was. "Who's your grandfather?"

"Cristobal Montbard. He was the dean of the history department until he retired recently. He's still on staff, though, and this is his office. I doubt he'd appreciate anyone moving in when he's not here."

She held up the key Cristobal had given her. The keychain had a gold coin on the end, and she finally studied it. The writing on it was Arabic, with a sort of flower at its center. This was an interesting family, or maybe it was only Cristobal. The later generation had plenty to learn in manners.

"He gave me this key and directions on how to get here." She put the key back in her purse and crossed her arms. "Are you sure you're related?"

"Ah, Dr. Hassani. He's been looking forward to your arrival."

Yasmine's skin tingled and she knew it was from anger, always anger and never from anything else, no matter what the romance books said. "Cristobal is different from most men I've met. He sees the world—why am I wasting my time? What do you want?"

"He didn't say you had such a short fuse." The woman sounded condescending, but there was a hint of a smile on her lips.

"Who are you?"

"Levi Montbard, and like I said, Cristobal is my grandfather. He must really like you if he gave you this place."

"Are you going to be barging in here every day? I'll rethink the accommodations if that's the case."

"I'll be gone in a minute, but I needed one thing out of here." Levi walked to the bookshelf and ran her fingers along the books. She pulled one, held it up, and tapped the cover. "I need a refresher on my old Arabic, but maybe you'd be better than a book."

"You just accused me of trespassing, and now you want help?" She shook her head and scoffed. "Are you that arrogant or that brainless?"

"This office—" Levi started, then put up her finger. "Better yet, let me show you."

Levi crooked her finger and opened the door. The dates under the pictures outside went back to the founding of the university. Most of them were men, but there were a few women, and they all had one thing in common. "There's been a Montbard in the history department as long as they've been teaching in this city. My father, Renaud, is the dean now, but he let my grandfather keep his office."

"Okay," Yasmine said, stretching the word. "It's impressive, but now it seems to be more about tradition than—"

"Picking the right person for the job?" Levi finished for her, but it was a good guess. "I only know my father and my grandfather in this job. My love is centered more around field work than the classroom, but my time here is something I won't ever forget."

The pictures of Renaud and Cristobal made it easy to see the strong family resemblance to Levi. "College is usually a time everyone likes to look back on."

"Their skill in weaving the past to make it come to life is what I meant. It's something your students say you do." Levi walked back into the office and retrieved her book. "Good luck, and I hope to make it back before you're done."

"Wait." Yasmine spoke louder than she meant to, but she didn't want Levi to leave like this. "What do you need help with?"

"Before we go on, I'd like to apologize for earlier. Enjoy the space." Levi smiled, and this time it appeared relaxed and genuine. "You're the only person who's ever reminded me of my family in the classroom. History, the way you teach it, becomes a living thing. When you get people to enjoy it, I think it helps us learn. By learning, we tend not to repeat our past mistakes."

"Did Cristobal tell you that?" She pressed her toes into the carpet and tried to ignore the warmth in her ears. Blushing wasn't something she did often.

"You did, actually. I sat in on one of your classes a few years ago. The lecture hall was big enough that you probably didn't notice me. I'm sorry for not recognizing you earlier. You're hard to forget."

Yasmine didn't know what to make of the statement or the wink Levi gave her at the end. "I'm hard to forget how?" When in doubt, ask.

"You're a beautiful and smart woman who doesn't seem…" Levi faded off and chuckled. "I think if I finish that, you might physically throw me out of here."

"Please, you must." She took a step closer and placed her hands on the back of a reading chair. "I'm curious now."

"How about you get to know me better, and then I'll be happy to tell you." Levi leaned against the desk and crossed her feet at the ankles. "Were you serious about helping me?"

"How else will I get to know you better? You've managed to insult me and compliment me all in the span of five minutes. That takes talent." She moved around and sat in the chair across from her. "What are you working on?"

"What I'm working on is something I found trapped in a book, and I'm leaving to see if it's total bullsh—ah, bull." Levi stopped herself from cursing, and it made Yasmine laugh. "I purchased some scrolls recently, and they're in an older language than I'm familiar with, but it's still in the Arabic family. It would be stupid of me not to ask an expert the Moroccan government depends on to do the same thing."

"Wow, I didn't think there was so much about me on Google."

"You'd be surprised, but I have my own kind of Google, and it's much more thorough." Levi grasped the book on her knee and smiled at her again. "I have to go, but perhaps if I'm done early enough, I can treat you to dinner or a drink."

"Where are you going?" If she wasn't so rusty in the dating department, she would swear Levi was sort of flirting with her, but that couldn't be the case. It didn't bother her since it was subtle enough to feel safe.

"It's about sixty miles from here, and I doubt few people who live in the city have even heard of it, but when you break a code and it puts an X on the map, it's worth the drive." Levi glanced at her watch and grimaced. "My team is waiting for me, so how about this." She stood, took a sheet of notepaper from the leather holder on the desk, and wrote something down. "Here's my number. If you're not busy tonight, give me a call."

"Give me a sixty-second scenario of what I'm getting into." She really didn't want her to go.

"The scrolls were supposedly written by a young girl, and then buried with her. I bought them, and an operative for Opus Dei tried to buy them and then hired some thugs to break into my house and steal them. Now one of them is dead and my friend is recovering from a knife wound. I doubt anyone would go through that trouble if these things contained the day-to-day diary of a young girl who lived a very long time ago."

"Interesting. What time tonight?" Yasmine took the paper and glanced down at the messy handwriting. At least the numbers were legible. "I think there's more to your story than that, but the Opus Dei angle does add something sinister."

"There's plenty more, but you already think I'm arrogant, and there's no need to add crazy to that. Good luck today, Dr. Hassani, and I should be showered and done by eight."

Yasmine watched Levi leave. It wasn't often that she met anyone who felt like an old friend, or at least someone she'd met before and liked. Maybe her subconscious mind remembered her in her classroom when she didn't. Either way, she was looking forward to making the call that night and talking to this enigmatic but aggravating woman.

Chapter Five

L evi followed the GPS directions to the exact spot where the small team would be waiting for her. Choupick was a blip on the map with perhaps seventy nice homes that must have housed some higher-ups working in the neighboring town of Thibodaux. One of her guys was on the road next to a cane field blowing slightly in the breeze. There were few houses, but the empty land was filled with cane and soybeans, making for lush green spaces.

"The farmer is waiting for you about a mile in, and he has some questions," Greg Grassley said when she stopped and lowered her window.

"As in, *am I going to get rich* kind of questions?" Private land was always iffy. People's expectations of compensation varied to the ridiculous or impossible at times, but places like this held nothing of value except as a jumping-off point to something else.

"I don't get that vibe." Greg pulled on his lip ring, making him resemble a hooked trout. The four people she'd picked for this trip were young and still in school, but time with her excused them from the classroom as long as they kept up with their work.

"Get in and let's go talk to this guy."

The recent rain made the dirt road between the rows of crops a muddy soup, but the four-wheel-drive Jeep made it fine until she reached an ancient man wearing overalls. If you looked up *farmer* in the dictionary, you'd find this guy. "Good morning, sir."

"My friends call me Bumpy," he said, combing down the small ring of white hair that went only an inch above his ears. Levi could tell him it wasn't going anywhere that needed any kind of smoothing down.

"Hey, Bumpy, my name's Levi, and I believe my assistant Pia

went over all the particulars with you. Did you receive the check she sent?" She felt the need to ask him about the nickname, but she was burning daylight.

"That wasn't necessary. The swamp out there doesn't really belong to me. Well, it does, but I ain't ever got anything of worth out of there. What do you think is hidden in all that muck?"

"The short answer is information. Muck surprises us sometimes. Think of this as the first stop in a scavenger hunt. If it's something other than what I think, we get a fair market value of the items found, and you get half that value." She took comfort in the way he was nodding.

"You thinking pirates?" he asked in a way that assured her the way to go here was to say yes. Bumpy was an old dude, but it took sixty years off him when he asked that question.

She couldn't blame him—pirates were the best. "How about you follow us out there and I'll give you the long answer, since you seem interested."

Bumpy seemed mesmerized as she gave him a short history of not only local pirates, but groups of people who explored the land way before Christopher Columbus was credited with discovering the New World. Old Chris had the better marketing team, so he was the one who'd ended up with the federal holiday. "You have to imagine the land hundreds of years ago, and also take into consideration the storms we've had since then."

"So this might've not been swamp back then?" Bumpy sat in one of their camp chairs and looked like he was in for the day.

"Maybe, and maybe not. If there's anything down there, it's going to take a minor miracle to find it, but my faith in locating the unknown has blessed me with a lot of patience." She zipped up her short wetsuit, and Pam Hebert helped her on with her tank.

The helmet she was using would allow her to communicate with the team. Pam was on equipment, Greg was in charge of logistics, Brad Jenkins was on the radio, and Blue Fitch was steering the small boat. Blue had grown up the only girl in a family of thirteen, and she was the only college student in a family of high school dropouts who all fished for a living.

"Good luck, Levi, and if you find something, maybe I could give tours out here," Bumpy said and laughed. "Might liven up the dreary farming days."

"Thanks. Feel free to hang around. I'm not promising a great view, but you can watch the feed coming from my helmet with Brad and Greg." She entered the boat as Bumpy moved his chair closer to the monitors. "Let's hit it, Blue."

They went out farther than she'd thought, and all the cypress trees they dodged made her nervous. If whatever the map pinpointed was buried under one of the old behemoths, their day was done. "This is the coordinates you gave me," Blue said, dropping the anchor. "We're in about eight feet of water, which is surprising for a swamp. I'll be on the lookout for all the less-than-friendly residents this place breeds."

"Thanks. Fighting off a gator isn't in my plans for today." Levi strapped the small GPS unit to her wrist as Blue placed her helmet on. She grabbed a type of police baton that telescoped out another five feet. The book code had put the time frame at exactly 1300 AD. Over seven hundred years of hurricanes and sediment were something she'd have to contend with, but you had to start at the beginning.

The brown water was surprisingly clear when she went over the side, and she put visibility at around six feet. She dropped to the bottom and stood still to let the water settle. The surface was only two feet from the top of her head, and the sun that penetrated the tree canopy came down in spears that lit up the area around her. There were a few fish, but she concentrated on the GPS at her wrist. She was six feet away from the spot on the grid they'd start with.

"What's it like, boss?" Brad asked.

"No current will make this much easier, and it's shockingly clear. If we bring the submersible I'm going to have to walk it around. There are a million trees growing out of this water, and plenty more still on the bottom. Maybe the treasure is really the wood that's probably worth a fortune. Tell Bumpy that might be his next big venture."

The thrill of standing on the exact spot someone did so long ago sent a chill down her as if a ghost had walked through her. This was what it meant to walk in the footsteps of history, and why she hadn't given it up for the classroom. That would come in time, and one day she'd think about days like this when she took her rightful place behind that big desk at Tulane.

She pressed the button and released the rod, stabbing into the muck. It went in easily all the way to her hand, and she tried again in a few more spots. Nothing. "Blue, send down some markers, please." The ten rebars were five feet long with orange tape at the top, and she drove one in the middle of the spot she'd just probed. The probing was slow enough that she had to come up and change tanks as the hours ticked by.

"We're burning daylight, boss," Greg said. "You want to call it for the day?"

"Give me another fifteen and I should be able to map out the northern direction." Her feet sank into the mud. It felt cool now that there wasn't as much light coming through.

She feared this was going to take more than the two weeks she'd planned as she held the last marker for the day. Her calculations put whatever it was in this vicinity, given the weather patterns and other factors that had to be taken into consideration. Her arm was tired as she jabbed into the mud, and there was nothing. The next probe, though, hit something hard, solid, and if her experience counted for anything, metallic.

"I got something." She said it softly and repeated it when Greg didn't say anything back. "Can you fucking believe it?"

"You're not kidding?" Greg asked.

"It's about four feet down, and there's a lot of roots, but there's something there." She lifted the probe out and went in from another angle.

It took her another fifteen minutes to go all around the top and get the dimensions of the find. When she finished, she had something that was roughly two feet by three feet. That it was metal didn't leave her with much hope that anything inside had survived. Not documents, anyway, and it was unlikely to hold silver or gold, given what she knew of what might be in it. Documents were what she'd hoped for, and she sighed in disappointment. It was too much time, and the introduction of water would make this a recovery of mush.

"I need you and Brad to set up in the boat and stay the night." She pushed off the bottom and surfaced. Blue was waiting and took her helmet off, making it easier to get back in the boat. "This is just short of a miracle." She combed her hair back, sweating despite the sun sinking fast.

"I'll stay with Greg tonight. Neither of those guys is great on a boat, and if they drift tonight, I doubt we'll ever find them." Blue started the small motor and got them back to shore. "That and I have a mosquito net in the truck. We'll be fine."

Bumpy was the first one waiting on her, and the size of his smile meant he was probably thinking of pirates again. "You found something?"

"I did, and tomorrow we'll figure out how to get it out of there."

She walked to the Jeep and stripped off the wetsuit. Her bathing suit was mostly dry, but it was still hot enough to sweat, and she felt like she needed a shower. "Is there any way to lock up the access road back here? I'm leaving my guys, but I don't want anyone giving them any problems tonight."

"Don't worry about that. My wife and I will come out and make sure everyone is okay. If anyone decides to give us a problem, then I have a shotgun that's a great deterrent to scumbags trying to take what isn't theirs." Bumpy appeared to have gotten a shot of adrenaline. If Levi was lucky, there'd be at least one piece of gold or silver in that metal box that she could leave him. It'd be something he could brag about to his friends and grandkids until the end of his life.

"Are you sure?" She didn't want to be responsible for someone else getting hurt since George was still on her mind. "Nights can be long when you spend them out here."

"I grew up in the swamp, and there ain't anything out here that scares me. Go on and get back here early with that fancy coffee. If I'm going to try new things, then I'm going all the way." Bumpy laughed and shook her hand again. "You can trust me with your group. I'll get my son to sit out there with them."

"Thanks, Bumpy, and I'll be back early with fancy coffee and breakfast." She told the group she was headed to the hotel to take a shower, but she couldn't get any of them to follow her. They'd have a night out in the swamp swatting bugs and being awed by the number of alligators that lived where she'd been swimming. She'd never ask them to do anything she wasn't willing to do herself.

"Give me a couple of hours and I'll be back. Greg, can you drive up the road and pick up whatever Pia orders for you guys?" She sent Pia a text asking her to find something good for dinner and sent the information to Greg. "Let me take a shower and I'll come back so you guys can do the same."

It wasn't that far to the hotel Pia had booked, and as Levi stood under the warm strong spray of the shower, she thought about the last week as a whole. There was something she was missing, but she couldn't narrow it down enough to figure it out. Her brain felt like a bundle of knotted cable, and she was having trouble finding the ends so she could start unraveling it.

❖

Yasmine cleaned up the kitchen and waved to Zara as she left for a long walk with Cristobal and Diana. They were showing her sister all the supposedly haunted spots in the Quarter that were close by and had promised to have her home early. The two lectures she'd given today had gone well and she'd enjoyed talking to students who were full of questions on the subject matter.

She glanced at the clock and saw it was ten to eight. As much fun as she'd had, she was still looking forward to talking to Levi. If it hadn't been for the commitment she'd made to teach, she'd have rented a car and driven out to wherever Levi was working. Her job had always been to study the past, but she'd never actually seen an operation to find it. Up to now she'd only seen the result in museums.

The house phone rang, and she stared at it. If it was her mother, she'd be on the phone for the rest of the night and wouldn't get to talk to Levi. "Hello," she said softly.

"Were you trying to ditch me already?"

The words made her laugh. "I said I'd help, and you told me to call you. Did you think I'd forget?"

"My grandfather will tell you I'm the impatient kind." Levi laughed, and it made Yasmine smile. "How did your first day go?"

"Good. I'm not used to so many questions, but I like curious students." She opened the refrigerator, took out the bottle of wine they hadn't finished with dinner, and poured herself another glass. "What kind of student were you?"

"I'm still in school, according to my parents, so I'll let you decide that." Levi sounded as if she was moving around, and Yasmine wished they could share a glass of wine together. It was totally insane, but it wasn't often that she met anyone who fascinated her so quickly. Levi was her complete opposite. "But if I'd been there today, you'd still be in that lecture hall answering questions."

"I don't doubt that. How did it go for you today?" She climbed the stairs and walked to the window to stare at the house she now knew belonged to Levi. "Did you find what you were looking for?"

"I found something. You have to wait until tomorrow to find out what." Levi sighed, and it sounded more like she was exhausted than from not wanting to talk.

"Give me a hint."

"It's metal and it's at the bottom of a swamp. I'm going to have to pry it out of the root system of some giant cypress trees. Had anyone told me I'd actually find something in that spot after breaking a code in a book that shouldn't exist any longer, I would have thought it was the by-product of a bad hangover." Levi sounded like she was on the move down some stairs.

"Where are you going?"

"My eager team is out there for the night, and I don't want to leave them alone. I came back to take a shower, but I've got a night of ghost stories and local wildlife ahead of me. Whatever this is, I'm probably going to bring it home to open it. The location is already compromised enough that it's doubtful there's anything left."

"You said this place is not that far from the city," Yasmine said, taking a sip of wine and getting on the bed.

"A little over an hour. What time do you finish tomorrow?"

"At one." She'd have to find a way of getting there, because she really wanted to see what Levi was talking about. "Now tell me about the scrolls you purchased?"

"I don't have much information except what the auction house gave me, but I have a hunch." The ding of Levi's car door came through and Yasmine gave her time to get settled. "I'm not putting you off, but can we wait until I get back to talk about what my crazy theories are?"

"If you're already admitting you're crazy, this should be interesting." She laughed when Levi did and took a sip of her wine. "Tell me about this latest job of yours, then."

"One thing our business specializes in is rare books. The ones I really like are the kind that had small runs or were personal dairies."

"You and I have something in common, then," she said. Those types of books had been her training ground for what she did for the government and had brought her to Nadil's attention.

"You're crazy too?" Levi teased. "It's so progressive of you to come out and admit it."

"I'm no such thing," she said but laughed. "I actually love old books and diaries. I'm not sure where you are, but that you were led to a place from an old code does seem unbelievable. I'm not as knowledgeable on early American history, but there were plenty of pirates working this area. Am I wrong?"

Levi laughed again. "That's the second time today that I've heard the pirate theory, only Bumpy seemed more excited about it."

"Bumpy? Is this a small child with an unfortunate name?"

"He's about eighty, but pirates are something that made him sound like a little boy again. Bumpy owns the land I'm working on, and he's also out there keeping my team safe from snakes and alligators."

"Would you mind if Zara and I came out tomorrow?" The question was forward, but perhaps her mother was right. Signs were thrown in your path to shake you out of the normal so you could start living what could be a more complete life. "I'll have to rent a car or something, but if it's not that far I could come after I'm done at the university."

"I'd like that, and don't worry about driving. Use the driver, I promise he won't mind, and your sister is welcome if she's interested." Levi paused as if thinking of something else. "If it's not too late once we're done, would you consider dinner?"

"I'd love to," she answered without a second of hesitation. "And I'll try not to take insult that you're questioning my driving."

Levi's laugh was full and open. "I have no idea about that, but when you get a look at this place you'll understand what I'm talking about. It's as out of the way as it gets, but if you're feeling adventurous, ask my grandfather for my car. There's no reason to rent one when mine is sitting in my garage."

"I might do that. My sister is the more adventurous of the two of us, but I'm learning." They talked until the signal started to get touchy, which had to be from Levi's end. It made Yasmine smile when Levi doubled back to make sure she could say good night and have her hear every word.

The next day she talked Zara into going with her as she drove Levi's SUV to the university. Having her sister with her would save her from having to go back to the French Quarter, and the car's GPS had the coordinates of where she'd find Levi.

The drive out to the site took them through some small towns that in no way resembled anything back home, and some large areas of swamp and marsh. Zara hadn't said much but Yasmine could tell there was something on her mind as they exited the highway for a two-lane road along a waterway. The houses they passed were a mixture of new and old, but all of them had large yards with moss-draped oak trees.

It was like they'd landed on a different planet compared to their home. The large homes and green spaces for as far as they could see weren't found in Morocco. There were plenty of places back home she found relaxing, but the area they were driving through made her exhale and enjoy the ride. The foreignness of it was beautiful.

"Is there something wrong?" she asked. Silence in Zara was such a rarity, she was starting to worry. She glanced at the screen and saw they had twenty miles to go.

"I'm enjoying the scenery, don't start channeling Mama." Zara laughed and slapped her arm softly. "I'm also trying to figure out why you're dragging us out of the city for someone you've never really met."

"We've met. I told you what happened, and I'm interested in what she found. She's Cristobal's granddaughter, so she can't be all bad. Right?" The road was curvy enough for her to have to keep her eyes on it, so it was hard to gauge what Zara was thinking.

"I don't believe she's bad at all, but I'm glad you've decided to come out of that shell of yours and make new friends. I worry about you sometimes."

"You don't have to. I'm not unhappy with my life, and before you say anything, I don't want to settle into something simply to have someone other than you to talk to. You remind me of Mama sometimes too." There were times she was lonely, but it was hard letting people in. Growing up in a society that expected such specific things from her made it hard to find like-minded people. People who didn't want to fit into the mold that everyone else seemed to aspire to.

"The last thing I want for you is what Mama wants for you, but I looked up the Montbard family. Levi Montbard is an interesting woman who's really good at her job."

She hiked her eyebrows at that. Zara wasn't known for her detective skills outside of her academic studies. "I gathered that much, but I have a feeling there's more."

"She appears to be as talented in romancing women as she is in acquiring things for their business." Zara sounded almost apprehensive, and it made Yasmine smile. It was times like this that highlighted their ten-year age difference. It wasn't a lot of years, but Zara seemed to see the world differently than she did.

"Are you worried I'll be banished, or appalled I might befriend someone like Levi?" She couldn't hold in her laughter when Zara turned in her seat to face her. "Don't worry. I'm not going to go insane on you so you'll get in trouble with Mama."

"That's not what I'm talking about." Zara stopped, then smiled. "Well, that is what I'm talking about, but I wanted you to know."

"It's like some scene out of a horror movie where you keep wondering why they're being so stupid," Yasmine said when the GPS told her to turn right onto an even smaller road. There were some abandoned buildings overgrown with vines, and some larger trees that looked ancient. They drove another five miles before seeing a young man waving on the side of the road.

"Dr. Hassani?" he asked when she slowed and dropped the window.

"That's me."

"Good, follow me. Levi's in the water trying to dig a hole, and it's taking some time."

They followed him to a clearing, and when she got out, she could hear Levi's voice where a group was watching a picture of some muddy water on a screen. Yasmine glanced toward the swamp but didn't see anything that would clue her in to where Levi was.

"Hey," another guy said when he noticed them. "Have a seat."

"Thank you." She couldn't take her attention from the screen, and she saw Levi's hands as she held a shovel.

"Your guests are here, boss."

"I'll stop cursing, then, so they won't think I'm a total idiot." The camera angle went lower to the bottom and they watched Levi's hand disappear into the hole she'd made. "If I can free the other corner, maybe we can try pulling it out with the Jeep."

"It's four-wheel drive, but I doubt it'll survive eight feet of water." The two guys and young woman laughed.

"We'll need a lot of rope, smart-ass." Levi grunted as she went back to work. "There's a big bunch of roots across the top, so pulling it might be our only option. Even if we cut the tree down, the root system isn't going anywhere."

"Let's see how much we have, and I'll go find some more if we need it." The guy who'd led them out there wandered off.

Yasmine and Zara watched as a small boat came into view with a young woman at the motor. "You guys interested in a swamp tour?" the boat's pilot asked.

"Yes, thank you." She stood and Zara didn't hesitate to join her. One of the guys put in a huge mound of thick rope and took the end before instructing them to unwind it so it didn't get caught up on itself.

They went slowly in the straightest line they could manage to get to Levi. The rope she and Zara stretched out as they went had about twenty feet to spare when Blue cut the engine. Yasmine startled when Levi popped up next to her.

"Hey." The word was muffled because of the helmet, and Yasmine had to bend down to hear it. She waved and handed Levi the end of the rope. She didn't know what she expected out of the day, but so far it was exciting. Finding history was not what she did, but she could learn to love it as much as Levi did.

The radio came to life as Levi's lips moved, and Blue nodded as she got the order to move aside. Levi didn't want them hurt if the rope snapped. They all waited quietly as Levi looped the end around her find and the rope pulled taut. It held as they heard a vehicle rev up in the distance.

"Did it move?" Blue asked into a handheld radio when the rope went slack again.

"Boss says if this is something someone threw overboard empty, she's going to be pissed," a guy said. "Stay put, she's repositioning the rope."

It took five attempts before Blue sent what looked like a hammock over the side. The box was about three feet square, patinaed, and came up muddy but appeared solid. Blue tied it to the side, then helped Levi with her tank and gear. Levi pulled the box up, and between the three of them, they pulled it into the boat before she joined them.

"You arrived in time for the good part." Levi leaned over and washed the mud off her hands. "Levi Montbard," she said, holding her hand out to Zara once she'd dried it. "It's nice to meet you."

"She's not rude at all," Zara said, mortifying Yasmine.

She felt the heat of her blush when Levi laughed. The only good thing was her dark complexion hid embarrassment well. "She can't keep a secret."

"It's no secret Levi can be an ass," Blue said as they neared land.

"You're hilarious," Levi said. "Bumpy, we got something."

The old man who'd introduced himself earlier came closer and touched the box. He did appear younger as he ran his fingertips along the surface. "What now?"

"Now you trust me to take it so I can try and figure out what's in there before we pry the lid off. If it's as old as I think, there's some steps we need to take beforehand to preserve what's in there if we can."

"You'll call me, right?"

"You and your wife are welcome to come with me." Levi unzipped the wetsuit and watched as the two guys filled a container with water and lifted it into the SUV before setting the box in it and sealing the top.

"We've got some stuff going on, but I trust you." Bumpy shook Levi's hand and stuck his cap back on.

"You can come visit me or the crew anytime. They'll be sticking around to map out the area and make sure I didn't miss anything."

Yasmine watched Levi give orders after she'd changed and gladly gave up the driving duties when Levi said they were heading back. She sat in the front seat with Levi but enjoyed the conversation Zara kept up as they drove. It sounded like her sister found Levi as likable as she did.

"Will you open it soon?" Zara asked the question on Yasmine's mind.

"Once we x-ray it, I can give you an answer." Levi had made it back to campus faster than Yasmine expected, and they followed her into the building. It didn't take much to convince a few guys to carry the heavy box inside and set it down in a lab.

"Dr. Hassani and Zara, I'd like you to meet my father, Renaud."

So far everyone Yasmine had met in the Montbard family was nice to talk to, and Renaud was no exception. He kept them entertained with a few stories of things they'd found as Levi worked to x-ray the box as well as run it through various tests.

"It's lead, and there's definitely something inside," Levi announced after an hour. "We'll have to lock the room down since it's swimming in something and there's no way to know if it's toxic or not, but there are at least two solid things in there."

The top took some effort to remove, and they watched from the safety of the observation room as the mercury that filled the box shone under the fluorescent lights. Zara and Yasmine stood on their toes to get a good view as Levi found hazard containers to put the stuff in.

"Why mercury?" Zara asked.

"Think of it as an old preservative. It preserves parchment as well as paper for years in the right conditions." Yasmine saw Renaud nodding as she spoke. "I'm not sure it handles hundreds of years of water, but we'll see."

Levi lifted out two flat stones and what appeared to be a leather bag. Their eyes met through the glass, and she could almost touch Levi's excitement. The stones were carved, but what held her attention was the lid Levi held up. After a cleaning solution had been applied, they could all clearly see the Templar cross engraved on the surface.

"What in the world?" Yasmine whispered the words, but a chill went through her. It wasn't from fear but from the impatience of not knowing. The Templars had been a prominent theme of their trip, and she didn't know what to make of it. "What's that doing in the New World?"

CHAPTER SIX

D ad, can we lock this up?" Levi prepared two pans of cleaning solution and put the stones inside. She then moved to the bag and opened it carefully. The leather had become almost rubbery, and the mercury had filled the inside. "I need to set it up to drain and see if we can salvage anything, but that's going to take time."

"This place has great security, but I'll get a couple of guards we use at the store to come and spend the night. If it drains off enough, you should know something by tomorrow." He placed his hand on the glass that separated them and tapped his fingers against it. "Is there anything else in there?"

She finished hanging the six scrolls with special clips, but she didn't unroll them. The mercury sheeted off them, and even through her gloves they felt strange. They were parchment but the kind made from animal skin, like the ones she'd purchased recently. That discovery made her want to rush, but she wanted to follow every step to assure they'd be able to read whatever was on them. The mercury as well as the time they'd been submerged had given them a dark appearance, so it would take some work to uncover what they said.

"That's it. Bumpy will be disappointed there was no pirate treasure, but maybe we can pay him in gold bullion. We have some around the shop, I think." The small room that separated her from the others allowed her to strip off all her protective attire.

"Bumpy has to realize this might be more valuable than a bucket of gold," her dad said.

"You had to see him talk about pirates, Dr. Montbard," Yasmine said.

"Please, call me Renaud, and all men keep that little boy we once were alive and well when it comes to buried treasure." This made them all laugh, and Levi hugged him once she joined them. "Go on, I promise all this will be fine."

"How about the dinner I promised you?" Levi asked, and the Hassani sisters nodded.

"Actually, how about we cook dinner and we can stay in and you can tell us a story?" Yasmine asked.

"That would require a trip to the grocery store, and one of us knowing how to cook. I know how to drive to the store, so hopefully one of you knows what to buy." Levi smiled and Yasmine gazed at her as if she didn't know what to make of her.

"Maybe that little boy lives on for more than just treasure. Let's go, I know how to cook and what to buy."

It didn't take much time to get everything Yasmine deemed necessary. Once home, Levi opened a bottle of wine, gave them a tour of the house, and answered questions about the antiques she'd collected along the way. Each of the three homes the Montbards owned was filled with the things the family had found through the years, and the Hassani sisters seemed to love the house.

"So?" Yasmine asked once they were done with dinner and they'd all moved to the study. The sofa and chairs made it one of the most comfortable spots in the house. "Tell us a story."

"Are you sure?" Levi smiled, knowing that what she'd be hunting for opened her to some teasing. No one in the academic world had believed all the clues she'd found led to two specific people.

"I said I'd help you and not think you're crazy, so I'm sure." Yasmine slipped her shoes off and folded her legs under her as she leaned back on the sofa.

"It started four years ago when I found an old diary in Florence. The shopkeeper had it translated. It didn't have a lot of entries and seemed like a type of poetry that sounded like gibberish." She laughed when she thought of some of the lines. "It was like whoever this guy was discovered the wonders of heavy drugs, and it made him love things like cauliflower."

"What year was it written?" Yasmine asked.

"Carbon dating put it between 1300 and 1400 AD, and it's written in French. When you read it, it sounded like madness, but my grandfather is an expert on code and taught me a few things." She went to the filing cabinet and pulled the file on the book, which was now locked up.

"If the poetry was that bad, the owner should've known it was code," Zara said. "At least realized there was something more to it."

"Believe me, he charged enough for that little bit of craziness that I don't feel bad," she said and laughed. "Old books and journals have become expensive, and prices continue to rise because of one certain industry."

"Art forgery," Yasmine said. The way the professor stared at her made Levi smile. Yasmine was either toying with her or indulging her. Either one was fine.

"It's not common, or not as common as the movies make it out to be, but old paper and cheap old art comes in handy when you're trying to fool the carbon dating of things. It's a crime that's hit book collectors the hardest, but anyone stupid enough to buy an unknown author just because it's old is asking to be ripped off." She flipped through the file and pulled one page. "This is the first page."

The copy had circles around certain letters with the complete translation at the bottom. This small and seemingly insignificant book had changed her life and started her down the rabbit hole that this chase for information had become. Once she'd worked out what proved to be a very complex code, she'd found the existence of the person she'd begun chasing through time.

"Who's André Sonnac?" Yasmine asked, not looking up from the page Levi had given her.

"A member of the Knights Templar from France around 1300 AD." She pointed to the notes in the margin. "The main key to unlocking the message this held was *Beau Ciel*. It was repeated in the first poem five times, followed by the number of grapes it takes to find happiness."

"Beautiful sky," Yasmine said. Moroccans, like other peoples occupied by the French, spoke the language beautifully. "I understand the key, but I'm still not sure what's special about one particular Templar Knight."

"Being as versed in the Templars as I am, you know how they began—why they were formed."

"They were escorts to nobles going to fight in the Crusades. Legend has it that while they were in the Holy Land, they found something that they used to bribe the Church into leaving them to exist without any papal oversight." Yasmine knew plenty about one of Levi's favorite subjects. "At first the Church embraced their legion of warrior monks—before they lost control of them."

"The Church has seen the error of their ways when it comes to the Templars, but their narrative revolves around these devoted men who fought to spread the word of God. An army of God is something to be proud of now, and the pope issued a mea culpa so everyone should forget what they did when they ordered God's army killed."

"I understand that, and I understand your love of the Templars considering your name. I told Cristobal the same thing." Yasmine sipped her wine and appeared at home on Levi's sofa. "What does all of that have to do with André Sonnac?"

"André Sonnac rose through the ranks and, from the information I've found, was as good on the battlefield as behind the pulpit. After the actions of Pope Clement V, the Templars were in danger of being erased from history, and only the actions of a few saved it for posterity. Today we know the contributions they made to modern man only because there were some who believed in their cause." She stopped and took a breath, smiling when Yasmine laughed softly.

"Should we run out and get you a soapbox? I believe that is the saying. History is always a double-edged sword, my friend, and a lot of my people died at the end of those pretty swords the Templars carried into the Holy Land." Yasmine kept her voice light, but she pointed at her. "But we wouldn't be earning interest on our accounts at the bank if it wasn't for your army of God."

That did make Levi laugh. Banking was usually the only thing people knew about the Templars, if they knew anything at all. "What if I told you André Sonnac gave up the sword and tried to find a quiet life at Beau Ciel with a woman from the Holy Land? They tried to make a life at the family's estate only to have it stripped from them by Pope Clement V when he ordered the Templars slaughtered. They ran before the papal forces arrived and took with them a full account of the Templar history, including their own."

"He loved a woman most people thought of as an infidel back then?" Yasmine's voice was softer but still disbelieving. "This dark skin wasn't considered acceptable, and in some circles that hasn't changed much."

"If I'm right, their love was epic, but I've shared all I know, and since the Church destroyed so much, a journal found in a shop in Florence isn't going to stand up to scrutiny."

"You sound like a romantic," Zara said.

Hearing her voice jarred Levi's attention away from Yasmine.

She'd almost forgotten the young woman was there. "If you knew me, I doubt you'd believe that."

Zara laughed and shook her head. "You should listen to yourself more often, then. As fun as tonight has been, I promised your grandfather I'd take a walk with him in the morning."

"Come on, then," Yasmine said.

"No, you stay," Zara said, putting her hand on Yasmine's arm. "You can't help if you're across the street."

"Let me walk you back," Levi said. She stood and was pleased that Yasmine stayed seated. "There's tea in the kitchen. Feel free to hunt for it if you want some."

Zara put her hand in the crook of Levi's arm, and Yasmine's eyes seemed riveted on her sister. "Come on," Zara said. They walked across the street as Zara moved closer to her so they could squeeze through some cars parked along the side of the street. "Thank you for a lovely time. Don't let my sister sink back into her shell. She needs something to get excited about again."

Levi took her keys and unlocked the door for Zara. "She seems old enough to make up her mind about things."

"She's no pushover, but sometimes she likes the safe road too much."

"I'll keep that in mind." Levi stayed still when Zara stood on her tiptoes and kissed her cheek. She waited until she heard the lock engage, then let out a long breath. "What the hell was that?" She shook her head at the question and had to laugh. Mysteries were everywhere.

Yasmine looked around the room and thought Levi fit here. They didn't really know each other, but that gut sense of knowing something without proof settled in her head, and she sighed. She had to pace herself and not get caught up in all this. In a couple of weeks, she'd have to go home, settle back into her life, and start thinking of all the things expected of her.

"Damn," she said out loud. Today was the first time since she'd worked with Nabil that she didn't feel trapped. When her mother spoke of responsibility and expectations, Yasmine could almost hear the doors of her jail cell slamming closed. Her life would be confined to a space that would grow smaller with time.

"I have to stop drinking," she said, laughing. She went back into Levi's kitchen and filled the kettle sitting on the stove. The large, open space was the exact opposite of her small apartment close to the university at home. It was a perfect contrast of her life and Levi's.

It took her a few minutes to find Levi's selection of tea and take out two mint tea bags. She heard the door open and close as the kettle whistled. The loose braid she'd put her hair in that morning was starting to come undone, and she combed the strands of hair that had escaped behind her ear. She didn't have to turn around to know Levi was in the room with her—she sensed her.

"Thank you for walking her back. Zara's adventurous streak scares me at times. She never knows when it would be prudent to be wary." She poured the hot water and finally faced Levi as she let the tea steep.

"You can't find treasure unless you're willing to take chances," Levi said. Her arms were crossed, and her hip was leaning on the granite-topped island.

"That might be true, but it's no reason to be reckless." She handed Levi a cup and mirrored her stance on the other side of the island. "Is there more to the story you told me?"

"Plenty, and you haven't heard the best part." Levi narrowed her eyes, but her smile was still in place. "Can I trust you, Dr. Hassani?"

"You might be sliding back into that rude persona I met at first." She narrowed her eyes too, and Levi chuckled. "If you need to hear me say it, you can trust me."

"Come with me." Levi took her cup and walked back to the study. This room, like the office Yasmine had at Tulane, had beautiful full bookcases and a feel of permanence. A stand close to the desk held five swords on display, and she held her breath when Levi picked one up.

"You don't have to threaten me to get my cooperation."

Levi flipped the weapon in her hand and laughed. "My grandfather tells me it's in the genes, but this is simply a big key." Levi drove the sword all the way to the hilt into a slot behind a copy of *Don Quixote* and turned it to the right.

Yasmine expected something to happen where Levi was standing but she was surprised when the case behind her clicked and swung out an inch. "You really are full of surprises."

"You have no idea. This place was built to hide something, but don't ask me what. The empty room through there came in handy, though, and people like the ones who broke in the other day would never find it." Levi swung it open so they could step through into a space more austere than the study, but still strangely comfortable.

Another great rug covered the floor, the furniture was all nice antiques, and the lights were a combination of overhead fluorescents and lamps. The bookshelves in here weren't as plentiful, but it made sense when Yasmine stared at the wall before her. On it was a map and history of André Sonnac's life, and at the center was a sketch of him in his Templar armor.

"Dr. Hassani, meet André Sonnac and Farah Elbaz." Levi placed her hand at the bottom of André's picture, and to the right of it was another of a beautiful woman in a djellabah, a type of loose-fitting dress still worn because of its comfort and coolness. "I found these sketches in one of the books I acquired, but I don't know yet if it's truly them."

"I'm sure your monks fell in love with more than one woman along the way, infidel or not. Faith isn't always adhered to when the heart and other things decide to go in a different direction. Why does this particular couple fascinate you so much?" She moved closer to the sketches and studied Farah's likeness. Even in the simple drawing, she demanded attention. It was as if her strength had been captured in the lines of her face.

"That might be true, but I didn't find any of the others, I found this one. Maybe it's the romantic in me I didn't realize existed, but their story sounds like one the world should hear. Maybe they went on to have a family, or it ended as quickly as it began, but I want to know. It's become something of an obsession, I suppose." She stood close to Yasmine but didn't touch her. "The other thing is that André sounds like he was an important part of the Templar history, but he never became a known part of Templar history. Bringing the unknown Templar history to light is something I'm passionate about. The church should answer for what happened."

"What?" She glanced back at Levi and then to the drawing of André. There was something in the eyes that didn't come across as cruel. With her eyes closed she could almost imagine the way André must've looked at Farah and what price they must've paid for it. "What do you mean?"

"Knowledge of the Templar history only exists today because there were men who were willing to defy the pope," Levi said, sitting in one of the two chairs that faced her wall of information. "To do that back then was considered sacrilege, and you gambled with your soul."

"Maybe, but you might be right in that there is a story here." Yasmine stared at the two sketches. "I'd like to know why he left the order. That might be the best story of all." She turned and joined Levi, sitting in the other chair.

"Look at her." Levi pointed to Farah. "I can tell you exactly why André left the order. Beautiful women have a way of making any one of us forget whatever belief system we have if it means being able to be with them."

"Is that your philosophy?" She smiled at how romantic Levi sounded.

"The way I look at it is, it doesn't matter what name you call God. Your faith should tell you that he created all things. So loving a beautiful woman and sacrificing for her isn't turning your face from God. It honors him in the best way possible by following his teachings of love."

"You're an interesting person, Levi." She pressed her back into the leather of the club chair and gazed at the massive amount of information that must've taken hundreds of hours to compile. "How can I help you?"

"I've only glanced at the scrolls I just acquired, but they're going to take me much longer to decipher them than it would take you. I'll be willing to hire you if you help me with that and also use your code-breaking skills to find what they really say, because clearly they won't just give up their secrets in plain language." Levi held her mug with both hands and looked at Yasmine as if she were the most important thing in the room.

"Is this related to what you're working on?"

"I have no idea, but when something like this becomes available, I like to acquire it if I can. It's good practice, if nothing else."

Levi smiled, and it made Yasmine think of passages in books when someone was described as roguish.

"So will you consider my offer?" Levi asked.

"I'm very expensive," she said, teasing. The Templars weren't her favorite subject, and she in no way admired them, but working with Levi wasn't something she'd pass up.

"Name your price."

"Dinner at Blanchard's. I read about it, and it was on my list of things I wanted to try." She winked and wanted to be embarrassed by it, but she couldn't find it within her to be. "When do you want to start?"

"Would you mind if I sat in on your lecture tomorrow? We can walk over to the lab and check out our find afterward." Levi smiled at her, and it made her happy to find a friend. "Afterward we'll have dinner at Blanchard's, and we can make a schedule over a wonderful meal. Does Zara also have a desire to try Blanchard's?"

Levi asked as if she were fishing for an answer that would fit a scenario that probably always ended with her dinner companion in her bed.

"I'll ask her, but I don't feel comfortable leaving her behind." She didn't mean to sound defensive, but she also didn't want to come out with a big announcement that she wasn't interested in where Levi might be leading her.

"I just need to know how many for the reservation." Levi's smile dimmed a little. "You have nothing to worry about, Dr. Hassani. I'd never do anything to make you feel uncomfortable."

"You don't, and please, it's Yasmine."

"Then, Yasmine, it'll be you, Zara, and the infidel for dinner tomorrow."

She couldn't hold in her laughter, and Levi joined her. "It'll be my pleasure." Yasmine winked again and decided she might be going a little insane. Her mother's voice in her head screamed at her to finish her job and stay away from the Montbard family before they led her astray. Her problem was the definition of *tempting* was *alluring and enticing*, and Levi Montbard was all those things. "And thank you for tonight and sharing all this with me."

"We're only just beginning."

She feared that was completely true.

CHAPTER SEVEN

Levi carefully wiped the surface of the stones and set them on a table that had a camera over it. She'd given Yasmine and Zara a ride in that morning, but the sisters had been running late, so Yasmine had left them to prepare for her class. Zara offered to walk over with Levi to see if any features on the stones could be made out. There was something there, but time had made it faint. They'd checked the scrolls, but they were still drying and dripping mercury.

"The camera will make this clearer?" Zara asked. She stood close to Levi and watched everything she was doing.

"It should, and we'll use different lighting and filters to enhance whatever's there." She took the cable trigger for the camera and started shooting.

The morning had been strange in that Yasmine had been quiet but Zara hadn't shut up in the car. It probably had to do with the night before, and Levi regretted teasing Yasmine the way she had. Flirting was something she did with women, but this was the first time she'd ever sensed that the woman wanted to run. It was a different headspace for sure.

"Is my sister going to help you?" Zara's eyes never left the stones. "She's good with languages, but my field is symbolism. If you want, I can help you with these."

"She said she's going to, but I promise not to hold her to anything if she's not comfortable. And I never turn down help. If you're willing, I'll gladly give you this assignment." She changed the filter and shot some more pictures. "I didn't think before asking that this is a vacation as well as a work trip." Maybe this was the scout sent out to scope a field that suddenly seemed filled with land mines. It sounded like the sisters had a close enough relationship to share what was going on in their daily lives. "You know both of you are welcome to stay at the house until you're ready to go home. It's no fun to come to New Orleans and work the whole time and then have to rush back."

"I'm trying to convince her of that, so I'd appreciate your help. This isn't the time to back down now, Levi. My sister is—" Zara stopped and didn't seem to know how to go on.

"Your sister is a good person, but maybe she's wound a little tight." She pressed the trigger again, hoping she hadn't just insulted Zara.

Zara laughed but shook her head. "I'm not sure exactly what you mean, but I think you might be right. You have to know how we were raised to understand."

They moved to the computer, and Levi brought up the pictures they'd taken. "I do understand, to some degree. I visited Morocco a few years ago to meet with some of the faculty for some research I was doing. I was surprised by the size of the class that was getting ready to begin and I decided to sit in." She started printing, wanting to get all this locked up before they left. "It was Yasmine's class, and she was so in her element, I told my grandfather about her. He's been trying to get her here ever since."

"I don't mean to share too much with you, but yes. She is a great teacher, but that's all she is right now. Do you understand what I'm having trouble saying?" Zara laughed and followed her out when they were done. "I want my sister to be happy."

"I wasn't finished. My grandfather wanted her here because she's a kindred spirit. Yasmine's as comfortable walking in the past as in the now." She waved to a few professors she recognized and glanced over at Zara.

"I think maybe you don't understand what I'm trying very poorly to say."

"You want Yasmine to open up to who she could be. That isn't a woman who simply teaches and finds happiness in only that." She stopped talking and Zara nodded. "We're both still dancing around what we're trying to say, but that's the best I have without spelling it out. I don't want to upset you or her by making assumptions I have no business making." They entered the building where the history department was located, but Levi stopped them at the vending machine. "Yasmine needs to take a step from the wings, and you'll get your wish. But only Yasmine can decide to do that."

"It's like you're talking in parables and I'm having trouble keeping up." Zara laughed and accepted the soft drink Levi offered her.

"Think of a play," Levi said, pointing in the direction of the lecture hall. "There are those who face an audience and put it all out there for the world to see. Then there are those who stand in the wings. They're just as important because without them the play couldn't go on, but they simply look on and never step into the spotlight."

"You could've been a philosopher." Zara put her hand in the bend of Levi's elbow and smiled up at her. "That's exactly true, but not totally accurate."

"It has to be one or the other." Levi laughed and led her to the seats for special university guests near the top of the hall. "It can't be both."

"She does step onto the stage and shines like no one I've ever seen, almost every day. Here in the classroom she can slay dragons, but it's in the rest of her life she stands in the wings, as you say."

The place was starting to fill up, so they lowered their voices. "What do you think I can do? I'm not sure how much about last night she told you, but she doesn't seem…comfortable…with me."

"Tell me you don't scare that easily." Zara's smile was coy, as only one side of her mouth came up. "New things can be scary, but it doesn't mean you shouldn't do them. Yasmine needs to learn that."

"I do want to work with her, but believe me, I'm going to behave. Last night was innocent, and I almost sent her screaming across the street."

"I doubt that, and she didn't talk about last night much. Thanks for telling me at least a little so that I can understand her mood this morning." Zara crossed her legs and rested her can on her knee.

"Can you explain that to non-Yasmine experts, then?" Levi's question made them both laugh, causing a few people to turn and stare at them.

"My sister only gets quiet when she's either trying to think of a way to avoid something or when she's thinking in general. You might fall into the general category of thinking." She tilted her head. "Or avoiding, maybe."

The room filled without either of them noticing, but they turned their attention to the bottom when Yasmine walked in and placed her bag down. "Good afternoon, everyone."

Yasmine started lecturing, and Levi sat back and let the sound of her voice make pictures in her head as the lecture went on. Her litmus test for any professor or teacher in her academic career was if the person could energize her imagination. Yasmine could do that without a problem. She noticed when Yasmine looked up in the direction they were sitting, and she smiled on the off chance Yasmine could see them.

"Thank you all for coming, and I'll see you all Monday." Yasmine answered questions for another hour after the class officially ended, and Levi was happy for her. That college students cared enough to wait that long to speak to a teacher spoke volumes for her talent in the classroom. "I hope you two didn't mind waiting, but I hate putting them off if I can help it."

"You're not done," Levi said, sitting on the first row. "I have plenty of questions."

"You can save them for dinner." Yasmine glanced at her watch, but Levi knew it was still too early to head over to the restaurant.

"I can, and I know it's early, so how about a little more work before we head over? That way we can change and start on the scrolls."

"That sounds like a good idea," Zara said, but Yasmine stayed quiet.

They followed her into the house, and she opened the secret room. When she was working on the Sonnac file she usually left the room open, but what had happened with George made her more cautious. The scrolls were sitting on the desk, and Yasmine seemed drawn to them.

"Do you mind?" Yasmine asked.

"Please, that's why I asked you over." She and Zara took the chairs in front of the wall and split the pictures of the stones. "Use a Sharpie and trace over whatever you see. We can always make more copies, so don't hold back."

It was nice that they could all work in silence, and Yasmine looked up at her when she stood. "Are you leaving?" Yasmine asked.

"I was going to make us a cup of coffee. Sometimes I need the boost when I'm slogging through stuff like this, but I can get you something else."

"I'll come with you," Yasmine said, but Zara barely moved her head. She was still working on her pictures, and they left her to it. "I don't know if I mentioned it, but you have a beautiful home."

"My family was lucky being able to buy so many places on the same street."

"Do you have siblings?" Yasmine took mugs out of the cupboard as if she already knew the layout of Levi's kitchen.

"My father and I are both only children. Seeing you with Zara makes me a little jealous, but my grandparents and parents have filled my life with all the family I've ever needed." She steamed milk as she waited for the espresso. "My mom's parents live in London, so I spent a lot of summers exploring places in Europe as well as the States. My grandfather Percy teaches history as well but spends some of his time in the field on different digs happening in England. Is it just you and Zara?"

"Just the two of us, and I'm the first in my family who decided on the teaching route. My father is in charge of the public water system in Marrakech, and my mother has never worked." The way Yasmine said it sounded as if that would be the worst thing that could happen to her. "Her job has always been to take care of my father and us, and no matter how old we get, she's still at it."

"My mother's still the same way, but I'm glad someone worries about me." She poured the coffee into three mugs and carefully followed with the milk, making a foam leaf on top of every cup.

"She sounds like a lovely woman." It was as if the wind had disappeared from Yasmine's sails.

"How about a family dinner this weekend so you can meet her? The table in here is big enough, and I can have something brought in." It wasn't probably what Yasmine wanted, but it would give Levi an excuse to spend more time with her.

"A family dinner can't be called a family dinner if you have someone else make it." Yasmine added sugar to two of the cups and shook her head. "You should know that."

"It's also not usually built around peanut butter sandwiches, but that's what I know how to make." She made Yasmine laugh, and it felt like a major achievement.

"I see another trip to the store. Zara and I will make dinner."

"I can't ask you to do that."

"You didn't," Yasmine said, smiling. "I offered, and you're not getting out of helping. The best chefs always have backup, and that's what you'll be. Your first assignment is to sharpen your best knives and get ready to work."

"It's the least I can do," she teased. "Thank you, and I'm sure my mother will love not having to do it. My grandparents will be thrilled as well, since my mother is a terrible cook. And it sounds like you didn't finish your debate on the Templars with my grandfather." Yasmine laughed again, and it lightened something in Levi she didn't realize was dark.

"Your grandfather isn't a man you'd want as an enemy, I'm

thinking," Yasmine said, picking up the other cup. "I'm glad he's my friend."

"We all are, and that's always a lifetime commitment for us."

"That's a long time." Yasmine stopped and stared at her.

"Remember, the only way I'll leave you alone is if you send me away. Only you have the power to do that." Levi's hope was that Yasmine wouldn't ever think about exercising it. There was something about her, something that called to her in a way no other woman had. It was scary, and confusing, but there was no way she wouldn't take a chance and explore it if the opportunity arose.

❖

Ransley listened to Baggio and Donnie and wanted to beat both of them until they bled and cried for mercy. Incompetence on this level was unacceptable, and they'd never get to where they absolutely needed to be if he had to rely on them. There were already five cardinals who were on board with their plans, and something like this could make them reconsider.

"How exactly did this happen?" Ransley asked. He was glad neither man took the liberty of sitting. If he had his way they wouldn't be staying long at all.

"We were about to open the safe when we heard a shout. The guy had a gun, and he shot when our guy threw a knife. I ran when the man called for help."

"Your stupidity has brought the police to my door. They came because the rooms were all booked by Baggio but paid for through my company. The New Orleans police are demanding you be sent back to the States for questioning, and I'm seriously thinking about it." He took a breath knowing that he could never do that. Both of these idiots would break in less than a day if the police got hold of them. "According to the police, it was Levi Montbard who suggested they talk to you two."

"Why?" Baggio asked as if he hadn't heard any of the conversation so far.

"Why? Perhaps because you tried to throw a bunch of money at her in Paris, then she saw you in New Orleans. You follow that up by breaking into her house. It doesn't take the skills of Sherlock Holmes to track them to my door." He took another deep breath, but his anger was only ratcheting up.

"I was doing what you asked me to do. If you think I'm some sort of clairvoyant who can predict that some armed imbecile was going to be waiting on us, then you're mistaken. In the future, do it yourself if you think it's so easy," Donnie shouted.

"Get out of here and don't come back. You botched this job, so your payment is me getting you out of harm's way." He opened his desk drawer enough to be able to reach inside. The man in Montbard's house wasn't the only one who was armed.

"You're going to regret this, and when it comes back to drown you, you can bugger off."

Baggio had a hint of a smile as Donnie slammed his way out. "If you'd like me to leave as well, I'd be happy to. Placing so much faith in someone like that won't serve our interests at all."

"Baggio, you do realize the only way you're leaving is in a box? You might want to keep the snide comments to yourself, since this was your mess-up as well." He pointed to an empty chair and turned his own toward the window. It was raining again, but not even that could calm him. "What do you know about the area where these scrolls were found?"

"Two weeks ago, you'd never heard of these scrolls. A few days ago, you acted as if you couldn't care less if these things were out in the world. At least that's the story you told me. What's changed? Lie and I walk."

"The climate in the Church under this new pope has changed. Our old guard who've held the sacred beliefs of our Lord the way they were originally written is being forced out. In order to recruit the next generation of priests who will tamp down rebellion in their parishes, we must have our generals lead by example." He ran his hands up and down his thighs to rid himself of the sensation of something crawling out of his skin.

"I understand all that, but it doesn't explain the scrolls." Baggio hardly ever raised his voice, and he admired him for that. Passions for someone who'd taken vows of celibacy and of the priesthood usually centered around books and the gospels. Real men let their emotions range from calm to murderous because they understood human nature much better.

"It wasn't until after the auction that something came to light about these scrolls. I can't tell you exactly what it was, but Cardinal Chadwick passed it along, and it was a mistake on my part not acquiring them. They might have something to do with Pope Clement V." He closed his eyes and tried to center himself. "He foolishly allowed others to dictate what should be done when it came to the Knights Templar because greedy men wanted the treasures they supposedly had. Clement realized too late what happens when you attempt to do a job and leave it undone."

"God's army killed by the Vicar of Christ," Baggio said. "I never understood his reasoning."

"It was King Philip of France. The idiot was in debt, and the Templar vaults were the easiest way out of his piss-poor decisions. Think of the power the Church would have now if the Templars still existed."

"Mistakes were made, but again, what does it have to do with the scrolls?"

"The Templars found something in the Holy Land under King Solomon's Temple. It was explosive enough to keep the Church at bay for hundreds of years, and Clement thought, with the help of the French king, that he had the power to take it and bury it." He shook his head and sighed. "I understand his reasoning, but the secrets the Templars had were swallowed by time and have waited all these years to blow up in our faces."

"And the scrolls have something to do with that? I was fascinated by books of the Templars and their hidden treasures in my childhood, but I doubt any of it still exists. All those caches of gold have been dug up and plundered by people who didn't realize what it was."

"Gold can make a man rich, Baggio, but information can make a man powerful. That kind of power can bring down empires. It's our responsibility to find this information before the throne of Saint Peter is destroyed along with the rest of the Vatican. These scrolls might have the power to unlock age-old secrets that would be better left to the fires that should destroy them." He pressed his hands together, trying not to get ahead of himself. "These scrolls might be the key to what secrets the Templars left behind. The cardinal tells me Montbard has found plenty already, but she can't be allowed to find any more."

"My fear is that with Donnie's mistake and my initial offer, Montbard has buried those scrolls in a hole so deep *we'll* never find them."

"We must, my friend, we must."

CHAPTER EIGHT

Yasmine slipped on the summer dress that was dressier than anything else she'd packed and studied herself in the mirror. At home she never wore anything sleeveless, and never showed her legs. She'd left her hair down tonight, and she pushed it behind her shoulders for now. It felt strange out of the ponytail she usually kept it in, but if she was going for a new look, this would complete the picture.

They'd worked for three hours before Levi walked them across the street and promised to pick them up in another hour. The scrolls were a long soliloquy of a young woman's love who'd gone to war. Not at all what she'd expected from a young adolescent girl who was born poor and died young.

"Are you ready?" Zara had on a minidress and heels and looked fantastic. "Wow," Zara said and whistled. "You're beautiful." Zara's outfit was also something she'd never wear at home. Every one of their friends and family would've found the clothes unacceptable, but they were far from unapproving eyes, so Yasmine was glad to see Zara relax.

"You think so?" She'd never carried herself with a lot of confidence in this area, but Levi had been nice enough to offer, so she was making an effort. "It's not too much?"

"Too much for what?" Zara asked and blew her a kiss. "This place is supposed to be nice, so I doubt you're overdressed."

She hardly ever wore makeup, but she chose a light lipstick and then slipped into the low heels she'd decided on. The last thing she did was put on the wide, loose belt that rested right above her hips. It gave more shape to the straight-cut dress but didn't reveal too much. The doorbell rang and she heard Zara greet Levi.

The way Levi's eyes followed her way down the stairs made her slow down. It was only an instant, but the only way to describe her expression was *desire*. This wasn't the first time she'd seen it directed at her, but it was the first time she didn't turn away. She didn't have time to analyze what in the world was happening.

"You look beautiful." Levi's voice was soft and inviting.

"Thank you." She noticed the nice linen suit and starched white shirt and thought her mother would be thrilled. Here was a successful, kind, and generous person, with only one glaring problem: Levi was a woman, and there was no changing that. Women dressed like this wasn't a reality back home. "I love this suit."

"Thank you. If you two agree to go out for Sunday brunch, I'll show off my seersucker. That's the most Southern thing I own." Levi opened the door and waved them out. "If you're ready, I'd be happy to take you to dinner."

The meal was wonderful, and Levi stayed for coffee at their place once she'd taken them back home. Zara had bid them good night before Yasmine brewed coffee, but Levi took her jacket off and sat on the sofa in the family room.

"Here, I think I remember how you like it."

"Thanks." Levi took a sip and nodded. "Perfect." She was looking at the work she'd done on the scrolls. It was still in Arabic, but Levi was staring at them like she knew what she was reading. "You made some progress here."

"It's a weird thing for a little girl to write about, but maybe she was enlightened. I doubt it, but anything's possible." She sat next to Levi and pointed to the first page. "Do you know Arabic?"

"Enough to get a decent meal and a bathroom," Levi joked. "For the rest, it takes a lot of research."

"Is it too late for me to read this to you?" Yasmine picked up the sheet and leaned back to get more comfortable.

"I don't want to keep you up, but I'm dying to know. Please feel free to read, but don't stay up too late for me."

"The good thing about starting in the middle of the week is that tomorrow is Saturday. I can enjoy the weekend and see some of the city." She folded her legs under her, then smoothed her dress down. "I'd love to see some of the out-of-the-way places." It was the only hint she was willing to give.

"I realize my grandfather loves giving tours of the city, but I do know my way around. If you're not too tired tomorrow morning, we can start then, and if you're not sick of me by Sunday, like I said, we can do brunch. Then we can do what most locals do on lazy Sunday afternoons." Levi stretched out and put her feet on the coffee table, showing off her socks. They were blue and covered in hula girls.

"And what do locals do on lazy Sunday afternoons?" The question had dozens of answers that were completely inappropriate, Yasmine guessed, but again her curiosity got the better of her.

"They wander in and out of the shops in the Quarter and look for treasures."

"Considering how you hunt for treasures, that seems almost like cheating," she said, making Levi smile.

"It depends on what you're hunting for," Levi said, and Yasmine let it lie. If she kept talking, it would only lead somewhere that might be dangerous.

"How about I start reading, and later you can make your plan where you'd like to take us." She hoped Zara was up for some sightseeing, as being alone with Levi was starting to feel risky. "For now, listen."

She began to read and was quickly immersed in a seven-hundred-year-old romance.

My love is leaving once the sun pierces the sky. The war that waits holds no promise of return, and for that I'm already dying inside at the thought of a world without him. I'll remember and hold the words he spoke to me this night. He held me, and I could see his heart shining in the blue of his eyes and feel the love he has for me in how he caressed my face.

"I'll not ask you to wait for me. We know not what tomorrow brings, and the pain of that is something I wish to spare you. If you find love with another I will understand, but know that I carry you with me in my heart. The memory of your face and how you look upon me will forever feed my soul."

His words feed and pierce me at the same time. He stands, and I gaze upon him in his tunic and pants. His thick leather undercoat and armor are right behind him waiting for the morning, and I pray it will keep an enemy's blade from piercing what I know is my destiny. I've known him only a short time, and my God made him only for me. There is no secret between us and still I love him. The world will never understand what I feel for him even though our people think it should be forbidden. Even they do not know how forbidden it is.

"How can you ask me to let you go? Even in death you will never lose what is completely yours. All I ask is that you stay true to who you are and fight with the will of your God. There can never be another who can own my heart, and if you fall, I shall fall with you."

There is a moment where I lose him because he shuts his eyes, hiding his heart from me. The pain of it squeezes my breath from me. I feel the agony of it as acutely as if a blade pierced my body. He seems resigned to the Fates tearing us apart, but I must give him a reason to come back to me. I can pray for all my days to help me find a way to go on without him, but he is the holder of my fate and faith.

"Please, love, you cannot say such words. They go against everything you believe. Even my God knows it is a sin."

"There can be no God if you do not come back to me."

He places his hand against my cheek and smiles in a way that makes me glad that I have life and the gift of sight. For a warrior he has such tenderness about him, but then he is different from the others. He understands the whole of me like no other, and I'm dying again and again that he will be gone.

"There is always God, and there is always you. My promise to you is that my blade will be swift, and though it will take time, I will return to you. You are the light that leads me through the darkness, and you are the beacon who will guide me home. But please, if there be another, go and be happy. Perhaps they can give you what I cannot."

"You think children will make me complete? No, love, only you can make me so. Fight for us as well as for what you believe in. When you return, I promise to give you the life you deserve."

His kiss was as always tender, never demanding. He is alone in the world except for me. He has no family, no one waiting for him except for me. He told me the story of his life when we first met, and he shared with me what little he had. He was raised by one of his leaders to be a warrior and nothing more. I have tried to pierce the armor that surrounds his heart from the moment I saw him. He loves the sword and the call of war, but neither of those come close to the way he is with me.

"If you believe the teachings of your holy men, loving me will damn you. You know the truth of me, and I will not be responsible for that."

"Leaving me to a cold that will never warm is damning me, my love. Trust me that I care not to see paradise if you are taken from me. The agony of losing my heart is what will damn me." I cling to him hoping he remembers the feel of my arms around him and the way my lips feel on his. If there were time, I would lay myself bare and beg him to pierce through my innocence and truly make me his.

"I will come back, and then we will leave this place. We will go back to where the sky is always beautiful and the fields are always green. I will love you forever, and no one can ever take you away from me. This is the vow I give you."

My heart believes every word. They are all the marriage vows I will ever need, and the last of my fear falls away. I step back and drop my dress. The way he gazes upon my nakedness makes me crave what only he can give me. Once this night is done there will be no turning back, but I am not afraid. My people will stone me if we are found out, but I must have him remember everything he must come back to.

"Are you sure?" He acts so hesitant, but the desire is plain on his face and in his voice. "This can never be undone."

I reach for his tunic and lift it over his head. His body is strong but soft to the touch, and the many scars that mar the surface only make me love him more. He has survived so much, and yet he is here with me. His touch is all I want.

"Please, André. You are everything to me."

❖

"Holy shit," Levi said. She'd been mesmerized by the sound of Yasmine's voice and she'd closed her eyes to concentrate on what she was saying. But with that final name came confirmation of all she'd hoped for.

"I wouldn't put it so colorfully, but yes, I agree with the sentiment. We now know why, perhaps, this man you saw in Paris broke into your home." Yasmine put the sheet down on her lap and took a sip of her coffee. It had to be cold by now, but she didn't seem to mind.

"Finding something that leads directly to André Sonnac and his first encounter with Farah was about as likely as getting hit by lightning every day for five years." Levi reached for the copy of the original scroll and studied it. "How did the auction house ever let this go?"

"The language was obscure. It's one that was, like these scrolls, lost to time. You'd have to be familiar with the languages of the tribes of the Sahara to figure out what it is." Yasmine put her mug down and put her hand on her bent knee. "Fortunately for you, I am."

Levi admired Yasmine's beautiful face, which, together with her incredible intelligence, made for an intoxicating package. The biblical story of forbidden fruit made perfect sense now, and resisting the temptation of taking a bite was taking an act of God. "You have obscure tribal languages at the top of your head? I'm impressed."

"I am impressive, but no," Yasmine said, laughing. "A recent project made me brush up on my languages, which makes me think of something."

"What?" She couldn't take her eyes off Yasmine as she brushed a lock of hair behind her ear.

"I could tell you, but then I'd have to kill you. That would be a tragedy before I get my weekend of sightseeing and brunch." Yasmine winked at her again, and Levi had to fight the urge to lean over and kiss her.

"I see how it is, but while you have your secret agent hat on, do you think there's a code? Or is this simply a hidden account of what I sometimes think I'm never going to find? André and Farah have left crumbs through time, but the whole story is elusive."

Yasmine reached over and put her hand on Levi's forearm. "Don't lose faith. You *did* find something. This is a big step in the right direction. Let's find your answer. Close your eyes and I'll read it again."

Levi did as Yasmine asked and let the words flow through her brain like a trickle of water. It was the best way to describe waking up the part of her mind she needed to zero in on clues. The flow of water down a fast-moving stream was all some people saw. But when she looked, water moved and rippled, making whirlpools and froth, and under the surface there were stones, sand, and pieces of wood moving along with it. They all belonged, but it was the stones and other things the water carried unseen that gave her the answers.

"*Pierce* and *God*. They were used correctly but there were plenty of other choices Farah could've used."

"That's right, and it won't work in the English translation, but it does in the original form. There's something in there, certainly."

"You're a cruel woman," Levi said, teasing. "I would've taken you out to dinner even after you told me all this. I can't believe you made me wait."

"Maybe I wanted your full attention at dinner and didn't want you bouncing in your seat like a little kid waiting for a toy." Yasmine seemed to want to sound like a scorned lover who resented having to share her with the work, but Levi could tell Yasmine was as excited as she was.

Zara's words not to let Yasmine shrink back into her shell came to mind, but flirting now would probably do just that. She couldn't help it, though. Some things simply had to be said. "Can I tell you something and not have you get mad at me?" She was surprised the energy passing between them wasn't making her hair stand on end.

"I'll try my best, but with you I can never be certain." Yasmine laughed and combed her hair back again.

"The sight of you tonight on the stairs when I first walked in was enough to keep me from thinking of anything else. Not even a map to the Holy Grail would've stopped me from being the one who took you to dinner." She didn't touch Yasmine, but her fingers twitched from wanting to. "I'm sure you've been told plenty of times just how beautiful you are, but you're so much more than that."

"It's true, I have been told that from the time it seemed important. My mother tells me I've been blessed with beauty, but it's all she and the world see sometimes." Yasmine glanced away as if the admission shamed her somehow.

"I'm certain you won't welcome this, but I do see you. All of you." Levi waited for Yasmine to face her again and smiled when she did. "You have been blessed with beauty, but your mind is what makes you unique. In my line of work, rarity and uniqueness are what makes something valuable."

Yasmine smiled and shook her head slightly. "And you have been blessed with the gift of flattery. You're really good at it, which I believe comes from plenty of practice, but thank you anyway." Yasmine sounded as if she didn't know how to respond to the conversation, and there was a moment of hesitation. "I'm glad I took this trip. Meeting you and your family, and hearing about your work, has made the travel worth it." The change of subject seemed to be a defensive maneuver, but it wasn't a declaration of anger, so it worked.

Levi didn't want to lose before they even started because of gossip about her past. "It sounds like you know a little bit about me." She held her index finger and thumb close to together. The way Yasmine's nose flared slightly confirmed it. "The most important thing you should know about me is that I never lie about someone's qualities or use flattery to get something over on someone. It's not my style."

"I'm sorry. It's hard for me to accept compliments."

"Why?" That Yasmine wasn't as confident outside the classroom was surprising.

"They're always offered because the person wants something I'm not willing to give."

The answer was so quick Levi knew it was something Yasmine believed deeply. "Let's make a deal." She held her hand out to Yasmine.

"What?" Yasmine took it without hesitation.

"I won't compliment you unless it's absolutely necessary, and you promise to try to accept that you're extraordinary." She squeezed Yasmine's hand and waited for her to take it back, but she didn't. "You also accept that my opinions are given only because they're true, not because I want something from you. I'd never push you in a way that would make you not want to be my friend."

"I think I can do that." Yasmine moved slightly toward her, but not enough for Levi's liking.

"The other thing is, you have to tell me what you uncovered."

Yasmine read from another piece of paper. *"I wait for my love in time in the land of Andraste's warrior queen. To find me you must face the serpent and defy the poisonous bite like my love defied the paradise of eternity for me."*

She stared at Yasmine's mouth and broke out of her haze when she stopped talking. "That's it?"

"I'm not holding back on you," Yasmine said, rolling her eyes. "It's all I have so far, but I have the other three scrolls to get through."

"Sorry, but for once I'd like them to say *go here, and there are all the answers.* Finding this, though, is enough to keep me going. It's exciting, don't you think?" She curled her fingers around Yasmine's and lifted her hand to her lips. "This is beyond anything I thought it would be. Some finds make you stay up nights planning to fly off to the next set of clues. This is one of those."

"I can see why you do this, and it was hard keeping it to myself all night."

"The odds of finding another clue when it comes to this mystery will make me lose sleep, but you need to go to bed and get some rest. I'm a spoiled child when it comes to patience, but I'm willing to wait until tomorrow or whenever until you have a chance to work on the other three."

"Thank you for a lovely evening, and for waiting. Not that I gave you a choice."

"Trust me, tonight was something special for me, and I'd like to do it again soon. Maybe if you're not too tired after I drag you around tomorrow you'll agree to have dinner with me again. I'm dying to know what's on the other three scrolls, but this weekend is for fun and not work."

"That sounds fun, and I'd love to." Yasmine stood and twitched her dress back into place.

They walked to the door together and Yasmine reached out and touched her arm again when Levi stepped out into the street. She took a step back and waited for her to lock the door to keep herself from succumbing to temptation.

"This should be torturous," she mumbled to herself as she walked across the street. Her instinct was to charm and win the woman over, but this was different. Yasmine wasn't a woman who'd ever allow anyone a night and be satisfied with that. Her upbringing, beliefs, and sexuality didn't give Levi much hope that they'd share more than friendship, but there was always *some* hope. All she could do was work with her and make a friend. That the friend was gorgeous, smart, and interested in everything Levi was would make this hard, but she'd let her go when Yasmine was ready to get back to her life.

Eventually, she might make herself believe it.

Chapter Nine

Yasmine stepped out of the shower Saturday morning and stared at her naked body in the mirror. She thought of what Levi had told her the night before and tried to convince herself she wasn't crazy for finding it comforting. She'd never cared about her looks, not really. It was like worrying about the color of her skin, or the size of her feet. Appearance was something you couldn't do anything about.

"Stop thinking about it. You'll be gone in less than two weeks and all this will be forgotten. She'll forget you as soon as you board a plane out of here." She spoke out loud to make it true. The words made perfect sense, but she couldn't make herself believe them.

"Did you say something?" Zara asked from the other side of the door.

"No, I'll be out in a minute." She put her hair back in a ponytail and put on the summer dress she'd chosen, realizing how hot it was going to be. They weren't sure where Levi was taking them, but if any of it was outside, she wanted to be prepared.

"Do you think she'll take us to one of those bars on Bourbon Street?" Zara was sitting on the bed in shorts and a loose blouse when she stepped out. "I doubt *you'll* take me."

"What kind of bar?" She'd read about Bourbon Street—there was no telling what Zara had in mind.

"One with classic New Orleans jazz." The way Zara was smirking at her made her want to laugh. "You have such a dirty mind."

"Yes, that's totally me. Get ready, I don't want to keep Levi waiting." She slipped into her sandals and grabbed her purse.

"Did she freak when you read her that translation last night?" Zara followed her downstairs.

"I'm not sure what reaction *freak* is, but she was about to run out of here and start preparing for some kind of adventure."

"I like Levi. She's nice and she doesn't treat me like the nagging little sister."

"You're not that young, and she is nice. The whole family is, and we owe Cristobal and Diana some time. Maybe we can invite all of them over for dinner." The doorbell stopped her, but Zara nodded at her suggestion. "Do you have everything?"

"I'm ready," Zara said as Yasmine opened the door.

Levi was wearing tan shorts that went to her knees and a navy-blue polo shirt that brought out the green of her eyes. It was those eyes along with her tan face that made her so incredibly handsome. That was the best description Yasmine could think of, and it was a better fit than anything more traditional.

"*Assalamu Alaikum*," Levi said in a horrible accent, and bowed her head slightly.

"Good morning to you, and peace be upon you as well," she said, smiling. Levi had mentioned her Arabic wasn't great, but she gave her points for trying the customary Muslim greeting. "You're early, but we're ready to go."

"I'm not in a rush if you need more time." Levi put her hands in her pockets and rocked on her feet. The hair on the top of her head was longer than the sides, and a lock of it had fallen on her forehead. Yasmine wanted to comb it back. "Do you feel better this morning?"

"Yes, thank you," Yasmine said. The jet lag had caught up with her and her sister, and staying up late the night before had left her fatigued but ready to go. "Lead on." She smiled when she saw the black BMW convertible parked in front of their place.

"I borrowed my mom's car, and I brought a hat for everyone. If wind really bothers you, I'll trade this out for my car."

"No way," Zara said, climbing into the back seat before Levi could open any door.

"Our first stop is a classic swamp tour, but it's a little out of town."

They listened to music as they drove, and Yasmine enjoyed the rush of wind that kept them all quiet so they could enjoy the vastness of open space once they'd left New Orleans behind. The swamp tour was interesting, and both she and Zara were amazed at how the alligators came out when the guide dangled chicken over the side of the boat. Levi had laughed when they both grabbed her arms as they were surrounded by what seemed like a hundred of the large beasts.

From there they went back to town, and Levi gave them a tour of the St. Louis Cemeteries I and II. She was so knowledgeable that some other people had trailed along with them and asked more questions than she and Zara had. They went on to Laffite's Blacksmith Shop Bar and sat for drinks. The crowd was impressive, so Levi had found them something outside and told them about the building as well as some of the other old structures in the French Quarter.

The sun was starting to set, and Yasmine was surprised at how fast the day had flown by. Lunch also seemed like it had been ages ago, and she was glad for the noisy convertible when her stomach growled. Levi jumped out to get their door, and Yasmine liked the attention.

"Is an hour enough for you both to get changed? I'd love to treat you to dinner again."

"How about if we treat you?" Yasmine asked as Zara waved over her shoulder, already heading up the stairs.

"Southern hospitality forbids me from allowing you to do that." Levi reached out as if not thinking about what she was doing and took her hand. It was an intimate gesture, but she didn't pull back. "When I'm in Morocco next, you can treat me."

"Do you go to Morocco often?" She doubted they'd see each other again, but there was always hope.

"More than you think, so start thinking of somewhere you'd like to take me." Levi let her go and waited again until she was safely inside.

"Allah preserve me." Yasmine pushed off the closed door and headed to the shower.

An hour later Levi was back, and Yasmine thought she was hallucinating for a moment when she saw a horse and carriage waiting outside. "This is a little taste of old New Orleans," Levi said, helping them both up. Zara sat facing them, and Yasmine teased Levi that she hadn't said a word at their transformation for dinner.

"*Zwina*," Levi said and flinched slightly.

The word was commonly used in Morocco for a variety of things, but its true meaning was *beautiful*. "Thank you," was all she could say without making a fool of herself.

"Did I pronounce it correctly? I could tell this morning that my accent isn't very good."

"For that word, it's the meaning behind it more than how you pronounce it that matters." It was another compliment, and she'd promised to try and accept them with more grace. "Where are you taking us?"

"When I travel to places like Morocco, one of the things that always hits me is the history that you can almost touch. Some things haven't changed in hundreds of years. Comparatively speaking, we're in our infancy, but there's still some history here."

"This is my first time in the city, and I agree." She could feel the warmth of Levi's body and figured she would've been better off sitting where Zara was. "The people here understand the importance of preservation."

They stopped in front of Antoine's and Levi hopped down and took Zara's hand first to help her out. When it was Yasmine's turn she took a breath and held it as Levi smiled up at her. The moment was over too quickly, and it was as if Levi had taken her request to heart. Once she was on the ground, Levi had let her go so fast she glanced down to make sure her hand wasn't on fire.

"I'm sure there are others who make this claim, but the same family who owns it now opened it back in 1840, making it the oldest family-run restaurant in the country. Their baked Alaska will make you glad the family is still dedicated to excellence." Levi escorted them inside, and they had another great meal.

"You might stop treating us to all this once I give you the bad news," Yasmine said once the dinner had been cleared away.

"Do you have to leave early?" Levi must've missed the lightness in her voice because she appeared worried.

"No." She reached out and touched Levi's hand, making Zara glance away. "I meant, I studied the next scroll last night when I had trouble sleeping, and it says the exact same thing, only in a different dialect. I need more time to make sure I'm right, but at first glance, that seems to be the case."

"That makes sense in a weird way," Levi said.

"It does?" Zara asked.

"You're too young to remember the gold records they attached to every *Voyager* spacecraft they launched about twenty-five years ago. They'd recorded the message *greetings to the universe* in fifty-five different languages. That way, whoever got them had a better chance of receiving the message."

Yasmine couldn't help but smile at Levi's delivery. Her new friend would make a great teacher one day if she ever settled down and concentrated on academics instead of treasure hunts. "I read about those, but Zara's right. What does that have to do with your scrolls?"

"They were put somewhere no one at the time wanted them found.

But they must've known they would be found eventually, and to leave bread crumbs you had to tell a story in as many ways as you could manage so someone would understand." Levi sat back but kept her hand on the table. "There was nothing different about them?"

"Word for word, and the code worked out the same. I'll look at the other two, but I'm thinking it might be the same. The first one I translated was from a northern tribe, and this one was more to the west." Yasmine stopped talking when the waiter carried over a massive platter of something on fire and set it on the table.

"Grab a spoon," Levi said. "Now you see why I only ordered one."

"Oh," Yasmine said, then moaned when she tried it. The heat of another blush made her want to cover her ears when she noticed how Levi was staring at her. It was everything her mother had told her about when you were attracted to someone, but in the face of someone her family would never accept. "This is delicious."

"It is," Levi said, her voice cracking. "Sorry." She cleared her throat and took a bite of dessert. "They're known for this and for inventing oysters Rockefeller."

"You are good at delivering great times," Zara said.

It was good her sister spoke up. Zara had broken the spell Levi had cast over Yasmine. "Yes, that's true."

Their dessert didn't last long, and they chose to walk back. The heat was still formidable, but it made her think of home and what was waiting for her there. Would staying someplace like this be something she could do? How would she survive if Zara chose to enroll at Tulane or some other university to finish her studies that would put miles between them?

"How about a nightcap?" Levi said as they stepped onto Bourbon Street.

If there was a place with every type of humanity, this was it, and every one of the people was in some state of inebriation. "Zara would like to hear some jazz," she said. It was hard to think with the sights she was seeing. This street was like debauchery come to life, but everyone around them was having a good time. It appeared to be normal to them that one place had nude dancers and the next had throngs of people dancing to loud music. There were only a few people who looked as overwhelmed as she was, which meant they weren't from here.

Her first reaction was to be shocked. There was no place in Morocco like this, and she was in overload trying to take it all in. Being lost in a crowd had been a fantasy in her college days, but she'd never had the courage to simply let go and not follow the rules. Here it would be easy to do that, but would she be able to go back to what her life was supposed to be if she did? The clearest answer when she looked at Levi was no. That would be impossible.

"After that dinner, how about something a little different tonight?" Levi said with that damn smile that showed off her dimples.

"I'm in," Zara piped up, surprising her not at all.

"Good, come on." Levi took their hands and led them to a bar full of dancing people.

Yasmine didn't recognize the music but the man on the stage was playing an accordion—that she recognized. The guy next to him was raking his hands up and down what appeared to be a crinkled metal sheet, and it both confused and delighted her. The large man at the door who seemed to be keeping an eye on the crowd slapped hands with Levi and pointed to the left.

"What is this, and what's that?" Yasmine asked, pointing to the man playing the metal board.

"That's called a rub board, and the music is called chank-a-chank or zydeco. It's a Louisiana tradition and it comes with its own kind of dancing. You two dance, right?" Levi looked pretty sure of herself, as if she'd found a way to get closer without appearing to walk over the line she'd set.

"Doc, how you doing?" a large man wearing denim overalls without a shirt asked. "It's hotter than my wife's titties. What can I get you to drink?"

"Ah," Levi said, shaking her head. "Bring us three madrassas, and I don't want to think about your wife like that." She waited for him to walk away before she turned her attention back to them. "Sorry about that. The man put the *c* in *crude*."

"Doc?" she asked, resting her chin on her hand.

"I have a doctorate in history like everyone in my family." Levi shrugged, and it was adorable. "Eventually I'll teach, but not yet."

"You have something against the classroom?"

"No, but I'm having fun in the field." Levi's friend dropped off three drinks, and they picked them up and tapped their glasses together.

"You can do both, you know." Whatever this was, it was delicious.

"Now you sound like my father, but enough of that for now." Levi offered her hand to Zara and cocked her head toward the dance floor. "How about a little two-step?"

Zara appeared totally charmed and gladly accepted. For the next couple of songs Yasmine watched as Levi taught her sister the steps. Zara was having a great time, she could tell by the way she was laughing as Levi guided her around the floor. They came back and finished their drinks as the band announced they were taking a break. Levi rolled her sleeves up and combed her hair back, clearly hot.

"That was fantastic." Zara seemed ready to dance some more, so Yasmine doubted they'd be home any time soon.

"Next time we'll have to opt for shorts," Levi said, mopping her forehead. She lifted her hand, and her friend came back with more drinks.

They talked now that it was quiet enough to be heard, but it didn't take long for the band to start up again. Yasmine stared at Levi's hand when she stretched it out, and it was Zara's poke to her side that woke her from her frozen state. "I'm not really a good dancer."

Levi took her hand and led her to the dance floor anyway. Once they were closer the music changed to a slower number, but it still had a little pep. "All you need to do is follow my lead."

Yasmine understood the words to the song "Jole Blon" and smiled as Levi put her arm around her and held her. There hadn't been much dancing in her past but she did know the basic steps to a waltz, and that's what Levi led her in. "Is there a pretty blonde in your past who went back to her family and left you all alone?" The song was all in French, and that was the gist of it.

"This is like the Cajun national anthem, and if there was a song called 'Jolie Noir' I'd have requested it." Levi leaned back a little and smiled at her again. "Right now, concentrate on this long rendition of the song and relax. I'm still trying to make up for all my rude behavior when we first met."

"You did that the same day when you apologized. There's no reason to keep at it."

"You're smart enough to know that's the excuse I'm going to keep giving you so you don't slap my face." Levi laughed, and the sound filled Yasmine's ears and her heart. "I like spending time with you and showing you a good time."

"The feeling is mutual, and I'm glad you do on both accounts." She did as Levi asked and simply enjoyed the moment. It didn't have to mean anything. There was no reason to sit and think about why being in Levi's arms brought her to life like nothing aside from her job ever had. She wasn't interested in women, and she definitely wasn't interested in Levi Montbard.

The song ended and she didn't move away from Levi even as the other dancers bumped them as they started what Levi had called the two-step. All that seemed to be was dancing on your toes in a certain pattern. Levi held her tighter and motioned for Zara. They all moved to the side and Levi danced with both of them. That's how they spent the rest of their night until Yasmine made the mistake of yawning at one in the morning and Levi walked them home.

"Thanks for everything," Zara said, kissing Levi's cheek before heading up.

It left them alone, and every ounce of exhaustion left her when Levi looked at her lips and swallowed hard. "I'll be here early, and we can walk to the place I'm thinking of, if that's okay."

"Sure." She was tired of all the voices in her head that weren't hers. "I had a good time tonight."

"Me too, jolie noir." Levi didn't seem to be able to help herself as she reached over and touched Yasmine's hair. "Call me if you need anything until then."

"Are you sure we aren't keeping you from something?" They'd monopolized Levi's time from almost the moment they'd met, and it didn't occur to her until now to ask.

"You think I'd want to be anywhere but here?" Levi asked. Her fingers threaded into Yasmine's hair, and the sensation made Yasmine close her eyes. She wanted to memorize the feel of Levi and keep it like a talisman. "If you do think that, then let me assure you, I do not."

"You do have a way of putting things that makes me feel good."

"You should never feel any other way." Levi kissed her forehead gently.

If Levi had lowered her mouth onto hers, she wouldn't have stopped her, but then the cool air returned when Levi moved away. "Good night," Yasmine said.

"It was an excellent night, and I'll be back before you have a chance to miss me." Levi hesitated, but then turned and closed the door behind her.

Yasmine locked it and tried to calm her breathing. Her heart was racing, and her nipples were so hard they hurt pressing against her bra. She was going crazy, but part of her didn't care. Her life would eventually return to the daily routine she found comforting, but right now, her only plan was to live and be happy.

The day would come when Levi would settle down with some lucky woman. The sad truth was that it wouldn't be her.

❖

Graham Tomkins entered the private house on St. Charles Avenue and headed for the small library on the second floor. The large old home a block from Audubon Park had been purchased from the Catholic Church a hundred years before, when the priest thought the land and structure worthless. It was close to Tulane and Loyola Universities, and they had visitors from all over the world.

"Graham," Cristian Bacon said when he lifted his head from the thick book he was reading. Cristian was the librarian for the order, and his knowledge of history was extraordinary. "It's been ages."

"The boss has had me running around on different projects. I stayed in the house in Paris, but their archivist wasn't nearly as interesting to talk to." He sat across from the old man and shook his hand. It had been Cristian who'd brought him into the order and mentored him until he'd become an important member the leadership counted on.

"Digby Nye said the same, so I'll remember to stay clear." Cristian smiled and closed the book with a puff of dust. "Are you ready?"

"Don't worry. I did my homework, and Digby was right. There's something going on, and we need to get involved."

"Come on, then." Cristian had trouble getting out of his chair, and Graham came around to help him. "They should be ready to start soon."

They walked together to the large room at the center of the house on the first floor. The place had four floors altogether, which gave them plenty of room to have guests like Digby Nye, who'd traveled from London. Graham had moved out the year before and now had a small shotgun house in the park.

Cristian went in without him since Graham would have to wait for their leader. Today it was his turn to light the candle of truth and tell the brotherhood what he'd discovered. Bartholomew Layton was this chapter's keeper of truth, the second person from his family to have that honor. The Priory of Scion had evolved through the years, and it was so much more than what they portrayed in the movies.

Everyone thought they'd been formed in the 1950s, but before that they'd gone by many other names. Their goal was always the same: to expose the Church for what it was and not what it tried to present to the world. They'd worked throughout history to bring to light what the Church tried to bury.

"Rise, brothers and sisters," Bartholomew said, and those in attendance stood around the large round table.

Graham bowed at the candle that was lit before every meeting. It was an honor to be the one who put fire to wick. "There is something going on here at home," Graham started. He told them about Baggio Brutos being in town, and the death at Levi Montbard's home.

"What do you think she has that the church would've sent their pit bull to get?" Bartholomew shook his head. "I should say what would've prompted them to send Cardinal Chadwick's fixer?"

"I've been following Baggio for a while now because I suspected he was up to something because of the travel he's been doing." Graham placed a map on the screen at the opposite wall from him. "He spent some time in Turkey but then rushed off to Paris. There was an auction at Drouot for some scrolls dated from around 1300 AD. Baggio wanted them but Montbard got there first. I witnessed the moment Baggio hunted her down and offered her a large amount of money, but she turned him down."

"I've kept an eye on Levi Montbard, and she's not one to suffer fools," Cristian said. "She's actually fascinating. Something set her on a course of acquiring a vast number of documents a few years ago, and I have yet to figure out what that was. The whole Montbard family is doing the same work we are, but they've never explored joining us."

"We've never come out of the shadows for them to inquire," Digby Nye said. Digby held the same position as Bartholomew, and it was his job to keep the order well hidden in Europe like Bartholomew and three others did in the United States. As far as the world knew, the Priory of Scion did not exist any longer.

"We've never done that because it wasn't necessary. The Montbard family understands the importance of uncovering and making public whatever they find, and they don't need us to do so. Baggio Brutos and his handlers are the complete opposite." Bartholomew stared at the map. "Graham, you need to stick with Levi and make sure she's able to work through whatever she's searching for. Baggio has left the country, and from what I can see, he left no one behind to give her a problem."

"And if there is?" Graham asked.

"Digby will be here to deal with that. He has some people he can call on in the States to take care of any problem you run into. You do nothing but report back. I need you to be able to travel wherever we need you, so make sure you remember that last part." Bartholomew looked at him until he nodded.

"You have no idea what it is she's after?" Digby asked. "Levi, I mean."

"I don't know, but this is a departure from her usual way of working. When she finds something, she writes about it. This time there's been nothing, and with Brutos in the picture I can only guess that whatever she's found will make an impact that will rock the Church. If it weren't for Brutos, it could be anything, but with that connection... Perhaps that's wishful thinking, but Levi was one of my students. If anyone can cause the Church a problem, it'll be Levi Montbard." Cristian had taught for years in addition to his responsibilities, and very few students had impressed him. Graham had been one of those, but Levi was the star who had eclipsed everyone else.

"Don't worry. I'll stay on her and make sure she's free to work without worry. I'll be sending in regular reports, and I'll make contact if I see anyone else on her." Because of this mystery, he wondered what the future held, but only Levi Montbard knew that. "You're right, what she's doing could be important."

CHAPTER TEN

The clock display read 5:15. Levi was sitting in bed studying the translation Yasmine had done, trying to calm the restlessness that had awakened her by focusing on the thrill of digging deeper. Her doorbell rang, and she chose to ignore it. Sometimes drunks thought it was funny to ring doorbells in the French Quarter on their way past. The bell rang again, and this time she went to answer it. The drunks usually only rang once. She opened the door to Yasmine.

"Are you okay?" She looked her up and down, searching for injuries. "Come in."

"I'm okay. I hope I'm not bothering you." Yasmine gazed up at her and balanced herself by putting her hands on her hips. "I saw your light on and wanted to come and work on the other two scrolls, if that's okay?"

She'd given Yasmine copies of all four, but the originals were in the research room. Whatever reason Yasmine was here, she didn't care. "Sure, but how about some coffee first? Or would you like tea?"

"Coffee sounds good." Yasmine followed her to the kitchen. "Why are you awake so early?"

"For the same reason you probably are," she said, and Yasmine laughed. "I'll probably be exhausted later, but I'm glad I got up early if it got you to come over for a visit."

"How would you feel if Zara and I cook for you and your family instead of going out for brunch?" Yasmine didn't exactly ignore what she'd said but had changed the subject like she always did. "I don't want your grandparents and parents to think I was ungrateful for everything they've done for us."

"Neither my parents nor my grandparents would think anything of the kind. Don't think you have to do that." She watched as Yasmine waited for the coffee to drip, combing her hair back.

"I'd really like to, but I need you to take me to the store again." The way Yasmine smiled at her made her want to give her whatever she wanted. "I realize it's not your favorite thing, but I promise to make it fun."

"I'll take you wherever you'd like to go." Yasmine could drive, and there was no reason she couldn't go to the store on her own. A flare of hope shot through Levi as she considered the ramifications of that.

"Would you mind if I use your kitchen?" Yasmine poured a cup for her and handed it over. Once Yasmine had finished with the other one, Levi unlocked the secret room and turned the lights on.

"Let's just use the lamps. It's too early for all this light." Yasmine sat in the chair she preferred and as usual folded her legs under her. "Will you be cold?"

Levi glanced down at her boxers and T-shirt, having forgotten to put on her robe. "I doubt that, but I'll run and get dressed if you're uncomfortable."

"Come sit and stop worrying about that. What I said before...I was nervous and didn't know you well. Now that I do, I doubt you could make me uncomfortable." Yasmine stood and picked up a copy of the third scroll. They'd numbered them; not that it would matter if all of them said the same thing.

After working in silence for an hour, Yasmine asked if they could move to the study since the couch was more comfortable. They opted for soft lighting again and weren't close together when they sat down, but when Levi woke up, Yasmine was in her arms and sleeping. She wasn't moving, so Levi closed her eyes and enjoyed what little Yasmine was willing to give.

She noticed the change in Yasmine's breathing fifteen minutes later and waited for the retreat she knew was coming. Yasmine surprised her when she reached for her hands, threaded their fingers together, and didn't move. They fell back asleep for another hour, and although they didn't discuss it, Yasmine only moved so she wasn't fully in her arms. She'd think Yasmine was teasing her, but she didn't seem the type.

"Do you mind if I go and get Zara?" Yasmine asked softly, her head still resting on Levi's shoulder. "I left a note, but I'm sure she'll be wondering by now."

"I don't mind at all, but here." She reached behind her to the drawer of the side table and took out a key. "I'll run up and take a shower, but if you finish before I do, come back in."

"How do you know not to ask any questions about anything?" Yasmine still hadn't moved away, and her question was vague, but Levi had a clue as to what it was about.

"Because you're not ready to answer them. If you think I'm an expert at all this, I'm not. You need to take your time and be sure, and I'm as confused as you are. I'm going to be your friend no matter what, and slow and steady will answer those questions we have better than if I put voice to them." She ran her free hand down Yasmine's back and tightened her hold before letting her go.

"That doesn't sound like your usual reaction." Yasmine exhaled against her neck and shook her head slightly. "I'm sorry. I don't know you well enough to make that assumption."

"Don't apologize, you're right." She'd had so many great experiences with so many great women, and she'd never regretted any one of those, but she'd realized something in the last couple of years. There was something she and Pia had in common, and that was the belief that there was someone out there who'd been made just for her. Granted, actually meeting that someone wasn't something she'd ever stopped and seriously thought about.

It was the most ridiculous notion because the world was full of beautiful women. Deciding on just one was as foreign to her as a nine-to-five job, but it didn't make it any less likely. All she had to do was look at her grandparents and her parents to see that forever was possible. Giving in to love didn't mean the end of the excitement of what attracted you to the woman in the first place, but she'd never wanted to give in at all. There hadn't been a woman who'd made her think otherwise, but now she glanced down at Yasmine and reconsidered. It might have been a stretch to say she completely understood, but seeing the truth was the first step.

"What? Tell me." Yasmine's intoxicating voice interrupted her ruminations.

"You're right, but once I find—" She couldn't say it out loud without sounding like a romance novel.

Yasmine lifted her hand and pressed it to her cheek. The urge to kiss her was so strong Levi lowered her head a millimeter, but she wouldn't go back on her word.

"Tell me," Yasmine said.

"My grandfather told me a story of what it means to find and fall in love with the one person who is your match. Each generation has that one epic romance that continues the chain that was started so long ago." She laughed at the memory of Cristobal telling her the story over and over. "My family doesn't believe in divorce, so once the choice is made, you have to be sure it's the right one. It's a lesson that's been passed from father to son, and it's tradition to tell the story."

"But in this generation there was no son," Yasmine said, moving her hand to her neck.

"True, but I'm still looking for a woman to treasure," she said and shrugged.

"That's beautiful." Yasmine closed her eyes and put her head back down.

Levi hesitated for a moment before letting Yasmine's hands go. "It's something I hope is true. It's nice knowing I come from a long line of happy people. So, you're right, this isn't my usual reaction."

"Why is it different?" Yasmine laid her hand on Levi's abdomen.

"I don't have a way to explain it, and I don't have enough information to make sense of it. All I'm sure about is that I want to keep going."

Yasmine pulled a little away from her and looked down at her. "You are something else, Levi, and I'm glad you don't scare easily."

"I offered to go to the grocery store twice in a week, so that's true." She touched the tip of Yasmine's nose and laughed. "Let me throw on some pants and I'll pick you and Zara up so we can go."

Yasmine nodded but didn't move right away. From her expression Levi could tell she was trying to think of something, and she didn't move when Yasmine lowered her head and kissed her cheek.

"We'll be waiting—*I'll* be waiting."

Levi watched Yasmine as she crossed the street and entered the townhouse, and then she went up to get dressed. "Hey, Mom," she called as she put her watch on and grabbed her wallet. "Call Gran and Papa and tell them you're all invited to dinner tonight. I'll call you with a time later."

"What's the occasion?"

"Yasmine would like to cook for everyone, but I have more room, so come over here. She finished the translation, so maybe we can go over it and come up with a plan." She took the steps faster than usual, but she had places to be.

"You have a woman cooking in your kitchen and you're not freaking out?" It was useless to try and deny anything. Madelena Montbard was a detective and psychic rolled into one small woman.

"It's a dinner, Mom, and I don't have time to talk about it right now. I'm on my way to the grocery store."

"Wait a minute," her mom said, her voice getting higher. "You're willing to go grocery shopping?"

"Yes." She pulled out of her parking space and double-parked in front of the townhouse.

"Great. I can't wait for dinner. Let us know the time."

Her mother hung up before Levi had a chance to say anything else, but she didn't want to think about that right now. Yasmine and Zara were walking toward her, and she got out to open their doors. It took them three stops at different spots to get all the stuff Yasmine said she'd need for a traditional Moroccan meal. Once they were back home, the sisters spent an hour chopping and preparing before putting a large casserole dish in the oven.

Yasmine assured them that it would be okay to leave the slow-cooking dish while they drove to Tulane so they could check the scrolls that were still drying. Zara walked ahead of them, and Levi was warmed when Yasmine placed her hand in the bend of her elbow. There weren't many people around because of the early hour on a Sunday, but a few jogged along the empty sidewalks. Even so, if they were in Morocco she doubted Yasmine would've done the same thing.

This had always been her favorite time of day when she was a student here. "Do you like the campus?"

"It's so different than home with all the old oaks and Southern architecture, but I could sit in Cristobal's office forever and look out those windows. I'd miss my students, but the kids here are just as curious." The lab was locked up and Levi handed Zara the key when she held her hand out. "I hope I get invited back."

"If I know my grandfather, he's devising a plan to keep you permanently." They got through the couple of doors necessary to get inside. "Wow."

The pan was half full of mercury, and the scrolls were beginning to look like the ones she had at home.

"You think it's safe to unroll them?" Zara asked.

"Let's finish the process and find out." Levi followed the steps it would take to safely open a scroll without tearing or damaging it.

They all gloved up and put on masks, and Levi picked up the special forceps that wouldn't stick to the parchment. Yasmine held the corners, and they slowly started unrolling. Levi carefully put more clips at the bottom to keep them from curling up again. If there was anything left on the scroll after all this time it would be a miracle, but if there was it would also prove the method of mercury could actually work. It had seemed to work with some artifacts, and others it had turned to mush. They followed the same procedure for the other four scrolls.

"That's amazing," Yasmine said.

Levi stared in wonder, breathless at the neat writing that started an inch from the top and continued down to an inch from the bottom. It was written in French, but from the script and the few words she recognized, it could be as old as the scrolls she'd recently bought.

"The language makes sense considering where they were found, but the process whoever hid these went through doesn't. This is old school, way older than should exist for anything found in this country." Her thoughts were coming at her so fast she was having trouble processing. Excitement and adrenaline prickled her skin like there was an electric charge running through her, and she had to concentrate to slow down and not damage anything. A find like this didn't come often in the States, and she couldn't wait to dive in. "This is a huge anomaly."

"It was written in the year of our Lord 1312 AD," Yasmine said, pointing to the second line from the top.

Levi glanced back at the stones. "So what are those for?" The stones appeared to be marble, were about a foot across and two feet long, and the edges were left raw.

Yasmine walked over to where the stones sat and studied them. "Maybe they were a backup in case the scrolls didn't make it. I don't recognize the language, though."

"There's a lot more writing on this than there is on there," Zara said, pointing between the scroll and stones. "I've been working on the stones, but the symbols aren't anything I've seen before, so it's been slow on the research end. I don't think they're the same thing at all."

"We'll need to find the answer because the stones might have something totally unrelated to the scrolls. If I'm right, that means they lead to somewhere else. I also have an idea on how to make a breakthrough." She'd been enjoying her tour time with Yasmine and Zara, but the new information on the stones and parchment deserved all her attention now. "Let me scan all this and we'll head back. Once you get to know my family better you'll figure out they're always early. *Way* early." She set up to print copies of the first scrolls once the scans were done, wanting to give the others time to dry.

The year surprised her, even more so since she'd been studying anything she could find in the same time period having to do with the Templars. That's where she'd find André and Farah, but the odds that something found sixty miles from her home would have something to do with that would be infinitesimal. When she'd followed the clues she'd been expecting gold or silver that would lead to the pirates Bumpy had hoped for. Finding this was like finding a McDonald's on the moon. She'd never dreamed that two different searches would come together this way. Coincidence or fate, she didn't care. But it heightened the desire to put the puzzle together.

"This is so amazing," Levi said, holding up the folder with the copies.

"We might have brought you luck," Yasmine said.

"There's no doubt about it."

❖

Yasmine stood next to Renaud as he mixed drinks for everyone. They'd talked about the find Levi had made and the writing on the first scroll. Levi's father didn't seem like a man easily caught up in the excitement, given the calm way he appeared to go about things, but she could see how he felt about his child and all he'd done to make her the person she was. Levi had been lucky to grow up surrounded by wonderful people.

"It's French, but with enough variation from the language we know today that it's going to take some time." Renaud handed Yasmine a glass of wine and brought Levi a glass of whiskey. "The other translation you did on the ones she bought at auction was fascinating."

"I was shocked to find the name André in that scroll, but not as much as Levi, I'm thinking." She left Renaud and went to check on dinner. "I need to buy you a tagine. It would make this much easier," she said to Levi.

"I'm sure Amazon carries those," Levi said, winking. She was preparing a peanut butter and strawberry preserve sandwich for George, who was telling Zara about all the pirate books Levi had purchased for him through the years. He was clearly older than Levi, but Levi was his hero.

"You know the only tagine I'm going to use is one made with Moroccan clay, so forget your Amazon." She swatted Levi with her oven mitt and laughed. The cooking pots with their conical shaped tops used in Morocco made food much moister, and the one she had at home had belonged to her grandmother. "Everyone ready to eat?"

Zara was dishing couscous into a serving platter, and Levi lifted out the lamb cooked in Moroccan spices for Yasmine.

"This is delicious, sweetheart," Madelena said, after taking a few bites. "New Orleans has every type of food, but nothing like this."

"Thank you, ma'am. My grandmother taught me some of what she knows through the years. She was glad one of us learned, since our mother is a dreadful cook." She laughed along with Zara and gave thanks that her work gave her an excuse to miss her mother's family dinners.

"Maybe you could do this again and put some weight on my kid."

"Mom, I'm sure Yasmine didn't travel all this way to cook for me. She's got better things to do," Levi said, appearing chagrined.

"Don't worry, Mrs. Montbard, I'll work on her. Though she's treated me and Zara to some wonderful meals, so I can promise you she's been eating well." She reached over and placed her hand on Levi's thigh and smiled.

"Please, Mrs. Montbard is my mother-in-law, a wonderful woman, but you're aging me. Both of you call me Madelena." She smiled at them. "Are you enjoying the city and everything Levi's found to show you?"

"Yes. You have a lovely city to call home, and Levi has been wonderful." Yasmine glanced at Levi, whose cheeks were a little pink. "I can't thank Cristobal enough for inviting me to teach here."

The dinner went on with Madelena and Diana mostly dominating the conversation and asking questions about her and Zara's lives. Their curiosity seemed to bother Levi, but neither she nor Zara minded. As they walked home, delivering Zara to their door before they did so, the rest of the family promised to reciprocate with a home-cooked meal. Yasmine stayed behind to help Levi clean up the kitchen, and it felt as if they'd been doing it for years. It filled her with something she could only define as happiness. With Levi she could be herself without having to put up the shields she usually did. There was no logic to it, given how short a time they'd known each another, but there was no question in her heart that it was true. The night was a glimpse of how it should be.

"Are you sure you're not tired?" She watched Levi turn on some lamps in the study, forgoing the overhead lights.

"You're the one who did all the work. If you want we can wait until tomorrow." Levi joined her on the couch after a quick trip back to the kitchen and handed her the cup of tea she'd made for her. "I know you have class tomorrow."

"Let's look at the first scroll from today and see how far we get." She patted the seat next to her and sighed when Levi sat. "Do you really get to Morocco often?" Having Levi this close made her brain seize at the possibility it'd never happen again.

"I have a feeling it'll be a lot more than the three or so times a year I go now. When I told you how often I go, I wasn't telling you a story, honey. I have a few dealers I do business with and I also have a few projects going on in that part of the world." Levi took her hand and pulled her fingers gently. "I'm not happy that you have to head home, but not seeing you again is unacceptable."

The pet name made Yasmine's heart swell. "Good." It was all she could say. "Let's see what's waiting for us."

The writing had run in a few places, but there was enough of what was left to decipher whatever story it told. They'd gotten comfortable, and she started working through what at first seemed like a laundry list of nothing. It was like someone sat and wrote every word they knew with no reasoning behind it.

"What the heck is this?" Levi said.

Yasmine tilted her head, thinking. As they'd shared one copy of the scroll, Levi had lifted her arm to the back of the couch and moved closer to her, and it made it hard to think clearly. "It could be some kind of puzzle like the one that led you to André, but let's not get ahead of ourselves." She leaned back and pulled Levi's hand down on her shoulder.

"What happens if we do? Get ahead of ourselves, I mean." Levi leaned back farther, taking Yasmine with her.

"It might lead somewhere wonderful." She leaned against Levi and didn't want to move. "What would you like to do?" It was all so confusing. She'd never been attracted to anyone, not really. She'd tried to bury that part of her life, but being honest with herself meant admitting there had never been *any* reaction when it came to men. Now finding the one person in the world who made her blood boil made her realize everything she'd been missing. The feel of Levi made her not want to stop it.

"So many things, but I'm not sure if we're ready for that. Let's scan this in and see what happens when I run it through the program I have. I'm sure your program is sufficient, but mine is much more sophisticated since I use it for more sensitive work. If we have faith, then it might show us the best path forward." Levi took Yasmine's hand and walked her to the research room. It didn't take much time for the scanner to input the sheet.

"Can I?" She stepped in front of Levi and glanced back at her.

"Go ahead." Levi pressed closer to her back to look over her shoulder when she typed in the words *pierce* and *God*. "You accuse me of being a romantic, Dr. Hassani, but I don't think I'm the only one."

"Sometimes you have to believe in a little romance as well as have faith. You've worked so hard, and you deserve to have that rewarded. It would be exceptional if your two finds were connected somehow, and it looks like they are. Of course, it could be unrelated but still lead to something truly interesting." She pressed Enter and turned around. "How long will it take?"

"It's going to be at least a few hours, and you can't stay up that long. Don't worry, I won't go over the results without you."

"I know, but I think you're starting to rub off on me. My impatience is growing." She wasn't ready to call it a night, but tomorrow was another day. The one thing she was beginning to realize was that her courage grew with each day she spent with Levi. She couldn't keep bottling up all the things she'd kept inside for so long, and that was a terrifying prospect. "You're a bad influence, Dr. Montbard."

"You have no idea," Levi said as she tugged her closer. "How about we let this work and we find something else to do?"

"Like what?" She followed Levi like there was no other option.

Levi turned the stereo on and held her hand out. "How about a little practice for the next time we go out?"

The song was slow and sexy, nothing like the music at the bar. This was the kind of music you seduced someone with, but Yasmine didn't care as she took Levi's hand. When they came together it was also different. Levi held her tighter, closer, hotter. She put her hands on Levi's shoulders and rested her head against her chest.

The music touched her soul, and the heat of Levi's body and the overwhelming sensation it caused in her made her emotions break. There was no ready explanation for why Yasmine couldn't stop the tears, and the way Levi held her only made her cry harder.

"Hey, what's wrong?" Levi tried to pull back but didn't let her go.

"I'm sorry," she said. The only thing she could do was cling to Levi and hope Levi didn't think she was insane.

"Don't apologize. If you're upset, you can tell me." Levi put her fingers in Yasmine's hair again and gently moved her head back so she could look at her. "You're safe with me, and you'll *never* have to hide who you are from me. I'm never going to think you're anything but perfect."

"But why?" Her tears turned to sobs, and she let her head fall forward again. It felt like thirty-one years of emotion had reached their limit and had to come out. "Why do you think that?"

Levi appeared genuinely scared, so Yasmine guessed she didn't have a lot of experience with hysterical women.

"Because it doesn't take long to see someone's heart when they give you the honor of showing you. Tell me why you're crying?" Levi put her arms around her and hugged her hard enough to lift her feet off the ground. "If I've made you uncomfortable, you can tell me and I'll walk you home."

"No, it's not that."

She cried until she tired herself out and appreciated how Levi simply held her. The night wasn't what she'd planned, but it was like a weight lifted off her, and it was Levi who'd taken it and thrown it off. "Thank you." She lifted her head and kissed Levi's cheek. "I never cry, and it wasn't anything you did."

"My grandmother says it's a good way to wipe the slate clean. You okay?" Levi's voice was gentle.

"I am, and she might be right." Yasmine touched the face that was starting to dominate her thoughts. "You have a way of undoing me, but it's okay. It's like I've been sleeping, and you've woken me up."

"Are you sorry that's happened?"

"No, and you're sweet to care. You're the one who's perfect." She sat up, and Levi lowered her hands. "I'm sorry for falling apart on you, and if you don't mind, I'm going to go home and be mortified in private."

"There's no reason for mortification. This isn't going to change anything between us. Hopefully you're comfortable enough with me to let go when you need to." Levi kept some distance between them when they stood.

"Crying is so out of my norm and it's always embarrassing, and it exhausts me." Perhaps she should have gone into all the complicated things going through her mind. Maybe she should have talked about family expectations, about religion, about culture. About her mother and the way Yasmine was expected to behave once she returned home. But she couldn't bring herself to do it. She was exhausted and couldn't bear to have that kind of deep conversation right now. Or, possibly, ever. Maybe some things were better left unsaid.

"Let me walk you home." Levi held her hand until they were across the street. "I'll see you tomorrow, right?"

"You will. We still have plenty left to do." She stood on her toes and kissed Levi's cheek again. "Thank you for everything."

She closed the door after that so Levi wouldn't see the tears that were falling again. "What the hell is happening to me?" For the first time in her life she was lonely. Not even having Zara there with her was making it better. She needed something else, and it was killing her that it would never be hers.

CHAPTER ELEVEN

Levi smiled at Pia when she came in the next morning. She'd slept like shit the night before, but she'd kept her light off, not sure if she was ready to see Yasmine again so soon. It was plain to her what Yasmine wanted but wouldn't allow herself to have, and the smart play was to let her go.

"Good morning," she said, trying for a smile. "How was your weekend?"

"It was good. I tried that dating app one more time and I've decided there are more idiots in the world than normal people. I might have to take a break so I can restore my faith in humanity." Pia poured herself a cup of coffee and sat across from her in the kitchen. "How was your time as tour guide?"

"It was good. We're making progress on the scrolls, and the computer is working on the stuff we found recently. Things are fantastic." She stood and poured her cold coffee in the sink.

"Ah," Pia said. "What's wrong?"

"Nothing's wrong. I'll be working from home today, so go ahead and take care of the end-of-the-month stuff. If you could check with the team at the swamp, that would be great." She needed to get dressed and drive Yasmine to school. She wanted to see her again but didn't think that was a good idea. "I haven't heard from them lately, and I'm not sure if that's good or bad."

"Something is wrong, and you don't have to tell me, but don't deny it." Pia sounded almost scolding, but Levi wasn't in the mood. The doorbell saved her from getting into this any further.

"Zara." Levi moved aside when the young woman walked past her. "Is Yasmine okay?"

"Not really. Tell me why she looks like everything she loves has died." Zara put her fists on her hips and stared Levi down even though she was six inches shorter. "She's not talking, and you look like she does, which is not good."

"She was tired last night, and I think she got a bit overwhelmed. I'm sure some sleep and getting back in the classroom will make everything okay." She turned when Pia cleared her throat, and the sight of her only made Zara's anger climb for some reason. "Zara, meet my assistant, Pia Adler."

"Was she here last night?" Zara asked in a low voice. The *you asshole* was implied.

"No," Levi said and glanced down at herself. She was still in boxers and the shirt she'd slept in. Not the kind of outfit you received guests in. "Could you give me a minute? I'm not moving too fast this morning and I have to get dressed."

She came down in jeans and an old Tulane T-shirt and found Pia and Zara squaring off. Neither of them spoke, but the tension was plain. Her keys and wallet were in the dish by the door and she faced Zara before putting both in her pocket. "Are you coming or staying?" That was all she was willing to ask because she wasn't refereeing whatever the hell was going on in her den.

"Yasmine wants me to work on the stones, so I'm staying. I'll use the scans rather than the real thing for now." Zara grabbed the front of Levi's shirt and pulled until she lowered her head. "Whatever's wrong, fix it. I'm sure you're not to blame, but you're not completely innocent either."

❖

Levi got out of the car and knocked on Yasmine's door. She'd thought that once Yasmine had gotten all of that emotion out, she'd feel better. But when she opened the door, her eyes were puffy and her smile was sad.

Yasmine could barely look at her in the car, and Levi drove in silence. Whatever had happened to Yasmine the night before had driven a wedge between them, and she was at a loss as to how to repair the damage. She parked and went around to get Yasmine's door, taking her hand for the walk to her classroom.

"Levi..." Yasmine gently pulled her hand away and shook her head but didn't say anything for the rest of the walk to her office.

"I think I know what the problem is." Levi closed the door to the office and turned Yasmine around.

"What?" Yasmine asked.

"This." She put her hands on Yasmine's hips and lowered her head. She moved slow enough to give Yasmine the chance to stop her if that was what she really wanted. Nothing in her experience had prepared her for the first time her lips pressed to Yasmine's. Whatever tenuous control she had snapped when Yasmine moaned. She pressed closer when Yasmine accepted her kiss and ran her fingers through her hair.

"Oh," Yasmine said when they broke apart. "That was, um—"

"Something we need to try again when you don't have a hundred students waiting for you." She leaned into Yasmine's touch and smiled. "I think our first kiss should've been more romantic than that, but I couldn't wait any longer. I slept like hell last night because I left you hurting—it's something I'm not proud of. I'm still not sure if this is something you want, but I couldn't help myself."

"You know exactly what I wanted, and I'm glad you gave it to me." Yasmine started the next kiss. "Will you come back and pick me up later? I don't want to be away from you."

"I'll be here." She wanted to stay and sit in on Yasmine's lecture, but that would be way too distracting for both of them. "I should've brought my laptop. I could've worked from here."

"Would your grandfather mind if you used his? I'd offer mine, but I have sensitive documents and it would go against protocol." Yasmine was running her fingers along her collarbone.

"Good idea." She sat and Yasmine took the arm of the chair. "Maybe you could call your sister before you go and tell her I'm not an asshole."

"What are you talking about?" Yasmine tapped her fingers against Levi's shoulder before snapping them.

Levi explained her morning and Zara's mood. "I'm not telling you this so you'll get mad, but I don't want her to get the wrong impression of me. Pia's worked for me since I started in the family business, and we have a strange history." It was better to be honest and up-front, even if it worked against her.

"Strange history? What does that mean?"

Explaining friends with benefits hadn't been on her agenda for the morning, but life was full of curveballs. Yasmine nodded a few times as Levi explained, and then accepted her phone to make the call. The conversation she had with Zara was all in Arabic, and she was talking so fast, Levi understood none of it. She was sure that was Yasmine's intent, but the good thing was she didn't sound upset or angry.

"Tell me, Dr. Montbard," Yasmine said, pulling Levi's hair slightly. It was an attention getter in so many more ways than just getting her to look at Yasmine. "This strange history, is it still being written?"

"Truthfully, I've never had a reason to stop seeing any woman." Yasmine went to move away from her but stopped at Levi's next words. "I said I've never *had* a reason. There is no way I'd disrespect you that way even if all we do is kiss. I'm not flattering you to get you to sleep with me, but you're different."

"Even if I leave soon?" Yasmine's question was reasonable, but it still made Levi's heart ache.

"Do you want to stop? We can part now as friends." She came forward and kissed Yasmine again. "I know you can't stay, but I think we should take the chance."

"But then what?"

"I don't know, but I don't want to stop. Do you?"

"No," Yasmine said and kissed her again.

She laughed when Yasmine pulled away from her and put the desk between them to prepare for her class. Once she was gone, Levi used her grandfather's laptop to access her computer at home to see if her program had yielded anything yet. If the two words she'd entered weren't the key, the program could take weeks to work through every possibility. The cipher for the clues they'd found so far had unlocked the secrets the scrolls held, but if the key had changed for these documents, there were infinite possibilities that the computer could test faster than they could.

These scrolls being related to the ones she'd purchased in Paris was a pipe dream, but the Templar Cross on the box had given her pause. Science and research were what made her successful, but at times she had to take things on faith. Thinking the key words that had unlocked the first scrolls would do the same for these was working on faith. Faith, and gut instinct. Somehow, she just knew they were connected.

The most frustrating thing was she didn't know exactly what André and Farah had hidden that they'd made so hard to find, but the treasure had to be something special, and something well placed, to not have been accidentally found already. There had to be another clue hidden in these scrolls, and it was the next step in her chase.

"Because it has to be something. Who writes random words until they fill up a poster-sized skin?"

She watched the screen fill up with what appeared to be a long narrative. There was no way she was reading it without Yasmine, but the first line was *I write this in the year of our Lord 1306.* She had to stop and take a breath because her heart rate had picked up at those simple words.

She closed the program and opened the map of every find she'd made related to coded books. Then she filtered out everything that didn't have to do with the Sonnac file but included the book that had led her to Choupick. She took into account that the books could've been moved, but the map showed an almost straight line from northern Italy into France, then south into Spain.

The leather of the chair creaked when she leaned back and stared. "Who are you and why have you left so many bread crumbs through time?" Her next idea was to bring up a sample from every handwritten book she'd found in her Templar searches throughout the world. One thing seemed clear. She'd need an expert to confirm her theory, but to her untrained eye, eight of the books seemed to be written by only two different people.

"Someone must really love me," she whispered as she looked at the screen. None of the books were long, but each held a clue as to where to look next. The book she'd found in Madrid had survived in beautiful condition, and at first she'd almost put it in the store. They'd discovered decorators loved old books for studies and office spaces, though they rarely ever looked inside. The book was written in Italian, and the story was complete but complex. That rarely led to any kind of code.

The tale of a young boy and his family wasn't Shakespearean, but the description was fantastic. When she'd run the text through the program, it took weeks, but the result was a list of coordinates. It wasn't exactly a GPS location—hardly surprising given its age—but a general location that then took time to refine. All the work, time, and effort had brought her to the one place she'd never expected to go, but here they were with scrolls found close to her home.

"Shit." What she really wanted to know was where the people who'd buried the box had come from, and how they'd ended up in south Louisiana. Did they come after the "discovery" of the New World, or was it before? It was times like this that she wished for a functional crystal ball that would give her a glimpse into the past. What was so important or explosive that they needed all this subterfuge?

"This makes no sense," she said aloud. It was as if divine intervention had guided her to the books, ensuring she found each one so that she would be able to solve the riddle of André and Farah and discover their connection to the Templars. "The only problem with that is I don't believe in divine anything."

"Then it's good that one of us is a little religious," Yasmine said from the door. "I think it'd make your family happy if someone is praying to keep you safe."

Levi glanced at her watch, amazed she'd been able to concentrate long enough to not drive herself crazy thinking about Yasmine. "Want to go home?"

"Not yet," Yasmine said, coming over and sitting beside her. "At home I have to share you with Zara and the interesting history of Pia. Right now, I have you all to myself."

"Did you lock the door?"

"Yes. I can't have my students thinking I've been bewitched by an infidel," Yasmine said and laughed. "What have you found?"

"The impossible, it seems."

"Do we need to go through it right this minute?" Yasmine said as she ran her finger over Levi's bottom lip. "You seem to have awoken a part of my brain I didn't know existed until now."

"Just your brain?" She ran her hand up Yasmine's leg to her hip.

"Stop teasing me and kiss me."

They took their time until Levi was so turned on she wanted to strip and start begging. This confused the part of her that was usually on autopilot when it came to this kind of thing. Yasmine was beautiful, but the sight and feel of her were doing strange things to Levi, and she was helpless to stop it. Before she completely blew something important, Yasmine's phone rang. She seemed to want to ignore it but reached blindly behind her and answered.

After she said hello, the other person did all the talking. Yasmine tried to cut in a few times but then just sat back and listened. Levi could hear the speaker's voice even from a few feet away, and she didn't sound happy.

Yasmine didn't seem happy either, so Levi tried to cheer her up as best she could without saying a word. This morning was a major breakthrough, but there was no reason not to take another step forward.

She moved her hand down Yasmine's leg to her ankle, but on the way back she followed the path up the back of her leg. Yasmine looked at her with narrowed eyes as she stopped on her backside.

"Mama," Yasmine said, and Levi understood that title even in Arabic.

She lifted her hand and Yasmine grabbed it and brought it up to her mouth. It took discipline not to moan when Yasmine bit her index finger. Considering where they'd started, Yasmine was a fast learner. The one-sided conversation went on for another five minutes before Yasmine put her phone down and sighed. What had Zara said? *You have to know how we were raised to understand.* Their mother sounded like a force not to be taken lightly.

"Are you grounded?" she said, and Yasmine laughed. "I'd hate it if you couldn't come over."

"My mother believes if she talks loud enough, we'll have no choice but to follow the line she's drawn for us. I love her, but we don't agree on much." Yasmine rested her head on Levi's shoulder and sighed again.

"Your outlook on life is something she should be proud of, and your students love you." She held Yasmine and kissed her forehead. "Shouldn't all that count in your favor?"

"My mother's friends have children, and they're all married and starting their own families. None of them went to university, much less went on to get their doctorate. I not only did that, but I've talked my sister into following my path." Yasmine twirled a lock of Levi's hair as she spoke, and Levi smiled. "She ended up with two unmarried daughters, and we've ruined her life."

"That's a tough one, but I don't see you bending on that."

"I love my parents, but they'll never bend on their beliefs. But…I can't marry simply to make my mother happy. I'd rather stay single forever." Yasmine pressed her hand down on Levi's abdomen and her lips to the side of her neck. "This will never be acceptable, and my courage will only go so far."

"I've visited Morocco as well as other Muslim countries enough to know that." Levi leaned back so she could see Yasmine's face. "I don't totally understand it, but I know what they want from you."

"It's not want, Levi, it's a demand. Your family is different, and for that you're so very lucky. They love you for you. In my country they love me for who they expect me to be."

"All I can do is stand with you, but only you can decide what's best for you."

"I only kissed you this morning. Give me a little time to think about all this. I don't want you to make promises that will make you miserable."

"Weren't you the one who said we have to have a little faith? Sometimes that has to do with things outside religion." She kissed her again. "Let's go home so you can talk Zara into liking me again."

"Shouldn't you be worried about *me* liking you?" Yasmine asked, smiling. She packed up her stuff and joined Levi at the door.

"I have a head start on that, but I'm not going to let up now."

"Is something wrong?" Yasmine asked. They were in the research room, and Zara had her laptop open to five different sites as she worked on the stones. Levi had run out to get lunch when she said they had too much to do for them to cook again.

"Nothing, but something is different. You're different from this morning."

"I didn't get a lot of sleep." Her simple explanation didn't change the expression on Zara's face. "Levi and I had a conversation last night, and it upset me. She didn't do anything wrong, but you know how it is."

"I don't know unless you tell me."

Zara was tenacious when she wanted to know something. It was why Yasmine knew Nabil would snap her up as soon as her education was done, and she knew that if that was the path Zara chose, she would love it.

"Everything builds up sometimes, and I need a release valve. Levi gave me that without judging me." She put her hands up and stopped Zara from saying anything. "There's nothing wrong. It all had to do with us having to go back soon."

"Levi said we could stay as long as we want. Why can't we take the rest of the summer and work in exchange for helping her with all this?" Zara stood and hugged her. "It's a good deal, and I think she's good for you."

She wasn't entirely sure about that but wasn't ready to get into it. "I'm not in a rush to go, but Mama called today. She thinks we should be home for Grandmother's birthday."

Zara's shoulders slumped. "That's in three weeks. We might as well leave now."

"I didn't give her an answer, but she's only going to keep calling, and I doubt her wanting us back has anything to do with Grandmother's birthday." She put her hand on the pages of text Levi's program had developed. They'd agreed to wait until they were all together to read them, but she was getting to be worse than Levi when it came to putting it off. "I don't want to go back early either, so don't start bugging me about it."

"I know you. She calls and you give in because it's the easiest thing to do." Zara shook her finger at her, and she couldn't argue because it was true.

Levi called them to the kitchen before they could finish, and Yasmine stopped Zara as she left. "I haven't told her yet, so don't say anything." She didn't want anything messing with the bubble she was in right now.

Their afternoon was filled with work, but being close to Levi and her sister grounded Yasmine after her mother's demands. It was pathetic that she was thirty-one and her mother still had a way of bulldozing her. She wanted to develop a spine and stand up for herself, but her mother knew how to pour on the guilt. All her life she'd been taught what her duty was, and she'd been happy to comply until the day she stepped on the university campus. It opened up a new world and gave her a thirst for something more. What she hadn't been able to do was leave her home for that new world, because her bravery only went so far.

"Do you two mind if I leave early?" Zara said at five.

"Where are you going? We were going to read the translations." It didn't matter how old Zara was, Yasmine still felt responsible for her.

"Pia asked me to go with her to a concert, and I didn't think you'd mind. I promise I'll read the transcripts tomorrow."

"Pia, my assistant?" Levi asked, lifting an eyebrow. "You two didn't seem to be getting along."

"We're not best friends, but I like the band and I'd like to experience an American concert, so I said yes. She's not going to drug me and rob me, is she?"

Levi laughed. "She'll probably buy you dinner and a T-shirt."

Zara left with a smile, and Yasmine went back to Levi and stepped into her arms. The worry of whatever came next melted away as Levi kissed her, and she wanted so much more. "Did you plan that?"

"I wish I could take credit, but Pia can surprise me sometimes. She deserves a raise, don't you think?" Levi held her and kissed the top of her head. "You want to tell me what's wrong now?"

"What makes you think there is?" So much for her happy little bubble.

"Just a few things," Levi said, wiping the tears that had fallen. She led Yasmine to the den, where they sat.

Yasmine told her about the call and her grandmother's birthday. "My mother and I don't get along as well as we should, but my grandmother's the reason I finished university. She encouraged both of us to not fall in line and to make our own way. I think she'd understand, but my mother is the queen of guilt."

"How old is your grandmother going to be?"

"She'll be eighty-one this year." She stretched out next to Levi on the couch, enjoying the heat of Levi's body.

"Then you have to go."

The ease with which Levi dismissed her made her want to cry harder. "You want me to go?"

"Let me explain. You have a few more days of classes, then I want you and Zara to fly to London with me and meet my mother's parents. I called them today with the clue we found about the serpent's bite, and my grandfather said he might have an idea. We're going to chance the serpent's bite and find our next clue." Levi moved her leg, pressing their bodies closer together. "Once we've done that, I'll be happy to escort you home so you can celebrate with your grandmother, then I'll have you all to myself for the rest of the summer. I can work from anywhere, and you can stop getting calls from your mother if you're home."

"Really?" She was rusty in the dating game, but what Levi was proposing sounded like she wasn't ready to brush her off. "You'd come to Morocco?"

"Yes," Levi said, smiling. "I'd like to meet the woman who's responsible for you."

"Thank you," she said, lowering her head to kiss Levi. "I can't stay away from you."

"You shouldn't." Levi rolled over so she was on top. "My advice is for you to get much closer."

Yasmine moaned when Levi squeezed her breast and kissed her like she really wanted her. "You are making me crazy."

Levi let up the pressure and moved her hand away. "I promise we'll go slow, but you make me crazy too."

"How about we do some reading?" It wasn't what she wanted

to do but she wasn't ready to strip her clothes off—well, she was, but that wasn't a great idea—yet. Levi made her crave being touched, but she had so much to work out in her head. Sex without marriage was a bad idea, and she'd been so good for so long. Was it worth it to give in simply because she couldn't control herself? The wise move was to wait until she understood what it truly meant to give herself to someone that way, in a way so outside of the cultural identity that was a part of her.

"Would you like something before we start?"

"Yes, but I can wait." Levi winked at her, and she couldn't help but kiss her again. It was like her hormones were a candle and Levi was the match that lit her wick.

Levi picked up the decoded pages and began to read out loud.

Year of our Lord 1312 AD

My story began in France years before now. My mother was a servant who was also a comfort to the man who owned the estate. That comfort resulted in a child who lost its mother the day she gave birth. I was left alone with a father who taught me only the ways of the Lord and of war. The rich history of my father's family spans generations that include the Crusades and the wars that came after.

The Holy Land seemed so far out of Templar grasp, and all was lost when they were driven from Jerusalem. In France, my father raised me to follow our leader back to the place where it all began, back to the Holy Land, to win back for our king what is rightfully his. We are to be the sacrificial lambs who will ignite the fight against the infidels who took so much from us. As I planned to enter the fight I knew my death was imminent, but I feared not, for I had dedicated my life to the Lord and to my brethren.

We left for Jerusalem a fortnight before my twenty-second season, and I spent my time remembering the years in my home. The fields were ready for harvest, and at sunset the grain flows like the ocean, making me close my eyes and pray for strength. My father's time is done, and he grew weaker before my eyes. I doubt he'll live to hear of my sacrifices. To the world I am only an orphan he took in and raised, but he is the man I honor with what will come next. His love is for

God, and he has served well and faithfully, and his reward will be eternal life.

To the one who understands what I leave unsaid, know that our history must be told. Our betrayal must be told, and the world must know of the evil that has slithered into the holiest of places and that feeds only on greed. The enemy of Christ will stoop to anything to stop the telling, but I have faith the truth will survive. Once it comes to light, the lies told by the false vicar will crumble so we can build again.

This is the true beginning of my story. I have left pieces in as many places as I can, with people I can trust, as we move toward the end of the world. There you will find it all.

CHAPTER TWELVE

L evi tried to absorb what she'd just read. The date matched up with what she was looking for, and the subject matter had to be the Knights Templar, given the references to infidels and sacrifice. The discovery of something like this in south Louisiana was exceptional, because although it was recorded that the Templars had traveled along the eastern coast of North America, there was no record of them having come this far inland. Who had made the voyage to bring them to this area? And why had they done so? That took the kind of dedication usually reserved for religion.

"What do you think?" Yasmine asked as she ran her fingers through Levi's hair.

"There's nothing written about the Templars going back to the Holy Land after they were driven out. In the months leading up to October 13, 1307, the Templars were preparing and sending some of their people away from what was coming. Pope Clement V sanctioned what happened, but we all know King Philip pulled the strings to get his hands on the Templar treasury."

"That treasure was never found, and you're right. There was never an account of any Templar venturing back into the Holy Land. By then the Muslim armies were too great to try anything like the Crusades again." Yasmine put the sheet down and concentrated on touching Levi's face.

Levi closed her eyes at the sensation of the soft fingers tracing her brows, then down her nose to her lips. There'd never been a time aside from when she was a child that this kind of thing was enough to make her content. They were in no way in love, but the way Yasmine touched her made her feel loved nonetheless. The way she did it calmed her so she could enjoy the gift of the moment. All of her restlessness subsided, and she wanted for nothing.

"Did you hear me?" Yasmine asked.

Levi nodded and smiled, not wanting to open her eyes. "I did, but this feels too good to think about work right now."

"That's so flattering," Yasmine said, leaning down and kissing her. "You seem like you're always moving, running to the next piece that will get you closer to your goal."

"Maybe I'm beginning to see that treasure can sometimes be a quiet night at home." She reached for the hand on her abdomen and threaded her fingers together with Yasmine's. "Say you'll come with me?"

"What's in London?" Yasmine's voice held no tone other than curiosity.

"Plenty of things, but right now we need to concentrate on something that happened way before André Sonnac was born. It's the secret to the first scroll you deciphered."

Yasmine pulled Levi's hair gently and laughed. "Are you holding out on me?"

"No, but like I said, I called my grandfather Percy and gave him the clue we found. His best guess as far as location, which came after three days of him thinking about the snake bite clue, is St. Mary's in West Somerton. He even offered to drive us, unless you prefer going by train."

"Are you going to make me torture it out of you?" Yasmine pulled Levi's hair again before dislodging her head and standing. Before Levi could complain, Yasmine lay back down on top of her and held her lips a few inches from Levi's. "Is that the route you're taking?"

"You can torture me all you want, beautiful lady." Levi closed the small gap between them and kissed Yasmine like she wanted nothing else in life. "You're going to like Grampie Percy and my grandmother Jane."

"I'm sure I will, but I don't want to talk about them right now."

The work was forgotten for the next hour as they kissed, touched, and talked. Levi walked Yasmine home and held her until she forced herself to go home. There was still time to pull back and protect her heart, but the more she saw of Yasmine, the more impossible that became.

"This is karma's way of biting me in the ass," she said as she locked up for the night. "I finally find someone I could love, and I can't have her." She knew from the way Yasmine spoke about her parents, especially her mother, that she'd never have the strength to leave. Things that were so engrained were hard to break away from, and a few weeks of seeing what their life could be couldn't compete with a lifetime of her mother's voice in her head.

Pia made all the travel arrangements the next morning, and for the next few days Levi took Yasmine and Zara to the university, and once Yasmine started her lectures, she and Zara worked in her grandfather's office until Yasmine finished. She enjoyed Zara's company and quick mind. The younger Hassani sister had a rebellious streak, but she loved her introverted sister fiercely. In the afternoons they went sightseeing, and Levi showed them all the things they'd wanted to see before Yasmine cooked for them at night.

Those nights together made it so that she didn't want to let Yasmine go home to an empty bed, but there was Zara to consider along with Yasmine's hesitations and fears. "All you can do is enjoy the time you have left," she said softly to the ceiling of her bedroom. The memories would have to do, and with luck they'd eventually fade into something bittersweet instead of heartbreaking.

She'd never forget Yasmine, but her heart would only heal once she did.

❖

"Don't forget," Cristobal said with his hands on Yasmine's shoulders, "you have an open invitation to come back and wow our students whenever you like. Say the word and I'll get you a job."

"You and your family have been so kind." Yasmine wiped away the tears the goodbyes had caused. She'd definitely learned how to cry, but it couldn't be helped. The Montbards had wormed their way into her heart, and leaving was painful. "Thank you for having me."

"That was a pleasure we'd like to have again," Madelena said when she hugged her next. "Remember one thing, sweetheart."

"What?" Levi's mother held her like she was trying to give her strength. They'd had a few conversations since her arrival. Madelena was easy to talk to and an even better listener.

"Follow your heart always. It's the only way to keep the demons of regret from taking root and ruining whatever happiness you can have." Madelena cupped Yasmine's cheeks and kissed her forehead. "Only you know what's right for you—only you."

"I'll try, but it's a lot to think on." She shut her eyes when the tears fell faster. "Thank you, though. You have a wonderful family, and you've raised an incredible daughter." She whispered that last part into Madelena's ear as she returned her embrace.

"My child is one of a kind, and all you need to remember is she comes from a long line of romantics who know how to love. They take commitment and their promises to heart, so if you wander off that path you thought you had to walk, you won't ever get lost." Madelena squeezed her again and pulled back to look at her. "Do you understand what I'm saying?"

"Yes, ma'am." She nodded as extra confirmation and turned to Diana. "Take care, and I hope to see you again."

"Oh, we'll definitely see you again, and probably sooner than later. Be careful and take care of Levi and Zara. I don't know your sister as well as I know my granddaughter, but they both seem the type to run into a hornets' nest, consequences be damned."

"I'll do my best," she said and laughed at the truth of that. She and Zara received another kiss from the entire family as well as George before they went through security. They were flying to New York, then on to London.

Everything Levi had found was securely locked in the vaults at the family store, but they carried the various copies of what they were working on. Levi had promised a layover in New York so they could see a play and enjoy dinner. Apparently, mentioning anything to Levi was like making a wish that came true.

"Thanks for the tickets," Yasmine said to Levi as they boarded.

"I'm coming out ahead on all this. Without your help I'd still be fumbling through a lot of this." Levi lifted their carry-ons into the overhead bin and pointed to their seats. She would be sitting across the aisle from Yasmine and Zara.

A beautiful blonde boarded, smiled, and pointed to her seat next to Levi, which made Yasmine lose all good humor. The woman immediately engaged Levi in conversation, and Yasmine had to relax her hand out of the fist she'd made.

"Since you and Levi are working on the same thing, why don't you two sit together?" Zara said as she climbed over Yasmine. She tapped Levi on the shoulder. "Switch with me."

"Are you sure?" Levi glanced up at Zara, who pointed to the empty seat.

"Move." She smiled sweetly at the other woman, who looked bemused.

Yasmine moved to the window seat and left Levi the aisle. "Is she always this bossy?" Levi asked and blew her a kiss so that no one else could see.

"I'm convinced she'll run Morocco one day." Yasmine put her hand on Levi's forearm.

They took off and she joined Levi in a nap, and when they hit turbulence she woke with her head on Levi's shoulder and their hands clasped in Levi's lap. Zara winked at her when she opened her eyes. The small sign of acceptance made her not let go and move. She closed her eyes again and imagined waking up like this after a night with Levi. How would her skin feel pressed to Levi's, and how would she go on without feeling it again once their time was done?

"Would you like something to drink?" the flight attendant asked, and she ordered them two coffees.

"Thanks," Levi said, kissing the top of her head. Yasmine stopped breathing and glanced at Zara again. If their position hadn't given them away, that move certainly would. "Sorry," Levi whispered and went to move away. "I wasn't thinking."

"No, I don't want you to start behaving now." She held Levi's hand tightly, and Zara went back to her laptop with a smile. The only one who appeared upset was the blonde sitting next to Zara. "I don't want to give my competition an unfair advantage."

"You should study yourself in a mirror sometime, honey. There's no competition." Levi spoke softly in her ear, and they stayed like that until their coffee and breakfast was served.

Their night in New York was fun, and Pia had booked them a later flight so they didn't have to rush off the next morning. The city was the definition of excess, and Yasmine couldn't see herself living there. She'd much preferred New Orleans and its special brand of a more relaxed crazy. Levi took advantage of the time they had and treated Zara to a drink at a place that overlooked the whole city. Yasmine liked the way Levi was thoughtful of her younger sister, and how Zara laughed with Levi. Their rooms adjoined, and Levi promised to keep her side unlocked in case they needed anything. They kissed good night while Zara was in the bathroom.

"Um…is there something you forgot to tell me?" Zara waited until they were alone to pounce.

"I don't think so," Yasmine said, stepping into the bathroom. She picked up her brush and started on her hair with Zara sitting on the counter.

"First of all, you looked like you were ready to kill that woman when she sat down, and you slept like you would've been happy in one seat." Zara held up two fingers before turning them and pointing at her. "So yeah, you forgot to mention a whole lot of things."

"I like her, and she has a way of making me—" She stopped and covered her face with her hands. "I don't know, she makes me want things that you probably think are wrong."

"No, no," Zara said, pulling her into a hug. "You don't get to back away in fear of what I think, but if you need to hear my opinion, here it is. She makes you happy, she fills you with life, and you look at her like you want to rip her clothes off."

"I do not."

"Yes, you do, and it's about damn time. You can't die a virgin, Yasmine. I mean, you're thirty, so I hope you aren't a virgin, but if you are, rev her up and let her loose."

"Are you serious?" She stared at Zara like she'd never seen her before in her life. "There are more reasons not to do that than there are to do it. Are you forgetting everything from our family and our upbringing?"

"Answer two questions for me and I'll give you my opinion." Yasmine nodded but Zara didn't let her go. "Is she a good kisser?"

"How did you know?" She shook her head and laughed. "Never mind. She is an excellent kisser."

"Good, and two, does she make you hot?"

"I can't believe I'm talking about this with you." Yasmine moved back and left the bathroom for one of the beds.

"Answer the question." Zara sat cross-legged across from her and snapped her fingers.

"Yes." She sighed. "Are you satisfied?"

"Not as much as you would be if you were next door instead of in here with me." Zara laughed and threw a pillow at her. "You can't think what you feel is wrong. Trying to conform to what the world wants will be like jamming a square peg into a very round hole. Stop hiding and start living."

"You know Mama will shun me. And the rest of the family? What about them?"

"She'll shun us both, because I'm not leaving you. I'm your family, Yasmine, and Levi could be your fate. Don't turn your back on that gift."

"I can't ask you to do that. Think about what you're saying. Losing everything we've ever known isn't something I even want to think about, and I'd never subject you to that." She put her arms around Zara and held her. "Thank you, though. I love you."

"Mama will fuss, but losing us completely, no matter what we've done, isn't in her. All you need to ask yourself is if you want to be happy. I do."

"Don't you think this is too much too fast?" Levi did make her feel alive, but she couldn't fathom having those people who'd shaped her life suddenly disappear. Zara was young and sometimes impetuous, so she'd have to weigh the consequences of all this because it affected more than just her.

"When you find someone to love, it's worth the gamble. I love you too, and I think it's time to be brave and think of yourself."

They went to bed after that, and she could hear Zara snoring twenty minutes later. Their conversation had left her wide awake, which would make the morning impossible to face. She picked up her phone and texted Levi since she could still see a light under the door. A few seconds later the door quietly opened, and Levi stood there. There were no words needed when Levi turned off her lamp and lay down next to her. She fell asleep in Levi's arms and her last thought before going to sleep was her new discovery.

Home wasn't a place, but a person.

❖

"Yes, sir." Graham set a small alarm on Levi Montbard's hotel room door that would alert him if she went out. He'd followed the small group to New York and with Digby's help had found that the city was a short stop before they traveled on to London. The flight wasn't full, so he'd be following them there as well and would have backup when some of Digby's men joined him.

"All they did was attend a play and dinner. The Hassani sisters are going with her, and Percy Breeden, her grandfather, has been making inquiries into the history of Queen Boudica."

"Why?" Bartholomew asked.

"I'm not sure, sir, but the academics who are loyal to us said he had a few questions about the warrior queen. Breeden's background is in Templar and British history as related to the Tudor dynasty, so we're not sure why he's asking."

"Are you prepared to travel?"

"Yes, sir. I don't need much, and the allowance you provided will be more than satisfactory. I'll report in again as soon as I have something."

"Good job, Graham, and be on the lookout for Brutos or any of his henchmen. If you were able to figure out their travel schedule and what Montbard's grandfather is working on, I can assure you Brutos and Cardinal Chadwick have as well."

"I'll watch over them, sir, and Digby's men will be waiting for me at the airport."

"I look forward to hearing from you." Bartholomew hung up and Graham headed for the shower. He would sleep fully clothed so he could follow at a safe distance once Levi was mobile again. Of all the assignments the order had given him, this was the most exciting. Most of his days were spent sitting next to Cristian going through books and compiling research. Jobs in the field, traveling to places he'd never been, didn't come along often.

CHAPTER THIRTEEN

Levi flagged a porter to carry their bags once they cleared customs. Her grandfather had already called to say he and her grandmother were there.

"Is that everything?" She waved Yasmine off when she went to take something from her. "Just carry my briefcase and we'll be set."

Levi's grandparents were easy to spot since Madelena was a carbon copy of Jane, her mother. "That has to be them."

"That's them, and if I know Grampie, he's double-parked somewhere." She made introductions and the Hassani sisters were treated to the same kind of greeting Levi got.

"Levi, go with your grandfather and get the cars," her grandmother said. "I refused to get towed again or get into an argument with official-looking people, so he's parked like a normal person."

"Yes, ma'am. Find a place to sit and I'll call when we're outside." Levi glanced back as they started to walk away, but Yasmine only smiled at her. She doubted Yasmine knew what was in store for her, since she'd bet heavily that her mother had already called Jane and filled her in.

"Don't worry so much. She won't embarrass you, and she's lovely." Her grandfather put his arm through hers and laughed. "They both are, actually, and I'm looking forward to one of your hunts, bear."

The nickname had come from her love of the teddy bear they'd gotten her as a toddler, and it had stuck. "I think we might actually get somewhere good this time, Grampie."

They piled all the luggage in the Land Rover and watched her grandparents drive off, as Levi and the girls followed in her grandmother's car. Thankfully, the traffic wasn't horrible and the trip to Chelsea would be quick.

"My grandmother didn't give you a hard time, did she?"

"Not at all, bear," Yasmine said and smiled. "She must be your biggest fan."

"My grandmother is the best. She's not as blunt as Gran, but she's good at getting her point across." She glanced in the rearview mirror and smiled at Zara. "If you're interested in symbolism, you should ask Granny a few questions. Grampie is a professor, but Granny worked for the government for years. Symbols don't come up often in that part of her life—she's more like Yasmine and an expert on codes. But Granny also does some work at the British Museum so she can dabble in the things she's passionate about, and a lot of that has to do with symbolism."

"Your family is like a real-life version of some kind of think tank. It's incredibly intimidating." Yasmine reached across the middle console and touched her arm. "I think our family will disappoint you when you meet them."

"Growing up with my family was an exercise in intimidation, but your family produced you and Zara. It doesn't matter if they teach at Oxford or stay home, they instilled amazing qualities in you." Levi took her eyes off the road for a minute and gazed at Yasmine. Her beauty really did have a way of making you stare.

"My sister's right," Zara said, breaking the spell. "You're good at flattery."

"I try my best, but with you two it's easy." She drove through the gates of her grandparents' home and waved to the gardening crew they'd had for years. "This is their summer place. They stay in a flat close to the university during the school year. Grampie refuses to retire, but that's good for us. He's got connections everywhere."

"This place is beautiful." Yasmine gazed at the house and didn't move to open the car door. "I love these places that make it easy to see what London was like years ago, and you don't find gardens like this back home. My grandmother loves plants, but most of hers are in pots and there's no grass."

"Both of them could've sat by a pool their whole lives, but trust funds don't have to breed laziness. That's Granny's philosophy, anyway." Levi opened the door for them and nodded toward the house as her grandfather helped her with the luggage. "The architecture is different, but Morocco has some beautiful homes."

Her grandmother led everyone to their rooms so they could get settled. She told them there'd be tea waiting when they made it back down. Levi handed her grandmother the whole file of what they'd found and smiled at how excited she seemed.

Sitting on the desk of Levi's room were some of the books she'd taken from the library downstairs, and pictures of all the trips they'd taken through the years dotted the shelves built into one wall. Summers with her grandparents had always been full of great adventures, and she had plenty of good memories to fuel her imagination. They'd spoiled her, but only to a point.

Her upbringing had been different than that of the Hassani sisters in that her family's traditions didn't revolve around religion and strictness of behavior. Her family's true religion was knowledge, and that's what she saw in Zara. She was looking forward to meeting the family if Yasmine allowed it. As her parents hadn't gone the university route, it made Yasmine and Zara even more impressive.

She knocked on Yasmine's door and stared at her when she opened the door and smiled. "Is the room okay?"

"It is now." Yasmine took her hand and tugged her inside.

"I have to admit to liking this new you." She put her arms around Yasmine and lowered her head to kiss her. "It's like I haven't kissed you in days."

"You're doing crazy things to me, Dr. Montbard. I'm not sure I can resist you." Yasmine stood on her toes and kissed the side of Levi's neck. "That flight did feel like days."

"Let's go have tea with my grandparents and we'll take Zara for a walk to the shops down the lane. We can get some snacks for our trip tomorrow." She put her hands on Yasmine's backside and tried not to let them wander further.

"Are you sure you don't want to spend at least a day with them? We just got here."

"If you think Grampie is staying behind tomorrow, you are not at all aware of Percy Breeden's streak of curiosity. Besides, he's the one who knows where we're going." She stepped back when she heard the door close to the room next door.

"You two ready?" Zara asked. She'd knocked before entering but made a shooing motion with her hands when they moved too slowly. "Your grandmother promised to show me some of her research after tea."

"Don't stand on formality here. They'll insist on Percy and Jane, and they mean it." She led them to the garden in the back and pulled out their chairs for them. "Granny, the flowers are beautiful this year." They had gardeners, but Jane planted all the bulbs and flowering plants in the yard. She insisted on giving them a proper head start in life.

"She says that even in the off years, but I love her for it." Her grandmother poured as her grandfather served biscuits. "Don't burn your mouth, but don't dally. Zara has made some progress on your stones by eliminating some things, but I think together we can crack them before dinner. Would everyone be okay with takeaway?"

"Granny's talents lie in using her head for things that don't include the kitchen," Levi teased. "Takeaway is fine. Grampie and I can go for something later. Did you get the files I emailed to you?"

"You are a remarkable human, bear," her grandfather said. "You've managed to roll together a hunt that includes the Knights Templar as well as our good Queen Boudica. The clue you sent talks about the land of Andraste's warrior queen, but not Templars."

"So how did you put the two together?" Levi asked.

"It was *defy the poisonous bite* that sealed it with me. The church we visit tomorrow should snap all the pieces together. I'd explain more, but I want to see if I'm right and if you see the same thing I do when we get there. I'm so excited, I won't sleep tonight."

"Then you're not driving tomorrow. Are you coming, Granny?"

"As much as I fancy a drive to West Somerton, I believe your stones are too exciting to ignore for a whole day." Her grandmother pressed her hands together, and Zara nodded.

"Would you all mind if stayed behind and worked with Jane? I would love to finish what I started with her help." Zara's question appeared to delight Jane. "I'll go if you need me, but I feel like we're running out of time. If we go home, we won't get to be part of the answer and I'd be filled with regret."

"Oh no, lovely," her grandmother said. "Once you start something like this, you must see it through. Stopping is out of the question. I'll have Percy write something up for you if it comes to that, but I'm positive time at Oxford will transfer anywhere in the world if you decide you don't want to finish here. Although, of course, I think a PhD scholarship to Oxford is rather a pinnacle, if I do say so myself."

The expression on Zara's face was like she'd been given a key to a room that held everything she'd ever wanted. She bounced a few times in her seat and squeezed Levi's arm. Yasmine laughed softly.

"Really?" Zara asked, as if wanting to cement the deal.

"Percy and I have a comfortable flat close to the university, and everyone will be fine if it comes to that. My Percy hasn't taught there for a hundred years for nothing. There has to be a scholarship available that'll cover you as long as you need to stay, even if it's not to do with these stones, but another project where we could use your input."

Her grandmother glanced at Levi and winked. Having the offer come from Jane instead of her would make it harder for Zara to turn down. From Zara's reaction, Levi had been right, and this was something Zara wanted.

"I just started my master's degree and was planning to go on for my doctorate after a gap year," Zara said. "But…that would be amazing."

"A master's in what?" her grandmother asked.

"History and ancient symbols. I decided to go in a little different direction than Yasmine, which is why I've been working on the stones in particular rather than the code."

If her grandmother hadn't been charmed before, that did it. "Finally, someone to follow in my footsteps. Not even our bear chose that exact route, and it'll be nice to have someone to talk to. It's decided, you're staying no matter what."

"Aren't the slots already filled?" Yasmine asked, and Zara looked like she wanted to shove a cookie or ten in her sister's mouth to shut her up.

"I wouldn't worry about it." Levi didn't want to put a wedge between the sisters, but she'd stand up for Zara if she needed to. She deserved the life she clearly wanted. "Grampie has enough clout to deliver what he's offering."

"You don't have to decide right this minute, but what we must do is go in and look at what you have so far." Jane stood and Zara popped up after her like she'd fallen in love. "Bear, make sure you order something early. You need to arrive in West Somerton way before daybreak."

"I might need to go to bed now," she joked.

"Really, bear, you know the Church frowns on anyone stealing from them. What you'll be doing won't exactly be stealing, but we need to borrow something they don't even know they have." Her grandfather shook his head as if what he was saying should've been apparent.

"Let's hope there isn't a lot of lightning tomorrow, then. I'd hate to get struck for theft so early in the morning."

❖

Yasmine stood in her bathroom and laughed at the turn this trip had taken. Their parents would blame her for what the Breeden couple had offered, but turning the opportunity down was something she didn't want Zara to do. A doctorate from Oxford would open so many more doors than if she stayed home, and at least one of the Hassani sisters should set out to wherever the wind blew them.

Jane and Percy were wonderful people, and they again made her think of the differences in their families. Levi had to be the luckiest person in the world when it came to the blessings of family. Their *bear* was a wonderful person, and the nickname fit. Levi was big and strong, and when she held her, Yasmine felt like nothing bad could touch her.

She came out and smiled at Zara, who was sitting on her bed. "Congratulations," she said, kissing Zara's forehead.

"Would you hate me if I said yes?" Zara brought her knees up to her chest and hugged them to her. "What will Mama say? Will she be crushed? Will you?"

"I would have a problem if you said no. Remember that I will always help you as long as it's something you want." She put her arm around Zara. "If anyone deserves this, it's you. Don't let anything stand in your way."

"I didn't think this would make you cry," Levi said, joining them and sitting on the other side of Zara.

Yasmine wasn't surprised when Zara shifted and pressed against Levi.

"I apologize if I overstepped, but I thought you'd appreciate having another option. If you'd be more comfortable in New Orleans with me, I'll get you the same thing at Tulane. With Granny, though, your education is going to be more complete."

"Oxford is a dream come true, thank you." Zara threw her arms around Levi and squeezed her. "I've been dreaming of finishing somewhere else, but it was only that, a dream."

"I promise I'll come and visit if you decide to stay, and Granny was serious when she said she has room. You're young and I'm sure you'll be interested in having a little fun. They won't get in the way of that, but it means you're not alone here either." Levi dried Zara's tears and didn't let her go. "I'll feel better if you stay for your first semester and get a feel for the area before you decide on going anywhere else. And there's one more thing, but I don't want to insult you."

"I doubt you could do that," Zara said.

"I wanted to give you a stipend to do some work for me. It'll be like a retainer. On-the-job training kind of thing."

"Are you trying to make me love you more than I already do?" Zara cried some more. "Thank you, Levi. None of this would've happened if it wasn't for you, so don't deny it."

"You're welcome. My grandmother knows how to get in touch with us tomorrow if you need us."

"I'm going to call my friends and share the good news." Zara kissed them both good night and closed the door behind her.

"Did I overstep?" Levi asked Yasmine when they were alone.

"You are the best thing that's happened to us. I'm not sure if you understand how happy you've made her, but you have." She slid closer to Levi and took her hand. "I didn't know how to deal with you when we met, but now I don't know how to let you go." The admission was more than she wanted to say, but there was no denying it.

"Promise me one thing," Levi said before kissing her with enough passion to make Yasmine want to strip her clothes off.

"What?"

"Take it one day at a time. Don't make any rash decisions."

"Levi, I only know what you've told me, and we're so different. You're used to living your life a certain way, and it makes me afraid that you'll get—" She couldn't be one of many and share Levi. No matter what happened, that she couldn't do.

"Bored? Is that what you were going to say? My track record isn't great, and I can see you might not want to take the chance, so I want to take it slow. Neither of us have any experience with anything like this." Levi kissed her again. "Am I right?" Yasmine nodded. This conversation wasn't filling her with confidence for the future. "All I'm asking is that you talk to me about the things you're thinking and feeling."

"Are you sure?" She wanted Levi to be sure because *she* wasn't sure of anything. "I don't want you to be unhappy because you feel trapped."

"Honey, to be honest I'm not sure what the hell I feel right now, but I'm not unhappy with what's happening." Levi held her like she had Zara, but her touch was hot. "Are you ready for bed?"

"I need to change," she said, not wanting to move away from Levi.

"Go ahead, I'll wait." Levi sat until Yasmine came out in her robe. She put up no resistance when Levi led her across the hall and pulled the covers back on her bed. "Let me hold you, if only for tonight."

"Why would you say that?"

"Because I want every moment I can get with you, and I'm willing to take it slow. I'll keep saying it until you believe me." Levi put her hands under the robe but kept them still on her hips. "Will sleeping beside me bother you?"

"No." She lay down and pressed herself to Levi's side. "If I didn't say it, thank you for Zara. She's been trying to escape from the time she started university, and you've given her a ticket out."

"What about you, honey? What do you want?" Levi started caressing her back.

"I don't know how to answer that." No one had ever asked her. From the moment she was born she'd been pulled and pushed in the directions everyone else had chosen for her. Her one rebellion had been Nabil, but even he'd had his own agenda.

"I'm asking you," Levi said, moving until she was leaning over her. "What do you want? What will make you happy?"

"I can't answer that now, but let's try what you said." Yasmine reached up and touched Levi's face. It had started to invade her dreams, and if she wanted not to suffer for the rest of her days, it was time to get Levi out of her head and, more importantly, her heart. "Let's take it one day at a time."

❖

"Yes, sir," Graham said in the back of the car one of Digby's men was driving. The exhaustion of the flight combined with sleeping in the back of this small hellhole was giving him a headache. They'd had no choice but to move when the Land Rover pulled out of the drive at a little after three in the morning. "Levi is driving, and the woman is next to her. Dr. Breeden is in the back and they're heading east."

Cristian flipped through some paper on his end and made a grunting noise. "Were you able to find out anything about what prompted her to travel?"

"They're traveling with what appears to be files, but the scrolls and everything else must be locked up in New Orleans, since I haven't seen any special crates. I'll call you when we see where she's going and what she's doing." The driver hung back but kept Levi in sight. It was too early for traffic, and they didn't want to get spotted.

"Hopefully you've watched Levi long enough to know how she works. There are never any unnecessary steps when she's looking for something. Moving this early means she's probably going somewhere close and doesn't want an audience." Cristian flipped through more papers.

"Has Digby heard anything about Baggio or Chadwick?" Europe was stricter about guns than the US, but Digby had taken care of that as well. None of them trusted the cardinal and what he was capable of doing to get what he wanted.

"Someone flagged Levi and the Hassani sisters' passports when they entered the country. They weren't stopped, but someone was alerted that they entered the country. It's not a stretch to figure out who wanted that information."

The man in the passenger seat had been focused on the side mirror for too long. "What's wrong?"

"Two cars back. It's been with us since we left the house. Stupid to try to follow us at this time of morning in no traffic."

"Cristian, let me go and I'll report as soon as we're done."

The knowledge they were being followed fired his adrenaline, and he turned and peered back. It was another large SUV with tinted windows. This was so much more than a treasure hunt, and they needed to find more information before they disappeared beneath the church's underbelly.

"Do you have any backup?"

"There's another team. I called when we started driving. It's going to take time for them to catch up."

Graham shook his head and turned to see Levi's vehicle. "We might not have a lot of time."

CHAPTER FOURTEEN

"Turn left at the end of this lane."

Nearly four hours after they'd set off from London, Levi did as her grandfather said and saw the church in the distance. She'd never been here, but her grandfather was good at finding needles in a field of haystacks.

It was still early and there was no way the church would be open, so Levi pulled over and parked across the street. "Looks old," she said.

"St. Mary's is one of the oldest churches in England," her grandfather said, pointing between the seats. "The only viable option for Andraste's warrior queen was Queen Boudica. She was way too early to have anything to do with the Templars, but her courage against the Romans is legendary. The Norfolk area is her land and takes care of that part of the clue."

"What about the serpent's bite? And how does this church relate to Boudica?" Yasmine asked.

"Is it inside or out?" Levi asked.

"Inside." Her grandfather had a big smile on his face, and he wiggled his eyebrows.

"I guess I should be happy you and Granny taught me how to pick a lock." She laughed and slapped hands with him.

"We're breaking into a church?" Yasmine sounded outraged. "Are you sure that's a good idea? If this were a mosque we'd be jailed. Why don't we wait until they open?"

"If we ask permission to take whatever is hidden in there, we'll never get to see it. If we go in there and borrow it, we'll get our next clue and eventually turn everything over to the proper authorities." This wasn't the best way to convince someone who obviously believed in following the rules, but it was true.

"Then let's go before you both have to talk our way out of jail." Yasmine winked at her, and it made her laugh. "If I go to jail, it will be a blow to our friendship." Yasmine was joking, but Levi figured there was truth buried in there.

They stood across the street and studied the church. It was a beautiful old building with a cemetery next to it. The best way in was through the gate to the graveyard, and once through, they headed to the side door. Levi made quick work of the old lock, and they followed her grandfather and the light of his flashlight.

The church was simply decorated and without a lot of embellishments. Percy pointed to the back corner. "The statue was a gift when the church was consecrated," he explained. "The records don't indicate who gave the gift, but the senior vicar told me it was from an old family in the area. They claim to have ties to Boudica."

"Makes sense. There are a lot of old families still in the area. Churches have always been good places to hide things." She walked around the statue of St. Michael, amazed at how realistic it was. It was like he'd come to life at any moment, and the serpent under his foot looked like it could kill you if you put your hand anywhere near its mouth. "Whoever donated this may have known of the clue and what's hidden here."

"I wait for my love in time in the land of Andraste's warrior queen. To find me, you must face the serpent and defy the poisonous bite like my love defied the paradise of eternity for me." Yasmine recited the clue they'd found, and the words echoed against the old stone walls. "I didn't think it would be this easy."

"Once you find the bread crumbs, it is pretty easy. I've always been struck by the beauty and mystery of this statue, and when Levi read me the clue, it felt right. If Levi hadn't found the scrolls and also found you to translate them, it would stay buried," Percy said.

Levi aimed the flashlight in the mouth of the snake but didn't see anything that would unlock anything. "If it's a trap, let's hope time has sapped the strength of whatever poison they put in here."

The inside of the mouth was smooth except for the outline of the forked tongue. She pressed on every surface, but nothing happened. They had to hurry, since it would be hard to explain what they were doing or how they got in if the vicar was an early riser or if the people in the housing estate nearby were out early. She dropped to her knees and moved closer. This view made her notice something she'd missed.

"Look at the eyes." She got even lower, and they pressed in around her. "They're Templar crosses."

"It has to be something, then," Yasmine said. "Otherwise they'd just use plain stones, right?"

"You have to defy the serpent's bite," Levi repeated. She moved her fingers from inside the mouth to the fangs and pressed hard on both. They moved a smidge. In the quiet of the church, the click was almost loud.

"You heard that, right?" her grandfather asked.

"We need to find what it opened." She handed Yasmine the flashlight and used the one on her phone to study the front of the statue.

The base was no different, but she glanced up when Yasmine gripped her shoulder. The sword St. Michael held had a hinged piece hanging open from the bottom. Something had come partially out of the hollow of the hilt. Levi reached up and pulled until a key emerged that was about four inches long and heavy. Once it was in her hand, the hinge popped closed.

"Great, what does this go to?" she said, holding it up.

"It looks like there's faint writing on the side," her grandfather said, looking at it closely.

"De Tourville." The name was familiar, but she had to think to place it. "Guillaume de Tourville was an English Master of the Templars in 1292, I believe."

"I think you're right, but what does it open?" Her grandfather studied the key more closely, running his fingers over it gently.

"If this place is nine hundred years old, then he could've had some history here." She stood and surveyed the inside of the church as a whole. "There." She pointed to a set of stairs in a shadowed, overgrown corner that led down. "Think *in the land of Andraste's warrior queen* and *eternity*. It's a tomb."

The key slid into the rusted lock and protested as it turned, the click audible as the thick ancient wood door slowly swung open. They went down into the total darkness, and from the beam of the flashlight saw about thirty sarcophagi covering the floor of an enormous room. It smelled of mold, damp, and dust. Green streaks on the external wall started at the slits in the brick. Levi could see dust particles floating in the light and scratched her nose in reflex.

The tombs were laid out around a central sarcophagus in a pattern that resembled a sun with rays emanating from the middle. A moss-covered relief of the person buried within, most of them holding swords, adorned each cover. One of them had to be de Tourville. She could feel it.

"Pick a circle and work your way around," she said as she walked to the middle holding Yasmine's hand. The chase of the unknown had grabbed her by the heart from the first quest she'd gone on, but this was why she continued to search. Opening a door and knowing the answers she'd been looking for were within reach made her head nearly explode. Finding what was lost or hidden was her life's passion, and having Yasmine along with her added to the excitement.

She started with the tomb in the middle, presumably the most important, or at least the oldest. The sarcophagus wasn't ornate, but the carving of the man was as exquisite as the statue upstairs. She crouched down and started at his feet. At first glance the only thing that differed from the tombs around it was the face and the coat of arms on his chest. The name carved at the top was de Tourville, so this was the right one. Nowhere, though, did it appear to have a spot for a key. She decided to take another approach and let her gaze roam over the whole sarcophagus, looking for anything that didn't belong, any minute detail out of place.

"What?" Yasmine asked, glancing up at her from the next row.

"I found de Tourville, but nothing on here marks him as a Templar. If we're right, though, then there has to be something."

Yasmine walked closer and shook her head. "The eyes appear as you'd expect them to."

Levi moved to the sword next and found a carving not much bigger than a thumbnail. "Here." She pointed to the space under the circle between the hilt and blade. It was the only cross she could see. She went to her bag, took out a small brush, and dusted it off.

"Do you think this one is too obvious?" Yasmine asked.

She nodded as she moved to the hands holding the sword. "Look at his fingers." The artist had sculpted the fingers as if he were holding the sword—except for two, which were extended away from the sword handle, flat against the other hand. The women turned in the direction the man seemed to be pointing and saw a row of four tombs that lined up perfectly.

There was no cross on the sword like the first one, but after dusting off the area around it, Levi saw a fine line in the circle at the bottom of the hilt. A tree of life, a representation of the afterlife or the connection between heaven and earth, was carved there. It was a common Templar symbol, but it wasn't usually found on the tomb of an ordinary Christian.

"The Celts believed certain trees were sacred because they were how their ancestors come back in a different form," her grandfather said as if reading her mind. "They held all the wisdom of those who lived before them."

"Let us hope that was still their belief when they buried this man," Yasmine said.

Levi ran her finger over the circle and the carving of the tree, then got a good grip on it. She had to apply some force, but like the hinged hilt upstairs, the circle slid to the side and revealed a large keyhole.

"Levi, can you believe it?" Yasmine's eyes were wide with wonder.

Levi wiped sweat out of her eyes despite the coolness of the room, and her damp hands made her almost drop the key. Her grandfather nodded as if he were impatient to see what was inside, so she put it the key and turned it. The coat of arms carved on the chest popped open. Inside was another leather bag like the one they'd found in the box in Louisiana. When she undid the leather thong, her hands shaking, there were three books inside. As desperate as she was to sit on the dirty floor and examine her find, she knew they were running out of time. "We've got to get going," she said, glancing at her watch.

She carefully placed the leather bag inside her backpack and put the tomb back the way they'd found it, and after making sure it was secure, she pocketed the key.

"You have plenty to do," Yasmine said.

"*We* have plenty to do," she corrected. She waited until her grandfather was going up the stairs before pulling Yasmine close and kissing her. "I'm not doing this without you."

They stepped out to a damp morning, and Levi relocked the door before they headed out through the cemetery. Two men stepped out from the large willow tree to their left and pointed guns at them. Levi stepped in front of Yasmine and Percy.

"Hand over the bag and I don't kill you," the shorter man said in a tone that held no argument.

"It's only books," she said.

Her grandfather acted as if he was held at gunpoint every day. He didn't look concerned at all. "I'll happily hand over my wallet, if you want that instead."

"If I wanted your wallet, bitch, I'd have asked you for it." The man sounded uneducated, and the coldness in his face made it clear he'd have no problem following up on his threat. "Give me the bag."

There was nowhere to run, but if she kept them engaged long enough, maybe Yasmine and her grandfather would have a chance to run. Before she could do anything about it, her grandfather took a step forward. If she got them killed, she'd never forgive herself, so she shifted to ease the backpack off. The men turned their attention back to her when her backpack hit the ground.

"Get ready to run," she murmured and prayed they both heard her. If the men took the bag, there was a good chance they'd still shoot them all. This was the only way to give them a chance.

She was much taller than the man giving the orders, so she picked him as her target. Her running start made the man widen his eyes enough that she noticed it even without any sun filtering through the dense fog. It was luck that got her to him before he pulled the trigger, and they fell to the ground with her on top, holding down his hand that held the gun. A shot cut through the quiet. For a spilt second she thought the other guy had shot her in the back, but there was no pain anywhere.

Percy ran to her, pried the gun away from the man she was pinning, and pointed it at the guy's head. "Move and you're joining your friend." He sounded utterly calm.

She glanced back and saw the other man not moving. She scanned their surroundings, trying to figure out where the shot had come from and who had possibly just saved their lives, but there was no one to be seen. Except, that is, an apparently furious Yasmine. In the distance she could hear sirens. The scene was going to be hard to explain, but the sight of two vicars coming toward them made her feel better. Witnesses would keep the guy under her from making more trouble.

"Are you okay, Dr. Breeden?" one of the vicars asked. "We saw you studying the tombs again when these men attacked you. We assumed you'd brought students and didn't wish to do your studying when other people might be about, so we left you to it. But you seem to have run into some trouble. Can we assist?"

Levi stared at the man, not quite sure how to take what he was saying. If he'd seen them walking through the graveyard and knew they'd been underground with the tombs, then he knew full well they'd also broken in. The younger man with him looked serene but interested.

"Yes, thank you, sir," Percy said.

Levi went back to Yasmine and picked up the pack. Yasmine's expression hadn't changed. "You okay?"

"Let's finish with the police and go back to your grandparents' home. I don't want to get into it now." Yasmine crossed her arms over her chest and wouldn't meet her eyes.

There was no time to keep asking questions when four police vehicles stopped by the gate and the graveyard filled with officers. Strangely, they talked to the vicars first and got their account, so all that was left for Levi's group to say was that they had indeed been held at gunpoint by both the guy in handcuffs and the dead one on the ground. They were free to go once the police got their contact information. Levi drove them back in a silent car. Her grandfather looked tired and fell asleep, and Yasmine said nothing for the four hours it took to get back, leaving Levi to her muddled thoughts and ebbing adrenaline.

Levi put the books on the desk in the study and hitched her shoulders when the door slammed behind her at her grandparents' home. She had yet to figure out why Yasmine was so angry. "What's wrong?"

"What's wrong?" Yasmine repeated at the top of her lungs. "What's wrong? Maybe it's the fact that you could've gotten yourself killed. That man could've shot you, and then what?" The simmering fire seemed to have finally become an inferno. "You idiot!"

Levi wasn't at all used to women screaming at her, but she could've stood there all day and watched Yasmine. In her mind, it had always been a myth that women were beautiful when they were angry, but she was quickly becoming a believer. "I did what I did to make sure you'd be okay," she said, coming closer. "I was trying to give you and my grandfather time to run."

"Do you think I would be okay if you'd died?" Yasmine pressed her hands to Levi's chest and tried to push her away, but Levi wasn't moving. "I would never be okay again. You…you…stubborn, reckless donkey."

Levi held Yasmine and didn't let go when she started crying. "Remember what I told you. I'm not going anywhere unless you send me away, and can you stop yelling for a moment so I can kiss you?"

"You think you should be rewarded for that kind of behavior?" Yasmine finally glanced up at her, and her volume came down. "You make me crazy."

"In the future, I hope in only good ways." She lowered her head and groaned when Yasmine kissed her like she wanted to possess her. It was good, hot, and sexy. "I'm sorry I scared you."

"Do you think your grandparents heard me yelling at you?"

"I doubt Granny heard anything over her yelling at Grampie."

The truth made Yasmine laugh a little, and her shoulders dropped. "What did you mean we were lucky?"

"I'm not sure who shot that other guy. I doubt it was the two vicars, and I didn't see anyone else there." The trip had been beyond bizarre in many ways. "First the break-in at my house, and now this. It can't be coincidental. We've got something that someone else wants, and that means we're being watched."

"I think you're right," Yasmine said, slumping against her. All the fight seemed to have died away, leaving only exhaustion.

Levi couldn't help yawning. It had been a long morning with plenty of tension. "Want to take a nap with me?"

"Do you think we should? Will your grandparents be upset if we do? Don't you want to look at the books? And maybe talk about the people who might have killed us?"

"Grampie is probably already sleeping, and Granny and Zara are leaving for the University of London to meet with one of her old friends. The books and conversation about intrigue can wait."

"Then I'd love to," Yasmine said, kissing her again. She went into the bathroom to freshen up, leaving Levi with her thoughts.

Zara came in a few minutes later and waggled her finger at Levi. "I'm not sure what you did, but I'd suggest not doing it again. She might lose her voice if she has to scream at you any more."

"Don't worry, I learned my lesson. Have fun and tell Granny not to stay too late. I don't want you two out alone after dark." She didn't want them out of sight, really, but that wasn't fair to them.

"She already yelled at Percy and offered to tell me what you two, and I quote, *baboons* did this morning. She also called some guy she worked with and said it was taken care of. I'm not sure what that means exactly, but I don't want to argue with her."

Levi wasn't sure either, but it was interesting. Yasmine came back into the room looking exhausted. "Stay out of trouble," she told her sister.

"Don't worry about me," Zara said and winked at Levi. "I think you have your hands full with this one."

"I'd argue, but that's probably true," Levi said, laughing. "Tell

Granny to keep an eye behind her. If you think someone's following you, call the police. Don't handle it yourself."

"Jane doesn't seem the type to scare easily, and I doubt she'd put me in any danger. Don't worry. We'll be careful, and I'll call in a few hours to see how you two are doing."

"These people want something from us. Promise me you'll be careful," Yasmine said.

"I will, promise," Zara said.

Levi nodded and kissed Zara's cheek. "What these guys should realize is I'm going to give them everything I have," she said. "Only I'm going to do it when I have all the answers, and they'll find out with the rest of the world."

❖

Yasmine opened her eyes and tried to figure out what had woken her. Levi was still pressed up behind her with an arm thrown over her waist. The slight snoring was new, but it was more endearing than aggravating. It was the buzzing that finally made her glance at the side table to see that her phone was lighting up.

She moved slowly so as to not wake Levi and reached for it. Her mother's picture made her sigh, and she saw that she'd missed six calls from her already. They'd come in five-minute intervals, but only a minute separated the last one from the one before it.

The snoring behind her stopped and Levi loosened her grip on her. "Go ahead and answer it." The burr of Levi's voice made her shiver.

"It's my mother."

"Then call her back. She should be happy you and Zara will be back for your grandmother's birthday." Levi kissed the back of Yasmine's neck and rubbed small circles on her stomach. "That should distract her enough that she won't notice when I take you two right back out of town."

"My mother is a woman not used to being defied. She'll definitely notice." She turned and faced Levi, wanting to see the green eyes that so captivated her. "For you, though, I'll chance it." She dialed and reached back to stop Levi's hand from going any lower. The mischievous smile she got in return made her shake her head. "Mama," she said, and let go of Levi.

"You're ignoring my calls now?" Her mother's name meant

daughter of the prophet, but she was more of a complainer than a religious icon.

"I was working and couldn't come to the phone. Zara and I had to stop in London for research, but we'll be home soon. You can tell Jadda we'll be there for her big day." She smiled when Levi threaded their fingers together and kissed the back of her hand.

"You're in London now? Why, and where is your sister? I gave you the responsibility of watching over her. She'd better be there with you." Her mother was starting to rev up, and Yasmine wasn't interested in an argument.

"Zara was able to sign on to a research project. She's fine and we're in London working on the same project. I hate to cut this short, but I have to get back to my work." There was a little guilt when she disconnected the call, but she was too contented to care. In all likelihood her mother had only been trying to reach her in order to nag her and didn't have anything she actually wanted to say. As usual. And for the first time, Yasmine didn't have the energy or desire to deal with it. "You are a troublemaker."

"I don't deny that at all." Levi let her hand go. "You know, the one thing we haven't done is go on a date. Just the two of us."

"I know, but I hate leaving Zara behind like she's an afterthought." For a brief moment she remembered the last time she'd been on a date, some disastrous thing her mother had set up. "Would you like to do that?"

"My grandparents would like to introduce Zara to some of Grampie's students. It'll be a good way to break her into life at Oxford without her big sister butting in." Levi winked. "If the three of them are doing that, then we'll be here staring at each other."

"There are worse things."

"True, but would you do me the honor of having dinner with me?"

"Yes."

Levi let her go and they went down to enjoy a snack in the garden. They talked until it was time to get ready. Yasmine was sitting in the tub when Zara returned from her trip with Jane. The animated way she was talking made Yasmine sure that she had found her place. She looked more excited than Yasmine had ever seen her. Granted, she'd never been away from home, but her sister had always been the more fearless one. She got out and dried off so she could start getting dressed.

"Today was so amazing. Jane introduced me to some of the people she used to work for, and they promised their help with the stones.

They think they've figured out two of the symbols we were stuck on, so maybe we'll have some answers before we have to go." Zara shook her head when Yasmine took out a pair of sandals. "I'll be right back."

"I don't know," Yasmine said when Zara came back in holding out a pair of heels. "I'll break my neck."

"Just hang on to Levi and you'll be fine." Zara dropped the shoes and sat her down. "I haven't wanted to embarrass you, but Levi has brought you to life. Finally, you're acting like a woman who's alive and desirable. I've known for a long time she was buried somewhere in that serious, obligation-based woman."

"You know as well as anyone alive that Mama and Papa will never understand, much less accept Levi or any relationship aside from friendship. I can't take it much further than I have already." She pressed her fist to her forehead. The guilt ate away at her sometimes when she went to the mosque and prayed for guidance, knowing full well none would be coming. To some their faith was the cornerstone of their lives, but once she'd been educated, her faith and devotion had shifted more toward the written word. It was blasphemy, but it was her truth. One she'd never shared with anyone.

"Stop it. For once think about what you want. Don't keep putting everything off only to make Mama happy. She's already married and not thrilled with that, so she wants to sow misery for everyone else." Zara held her hand and kissed her cheek.

"Zara, you know that's not true."

"Isn't it? If you don't start speaking up for what you want, I'll have no choice but to stay with you. I'll lose all of this if it means keeping you company while you come to your senses."

"I won't let that happen, but I'm still not used to talking about Levi as anything other than my friend."

"Your friend looks at you like she wants to tear your clothes off with her teeth, so you might want to open your eyes before you break your neck in these things." Zara pointed to the heels.

"You don't have to say all that simply to get me to talk you up at home. I said I'd help you and I meant it."

Zara hugged her. "Is that what you think? It's not. I want you to wake up before you push her so far away she'll have no choice but to let you go. Women like Levi are not common, and you'd be a fool to not do what I know you want to."

"Thank you." Yasmine squeezed Zara before letting her go and slipping into the leopard print heels. They weren't at all something she'd pick for herself, but she'd seen them on her sister, and they were beautiful.

Levi was waiting downstairs with Percy, and when she turned and faced her, Yasmine stopped. Zara was right, and she wondered how she'd missed it. There was something in Levi's penetrating stare that made her want to reexamine her opinion of herself.

Right now, though, she'd never felt more attractive to another person, and she didn't want Levi to look at another woman like this, ever.

"Are you ready?" she asked. Levi nodded but stayed quiet. "You're so handsome," she said softly when she reached the bottom and walked close to Levi. She was wearing another suit but had added a bowtie this time, and it was the perfect touch.

"I'm blown away by you." Levi took her hand and tugged her closer. Yasmine thought to be embarrassed, but when she pressed against Levi, the rest of the world didn't exist. "You are a brilliant brain wrapped in a gorgeous package."

"Can I admit something to you and you not think I'm insane?" She ran her hands up the lapels of Levi's jacket and kept going until they were in Levi's hair.

"As if I'd ever think that." Levi kept her hands still.

"You make me feel beautiful. That's never happened before."

Levi cocked her head back. "You might be a little crazy if that's never happened before."

"You are the only one," she said, pulling Levi's hair. "No one has ever looked at me the way you do, and I like it."

"Come on, then, and I'll treat you to a whole night of my awestruck expression."

"I can't wait."

CHAPTER FIFTEEN

Levi drove to a place she'd only visited once, but she thought Yasmine would love it. Clos Maggiore was a great French restaurant, but it was also a conservatory, and the large trees growing inside were strung with lights, adding to the romantic atmosphere. Yasmine deserved to be romanced, and Levi was planning to do it as often as she'd let her.

"Where are we going?" Yasmine asked. She'd taken Levi's free hand when she'd started driving.

"Covent Garden." The drive didn't take much time, and she handed off the keys as she waved off the other valet from Yasmine's door.

Yasmine let out a small gasp when they walked in and held on to Levi's arm as the hostess led them to the most private table in the place. Levi had ordered a bottle of white wine knowing it was one of the only things Yasmine drank, and once the waiter had poured, she lifted her glass and smiled.

"To finding answers hidden too long," she said as she tapped her glass against Yasmine's. "And to my luck at being here with the most beautiful woman in the place."

"You say the sweetest things." Yasmine took a sip and nodded in approval. "What do you think our next step should be?"

"The books were important enough for someone to go to such drastic measures to hide them, so we should start there." She pointed to some appetizers they'd both enjoy and pushed her menu aside. Tonight, she was in no hurry. "Do you mind staying with my grandparents?"

"If they don't mind, I'd love to. I think if I try to take Zara away from them she might turn on me."

"I hate to bother you, Dr. Montbard, but there's a call for you on the house phone. They apologized but they didn't know your cell number," the hostess said. "If you'll follow me."

"Excuse me a minute." Levi stood and kissed Yasmine's cheek. "I'll be right back."

The hostess pointed to a booth with a phone inside, and Levi nodded. Pain shot through the side of her face before she could protect herself from another blow. Her vision was blurry, but she could see it was a man, and he'd brought a friend who pinned her arms behind her back as the guy punched her again. She let out a whoosh of air and spit up the little wine she'd drunk. A large hand clamped over her mouth, keeping her from shouting.

"Take her."

She slumped, trying to be dead weight and frantically trying to figure out her next move.

They dragged her outside and the valet came forward. She could tell through her unswollen eye that he appeared concerned. "Is she all right? She's bleeding."

"Bring the car around," the man to her right said. "We're taking her to hospital."

"Do you need me to call anyone?" the valet asked. She wanted to kiss the guy for stalling enough for her head to clear a little. The tip of a large knife was pressed against her side, keeping her from making a sound, but hopefully she could do something to avoid being put in the car.

She took a quick breath, then slammed her weight into the guy giving orders, knocking him back before she wrenched her arms free and slammed into the other guy, dropping him on the first. They were in a pile as she punched and tried to pin them down. A car speeding toward them left little time.

"Call the police," Levi yelled. Her shout brought the rest of the valets, who jumped in to help her as the first guy made the call.

"Get off me," the man under her ordered. The other guy had shoved the valets off and run to the waiting car. "Get off me or I'll make you sorry."

She shifted and slammed his head into the pavement. It only took that one hit for all the fight to go out of him, and she flattened herself over him in case there was any shooting. When the sirens were close, she rolled off the guy and sat trying to catch her breath.

"You okay?" one of the young valets asked. "This asshole did that to you?" He pointed to her face.

"He did, and your hostess witnessed the whole thing. Make sure the police pick her up as well."

"I always said that bitch wasn't right in the head."

The police cuffed the unconscious man, and a few officers went inside the restaurant. It didn't take long for Levi to give her statement, although she decided not to mention the treasure hunt they were on and the attack's likely connection to it. She promised to answer any more questions if they'd allow her to go inside and talk to Yasmine. The moment Yasmine laid eyes on her she was out of her seat and pressing her napkin to the side of her head where the cut from the first punch was still bleeding.

"What happened?" Yasmine said. "Who did this?"

"I'm not sure, but that hostess was in on it. She watched the whole thing and did nothing." Her head was killing her and the last thing she wanted to do was get stitches, but she was going to need some to stop the bleeding. "I hate to cut the night short, but I think we need to go."

"We need to rethink everything and figure out a new plan," Yasmine said as she wrapped her arm around Levi's waist. "Let's go. We need to call Zara and your grandparents."

Yasmine followed Levi's directions and drove to the hospital as she spoke to Zara, who was still at the small party with Levi's grandparents and hadn't experienced any trouble. They promised to go straight home after Yasmine promised that's what they were doing as soon as they were done in the emergency room.

Levi looked at Yasmine standing next to her gurney. "I should take you and Zara home before anything else happens."

"I've already been angry with you once today, let's not make it a habit." Yasmine took Levi's hand and pulled on her fingers as if to get her full attention. "I'm not leaving you, and you can't ask me to."

"Whoever these guys are, they're not playing by the rules." Levi closed her eyes when a stab of pain lanced through her head. "If something happens to you, I won't be able to explain that to your parents. There's also your grandmother's party. It's not forever." She sounded pretty convincing even with her brains scrambled, but Yasmine didn't appear to be buying it.

"You have to be the most aggravating person I've ever met." Yasmine's voice was low, but Levi could still make out the irritation.

"I don't know what kind of women you've dated, but I'm not someone who appreciates anyone doing my thinking for me. It's why my mother and I don't get along like a mother and daughter should. I'm not leaving you." She said the words slowly.

"But—" Before Levi could say anything else, Yasmine leaned over her and kissed her with passion.

"Don't say that again."

"Yes, ma'am." She smiled and gazed around Yasmine to the doctor at the door. "Hello."

"Dr. Montbard, let's take a look." He didn't take long to place six small stitches along her temple, along with giving her some shots that would prevent infection. "I'll make you an appointment to get these removed, but I'd like to keep you overnight for observation."

"I'll come back if I need to. Right now, I'd like to go home."

The rain had started while they were inside, so Levi took her jacket off and put it over Yasmine's head. "We need to get home and see if we can call the inspector in charge of the case. I want to know who those guys are and who they work for."

"Can we do that in the morning? You need to get some sleep, because if anything else happens, you're in no shape to handle it." Yasmine laughed when Levi picked her up and hurried to the car. "What are you doing?"

"Those are some great shoes, honey, and I don't want you to mess them up."

Yasmine waited until Levi had her seat belt on before heading back to the house, her mind in turmoil. She turned right at the corner, and they jerked forward violently when a car slammed into them from behind. The car spun on the slick road, and they stopped in a screech of metal when they hit a parked car.

The next jolt made Levi moan, and when she looked in the side mirror, she saw more men running for them. Yasmine's eyes were closed, her head against the window, and Levi wanted to scream for being the one who'd led her into danger.

"Leave her alone," she said to the guy who opened Yasmine's door, a gun in his left hand as he reached with his right to undo her seat belt.

"Don't worry," the man said, and she recognized him. He was the guy having dinner with Baggio the night George got hurt. "Once you give up what I want, I won't touch her…much."

She grabbed Yasmine's hand, but her own door opened and she fell to her knees when the guy yanked her out. She heard Yasmine cry out and was thankful that at least she'd woken up. "Who are you?" There was no one coming to help them this time.

"The hand of God," the man said and laughed.

The guy behind her laughed as well as he grabbed Levi by the hair and yanked her head back. Levi looked up just in time to see the man's brains hit the window behind him. The others went down just as fast, except for the one who held Yasmine.

She looked around but couldn't see the shooter, and she took her chances that whoever it was wasn't after her. She grimaced as she got to her feet and moved around the car to face the man who'd broken into her house. "Let her go," she said. The guy looked worried now, and he pointed his gun at her. That was getting old. "Let her go, or I'll have you join your men."

He shoved her toward Levi. She caught Yasmine and pulled her behind her so she was between Yasmine and the guy with the gun. Yasmine gripped the back of Levi's shirt and rested her head between her shoulder blades.

"You know we're never going to give up. What you found is ours, it belongs to us."

"It belongs to the world, so fuck off." Levi was tired of running from people like this.

"That's a funny thing to say for someone getting ready to get shot in the head." He got back in the car but kept his gun pointed at them.

Yasmine pressed closer to her. "No!"

Levi imagined how white his finger was from the pressure on the trigger, but she didn't close her eyes or beg. She had a feeling she didn't need to. The shot came a moment later.

Yasmine screamed when she heard the shot and felt Levi tense in front of her. Why was this happening? She'd finally found herself in Levi's eyes, and if Levi died she'd take so much with her. It was the oddest of things to finally realize what she'd known all along but could never admit to herself. She didn't fit. Not in her family, and not in the life she'd convinced herself was fulfilling.

No, she didn't fit anywhere but in Levi's arms, and someone had stolen that from her before she could tell Levi everything she needed to know. "Don't leave me," she said, hanging on to Levi, shocked she was still on her feet.

"Honey," Levi said, turning around and holding her. "Look at me." Levi's voice rose and she pressed her hand to Yasmine's face. "Open your eyes and look at me."

"Are you hurt?" Yasmine asked. Levi was a mess, but there didn't seem to be a big gaping hole anywhere. "Are you?" she asked again, running her hands over Levi's body. Her tears were making it hard to see anything, but Levi didn't act like she was in pain.

"I'm okay, sweetheart. Take some deep breaths so we can try and figure out what the hell is going on." Levi took out her phone and called the police while continuing to scan the darkness around them.

Yasmine thought they should put the authorities on speed dial, since calling them was becoming a habit. "Who are these people?" There were three dead men on the street including the guy who'd dragged her from the car. "And what in the world have you found that they think is so important?"

"There are only two things that make men like this crazy enough to try stuff like this. We're either sitting on the clues to a vast treasure that will make them rich, or we're sitting on a treasure trove of information that doesn't jibe with their zealot thinking." Levi led her to a home where the lights were starting to come on. "Did you hear that guy?"

"I didn't hear anything over the panic in my head," Yasmine said. She was still touching Levi's chest and back as she tried to convince herself that she was okay.

"When I asked who they were, he said the hand of God. That makes me lean toward the zealot side of the equation." Levi stepped in front of Yasmine when the front door opened and an elderly man stepped outside.

"Are you two hurt?" the man asked.

"I'm sure tomorrow we'll have some pains from that accident, but would it be okay for us to sit inside until the police arrive?" Levi asked.

"I was about to take Rupert for a walk when I saw what happened," the man said, pointing to the street. "That car deliberately hit you. Once the bullets started flying I got on the phone and called the police. I watch the news all the time and see the terrorists at work, but I never guessed it would be in my own front yard." A cute corgi came and sat at the man's side, bouncing from paw to paw as if he were anxious to come out and meet them.

Yasmine smiled at the surreal bit of normality in front of her. "Is that Rupert?"

"Yes, ma'am, and please come in. I apologize for not coming out sooner, but I don't move as fast as your friend there." The front room of his home seemed to be a study or library, judging by the shelves filled with books. Whoever the guy was, he was a kindred spirit.

"She's not having the best luck tonight." Yasmine placed her hand over Levi's heart, happy she'd have time to say everything she needed to. "Let me have your phone, darling." The endearment made Levi smile at her in a way that conveyed how much she cared.

"Tell everyone not to worry," Levi said, handing it over. She closed her eyes and leaned back into the sofa, looking exhausted.

"Zara," Yasmine said when her sister answered. "Something happened—"

"How did you know? Did the police call you or something?" Zara sounded winded and agitated.

"What are you talking about? Levi and I were attacked again, and we're waiting for the police because of three more dead men. Is something wrong there?"

"We got home and found someone tore the place up. It's a mess." Zara lowered her voice and sounded like she was moving. "Percy is talking to the detectives, but he's not giving up too much information. I think considering what's going on, that's a good idea."

"Did they take our work?" She tried to think what she'd left in her room.

"Jane told me not to ask right now, so I haven't." Zara was still whispering, but wherever she'd moved, it was quiet. "What happened?"

Yasmine gave Zara a short explanation. She wanted to get back since they were all clearly in danger. "Make sure you stay safe until we get there. We've got to figure out what they're after."

"Don't be long," Zara said. "Do you need us to come and get you if the car's wrecked?"

"I'll let you know. The police are here." Yasmine listened as the police gave them a rundown of the situation. They'd gotten the old man and Levi's accounts and seemed satisfied. One man who stood close to the detective didn't appear to be listening. He was staring at Levi as if trying to read her mind.

"And you've never seen these men before?" the inspector asked.

"The man who grabbed Dr. Hassani was in New Orleans recently. He broke into my house and hurt someone I care for." Levi put her hand up and Yasmine took it. "I don't know his name, but the other man with him in New Orleans was Baggio Brutos. Perhaps he can answer your questions."

Levi was reticent with information, just as Zara said Percy was at the house. Yasmine found it interesting that the only time the silent partner had moved to write anything down was when Levi had offered the name of the man in New Orleans.

"How long will you be in town?" the detective asked.

"At least a week. We'll be at my grandparents' home until then. Dr. Percy Breeden and Dr. Jane Breeden." Levi stood and didn't let go of Yasmine's hand. "Thank you, and we'll be available to answer any other questions you have."

"Can I offer you a ride?" the silent partner asked.

Yasmine tightened her hold on Levi's hand and hoped she understood the quiet warning. Levi glanced at her briefly and smiled. "I appreciate the offer, but I'm sure you're going to be busy with the investigation. There are three dead guys out there. Add that to what happened at the restaurant—well, we don't want to take up your time."

"I don't mind," the man said, and his accent was off. To Yasmine's ear it sounded like an American trying for an English accent.

"That's okay," Yasmine said. She put her other hand on Levi's arm and pressed closer. "Come on, darling." They could walk away from this place, then call a cab. "Did that man make you uncomfortable?"

"He did raise my creep level," Levi said, leading her to the back garden.

"What does that mean?" Yasmine followed Levi into the shadows.

"He made me uncomfortable." The house was still lit up, and the police were still inside with the old man, as well as around the bodies in the street. "We need to get back to my grandparents' place, and I don't want to be followed."

"I believe these people have already found your grandparents, so maybe we should go somewhere else." Yasmine told her what Zara had said and grimaced when she gazed at Levi's face. She'd really taken a beating tonight. "What do you think all this means?"

"The guy who offered us a ride, I don't think he's with the Church. Baggio Brutos, though, is definitely with the Church, or at least a very conservative branch of the Church." Levi pushed them closer to the side of the house when they heard the front door open and close and the two men bidding the homeowner a good night.

"How do you know that? All the men who've come after us give

orders and use their fists. Explanations haven't been a big part of it."
Yasmine followed Levi to the neighbor's yard, and again they stayed
in the shadows.

"Brutos wears an Opus Dei lapel pin, and it isn't a stretch to
think that all these guys work for him. To do that they either have to
be equally devoted or have plenty of money to stay on the trail. Think
about who has that kind of money."

"The Church," Yasmine said.

"I think the more accurate answer is the Catholic Church.
Something about what we have has them in a twist."

Yasmine shook her head and smiled despite the night they'd had.
"What does that mean exactly? Sometimes I hear you but have no idea
what you're talking about."

"Brutos works for someone in the Church or someone very
loyal to the Church. Knowing that we have this information has them
worried." Levi took her phone out again. "Don't worry, I'll teach you
all my slang." Levi had a short conversation with Percy, nodded a few
times, and hung up.

"How are you feeling?" Yasmine touched the bandage the doctor
had put on Levi's temple. It was bloody, which probably happened after
the accident. "I was so scared."

"I'm okay." Levi kissed her palm and Yasmine's body came to
life, which was inconvenient considering where they were. "Now you
can see why I asked you to consider going home until I'm done. I don't
want you in danger."

Levi lowered her head and kissed her. The danger they were in
and the reasons why flew from Yasmine's mind while she opened her
mouth and reveled in the feel of Levi's tongue against hers.

"How many times are we going to have this conversation?" she
asked when they finally parted. A horn sounded in the distance, and
Levi smiled instead of answering her.

"Sometimes I'm a slow learner. We'll talk about it later." Levi
took her hand and led her out to the street. Percy was waiting, along
with Jane and Zara. "Did they find everything?" she asked once they
were settled in the car.

"Bear, you insult me," Percy said. "It's time to go back home."

"But isn't the house torn up?" Yasmine asked, putting her arm
around Zara in the back seat. Percy drove off, and he wasn't worried
about speeding. It was late and the streets were mostly deserted.

"Grampie's family is English, but Granny's family is French.

Granny and my mother were raised in London, but my mom spent summers learning about the other side of her family." Levi leaned her head back and Yasmine wanted to run her fingers through her hair to make her feel better, but she was too sore to lift her arms at the moment.

"Are they another group of history lovers?" Zara asked.

"They're fishermen who became successful enough to become Parisians, but they've never forgotten where they came from. Their estate is empty and mostly forgotten," Jane said.

"Levi, how did one person luck into such a diverse family?" Zara asked.

"I was blessed, and if you believe the Montbards, we were pledged to always follow the truth and share our wealth of knowledge with the world." Levi closed her eyes and sighed. "That gave me permission to stay an adventurer."

"I'm sure Cristobal has a different definition of adventurer, but you've finally found your place, bear." Jane did the same as Levi and leaned her head back, closing her eyes. "We need to get to the place in the city, and we can move from there. It's obvious someone is anxious to get to you, and if I let something happen to any of you, Madelena will have me strung up."

"Granny, did the thieves take anything?" Levi asked again, since Percy hadn't answered her the first time.

"Don't worry. Would you leave a Gutenberg Bible outside for someone to take? They took what they needed to take, and that should buy you some breathing room." Jane nodded sagely.

Yasmine glanced out the window at Kensington Palace. It was a strange time to sightsee. "I thought we were leaving?" she asked.

"We are, but I travel better without a headache," Levi said.

Percy stopped at the gates of a nice apartment building, and the guard waved him through. They went up to an apartment on the top floor. Their luggage was already inside, and Jane pointed out the two guest rooms.

Everyone else went to their rooms, and Levi stayed in the hall and smiled at Yasmine. "Aren't you coming in?" Yasmine asked.

"Get some sleep." Levi came closer and kissed her. "I'll be in the apartment across the hall. It's a smaller place, so I'll be close."

"You can stay with me," she said.

"I don't think I could resist you tonight, honey. I'm weak, but I'm only human." Levi kissed the side of Yasmine's neck. "I'll see you in the morning."

"Levi, don't." She laced her fingers behind Levi's head and hung on.

"Zara was right—when it came to families, I lucked out." Levi put her hand on the side of Yasmine's neck and ran her thumb along her jawline. "I've been taught from my first memory how we're all connected as people no matter where we're from. How we should search for those things that give us a better understanding of who we were so we can plot a course for the future." Levi stopped her other hand at the slope of Yasmine's butt.

"I know that about you."

"The other thing I've been taught, though, is the most important things I have are my honor and my word."

"It's just a night, darling." At that moment Yasmine didn't care if that was all they got. She needed Levi, needed to touch her, feel her, and please her. All those things consumed her to the point of making her chest ache, and Levi was the only balm that would soothe the pain.

"I may be new to all this, but I want so much more than that, and I know you can't give it to me." Levi pressed her forehead to Yasmine's and closed her eyes, defeat and sadness in her tone. "You're no different than me when it comes to your honor and your traditions. You take them to heart, and you're devoted to them. It's why I know I'll never fit into your world."

"How can you be so sure?" She'd never cried so much in her life, but the tears were back and her emotions were haywire.

"It's not because I think that's true, sweetheart—it's because *you* think it's true. I can't change that because I can't change your heart. Given the chance, I could make you happy, but sometimes giving someone their freedom is what's best for them. I'd never ask you to change or give up your beliefs, but that creates a place where we can't meet in the middle."

Yasmine was convinced Levi had gotten a glimpse into her head and seen the truth of her. Her fears, beliefs, and truths were laid bare, and Levi was giving her what she'd sworn to herself she'd wanted all this time. Freedom from the mistake she was making—the mistake of what she felt, which she'd never be able to recover from if her family learned the truth. That was what she'd wanted, and Levi seemed to understand that, but why was her heart cracking into small pieces at the thought of Levi giving up?

"Don't cry. This isn't easy. Saying all that was the hardest thing

I've ever done, but I won't be the reason you turn your back on what's important to you." Levi held her until she stopped falling apart, but her tears started again when Levi closed the door behind her.

"You know," Zara said in Arabic from behind her, "you see and hear stuff like that in the movies, but you never think people still exist who talk like that, much less think like that. The world is cruel, and people act only to protect themselves. It's not often you run across someone who makes stupid sacrifices for the good of someone they care for."

"I'm sure you think I'm making a mistake, but this is for the best. She's not—" Yasmine didn't know how to finish that.

"She's not worth it? She's not the one?" Zara was blunt as usual. "You can be truthful when it's just the two of us."

"That's not it."

"Of course it is. Her expression when she left means she's smart enough to know it too. You not stopping her was probably more painful than everything else that happened to her put together, and you let her go." Zara went back to her room and closed the door. It was as if she couldn't offer her usual comfort this time because she didn't want to argue with Yasmine.

"It's for the best," Yasmine said out loud, trying to convince herself. "Shit." She seldom cursed, but it was warranted.

❖

Baggio sat in his car outside the apartment building. He motioned to his companion to start the ignition when the security guard stepped out of his small shelter and stared at them. Security in this section of town was tight because of who lived a few blocks down. The royals were also traitors to the Church, but their popularity had only grown in recent years. That proved to Baggio that the world needed the discipline he and the order wanted to provide.

"I can't go back to Ransley with another failure," he said to the man next to him. He'd never seen him before. Ransley and Cardinal Chadwick liked to send these compliant priests on missions on occasion because of their loyalty. Baggio was sure one of them would eventually put a bullet in his back and receive absolution from the cardinal for the grievous sin.

"There was someone else in the shadows. We had them both,

Montbard and the Arab woman, and our men were killed." The priest made the sign of the cross and kissed his hand. "It's as if some dark force is protecting them."

"Evil does exist, but it's seldom this loyal to its followers. The devil is fickle, and they are only women. Weakness is their lot in life. We must keep an eye on them and concentrate on what we found at the house." They drove back to the home the order maintained nearby. If Montbard moved, they'd hear about it from their brethren in law enforcement. "Are you sure you sent the best men so nothing was missed?"

"Our men found every hidden room and compartment. The search wasn't that hard. They left everything in the study as if they were coming back to work on it." The priest never took his eyes off the road, but he sounded boastful. "I'm not sure why the operation in New Orleans was so hard. Success has a lot to do with timing, and we got it right."

"And you believe this?" Baggio tried to sound nonchalant, but his right hand tightened into a fist.

"You are a hero to the cause, Brother Brutos, but we cannot win every battle. Mistakes in New Orleans have been smoothed over by what we did in London."

"That's true, and a true army of God has leaders willing to take the blame when needed. Remember that when you take my place seeking glory and heroism. Our job is not only to carry out the deeds that will make us victorious but also to offer our heads when we lose the battles." He stretched his hand out. This idiot wasn't worth it. "When you see the jihadists who are willing to blow themselves up for what they believe, keep one thing in mind."

"Those people are an afront to God. What's your point?" The priest glanced at him.

"It's always the foot soldiers and never their leaders wearing the bombs. We are no different. We fight for what we believe in, but it's we who make the sacrifices, never the generals."

"Mr. Hastings is waiting to see you." The priest glanced at his phone. "He sounded disappointed this has taken so long."

"I'm sure he was, and congratulations. I'm sure you'll be a fine stand-in for me. I'll see you in hell, eventually." He laughed when the priest scowled.

"My reward for serving the cardinal is the kingdom of God. Of that I have no doubt."

"Keep one thing in mind. Finding such glee in the downfall of others will pave your way to hell. The Lord was never boastful."

Baggio slammed the door closed and entered the house. Ransley was waiting for him in the formal living room, drinking a scotch. "What a surprise. You don't usually come down from that ivory tower of yours."

"All these dead bodies are getting harder and harder to hide, Baggio. Are you making any progress at all when it comes to reining Montbard in so she's no longer an issue?" The amber liquid coated the sides of the crystal as Ransley twirled his glass. "Now that the priests have the information we wanted, I'm not sure if we should keep you on this case."

"Can I make it easier for you? I spoke to the Holy Father's second, and he'd appreciate my help in the archives." He poured Ransley another drink and sat down. "I won't stand in your way. The sycophant with me tonight sounded happy to take my place. He gave me a lesson on how things are done."

"You'll forget everything you've done for me and Cardinal Chadwick?" Ransley smiled to accentuate his sarcasm. "Please, Baggio, you're a smart man. This was a lifetime commitment."

"My commitment hasn't changed. It's your commitment to me that's changed. You've done everything to clear the way to what you want, and you've committed a number of sins to do it." He poured himself a little scotch. "I've prayed for forgiveness, and I'm at peace that I've done all I can."

"You haven't done an iota of what you need to, and you also have to understand that there is no leaving. You belong to me until I say the work is done, and the work is not done." Ransley slammed his glass down, and the crystal cracked up the side. "Get me what I want, or I'll replace you with someone who is dying to carry out our wishes. We have the manuscripts and I demand to know what they say."

"I'll finish this, and then I'll be out of your reach." Baggio stood and buttoned his jacket. His hatred for Ransley Hastings rivaled his passion for the Lord. "Kill me if you want—I can't stop you—but careful what floodgates you open doing that."

"What does that mean?"

"Tonight, your minions found what Donnie couldn't, and you should ask yourself why it was so easy. Does that sound like Montbard at all? She and I understand something you and the others do not."

"Enlighten me."

"Despite all you've done, all you've tried to hide and destroy, there is still plenty left to open the Church to change. There are numerous people throughout history who believed more in the truth than in blind faith."

Ransley lifted his fist. "Is that a threat?"

"It's a fact. You need to remember all the things that can hurt you."

CHAPTER SIXTEEN

L evi stood in front of the refrigerator trying to decide what to eat. The apartment, owned by Granny's family, was always stocked with ingredients for sandwiches and other easy meals. It wasn't until now that she realized she was starving. Dinner was hours ago, and she'd been hit before she could eat. She opted for a ham sandwich and a beer, and she stripped down to her underwear while the bread toasted. The pain in her head had lessened, but her body was starting to stiffen up, and she didn't want to take time for a bath.

"I'm such a fucking idiot." The conversation with Yasmine had been her way of ripping the Band-Aid off quickly, and it had left her bleeding to death. This time she'd have to watch Yasmine walk away. "You could've left it alone and enjoyed what she *could* give." The disappointment in herself made her forget the food, and she took only her beer into the bedroom. "But no, you opened your mouth and it's done." She'd slap herself in the head, but with all the injuries that wouldn't be a good idea.

She glanced out the window and studied the street but didn't see anything out of the ordinary, so she finished getting undressed and lay down. Her eyes were closed, and tears fell down her cheeks to the pillow. It was the last thing she remembered until she entered a dream where Yasmine was waiting. She was sure beauty like Yasmine's was what fed the poets and artists throughout time.

The movement of the bed made her open her eyes slightly, and she waited to see if this was going to be another problem. She was done being everyone's punching bag for the night. Someone sat next to her, and the feel of a hand against her back stopped her breathing. She prayed it was Yasmine, and if it was, the morning could kiss her ass if this was still a dream.

"Levi." Yasmine's voice was like silk, and her skin was even softer.

Levi rolled over but didn't reach for her, afraid of scaring her off. "Hey," she said, sounding like her brain had leaked out her left ear.

"I'm sorry," Yasmine said.

"For what? You have nothing to be sorry for." Yasmine's eyes swelled with tears, the last thing Levi wanted. "Knowing what you want and not compromising isn't something to apologize for."

"I'm not sorry for what I feel," Yasmine said. "I'm sorry for making you doubt yourself and me. You believe I don't care for you, but that's not true. I do, and I can't hold back any longer. I don't know what that will mean going forward, but you make it impossible to worry about the future."

"Don't make decisions you can't live with. Regret will eat you alive."

"That is true, but my life has always been about duty to God and family, and never myself." Yasmine sounded as if she were on the very edge of a cliff that she was about to step over. "None of that matters if I hurt you for being honest. I'm sorry I hurt you."

The curtains let in just enough light for Levi to see Yasmine's expression. All the fear she'd seen earlier was gone, replaced with what appeared to be certainty. "I'm sorry too."

"I'm too late," Yasmine said, sounding miserable.

"No." She sat up, grabbing Yasmine's hand when she went to stand. "I'm sorry for voicing my frustration. I shouldn't have said all that stuff earlier. We can go at your pace. You're so much more important than the work and everything else. All I want is you."

Yasmine broke Levi's hold and stood up.

"Don't—" All the air left Levi's lungs when Yasmine pulled the tie on her robe, opened it, and let it drop behind her.

"Will you touch me?"

Levi had to press her lips together to keep from screaming "hell yeah," so she went with "thank you for trusting me."

"If I listen to what I've been taught, this will damn me, but if I listen to my heart, I know it's the way to happiness. I want to know what it is to be the woman I want to be, if only once."

Levi lifted herself onto her elbow and touched Yasmine's face before letting her fingers trail down to her collarbone. Yasmine's skin was soft and her dark brown nipples puckered. It was as if Yasmine's desire couldn't be contained any longer and her body was ready to be touched. What she'd just said gave Levi pause, but stopping wasn't an option.

No matter how turned on Levi was at the sight, she was going to go slow. She started with a kiss, liking the way Yasmine combed her fingers through her hair and hummed against her mouth. Pleasing someone and being pleased in return was a wonderful thing.

"You're so beautiful." She released Yasmine's lips and kissed her cheeks and eyelids. Yasmine pressed her chest to Levi's at the compliment, and all the aches fell away. Levi wanted to turn the lights on to see Yasmine's body, but she didn't want to move. This time when her hand went down past the small of Yasmine's back, Yasmine didn't stop her.

"I like hearing you say that. I want to be beautiful for you," Yasmine said. "I want you to look at me, and only me."

"Good." Levi brought her hand up and cupped Yasmine's breast. The way Yasmine reached up and placed her hand over Levi's made her kiss her again. She took her time here as well, wanting Yasmine to feel cherished.

Yasmine moaned when Levi kissed her neck before sucking her nipple into her mouth. One taste was never going to be enough. Like all the treasures Levi sought that had been buried, waiting for their time, Yasmine had been waiting until they found each other. Walking into that classroom a few years back was the best thing Levi could've done.

"Oh," Yasmine said. "Please, darling, touch me."

"Where do you want me to touch you?" she asked, and Yasmine covered Levi's hand with hers and squeezed, applying pressure to her other breast.

"I don't know what to ask for. Touch everywhere."

"Tonight's about you and what you want. I want to make you feel good, touch you, and make love to you, but tell me to stop if you need me to." This had to be about Yasmine and her wants. She'd never said anything, but Levi figured she didn't have a lot of experience in this arena.

"I don't want to stop, but I don't know…" Yasmine stopped talking, and her lack of confidence broke Levi's heart.

"Look at me," she said, coming up and kissing Yasmine again. "Feel me," she said as she let Yasmine's breast go and moved her hand between Yasmine's legs. The sensation made Yasmine moan, and she stopped. Whatever mental hang-ups Yasmine had, her body didn't share them. "Please tell me you don't want to stop."

"I don't. You're making me crazy." Yasmine's hands tightened on Levi's shoulders, and if she squeezed any harder, she was going to leave a bruise. "Oh, Levi," she said when Levi pinched her clit and tugged. "That feels so good."

Levi moved so she was on top, and Yasmine kissed her. Yasmine was so wet, and her hands on Levi's back were driving Levi crazy as well as reminding her to go slow. This had to be Yasmine's first time with a woman, and Levi wanted to give her an experience that would leave her open to so much more. It scared her, but she didn't want just a night. She put her fingers at the opening of Yasmine's sex and stopped. "Can I touch you?"

"Yes, please." Yasmine spread her legs wider, wrapping them around Levi's waist. "Touch me."

Levi entered Yasmine and stopped cold. This wasn't just her first time with a woman, but her first time with anyone. Yasmine turned her face away from her, which Levi took as a sign of shame. "Look at me, honey."

"I've never—" Yasmine couldn't say any more, but she finally made eye contact. "I know you're used to women who—"

"Forget about that right now. Right now, it's only you and me, and I want you. Are you sure? This can't be undone, honey." As much as she wanted Yasmine, she'd never take something like this from her if there was even a bit of doubt. Yasmine had waited all this time for something or someone, and Levi doubted it was her.

"I waited because there's never been anyone I wanted like this. No one until you." Yasmine placed her hand on Levi's wrist and didn't look away. "I want it to be you."

She took her time and tried her best to ease in without hurting Yasmine. She kept stroking her clit, and Yasmine closed her eyes. "You feel so good," Levi said as she bit down on Yasmine's nipple and pushed through the last of her innocence.

"Oh…oh…wait. Wait," Yasmine said, her eyes flying open. "I feel so full."

"Relax and let me in," Levi said as she came up to kiss Yasmine. She never stopped her strokes, and Yasmine rubbed her hands up and down Levi's back, moaning as she pressed into Levi's hand.

She felt Yasmine open up to her, and her soul sang. She wanted Yasmine to come for her, so she pressed down with her thumb and whispered in her ear, "Let go for me, beautiful."

"Please." Yasmine ran her fingernails up Levi's back. "I need…

oh, Levi." Yasmine let out a loud moan and bit Levi's shoulder. "I don't know—" She let out another loud moan as her body tensed, her nails digging into Levi's back, her head thrown back like a goddess. Slowly she stilled and took a shuddery breath. "That was wonderful," she said a few minutes later.

"It gets better with a little practice," Levi said. They shared another kiss before she moved off Yasmine and carefully withdrew her fingers. "Are you okay?"

"I'm wonderful, despite the truth of you thinking I'm pathetic."

Levi lay back and held Yasmine, liking that she put her leg over Levi as if to hold her in place. "That's the last thing I think. I've never been a jealous person, but thinking of anyone else touching you makes me nuts. I've never felt that way before."

"But I have no idea how to please you."

"It's not hard, and those lessons will start tomorrow." She relaxed and took a deep breath.

"Don't you want me to…you know?" Yasmine rose enough to gaze down on her.

"More than I want anything in my life, but it's three in the morning, and knowing Granny, we'll be moving early." She reached up and caressed Yasmine's cheek. "Once we arrive tomorrow, I promise we can take our time."

"Aren't you in need of something?" Yasmine used her index finger to trace a line from Levi's neck down her chest to the top of her sex. "You've been looking at me for days, and now you want to sleep?"

Levi smiled at what a difference one orgasm made. Yasmine had shed some of her shyness and was doing a great job at seduction. "I've been looking at you for days because I wanted to show you how I feel about you."

"Can I touch you?" Yasmine's hand was frozen as if she wasn't sure what the protocol of this was.

"You don't ever have to ask me that. If you want to touch me, it'll be something I'll enjoy." She bit her bottom lip when Yasmine's finger moved down between her legs. All the pent-up frustration of keeping herself in check unraveled when Yasmine moved her finger over her hard clit. "Fuck." Levi raised her hips slightly, trying to alleviate the beautiful pain.

"Do you like this?" Yasmine's smile was soft and teasing. It was the first time Levi had seen this version of her, and it did something to her heart. She held Yasmine's waist and encouraged her on top. "Do you?" Yasmine pressed down, and Levi had to clench her teeth.

"I do." She pinched Yasmine's nipple and smiled at how Yasmine's mouth opened. "Keep your hand right there." She moved her hand between their bodies and back between Yasmine's legs.

"Let me touch you." Yasmine's butt came up slightly as if to give Levi better access.

"Come with me," Levi said, rubbing where Yasmine needed her most. The action made Yasmine copy her movements, and if the sight of Yasmine claiming what she wanted was the last thing Levi saw in this life, she'd die happy.

She held her hand in place as Yasmine pumped her hips at the pace she wanted while also touching Levi. "Harder, baby." The orgasm was right there, and Levi couldn't hold back the tightening in her stomach. She squeezed Yasmine's ass with her free hand and jumped off the cliff Yasmine had driven her to, holding Yasmine as she came with her.

"No one ever told me it could be like this with a woman," Yasmine said. After her second orgasm, Yasmine slumped on Levi in a dead weight with her hand still between Levi's legs. "I should have never waited so long."

"I'm honored to be your first, and I'm glad you waited." She held Yasmine and kissed the top of her head. "If I'd known you existed, I would've waited as well."

"You're still a sweet talker."

"Later on, I'll teach you the meaning of how sweet I am, but for now, go to sleep." Tomorrow was a new day, and no matter what they faced, this made it all bearable.

CHAPTER SEVENTEEN

The brightness of the room made Yasmine squint when she opened her eyes. In the light of day, she should regret what her emotions had led her to, but the sight of Levi sleeping next to her made her grateful for her decisions. All the excuses she'd used throughout her life hadn't worked on Levi, and she'd had to have her. What would happen next wasn't something Yasmine wanted to worry about now. Their night had forced her to face who she was, but losing her family, no matter how exasperating, gave her pause.

"What are you thinking so hard about?" Levi's low voice made her shiver. "I thought I was dreaming when I woke up, but I pinched you and you were real."

That made Yasmine laugh and lift up so she could see Levi's face. "Has anyone told you how wonderful you are?"

"No one who's ever mattered." Levi tugged Yasmine's head down and kissed her. "Thank you for last night. It *was* wonderful."

Yasmine could've spent the rest of the day in bed, but she didn't want to be naked when Levi's grandparents and Zara were ready to go. "Should we shower?"

"Let's do that and go across the hall for breakfast. I'm starving."

Zara stared at them when they walked in and smiled. With any luck, no one would figure out what they'd spent most of the night doing.

"Good morning." Yasmine took the plate Levi prepared for her and sat across from Percy. "What is the plan?"

"We're going to extend your vacation, but we're heading to the beach this time." Jane placed a cup of coffee in front of her. "The house is remote but also guarded, so we'll be fine."

"Can we tell our parents where we're going?" she asked.

"Why not call this morning and check in?" Percy's suggestion was strange, and it meant once they left there'd be no contact. "The fewer people who know, the better off we'll be."

"Leaving will hopefully knock these people off our bums," Jane said.

"Someone has been following us, and I've been too stupid to notice." Levi shook her head and ate some eggs. "Up to now, nothing I've found has attracted this kind of attention. We're not taking any chances. This is important, but it's not worth dying over. We need to be hypervigilant from now on."

"The Church as a whole isn't evil, but some parts of it are misguided. What we need is a place where we can work without anyone shooting at you. Sometimes the best place to do that is at home," Jane said. "You're not to blame for not noticing anyone was out to get you."

"Who is to blame, then?" Levi asked.

Yasmine placed her hand on Levi's thigh and squeezed. "It's their fault. Like you said, if they're afraid of something, we must be on the right track."

"I hope you like the beach." Levi held her hand and smiled. "What's the best way to get there? I don't want anyone coming who isn't invited."

"Leave that to Granny," Percy said.

Once breakfast was done, they all packed while Jane made a few phone calls. Yasmine checked her email and opened the one from Nabil. He asked her to call when she received the message, no matter the time.

"Do I have time to make a business call?" she asked Levi.

"Take all the time you need, honey. It's going to be a minute." Levi led her to the office and closed the door to give her privacy.

The view out the window was the tree-lined avenue. The leaves glimmered in the slight breeze and bright sunlight. It was a sight she'd seen so many times in her life, but today everything appeared new and somewhat strange. She was no longer a virgin, and instead of overthinking that, she wanted to be with Levi again. She wanted them to be alone so Levi could touch her and make all the cells in her body come alive.

She waited for the operator to go through the steps of connecting her to Nabil. Whatever he wanted had nothing to do with work because he was willing to chance her using her phone. He'd been a good but tough boss, and she'd found him fascinating. With time, that hero worship had tarnished a little, but she still liked him as a person. Right now, she didn't want any other complication when it came to work.

"What have you been up to?" Nabil asked in a booming voice.

"Working," she said, laughing at his directness. "I'm helping a friend with a project."

"Does that friend work for some branch of the government? Academia doesn't make you a target unless you've chosen a job at a terrorist training camp. So I repeat, what have you been up to?"

She cocked her head and stared at the ceiling. "I'm working on decoding some old scrolls for a friend. Why someone has a problem with that I can't tell you, although they very clearly do. How did you find out what happened?"

Nabil laughed, and she could imagine his shoulders shaking. "You're important enough to me that I keep some tabs on you. When your name comes up in an incident like what happened last night, my people report in."

"You're stalking me?" That got another laugh.

"Yes, and you're in interesting company. Jane Breeden is retired, but not really, and she's good at her job. That job is with British Intelligence, and she's worked with us on some projects where we had a common interest." Nabil stopped and spoke to someone on his end, but it was muffled. "I called because I'm worried. Promise me you'll call no matter what if anything else happens. This isn't something to play around with."

"I promise," she said, glancing at the door. "Have you met Jane?"

"I have, and she's a force to be reckoned with. From the report I received, though, whoever chased you down last night wasn't messing around. That spells professional, so think about coming home soon. There's not much I can do to protect you if you're in England."

"We're coming home for Jadda's birthday."

"I'll be more help when you do. You sound not yourself, so take care. The work you finished for us was wonderful as usual. Remember that you always have a place with me."

"Thank you, sir, and I'll call if I need to." She disconnected the call and tapped her phone against her chin. Nabil was a good friend, but he didn't always tell the full story. Asking him to fill in the gaps, though, was a waste of time. He only shared what he wanted and there was no forcing the rest. She opened the door and saw Levi with her bags coming out of the room Jane had given her the night before.

"Everything okay?"

"Just a check-in kind of thing. Are we ready?" Yasmine waved Levi into the office. When Levi closed the door, Yasmine smiled at the chance to kiss her one more time before they had to go. "Is it a secret where we're going?"

"We're headed to the French coast and the old Caron beach house. It's seldom used, like this place, but it'll be comfortable. It's in Ault, France."

They went down together, and Yasmine stared at the man who was waiting at the service entryway. He loaded their bags into a van with the logo for a cleaning company, then pointed to the dark SUVs waiting behind him.

"They'll take you out the back, and we'll have these delivered to the house. It's all set up for you."

"Thank you, Chuck. Drive safe and make sure you stop for croissants. I know your little boy loves them." Jane kissed the young man on both cheeks and followed Percy to the first car.

"Come on," Levi said, opening the door to the second vehicle. They got in and Yasmine leaned into Levi. The car Percy and Jane were in turned in the opposite direction they did, and the other three cars behind them did the same thing.

"I feel like I'm in a spy movie," Zara said.

"I'm glad all that happened to you is finding the house ransacked," Levi said. "Last night wasn't a great time. It was certainly a memorable date."

"I'll give you another shot," Yasmine said softly to Levi. They all laughed, but Levi spent most of the trip glancing over her shoulder.

The driver seemed to be giving them a tour, stopping at the oddest locations and getting out as if he were running errands. If anyone was following them on the off chance it was them, they must have gotten bored by now. They finally arrived at the Eurotunnel Shuttle entrance. Once loaded, they sat in the car until they were in France. It didn't take much time to get on the road, and no one seemed to be following them.

Yasmine drifted off and woke wrapped in Levi's arms with Zara's head on her shoulder. A spectacular view of the coastline was visible through the trees, but the road was much higher than the water. She slid her hand into Levi's shirt and contented herself with the feel of her skin as she admired the scenery.

Levi took a deep breath and it made Yasmine smile. It was a wonderful thing to be awake after so many years of sleepwalking through life when it came to caring for someone this way. Her smile widened when Levi kissed her temple, but she stayed quiet for a few minutes anyway.

"We're almost there." Levi pointed to a road that led down the coast. The exit was the straightest part. They went through a series of hairpin turns and didn't pass many homes. The open land had plenty of trees and rocky terrain and seemed untouched by time.

"The family owns most of the land along here, and the places you see have been inhabited by the people who have tended to the estate for generations."

"All this from fishing?" The Montbards, Breedens, and Jane's family, the Carons, were a different breed from anyone Yasmine had grown up with. The money was evident, but their attitude about it intrigued Yasmine. They weren't exactly dismissive of their wealth, but they didn't flaunt it.

"Sardines are popular, or at least that's what Granny's people keep telling me. She's on the board of the company, but her nephews run the day-to-day operations. Once her brothers passed away, my French cousins stopped coming out here." Levi pointed to the left. "The townspeople are very loyal to Granny, so if anyone comes looking, we'll know about it."

The beach house, as Levi put it, was ridiculous. The sprawling mansion with turrets, surrounded by a stone wall, also appeared to be made of thick stone. The high white cliffs that backed it and the ocean that fronted it added to the dramatic appearance. Yasmine guessed it would make an excellent location for a mystery movie, and she couldn't wait to see the inside.

"This is amazing." She took her hand from Levi's shirt and shook Zara awake. "We're here."

"Welcome to Maison des Vagues," Jane said moments later, opening the door.

House of Waves was a good name, and the inside was much warmer than Yasmine would've guessed. The tapestries on the walls appeared old, but the furniture was new and comfortable looking. The best part of the house was the sweeping view of the ocean from the large family room to the right of the entrance.

She and Zara followed Levi when she offered a tour, and they walked around for half an hour, ending outside on the third floor. The overlook provided a panoramic view of the land around them as well as the water.

"There are plenty of bedrooms, so if you don't like the ones the staff picked out for you, let them know and they'll move you," Levi said, combing her hair back because of the stiff wind.

"Is the staff here for us?" Zara asked.

"It's not a large number, and they actually live here. They enjoy this place more than anyone, but my parents and grandparents try to visit at least a couple times a year. Come on and I'll show you the best room here."

They walked down the spiral steps, and Levi led them to the center of the house on the second floor. The library was huge and full of books from floor to ceiling. A couple of computers to the side didn't take away from the beauty of the space with the fresco of Athena on the ceiling. The books they'd found, along with the copies of all the scrolls and the stones, were already on the tables waiting for them to decipher their secrets.

"Let's have lunch and we'll start," Levi said.

Before they went down, they all went to change. Levi opened the door to her room and winked at Yasmine as she closed it. Yasmine's bag was inside, and the open door to her left was the entrance to her own bathroom. It was like a nice resort with the antique canopy bed and beautiful view, but as she removed her skirt she heard a light knock.

She opened the door and saw no one in the hallway, but when she turned around Levi was sitting on the bed, barefoot and grinning. It was the open closet door that gave away how she got in there. The open trapdoor connected to the room next door.

"I've been with you all day and yet I miss you," Yasmine said.

"Tonight, you'll have my total attention if you invite me in," Levi said, watching Yasmine as she dropped her skirt to the floor. "Though you have my total attention right now."

"Good, but we're not going to keep your family waiting, so behave."

Once lunch was over, they all went up to the library, and Levi asked Yasmine to take the books they'd found out of the leather bag. If she had to guess, both Levi and Percy had called on all their willpower not to sit in the crypt the previous morning and start reading through their treasures.

"Thank goodness the thieves didn't find these," Yasmine said to Jane and Percy.

"After what happened to George, I took some precautions. If these idiots were going to hit again, I figured it was when we'd all be out of the house. I had all of the information you brought with you shipped here." Jane motioned to the room. "This place is much older than our family's ownership, and the man who built it in the fourteenth century put this room at the center to protect the contents from storms and thieves. It was brilliant, really."

"Shall we begin?" Levi asked.

They all put on gloves to handle the books, which didn't have many pages. The thick leather stamped with the Templar Cross at the center of each had held up well for their apparent age.

The book creaked loudly when Yasmine opened it, and Levi shivered. Whatever this was, it would change their lives. She didn't have to be a psychic to know that.

"It's in Arabic again," Yasmine said. She adjusted her white cotton gloves as she stared at the page. "With all the stuff I've translated lately from this tribal dialect, this shouldn't take long. There isn't much here, really."

"It would've made more sense to combine these into one volume, but if it's like the scrolls where each one says the same thing only in a different language, it makes sense," Levi said.

"Do you need us to leave and give you some quiet?" Percy asked.

"No, sir. If you don't mind a few gaps for things I have to look up, I can start reading." Yasmine glanced at Levi. It was as if she knew how much Levi wanted to hear the story, to figure out what the next clue was going to be and where it was going to lead them.

"You want to get comfortable?" Levi sat on the Chesterfield and rested her arm along the back. It wasn't exactly a challenge, but Yasmine raised her eyebrow, taking it as one. "Or stay there?"

There was another couch across from the one she'd picked, and that was where Levi's grandparents picked to sit. Zara sat on the opposite end from Levi. She smiled when Yasmine joined Levi and leaned against her. As usual, Yasmine slipped off her shoes and folded her legs up on the sofa, using Levi as a backrest. Zara closed her eyes like she was waiting for a good story.

"Written in the year 1312 AD." Yasmine cleared her throat as she began reading.

❖

I remember the first day he came to our village. He wore the white tunic with the red cross with pride. I could tell his sense of superiority from the way he sat in the saddle. He was proud even though most of my people would kill him for showing that symbol so openly. The history of that simple piece of clothing in my land carried only hate and death.

"You have no need to fear us," the man leading the group said when he noticed me looking. "We come in peace."

The lie fell easily from his lips, so my family and I said nothing even though we understood him. This was one of the jackals who'd spent so much time here taking so much from us. They had been gone for lifetimes, but the stories lived on. I could see his cruelty in every line of his face and the coldness of his eyes. The young man with him stared at the pommel of his horse, and that did not fit with my first impression of who they were.

That first bolt of emotion that kept me from turning away gave me pause, and my gaze manifested into something I could not fight. Our story is in these books, and my hope is that they will be treasured for what they are. It is our life together in words, and they hold the key to what is most important. I pray you listen and learn of who we are.

Yasmine stopped talking and sat up enough to be able to look at her. "Do you think this is a complete history of their life together? Simply a journal of sorts?"

Levi glanced at the book in Yasmine's hands and the other three on the library table. "If it is and this is all that's left, I'll be happy. Sometimes the greatest treasure is the knowing. To know the why of things is better than gold. But if that's all they were, I don't think there'd be people after us."

"It's like intruding on someone's private thoughts, but you're right. This is a treasure worth more than gold. Their story can't be lost again." Yasmine sounded as passionate as ever, and it made Levi happy. Saying that meant she understood Levi on a basic level like no other woman ever had. That opened a door in her heart that had stayed firmly closed from the first time she looked at a woman with desire.

"Believe me, we'll use every resource we have to make sure they're appreciated for what they are."

"It's obvious it's written by Farah, and from that first section, it's in story form, like she thought that would be the best way to put down what she needed to."

"Maybe she was a teacher who understood the best way to keep her students enthralled." Levi forgot herself and kissed the tip of Yasmine's nose. "She's a lot like someone else I know."

"I don't enthrall people." Yasmine smiled, but Levi could tell she was embarrassed.

"I've been completely under your spell since before I met you."

"You can sweet-talk each other later," Zara said, rolling her eyes. "Right now, I want to know the rest of what Farah has to say."

"Buzzkill," Levi said, sticking her tongue out at Zara. "Keep going, honey."

Their tents were clustered together, and the soldiers kept to themselves after arriving. All of them had taken off their white tunics and armor no matter what they were doing, and they came and went in small numbers, never divulging where they went. Our elders have left them alone and have not sent word that they are here. It was as if they were trying to hide in plain sight and we did not want to invite trouble.

During the invasion of these infidels, most hated them for what they'd done, but some of our people had grown rich off these supposedly holy men. Warrior monks who fought for their god were still killers of women and children, and I hated them because of the stories I'd heard. I watched them every day, and yet there was one who stood out. The young man who had caught my eye that first day wore the garments of a worker. He still didn't fit in with us because of his tall strong frame, black hair, and blue eyes. He was handsome, but I tried not to forget that the beauty of a man could hide despicable things.

"Our well needs to be deepened if we want to have enough water for the rest of our stay," my father said one morning. We'd gathered for prayers and our breakfast, and it was one more chore in a long line of them. Our life is simple but hard.

We are nomads, but this was our winter home, and we would not move until the spring. Our animals as well as the rest of our tribe depended on the well that had been dug years before. Water was life, but the men who stayed so close to us cared not how much they used. It was still early, but the elders were gathered to assign the hard work to the younger men who would have to shovel buckets of sand to make the water flow again.

I went to gather our water for the day and stopped at what I saw. The young man was standing next to the well filling buckets for the women who had gathered, and there was a shovel resting against the stones that marked the opening. His Arabic was good, but the accent was still there as a reminder not to trust, not to let my guard down, and to not believe anything that came from that handsome mouth.

"Good morning," he said, hauling up the well bucket and filling the vessels I'd brought. "Take enough water for two days."

"Why?" The anger in me was hard to hide.

"When we dig, the water will become muddy. If we finish today, in two days it should be clear again." He acted as if I had asked my question with honey in my mouth. "I can help you carry those back if you have more to fill."

I saw that he had done that for some of the others, but I did not want his help. "I can do it."

For the rest of the day I sat in the shade of our tent and watched as the pile of sand grew. The monk had volunteered to go down and shovel, and he never tired as the men in our village pulled up bucket after bucket until the man said he could not touch bottom and the well was filling up again. It took four men to pull him up, and he was soaking wet when he climbed out. My father was the first to embrace him for his hard work. I did not want to see this. I felt it a betrayal of what we believe.

"Take him this," my father said that night. The plate of food was his way of repaying what the jackal had done. It was my place to serve my father, so I went.

The camp full of men was the last place I wanted to go, but my younger brother pointed to the top of a dune. There he sat as if he could see into the vastness of our homeland. The moon was full that night, and my mother watched as I climbed up with his reward. He smiled at me when I offered it to him.

"Thank you. Would you sit?" He took a date first,

making me think of the small boys in the other families. They were all different, but the one thing they had in common was a sweet tooth.

"Why?"

"I have heard of this place from my father for years, but the sight of it makes me feel like a small boy on an adventure. It's beautiful." He pointed to the horizon. The full moon illuminated everything around us. "My name is André."

All my life I have heard the legends of the fierce battles and how many of our people had to die before the Prophet sent Saladin to drive the evil men out of our lands. That was so many years ago, but people still sing of the bravery of our people, and the jackals who tried to tear our lands apart. This man, though, seemed nothing like the stories, with his handsome face and beautiful eyes that held nothing but kindness.

"You do not have to tell me your name, but I have seen you with the children. You teach them your words, and you tell them stories. Where did you learn this?"

I stopped his hand when he reached for another date. "First the lamb and bread, then the dates," I scolded like I did with my little brother. "My name is Farah, and I learn so I can take the place of my grandmother. She is the keeper of our history, but she grows old."

"I do not know your written words well, but my father taught me the language. It is not very good, I know, but I hope you understand me." His smile could melt even the coldest of hearts, but I must hold firm. No pretty words can sway my hatred.

"Why are you here? I doubt you will tell me, but I want to know."

"My father served all his life and raised me to be a sacrifice." His smile disappeared and his hands fell to his lap. "I did not mean to say that."

"Is it true?" My question made him stare out into the night as if the answers were written in the sands.

"I came because it was his dying wish, but I mean you and your family no harm." He spoke like he wanted me to believe him.

"What is your wish, André?" His name is so foreign on my tongue that hearing it from my lips makes him smile.

"My wishes are foolish, so I will not burden you with them." He took a bite to put me off, but he is an enigma I want to understand because I am sure there is kindness in him.

"How can we learn about each other unless you tell me? I doubt it can be foolish if it is something you truly wish."

He stared at me for a long while, then sighed. "I wish to return home to the green fields I played in when I was a boy. It would mean death from my brethren and bring shame to my father's name even to say it out loud. You hold the sword that can kill me."

I tapped the side of the platter and encouraged him to finish. "Why tell me all this?" It had to be a trick. "Do you think I would swing the weapon you have given me?"

"I saw you that first day, and you hated me solely because of what I wore. The symbol that I am proud of means nothing to you, and it makes me sad that we see no other way than battle to share our beliefs." He stretched his long legs out and leaned back on his hands. "I have chosen the life of a monk who serves God, but you follow a different belief. Neither of us should die because of it."

"Do you speak the truth?" It was a foolish question, but there was something in me that wanted to believe him.

"It's a sin to lie." He smiled again and offered me one of the dates. "You do not want me here, and I want not to be."

In the weeks that came, André helped with whatever the elders asked of him. My father fed him every night, and I sat with him as he ate. We talked and he told me of his home, his father, and the wine they made. If this was the man I was taught to hate, I could not see it.

The other men kept to themselves, and from the way they spoke to André, I could tell the teasing was not done in jest. If they were supposed to be holy men, André was the only one who learned the lessons of their god. In the mornings when it was his turn to preach, I would sneak close enough to hear. I did not understand his words, but I heard his devotion in every one.

"Do you have a woman at home waiting for you?"

He walked with me and my two brothers as we tended our goats. Half of the men with him had left on their horses days before, and the ones who stayed behind lay about drinking wine and speaking in low voices.

"I took a vow to God, so there is no one waiting for me. Love, a wife, and children are not possible for me." He lifted his shoulders and glanced away from me. "I have no one who cares for me aside from God."

"Your father was a man of God, and yet here you are." My logic made him smile, then laugh. It was a sound I cherished.

"Our God says that sometimes the will is strong but the flesh is weak. I am proof of that, no?" His explanation made me laugh, and when he joined me I felt as if we'd crossed some barrier and become friends.

Our talks went on for days, and he was the only one who never left their camp overnight. I was suspicious at first, but André never asked me anything that would betray my trust. Much later, as we sat under another full moon, he asked me, "Is there a man you have been promised to?"

"Why do you ask?" I held up a date my mother had soaked in honey.

"I see how some of the young men look at you, and it makes me think our time will end."

I turned my face away so he could not see my smile. Perhaps he had something in common with his father, and the needs of the flesh were stronger than his devotion. "I study to take my grandmother's place. I have told you this."

"Yes, the way you make the letters makes me sad, for I do not understand them though they are beautiful on the scrolls."

"Because I chose this, I do not have to marry if I do not want. The men can look, but I must decide."

My answer brought his smile back, and I returned it. I had never spoken to one man so much before, and despite my wishes, my heart warmed at the thought of him. He was what I thought I would never find, and I loved him. It would damn us both to admit this, but he was right. No matter how hard I fight, the flesh grows weak with the want of him. "Our time is in no danger of ending."

"Good," he said, accepting a date from my fingers. Our fingers touched, and neither of us pulled away.

The truth of who we would become came much later. Storms in our lands are not common, but at times they come with the fury of a dangerous animal. On such a day the sky lit up as if it were on fire, and André saw my brothers trying to gather the herd. He ran with them to drive the goats toward the pen my father had built but seldom used. One of the larger goats pushed him in fright, and André's head slammed against the gate.

My breath left my body when he did not get up. It was then I knew what I could not admit until that moment. I loved him. I loved him and I could not lose him. "André," I screamed into the rain. My brothers carried him to our tent and laid him carefully so my grandmother and I could tend to him. It was only the two of us, and my tears fell as I wiped the blood from his face.

"Fight," I whispered in his ear, hoping to see his eyes open. The piece of wood sticking from his chest worried me, and my grandmother ordered me to stay by his head. "Come back to me," I said in his words. He had taught me, and I hoped he understood me. "Come back to me."

CHAPTER EIGHTEEN

Yasmine wiped her eyes, and so did Zara and Jane. Farah's story proved to her that despite what the head said was important, it was the heart that ultimately ruled. Love defeated fear when it seeped into every ounce of someone's being.

"There is one section left, from what I can tell," Yasmine said, gently thumbing through the other pages.

"Let's take a break and think about the first part." Levi wiped Yasmine's cheeks for her and smiled. "Do you think there's code in there, Granny?"

"I hope you don't mind, Yasmine, but I recorded you as you read. It makes the transcription easier."

"I don't mind at all, but if there's a code it will be in the language it was written in. I promise I'll work as fast as I can."

"Can you point out the words *jackal* and *beautiful* as well as *handsome*?" Jane asked, handing over the copies they'd made of the books. "Those might be the key, but we still need you to figure it out."

Yasmine scanned the pages and circled all three words.

"Let's go for a walk while Granny puts that through the system," Levi said. She stood and offered one hand to Yasmine and the other to Zara.

"I'll pass this time. Jane was supposed to receive some information about the stones, and I want to be here in case it comes through." Zara waved to them and followed Percy and Jane into the kitchen.

Levi held Yasmine's hand but stopped in a small room by the back door to grab a bag. They followed a path down to the beach, and Yasmine left her sandals where it ended so she could go barefoot, like Levi. They walked in silence until Levi led her through a break in the protruding cliff to a secluded cove.

"Unless you're in a boat and look just right, this place is as private as the bathroom in your room." Levi dropped the bag in the sand and took Yasmine's other hand.

"And you're telling me this because? If you want to go swimming, I didn't bring a suit."

"Neither did I," Levi said, wiggling her eyebrows. "Sometimes, though, if the place is private enough, you don't need a suit."

She laughed at the mischievous smile on Levi's face. Life with Levi would never be boring. She stepped back and lifted her blouse over her head. The skirt came next, and she pointed at Levi to get her going. This was a different experience in the light of day, and she couldn't help but look at Levi's body. A few scars had to be from her past adventures, and her face was a road map of bruises, but none of it took away from Levi's looks. Last night's nerves had made Yasmine miss so much, but now she saw how stunning Levi really was.

"You're so damn beautiful," Levi said. She came closer, lowered the straps of Yasmine's bra, and kissed both shoulders. "Want to swim?"

"That'd be the only way I'd cool down."

"That's the last thing I want."

Once they were both naked, Yasmine followed Levi into the water and wrapped her legs around her waist once they were deep enough.

"Maybe this story Farah left is a warning to good Arab girls like me." She moaned at the feel of Levi's body against hers.

"What warning do you think she's trying to give you?" Levi sucked on Yasmine's neck, and she was instantly wet.

"That those handsome infidels who have more charm than Allah meant for anyone to possess are hard to resist." She let her head fall back and hoped Levi didn't stop what she was doing.

"Why would you want to?" Levi lifted her head, and Yasmine was about to complain until Levi put her hand between Yasmine's legs. "Jesus," Levi said when she put her fingers over Yasmine's clit.

"Let's leave religion out of this," Yasmine quipped, making Levi laugh. "I can't help it, you make me crazy."

"I plan on keeping you that way." Levi's fingers moved in a steady cadence.

"Ah…please," she said, wanting all the things Levi had given her the night before. It was like she couldn't breathe until Levi filled her up, and she rocked her hips, chasing the high Levi was building slowly. "Please, darling, go inside." Her face burned from the request, but it couldn't be helped. She couldn't wait any longer. Desire was making her crazy and robbing her control.

The calm of the water was disrupted by their movements, and the last part of her brain that wasn't focused on those long magical fingers noted that they were moving. She started to complain as Levi walked out of the water and laid her on the towel she'd taken from the bag. Levi shook her head when Yasmine reached for her, hoping Levi would lie on her and keep her grounded. She was afraid of floating away and needed Levi to hold her.

Yasmine gazed at the sky and lifted her hips to try to get Levi to focus, but Levi calmly kissed her way down Yasmine's body, making her hiss when she sucked in one, then the other nipple. How could something so simple make her want to beg? She was getting ready to when she felt Levi's shoulders against her inner thighs. She lifted onto her elbows and watched Levi spread her sex and lower her mouth.

The first touch of Levi's tongue made Yasmine's hips shoot up and her body drop back. She spread her legs as far as they would go. The sensation was so good she would've never been able to adequately describe it. She tentatively placed her hands on her nipples and moaned at how hard they were and how good it felt.

"Go inside me," she said, hoping Levi would give her what she wanted. "I need…oh my…you. I need you…ah," she said as Levi slid her fingers in and her body instinctively tightened around them. It was an overload of her senses, and she shook her head as Levi sucked her in. The orgasm was right there, and all she could do was buck her hips and beg with nonsensical repetition. "Yes, yes, don't…yes."

The orgasm almost hurt as her body tensed and she cried out, her back arching off the sand as her world shattered into a thousand glorious pieces. She fell on the towel, limp and replete. It had been so good and Levi had taken such care with her that she couldn't help the tears that started. She had no idea why she was crying, but the overwhelming emotions filled her with as much uncertainty for the future as the perfection of the present made her weep with its beauty.

"I'm sorry," she said when Levi moved up and held her. "I never cry. Now I can't seem to stop."

"You don't have to hide your feelings from me." Levi pulled her close and didn't ask for anything. "This is all new, so give yourself time to get used to it."

Farah might have had a point. When you found someone so different from you, and they were noble and kind, it was hard to believe that it could be true they cared for you. Levi was smart, driven, handsome, but also incredibly sweet. Would she always be that way, or would she change once the thrill of conquest was over? The guilt of even letting that go through her head shamed Yasmine, but she had no experience to draw from.

"You need to keep one thing in mind." Levi reached for another towel and covered them.

"What?" Yasmine used the edge of the towel to dry her face.

"What I want from you is so much more than this." Levi stopped and kissed Yasmine's eyelids. "We haven't ever talked about what comes next, but when you're ready, I'll be happy to tell you what I want."

"Will there be anything else?" Her chest hurt from the cowardice of the question, and it was hard to miss the way Levi flinched.

"That's up to you...to us. The important thing is I won't push you. Like I said, this is new, for both of us really, and you need to take the time to make sure it's right for you." Levi rolled away from her and sat up. "It's getting late. We should get back."

Something inside Yasmine was changing, and she was having trouble keeping up. Her instinct was to freeze and withdraw, but watching Levi walk away from her started a pain in her chest that brought more tears. She'd hurt her, and it was unforgivable. Levi had gone out of her way to be kind, and she didn't deserve Yasmine's usual aloofness.

"Levi, wait." She sat up, having come to the truth of who she was and what she wanted.

"Look," Levi said, turning around. She shut her eyes and pursed her lips as if trying to protect herself from what was right in front of her. "I'm sorry I upset you. I shouldn't have said anything."

"Please, darling, you didn't say anything wrong." Yasmine held a hand up. It was time to bridge the gap her words had caused or live with pain the loss would inflict. "You make me want all those things that come next."

Levi let out a long breath of air and smiled as she came back and sat next to Yasmine. "You know, all my life I've dreamed of finding things that no one thought existed. I've been through jungles, deserts, and caves, and I love the chase."

The things Levi was saying didn't give Yasmine a clue as to where she was going. Perhaps her hesitance had killed the feelings Levi had for her.

"The one thing I never chased, because I thought it didn't exist, was love. I've been with more women than is probably smart if I want a future with someone, but when I settle down, I want it to be forever."

"I can understand that." She hugged Levi's arm and pressed close to her.

"I want her to fit with me, in every aspect of my life, and that's never happened." Levi rested her head on Yasmine's. "On the flip side of that, I want to be the kind of partner who fits into her life."

"What would your life be if you found that woman?" Their worlds were oceans apart in more ways than one.

"All the things that makes a life worthwhile. Love, romance, a home, a family, and commitment." Levi didn't move when Yasmine straddled her lap.

"I'm sorry I'm so full of fear, but I've tried all my life to be a good daughter, a good soldier, and a good teacher. All that can only be possible if I give up parts of myself, and I did. I didn't think giving up only little bits would make a difference, but they have." It grounded her when Levi put her arms around her. "Then I met you and it was impossible to ignore what *I* want any longer. Please forgive me for being such a coward."

"When you love someone, honey, forgiveness is a given. And the last thing you are is a coward." Levi lifted Yasmine's head and wiped her tears. "I know what I want, and when you're ready to hear it, I'll say it as many times as it takes for you to believe it."

"Tell me," Yasmine said, choking off a sob.

"I love you." Levi's eyes were bright and her voice was strong. "I love you and I want to build a life with you. Everyone else might think this is too fast, and we might need more time, but I know what I want. I want you."

"I love you. I love you enough to know I can't give you up." The words lifted something in Yasmine's heart, and it set her free. Her problems would begin when she got home and her family figured out what was responsible for the lightening of her soul. "I hope that's okay with you."

"Are you happy you love me?" Levi always seemed to know what to ask. "I couldn't stand it if you're not happy."

"My love." She grabbed two fistfuls of Levi's hair and shook her head gently. "I've been happier in the last weeks than in all my adult life. I finally fit, and it's with you."

"I love you." Levi kissed Yasmine and held her as if she'd never let go. "That means I'm always going to stand next to you no matter what. When you go home, you won't have to do it alone if you don't want to."

"How do you always know what I'm thinking?" Being with Levi meant leaving Morocco and the only life she'd known. It wasn't a sacrifice but a choice that would make their future possible. With Zara going to London, being home would be a battle from the moment they arrived. Their life wouldn't be impossible in Marrakech, but it'd be perfect back in New Orleans.

"Because I know you. I know your heart, and I also know what you've said about your mom. The future is ours, and I'm not giving it up."

"I'm so glad you stepped into my classroom that day. It's because of you that we're here." For whatever came next, she had Levi's love, and nothing had ever been so right.

❖

"Where are you?" Cristian asked.

"I'm on the coast of France. Levi's grandmother has a family home here, and it's remote. We drove through town and have camped out on the cliffs." Graham looked through his binoculars but couldn't see Levi and Yasmine. "She's here with the two Hassani sisters and her grandparents."

"Is there any sign of Baggio's men?"

"We helped them lose them in London. It's going to take some time to find them, but they'll get here eventually. Here, though, they won't be able to hide."

"Try to stay in the shadows, but in this special case, we might have to eventually come out in the light. They deserve to continue the hunt, and it might be easier if they know someone is on their side."

Graham nodded and sighed when he saw the two women walking back toward the house holding hands. "We'll try to abide by our rules of no violence. I want them to succeed. Tonight we'll try to get closer to the house and keep an eye out for any threats."

"Good. You have our permission to deal with whatever issues there might be, as you did in London. We've also gotten some word that she did have a significant find in Choupick, of all places. It might have something to do with why she's there."

He saw Levi stop and turn Yasmine toward her. The kiss they

shared was much different from what he'd witnessed so far, and it reflected their deepening relationship. "We'll keep digging from our end, and I'll call if we find anything."

"They're lucky to have you," Cristian said.

"Thank you. You'll be happy that your favorite student might have found someone special in Dr. Hassani. They seem close."

Cristian laughed. "I loved you in the classroom the same amount I did Levi. Together you'll make an awesome team, even if she never knows you exist. You have been a gift, Graham."

"Thank you, sir. I'll talk to you soon." He ended the call and kept watching the women on the beach. He envied how comfortable Levi seemed in her skin. "Have you noticed any security on the property?"

"We might be able to get a few thousand yards closer, but that'll be it. Look," his colleague said, pointing to a spot in the yard. Security sensors meant there would be no close-up opportunities.

"We'll take what we can get. Once it's dark, we'll move." He scanned the water and the area behind them. There was no way he wanted someone to get the jump on them. "Anyone who comes here with a gun needs to be eliminated."

"It'll be our pleasure, sir."

"Yes, that it will be."

Chapter Nineteen

Dinner was a family affair, with Yasmine and Zara helping Jane in the kitchen while Levi and her grandfather looked on. The afternoon on the beach had left Levi buzzed, and she was still giddy from Yasmine's admission that she loved her.

"You look happy," her grandfather said.

His voice broke her gaze in Yasmine's direction. "I am." There was no denying it, but she had to get her head back in the game. "This has been a wonderful summer."

"I do believe it has, and I'm happy for you. We've waited for you to get struck by that rock that hits us all in the head. There's no cure from what it does to us. I doubt you need any input from this old man, but she's beautiful. Beautiful and smart will keep you on your toes, bear. Don't screw it up."

"I'm planning to be a good partner, not to worry." She laughed, and Yasmine glanced in their direction. That smile made Levi want to send everyone to their room so she could take Yasmine to bed.

"I doubt I've ever told you how proud your granny and I are that you're our grandchild. You've been such a joy, but it's time for you to get ready for another generation."

"Great-grandchildren?" The thought would've sent her running a few months ago, but now she thought about all those things that made a family.

"Exactly, and what beautiful babies you two will make."

"I don't need to explain biology to you, do I?" She laughed but stopped when Yasmine brought them both a fresh drink. "Thanks, honey."

"What are you two whispering about over here?" Yasmine combed her hair back and rested her hand on Levi's shoulder.

"We're hoping you're not too tired to finish the first volume we found," Percy said.

"I'm sure that meal would revive the dead. Jane is an excellent cook." Yasmine played with the hair at Levi's neck, and Levi put her arm around Yasmine's hips. "Your grandmother said there's an excellent wine cellar under this place. Want to hunt for something to go with steak?"

"You haven't seen the wine cellar? You're missing out."

Any plans for kissing Yasmine disappeared when Zara came down with them. Yasmine moved away from her a little, but hopefully the smile on her face meant she wasn't ashamed. It would take time for Yasmine to be fully comfortable, and that was okay.

"This is amazing." Zara impulsively hugged Levi when she saw the wine cellar. "You're the best thing that's ever happened to us."

"Thank you," Levi said, laughing.

"Promise me one thing," Zara said, letting her go.

"If I can I will."

"Don't ever hurt my sister. You two were meant to meet, but I've heard about your women and good times. All that ends now. From now on you have one woman, and she's the only good time you need." Zara was completely serious.

"I promise she's safe with me, and I'm going to love her until my heart stops beating."

"That was rather poetic. No wonder she fell in love with you."

"Um…how do you know?" Yasmine asked.

"*Please*," Zara said, rolling her eyes. "It's written all over you. Going home should be interesting. If you crumble under the onslaught, I'll never forgive you." Zara turned and kissed Yasmine's cheek. "I'm happy for you both, so stop trying to be careful. Everyone in this house is thrilled for you."

They selected a few bottles, returned upstairs, and ate the steaks Levi grilled. As they ate, each of them gave their take on the story, but none of them had a clue where it would lead. Farah was a good writer who had laid the groundwork of how she and André met, but the group could only follow what she gave them to find out what came next. Levi was sure of where they ended up—they'd fallen in love, meaning André would've had to give up his calling to take a wife.

"Are you ready?" Levi asked as Percy poured them all a brandy. Dinner was over and they were back in the library.

"If I said no I'd fear for my life. Zara would be the first to take a shot at me." Yasmine was ready to finish the book they'd started earlier too.

"I'll keep you safe, but the three-year-old that lives in me can't wait."

Yasmine leaned against Levi and began to read.

❖

"Come back to me."

My grandmother ordered me to gather certain herbs and to be quick about it. I had to get some of them from the other women, and they wished me well. It was as if they all knew what I could not admit until I saw him close to death. When I returned, the stick was out of his chest and he was still breathing. For the moment, he lived.

I took his hand and pressed it to my cheek. My grandmother mixed the herbs I'd been sent for and hummed as she worked. There was a blanket covering André's chest, and I had the urge to lie next to him in the hope he would feel me and come back.

"My beautiful girl," my grandmother said. "You love this man?"

"I care for him." It was the only answer I wanted to verbalize. Something held me back even though I knew myself and what I felt.

"Caring will not bring him back. He is special."

The words made me look at my grandmother. I was named for her, and she'd been teaching me the work of an archivist. She chose to marry but lost my grandfather young. Her strength had held our family and village together for years, and she had always spoken the truth to me even when I would have been happier not to hear it.

"He is kind, and he listens to me. Would I disappoint you if I told you I love him?"

"I would be disappointed if you lie to me. Tell me if you love him or go out and let me finish."

"I love him," I said softly. At my admission she lifted away the blanket that covered him, and I didn't know how to process what I was looking at. My sweet André, who had encouraged me to give my opinion and who was jealous when he thought I was promised to someone else, was a woman. This man of his god, a warrior for his faith, was no man at all. I fell back on my heels and let go of his hand. How could I have not known?

"He is still the person you love. To say what he is will mean his death at the hands of the infidels he is with. If they do not kill him, your father will call for his head. My son is quick to dismiss what he does not understand, and he is quick to anger. If he sees this as an insult to you, your love will not live out the night."

What my grandmother said was true, but I could not understand what my eyes stared at. "Why are you not calling for the same thing? You approve of me loving André?"

"He is a changeling, and you will tell me his story while we bring him back to the land of the living."

My grandmother worked while I spoke of all the things André had shared with me. I felt it a betrayal of his trust, but my grandmother only nodded as I spoke. "He told me his father raised him to be a sacrifice. I think if he did as he wished, he would go home and be happy in his fields."

"He is a product of the failure of a holy man. His father picked a woman over his god, and the child was proof of his indiscretion. He used that failure to punish what was left behind when the woman died. André was raised to erase his mistake while trying to appease his god. His destiny was supposed to be dying here, but then he met you." My grandmother's words were soft but strong.

"So, you do approve of my love?"

"The men of our village will never make you happy, my little flower. You must give him something to live for. I believe his honor will make him carry out what his father wants, but dying on a battlefield should not be his fate. Give him hope, or bid him farewell and we will watch him die."

My father sent word to the jackals' camp that we would take care of André until he was well. He did not object when my grandmother assigned me to care for André, and I thought I would never be able to ask my questions because of the fever. I worked with my grandmother to cool him. On the third day he finally opened his eyes, and I was lost.

It mattered not that he was not the man I thought. All that mattered was that he had come back to me. *She* had come back to me.

❖

"What?" Zara said with her hands up. "What the hell?"

"I could've gotten some of it wrong, so I might have to go back and make sure I didn't just tell you a story that wasn't true at all," Yasmine said, carefully closing the book. She glanced back at Levi, who had stayed quiet. "What do you think?"

"I think a woman was raised to be a Templar, succeeded in being admitted, and preached the word of God. She gave communion, heard confessions, and acted in accordance with her vows." Levi flattened her hand on her stomach and bit her bottom lip. "I believe that, but something doesn't make sense. This isn't something the Church will be happy to hear, but André couldn't have been the only one. It's not the kind of scandal that you hire thugs to hunt people down for."

"Then what is it?" Yasmine asked.

"It's got to be in the other three books or in the other things we've found so far. We need to figure out what the key is, if there is a code. If Farah spent all that time with André, she knew how to hide things in her writing."

"We're not going to figure it out tonight, so let's go to bed and start again in the morning," Jane said. The books were on the table, but Percy picked them up, as well as the one Yasmine had read from.

"Do you not trust us to move ahead without you?" she asked, joking.

"I trust you with my life, sweetheart, but the bastards who attacked you are another story," Percy said. "It's best we keep everything locked up when it's not in our hands."

Yasmine followed Levi up and kissed Zara good night. She wanted to lie down and absorb what Farah had written. The story was in no way like hers and Levi's, but Farah had possessed the strength to accept the gift of love.

Yasmine smiled when Levi stepped behind her and unzipped the capri pants she'd put on after their time on the beach. They were naked a moment later and in bed. "What do you really believe?" Her head was on Levi's shoulder, and she was so comfortable she hoped not to fall asleep.

"I'm having a hard time wrapping my head around this." Levi yawned and held her tighter.

"You, of all people?" She laughed at that.

"Trust me, finding that André was a woman is like finding a friend, but I've had a picture in my head of who they were. It's going to take a little adjustment to my thinking. That shouldn't take any time at all, since this makes for a much better story. Don't you think?"

"It's like finding us, but with less drama." Yasmine was tired, but the feel of Levi's skin reminded her again of all the things she'd put off for so long. "The other difference is I knew exactly who you were from the very beginning. You made quite the first impression, but I still noticed this gorgeous face." She rose high enough to see Levi. "I wanted to be angry, but you made me crave more."

"It's a good thing. I saw you and tried to find ways to make you want to spend time with me. That night we talked on the phone when I was in Choupick, I felt like I was in high school again, fumbling for the words to make the pretty girl like me." Levi took advantage of her position and cupped Yasmine's breasts. "I like that we got to know each other before we ended up here. Things you build with care and time last forever."

"I love the way you talk to me." Yasmine moved on top of Levi and spent a long while kissing her. "I love the way you make me feel." She bit Levi's lip when she reached between them and touched Yasmine. "And I love you."

"I love you too."

The passion that Levi was able to build in Yasmine was amazing, and the more they made love, the more she wanted.

"I've got you." Levi held her after she came, and she slumped against her, not having the strength to move.

Yasmine slipped into sleep without remembering it and woke when the room was filled with light. It was morning but she didn't want to move. Levi was behind her with her arm around her waist. Waking up like this was better than anything she'd ever experienced. She turned slowly, trying not to wake Levi, and gazed on her face.

"I love you," she said softly, and Levi's mouth twitched. A glance at the clock showed it was early, but it was nice to be able to look at

Levi without any audience. She moved her head closer and shrieked when Levi grabbed her and rolled on top. "You!" She laughed.

"Me, and you are beautiful in the morning."

When they went to the library after breakfast, the books were out. Percy had put the second one aside. This one was longer, and the first part spoke of the time Farah and André spent together as the wound on André's chest healed. The story was woven with the growing love that Farah obviously felt for André.

"She did a good job of describing how it began and how it grew," Yasmine said when she finished the first section. "What do you think of the grandmother?"

"She was a trailblazer," Zara said. "The elder Farah understood what would make her granddaughter happy, and that is a progressive way of thinking even now. Right now, it's innocent flirting and acknowledgment from Farah that she loves André, so we'll see when it becomes something more."

"There has to be something more, much more. If there wasn't, why all this?" Jane asked.

"I might be reading that wrong, but you're right. André was born a girl but never identified that way, so falling for Farah would be natural. She was as much a man as all the ones she traveled with. What I can't figure out is if the men realized who she was. It might account for the teasing Farah mentions that had an undercurrent."

"They would've never allowed her to preach if they knew she was a woman. The Templars didn't always play by the rules, but they were men of faith. Even today, that faith can only be administered by a man." Levi was right, and that went well beyond the Catholic Church. Why men couldn't bring themselves to follow a woman was beyond her, but that was the way of life and had been since the time of Adam and Eve.

"They should allow women to lead the churches and mosques," Zara said. "The men have made a mess of what is supposed to be a beautiful thing. Our mother fusses all the time when it comes to our devotion to Allah, but I've found my own way of praying, and it doesn't have anything to do with our mosque."

"Faith is personal, so however you choose to practice it isn't wrong," Levi said, taking Zara's hand. "We all like to think we're unique, but maybe there have been different versions of us through time. This story sure proves that."

Levi looked into Yasmine's eyes, and she nodded. It was easy to place herself in Farah's place and feel that who she loved wasn't wrong. All it was to her was the universe putting this perfect person in her path and saying *here, I made this one just for you.* That's who Levi was. She was her match, her other half, and all the other things people said when it came to the right person finally coming into their life.

"Maybe it gets better with each new chapter of the story. Theirs and everyone else's."

Levi smiled at her and seemed to act without regard for where they were and who they were with when she leaned down and kissed her. The applause made Yasmine blush, but she held on to Levi and pressed another quick kiss to her lips. Zara winked at her when they came apart, and it made her happy to have someone in their corner.

"It's good you finally got it right, bear," Jane said. "But enough with the mush. Get back to the books. Perhaps by the time you're done, the computer will have something."

"Let's get back to it, then. We need to know what the rest of the story is and where it will lead us."

❖

He is back to full strength, but still he stays close to us. There has been a change in him and he seems nervous around me. A secret as large as the one he has kept would come with all the fear one person could hold. I could not stand to see him suffer another moment, so I asked him to tend the goats with me at dusk. He nodded and we walked the herd to the oasis close to our home. The world felt alive. The grass was green and there were a few trees. He leaned against one and gazed off as he always did, as if his eyes could see into the vastness of our world. Finally, he looked at me, and a small part of that hunger I was used to seeing was back. It was what I was waiting for, and I took his hand and led him deeper into the desert darkness.

"Farah," he said as he stared at our joined hands. "I am sorry I lied to you."

"Did you?" I touched his face. "Are you not André?" I moved my hand to the side of his neck, and he hid those blue eyes from me. "Are you not my friend?"

"But you know the truth of me."

"Yes, and your secret will be safe for always. The truth

does not change how I feel for you." My words made him open his eyes, and I suffered at the tears. "Do not fear me."

"How can you feel the same? My father always said I was an abomination that needed to be cleansed in battle. I was his punishment for what he did, and I have never known love or acceptance."

That brought tears to my eyes. How could such a pure soul believe his god would think him wrong? "You will know it now. I have made my choice, and it is you. My fate was to write the history of our people, but I cannot go on without you." I pulled his head down and kissed him. It was my declaration, one that could not be misunderstood.

"I cannot commit you to a life of lies. You are too precious to me."

"Can you ask me to give up something I want? You have changed my life and brought me out of my loneliness."

I saw the battle in those eyes that haunted my dreams, and he finally lowered his head and kissed me again. It was the start of my life with my love. I loved all the time we spent talking of different things. My grandmother was correct—having someone who not only hears you but sees you as well is a gift. André was that to me, and I loved him. Still now I cannot believe how lucky I am to have found such a special person.

All those wonderful feelings ended the day André told me the morning would mean our separation. Her group was ready to move and start what they said would be the beginning of a new Crusade to bring their god to our lands. I begged André not to go, to stay with me and make a life with me. His father had a stronger pull than I, and he had promised. His sacrifice would wipe away the sins of the father but steal my love from me.

I did all I could do to sear myself into his heart. The morning was so far away, yet so close, and in that little time I gave him my innocence. It was the only way to give him the will to come back to me. When he left me before the dawn, my heart broke as he donned his armor and white tunic. He had taught me the word *Templar*. That was who André was, and I cared not. All I needed was for him to live.

The weeks passed, and with each passing day, I died a

little more. One morning my brother ran to me and led me to the place we had shared our first kiss. There André lay, the tunic torn from his body and blood everywhere. He was alone, hurt, but he had come back to me. My brothers carried him back to my grandmother, and like before, we brought him back from the grasp of death.

"I cannot stay," he said when he was finally able.

"You are safe now. You are home." His fever worried me, but he was so adamant. He had to go because it was not safe.

"I cannot bring you harm. I love you." He reached up with what little strength he had and touched my cheek. "You must send me away to keep you safe."

We went on like that for days until the fever broke and his many wounds started to heal. The story he told me and my grandmother was one of betrayal. His own church had killed the rest of his men. Their battle had been waged against their own, and André was the only survivor who could tell the tale.

It took months for him to heal, and my grandmother oversaw our joining. My father was not sure, but I told him it was my choice. She was my choice. Word came soon after that explained what André was saying. There were men visiting all the tribes looking for the one who got away. The secrets he knew had to die with him.

"I must go," André said.

"You are mine and I am yours. Where you go, I go with you." It was the start of an adventure that would open the world to me only to lead me right back home.

Chapter Twenty

"If this battle happened, there's nothing in the history of the Templars about it," Levi said. "I would have remembered the slaughter of Templars by the Church. Well, aside from what the church did to them."

"There is no mention of it in Arabic history either. The Templars were driven out after the Crusades were over. I can't remember a reference of anyone trying to revive the Crusades the second time around." Yasmine stood and typed in a few things into her laptop. "See, there's no reference to it."

"But there's no reason for Farah to write all this and go through what they did to hide it if it wasn't true," Zara said.

"This was written five years after the end of the Templars as we know them in history. The church as well as the French king executed their plot to kill them off and plunder their banks. I think the reason Farah wrote this was to make sure whatever betrayal started with André didn't end with the two of them." Levi joined Yasmine at the table and motioned for her laptop. "I've looked through the rosters of Templars and never found André Sonnac, but perhaps there is a history of Farah's family."

"I thought of that," Yasmine said. "I'm still looking, but nothing yet."

"The answer of what exactly happened to this troop of Templars has to lie in the vast archives of the Church. Who exactly sent them back to the Holy Land, and why that subterfuge? The problem with that is, if it is damaging, they're never going to share it with us," Jane said.

"That's true, but there might be something else they didn't count on." Levi glanced at the other two books.

"What?" Yasmine asked.

"The bread crumbs Farah has left through time. I'm sure she used her talents as an archivist to pen this story, and André is in there. It was something they did together, and they had sufficient resources to spread the clues far and wide enough that some of those things had to have survived. I doubt I've found every single thing they left behind." Levi pulled up the map of everything she'd found. "For everything we've found about the Templars, and all the insanely vague clues we've already got in hand, there has to be that much more that leads us to the final destination. I just haven't cracked the code to be able to figure out what that might be."

"It could be in here," Yasmine said, pointing to the other two books.

"The rest of their history is in there, but the answer to what she and André are really talking about is in the code. We need to find that." Levi glanced up when an alarm beep sounded. Someone was coming up the drive. "Take it all with you," she said, and everyone in the room picked up something. She was done taking chances.

"What are you doing?" Yasmine asked, holding the books against her chest.

"Let me see who it is, but you need to follow Granny and Grampie." There was no time to argue. "Please, honey. I promise I'll be okay."

"You'd better be. Don't make me have to come after you." Yasmine kissed Levi and followed everyone through the secret passage Jane had opened. Once it was locked from the inside, there was no way someone could open it from the outside.

Levi went to the security monitors and stared at the three cars headed in their direction. She didn't recognize them, and they didn't appear to be local. When they stopped, two men stepped out of the first car. She didn't recognize them either, but she did catch a glimpse of the guns they wore. The driver walked to the heavy oak front door, rang the bell, and held up his credentials to the camera.

"We're here to see Dr. Jane Breeden. We have some information on what happened at her house and with her granddaughter. The director sent us."

The identification said MI6, but she wasn't in a trusting mood. This many agents wouldn't show up to brief someone on a break-in. "Granny, are you expecting company from your former bosses?" She used the house's intercom system.

"How many Land Rovers?"

"Three, and their suits are nice." The men didn't ring the bell again but did appear ready to stand there all day if necessary.

"Give me a moment," Jane said, and was soon in the room with Levi. She quickly made some calls, then said to Levi, "Let them finish this sequence. Echo, Zulu, Lima, Papa."

Levi repeated the words, and the guy who'd spoken glanced up at the camera again. "Charlie, Kilo, Quebec." He followed that with a string of numbers.

"Come with me, bear," Jane said.

"Thank you, ma'am," the tall guy said when they entered the library. "Director Witherspoon wanted us to come and update you on the investigation."

"A phone call would've sufficed," Jane replied.

"Usually that is true, but this was a coordinated attack that still has moving parts. We'd like to set up a perimeter to keep an eye on things. I promise you won't know we're here, but Director Witherspoon insisted. He knows how valuable you are to the agency."

"How many men?" Jane asked.

"We brought six. That should be plenty, since from what we could tell no one knows exactly where you are or what you're doing. They want something but didn't find it at the London home." The other man was all business.

"We flagged some inquiries run by unknown players to see if you've used credit cards. It's the easiest way to track travel."

"If you're a complete imbecile," Jane said. "Set up wherever you like as long as it's not in the house." She escorted them back outside and bolted the door. She made a call, going through different channels until she reached the person she wanted to talk to. "Harrison," she said.

Levi recognized the name. Harrison Witherspoon was the director of MI6. That her grandmother could so easily get him on the phone meant her role in the government was a little more than she'd always alluded to. After reporting about the men outside, Jane was quiet for a bit and then made some notes.

"Find out and let me know. They said you were the one who sent them, and I will practice my shooting if they approach the house again." She sounded peeved. "And have it done before nightfall, please."

"What's this about?" Levi asked once they'd given the others the all clear.

"The team outside is MI6, but they weren't sent by who they said they were. That means they used their position to find us for someone not involved with British Intelligence." Her grandmother walked to the window and glanced out. "I can't know that for sure, but when their boss has no idea why they're here, I can jump to any conclusion I want."

"Do you think they will try and harm us?" Yasmine asked.

"No, but if you want information on someone and what they're doing, they chose the best in the business to do that." Jane tried to sound calm as Percy walked to her and put his arm around her.

"Should we stay or go?" he asked.

"The house is secure," Jane said.

"Is secure enough if they're here and want what we have? We need to figure out how to get out of here without having anyone follow us. These guys just showing up without warning doesn't sit right with me." Levi's mind started whirling.

"I agree with you, and you know the best way to proceed," her grandmother said. "Leaving won't be a problem."

"I do, but I need you to finish this." The answer was for them to split up.

"Bear, there are ways to send information through secure channels. All you need to do is get away clean."

"How exactly do we do that?" Yasmine asked.

"It won't be as hard as you think," Levi said with a quick kiss. "Right now, we need to finish the books before we go. Our best bet is getting you home early for your grandmother's birthday. Morocco is one of my favorite places, and we can work from there with no problem. I have more contacts there than in the boonies of France, and if we fly a little under the radar, we might get a head start."

They took their regular seats and Yasmine opened the third volume. It was another list of words that had no message at all. The book only had three pages of just words and nothing else, like the scroll locked up back home. Considering the story that Farah had started, this didn't make any sense. Levi opened the fourth book. It also contained three pages, only this time in French and in different handwriting.

"André must have had something to add," Levi said, handing it to Yasmine.

"Oui," Yasmine said and laughed. "How do you deal with all these frustrating turns?"

"I try to concentrate on the end of the hunt and how it will be worth it. When someone makes it this hard, it captures my attention. It meant whatever they hid is a true treasure they valued." She framed Yasmine's face and smiled. "It means it was me who was meant to find it and no one else. Then we can share it in the classroom as well as with the world so we can all learn from it. I'm a treasure hunter, honey, but I also have the heart of an academic."

"I believe you."

"Good. Now, start reading."

❖

Written in the year 1312 AD

The battle I had trained for all my life was a lie. We traveled for days to the place where my superiors had been scouting and waited. There was little doubt in my heart that I would be left to rot in this dry, unfamiliar place, but I had given my father my word. The sun streaked the sky in shades of pink, and I thought of nothing but Farah.

The doors of the military compound opened, and I looked to my brothers. It was not the enemy they expected but the soldiers with the pope's colors. The pope's men took swift action and cut us down without thought. My rage at seeing men I had tried to emulate growing up because of their devotion to God kill my brethren was hard to contain. I wielded my sword and tried to send as many of them as I could to the bowels of hell. Every cut sliced away a piece of my soul, and the only thing that kept me from succumbing to death was Farah.

In her eyes I have found my paradise, and unlike God, Farah has faith in me. The Vatican soldiers still alive left me for dead. As night fell, I thought that might be true as the light of the world dimmed and I lay down and waited for the peaceful darkness I knew was coming. After watching the soldiers of the Vicar of Christ kill my Templar brothers, the faith I had devoted my life to was dead. There would be no heavenly hosts to welcome me to the kingdom of God.

When the sun warmed my face, I looked on a new day and knew what my future would be. The ride back to Farah was four days, and I remember nothing after seeing the oasis in the distance. I woke days later and saw her face. If this was heaven, I was glad to be dead.

"You came back to me," she said as she touched my face. She used the words I had taught her, and my world filled with joy at the happiness she brought me. My future with Farah meant following the village and serving our community. We would never have children, but we would have each other, and she tells me that is all she needs.

The dream came to me one night, and the messenger who told me the pope's soldiers were hunting me down. I had never dreamed of her, and I believed what she was saying. The infection of one of my wounds sent me into another fever, and my mother came to me over and over. She said they knew I still lived. I was a voice who could tell who the pope was and what he was capable of. That could never happen.

My wounds finally healed and I left with Farah to travel back to my home. There I would take the information my father kept of the Templars and who we were. Where I would hide this to keep it safe, I did not know, but I cannot see it destroyed. The year I started my return for home was January of 1307. We appeared like every other couple on the road to Avignon. We left the sands behind and rode through the green fields of my youth.

Seeing the world again through Farah's eyes gave me renewed hope for the future. Farah was not only my love but the person who brought me back to life from the death I had been running to. My return home was a time to rejoice for the workers who had worked the land in my absence. I made love to Farah in the home of my ancestors and in the rows of grapes. It was three months of love and happiness until that last day.

The only thing that saved us was the loyalty of the people who loved my family and the land. They brought word that the soldiers were riding hard toward us, giving us time to escape. The death of my Templar brothers was only the beginning of the treachery of the supposed voice of God on earth. Farah and I fled with a few of the families who knew their connection to the Sonnac family would mean their death. Most of the army of God was dead by the time we left France and the pope had declared my family home as belonging to the Church. He had become a puppet of King Philip IV.

I knew what treasures the soldiers sought, and I carry

a part, and three other surviving Templar brothers carry the
rest. We travel until we are far from the church's reach, and
my only prayer now is for the safety of my wife and of the
papers we carry.

For you who reads our words, do what you must. Know,
though, that the Church is full of men capable of great sin,
greed, and evil. The story of my love and what she helped
me to do deserves to be told. Follow us home and shout out
the truth of what happened and of the men who chased us for
no other reason but to kill us to ensure our silence. To find us
you must go through what you already have.

I will fight until the end for Farah and for myself. That
is my belief now. Her and nothing else.

❖

"I think you were wrong," Yasmine said to Levi. "The stories they
wrote are just that—their story. The answer lies in the third book. That
list of words is where the answers are."

"See, Granny, beautiful and smart." Levi's compliments weren't
unexpected, but in a way they were, and Yasmine blushed every single
time. "Put the key words in and let's see what we get."

They all glanced up when the alarm rang again. "They're moving
closer," Zara said, looking at the monitor.

"How thick are these walls?" Yasmine asked. "If they were
listening in, they know what I just read. If those men are working with
the church, we're in trouble. These people are trained to achieve all
their objectives. There's no way we're leaving here without an escort."

"Let's go back inside that room and finish this," Levi whispered
in her ear.

The soft voice and warm breath in Yasmine's ear made her nipples
hard. Her craving for sex was getting ridiculous, but she wouldn't
change a thing.

"Later, honey, I promise."

Yasmine had to laugh at that and pressed herself to Levi's chest,
not wanting to show everyone in the room how turned on she was.
"You're incorrigible," she whispered back.

"But you love me anyway."

"But I love you anyway," Yasmine said, laughing. That proved
she was losing her mind. They were in real danger, but all she could

think about was being alone with Levi, learning what would please Levi most.

"*I* would love you both more if you stopped making out and figured out what to do next. We'll never eat otherwise," Zara said as if she realized she had to watch her words.

Yasmine put in the two words they'd used from the previous scroll and ran it with the new list of words, and they all stood around waiting. *Pierce* and *God* weren't on the new list from what Yasmine could see, and running the program took no time at all. It left only one paragraph, and she had no trouble translating.

"*Follow the path of the devil. Begin where the land falls away to the sand. Find the high point in Zagora and the map of our life will be written in the sand. It will be three cycles of the moon to the trees of life. Look where the shield points to find our secrets. It is where you will find the victory that leads to eternity.*"

Yasmine finished reading the translation, which Levi had written down as she spoke. The notes Levi always took reminded Yasmine of her most eager students, and that enthusiasm was endearing. The clues Farah and André left were not.

"Where the land falls away to the sand has to be the Sahara, if this is anywhere near Zagora," Levi said.

"You do realize the Sahara is like three and a half million square miles? That, my love, is a lot of sand."

"We have to think of the year they wrote this and think like a treasure hunter," Levi said, pointing to her laptop.

"Not here, bear." Jane stopped her from typing anything. "If they are monitoring the house, they can tap into the Wi-Fi and figure out what we're up to. Let's not lead them right to the spot with the big X before we get a chance to see what it is."

"We have the answer to the next step, and hopefully it's the final one that will lead us to our answer. All we have to do is get out of here and find it." Levi unlocked another small compartment in the room and placed the books inside. The copies of what they had would have to do.

"That might be harder than leaving London, no?" she asked as they locked the room again and stepped out into the library.

"Let's finish dinner and we'll talk about it." Levi walked Yasmine and Zara upstairs and whispered for them to get packed. Once they were ready, Percy helped Levi carry everything down to the wine cellar. Jane was already waiting for them and pushed a section of the wall to open another secret door behind a shelf full of wine bottles.

"They don't make houses like this any longer, do they?" Jane turned on the light to the passage that appeared to have been carved out centuries before. "Get going, and don't worry about what you're leaving behind. We'll keep it safe and try our best to join you in a few days once the cavalry arrives."

"Cavalry? You're not coming with us?" Yasmine asked.

"The director is sending in reinforcements to ask these guys some questions. If you take a job with British Intelligence, they expect you to be loyal to the company and only the company. That supersedes any religious beliefs or family matters." Jane opened her arms, and Zara hugged her first. "Take care, my lovely, and keep your sister and my bear in line."

"I'll try my best." Zara held on to to Jane for a long while. "Stay safe. I'll need you to help me get through my next year at Oxford."

"Don't worry, she's an old dog, but she knows every trick in the book," Percy said, hugging Zara next.

It wasn't a long goodbye, but Yasmine felt the separation keenly. They hadn't known each other long, but Jane and Percy had made them feel so welcome that she embraced both of them like Zara had.

"She's a mess of trouble sometimes, but she's the best of all of us," Jane whispered in her ear. "No matter what comes, she loves you. Take good care of each other."

"I will, and I feel the same."

"I know you do, and I'm so glad."

Yasmine and Zara watched Levi load all their luggage into a cart close to the door and then followed her down the passageway. The floor was damp, but the space was roomy enough to walk comfortably in, and the lights overhead made it less gloomy.

"What is this place?" She had her hand in the back of Levi's belt, and Zara walked on the other side of the cart.

"There was never really Prohibition in France, but that didn't mean some folks didn't like to run illegal liquor to make a few dollars. I can't say if anyone in Granny's family ever did, but that's what the tunnel is for. It's also a good way to leave the house without anyone seeing you even if they have a good vantage point on the cliffs." Levi stopped at an ancient-looking door, but the thing still appeared to be solid. The only odd thing about it was the modern lock with a keypad.

"Are we swimming out?" Zara asked.

"I think we're a bit more prepared than that. Pirate alleys are only effective if you can leave via the water." Levi swung the heavy metal gate open and pulled the cart to a concrete dock. There were two fishing boats tied up. "Give me a minute to lock up."

Levi handed both of them raincoats and hats before cranking the motor and maneuvering past the large cliff rocks that jutted out from the ocean floor. They left the cave and headed into open water and sunshine. Their bags were under a canvas, and Yasmine guessed if anyone did see them, they looked like some fishermen going out for the day. Levi followed the coastline until she reached a marina, where an older gentleman loaded their bags onto a large sailboat.

"You sail?" she asked Levi.

"I do. It's the easiest way to get you home without leaving a trail. This thing also has Wi-Fi, so we can work as we go. I promise I'll get you there in one piece. We'll stay close enough to the Spanish coast to avoid rough seas."

Levi guided them out of the harbor. The sails were controlled by a push of a button, so they picked up speed as soon as they were clear. The beauty of the shore made Yasmine almost forget that they were being chased by some crazy people. She stood behind Levi with her arms around her waist as she set their course. Zara, of course, was exploring every inch of the boat, so Yasmine kissed between Levi's shoulder blades.

"How long will it take for us to get there?"

"Since neither of you sail, it'll take about three days. I'll anchor at night so we can get some sleep, but we're fully stocked so we won't need to dock anywhere, which means we don't leave a trail." They stood together for a while before Levi tied off the wheel. "Let's start with the key to everything, which is the clue Farah left us," Levi said, taking out her laptop. She wanted to work but also kept an eye on their path.

"What do you think the first line means?" She brought up the paragraph they'd figured out.

"Follow the path of the devil," Zara said.

"Think the pits of hell," Levi said, and Yasmine stared at her. "Hell, in all the biblical references that's down, so it's another reference for south. I could be wrong, but Ait Benhaddou in Morocco makes me think I'm not."

"So this treasure is buried in Morocco?" She couldn't believe that could be the case. "Crusaders didn't go through Morocco to get to the Holy Land. I wouldn't think it was a logical place to hide something important to them."

"That's the part I couldn't put together, but I think André and her troops were somehow tricked into going a new way. A way that would take them through the Sahara where no one would see them and it would be easy to ambush them. The Church already knew about it, and they started culling some of their most devoted Templars to be slaughtered. They picked a place where no one would see what they were doing. No witnesses means no historical accounts."

"The middle of a Muslim country far from where the Templars were driven out would be a place where no one would care if some of them were killed by their own," Zara said. "They were encouraging them while planning their deaths. What they didn't count on was André surviving. Once the Templars were wiped out, the Church didn't mount any other Crusades in the Holy Land. That would make it a good place to hide something from the Church."

"Exactly," Levi said. "We can't know what the next step is until we get to Ait Benhaddou. It has to be something more than being written in the sand."

"It will be three cycles of the moon to the trees of life. Look where the shield points to find our secrets. It is where you will find the victory that leads to eternity." This part was filled with true Templar references. "Victory and eternity make up the bottom right branch of the tree of life. If we use that as a base, we can follow the rest of the tree of life like a map."

"The answer lies in the tree and in the stars. *Look where the shield points to find our secrets* might be the warrior constellation. The land changes in time, but the heavens do not. A star map makes more sense than putting land references, and just like the tree of life, it's about symbols that lead to understanding. We have to map where the warrior constellation was in 1307 AD." Levi went to type that in when Zara told her she would take care of it.

"Once we have an idea, it could still take months to find wherever it is it could be pointing to," she said to Levi.

"Let's see what we find in Ait Benhaddou, and we'll assess from there." Levi got some binoculars and scanned the water around them.

They seemed to be alone for the most part, but Yasmine was glad Levi was being so careful. "No matter what, you know I'm with you." She sat in the circle of Levi's arms and kissed the side of her neck. Zara had gone down to work on the symbols on the stones, and they were enjoying the sun and calm seas.

"It's always good to have someone who knows the desert better than we do. We need a Berber nomad, and I happen to know one," Levi said, taking out her phone. She glanced at it and reached in her bag for another phone. This one looked like the kind you bought in a box that you bought minutes for. "Ibrahim," Levi said loudly.

The man spoke loud enough for Yasmine to hear, and it sounded like he and Levi were old friends. Whoever he was, he was in Marrakech and owned an antiquities store. She'd heard of the place, but her small apartment had no room for finery.

"When can you be ready to go?" Levi asked. Even though she was on the phone, her hand was trailing up Yasmine's stomach to her breast. "Good. Let's keep it simple. The fewer people who know about this, the better chance you get some new inventory for the store. Or maybe you'll get an audience with the king and he'll pay you in gold for your good deeds." Levi laughed and hung up.

"You can stop that hand from moving any higher. I'm not giving Zara any more ammunition to tease me."

The sun was starting to set, and Levi kissed Yasmine, then got up and checked the GPS to see where they were. They'd gotten a good wind and they were off the coast of Spain when they dropped anchor. Lights were starting to dot the coastline and Levi pointed to a pod of dolphins playing close by. The water looked inviting, but Yasmine wasn't taking her clothes off to jump in with Zara aboard.

They traveled on for another two days down the coast of Portugal, and she recognized the tall minaret to the Hassan II mosque. It was the largest functioning mosque on the African continent and fairly new. It had been built to bring people to the industrial town of Casablanca, which was not the romantic place of Humphrey Bogart and Ingrid Bergman.

"Levi," a man yelled when Levi tied off.

"Omar, right on time, my friend."

"Ibrahim would skin me if I was late. You ready to go? We set you up."

The drive to Marrakech didn't take long with Omar's heavy foot, and Levi gave the Hassani sisters the option of going home first. That was the last thing Yasmine wanted, and Zara said the same. Yasmine had her small apartment, but Zara still lived at home, and neither of them wanted the adventure to end just yet.

"Ibrahim will be by in the morning for tea. He said to meet him by the pool." Omar stayed in the driver's seat as the staff at La Mamounia hotel collected their bags.

Yasmine had only been on the grounds a few times for lunch, but the palace turned hotel was in the medina and not far from the souk. She smiled at the sights of the old city and the noises that made her feel at home. Even so, being with Levi made her feel like she was still in a bubble where she didn't have to face her family or the future.

"Do you need to go by your place and get some clothes or anything?" Levi asked.

"Would you come with me?" Yasmine asked. Zara had gone to her room and announced she would be in the large clawfoot tub until it was time to check out.

The cab ride was short, and she couldn't help but compare her place to Levi's home. "When you see how small my home is compared to yours, I don't fit with you, do I?"

"I doubt you live here because of a lack of money," Levi said, putting down a picture of her family. "And you fit with me better than anyone ever has, no matter where we are."

"Being back here makes everything seem so impossible."

"Remember one thing before you let everything overwhelm you: I love you." Levi made everything seem like it would never be a problem. "Right now, though, we have dinner reservations and a suite with a large bed in it."

"You're a good motivator." There were important things to be dealt with, but for tonight there was dinner and then Levi. A perfect night.

❖

"How is this possible?" Cardinal Richard Chadwick asked as he tried to calm down. His whole career had been a process of meticulous planning to reach the pinnacle he wanted most, and these idiots were about to derail that. "I chose you for this because you're supposed to be the best, and frankly, Ransley, your group has been an utter disappointment."

"You never mentioned how important it was to acquire the scrolls to begin with, Dick," Ransley said.

Ransley only used the nickname he hated when he was pouting. Being called before him like a misbehaving schoolboy had done the trick. "When I give you an assignment, it's important. If I didn't make myself clear on that, remember it going forward."

"They still have to be in the house," said Lawrence Royce, who was leading the British Intelligence team in France. "My men covered every exit, including the beach."

"Have you heard from them again?" Richard said, sighing as he looked at the speakerphone.

"No, but they haven't come out. Jane Breeden didn't reach the rank she had with us by being an idiot, Your Grace. She's smart, and I've already made her suspicious."

He looked away from the phone and motioned toward the door. "Everyone out. Make sure you remember what I said and what your role is in cleaning up this mess." He waited until the room cleared and took it off speakerphone. There was no way he was taking the chance of being overheard. "Do whatever you need to do, but get all the information and bring it to me. Do you understand what I'm saying?"

"This place was a good choice for them to run to. It's a fortress, so getting in isn't going to be easy."

"Lawrence, you know what your life will become once all this is done. Your family's devotion to this cause started way before you and me, but in this generation we will both fulfill our destinies." The cardinal spoke softly, but it was hard to contain his excitement. Lawrence was the only one who knew every step of the plan, and he trusted him implicitly. "Nothing can come to light that would cast our families in a negative light."

"I understand that, but killing a retired but vital part of our organization is not going to be looked on favorably. We will be the first under the microscope. I'll try my best to get you what you want and avoid that option if at all possible."

"I trust you, but remember, you made promises and took an oath. What we're doing is for the good of the Mother Church. If a few must pay with their lives, it's the way of the Lord." He stared at the picture of the pope. He was a cancer to the faith, with his liberal ideas and apologies for the past. He had to go.

"I'll honor my oath and promises, but I'll do it my way."

"For now. Be prepared to admit your mistakes when it doesn't work out."

Chapter Twenty-One

Levi woke with Yasmine plastered against her front. She smiled when she realized her hand was cupping Yasmine's breast and the nipple was rock hard. They didn't have time for a morning of leisure, but she couldn't help running her hand down and spreading Yasmine's legs. Their night had ended in lovemaking, and the more she got of Yasmine, the more she wanted.

"Are you trying to kill me?" Yasmine asked but didn't move Levi's hand.

"You're wet and ready, so stop protesting." Levi ran her fingers from Yasmine's sex to her clit and groaned when Yasmine's ass pressed into her groin. "You do know how to get my attention."

Yasmine reached back and flattened her hand on Levi's ass, pulling her closer. "You are good at that." The way Yasmine was rocking her hips made Levi smile. "You make me feel so good…ooh."

The timing of the insistent knocking on the connecting door was horrible, but Levi doubted Zara would interrupt unless it was important. "Hold that thought," she said, getting up and putting on a robe. "Yes?"

Zara stared at her before standing on tiptoe and looking at her sister over Levi's shoulder. "You might want to get dressed so you can meet our Jadda. I would recommend a shower."

"Jadda?" Levi turned around and gazed at Yasmine.

"Our grandmother. She's in the garden restaurant waiting," Zara said and left.

"Should I wait here?" Levi asked.

"No, I'm not going to hide you away. If I do that, this isn't going to work." Yasmine smiled and accepted her help out of bed. "She could've given us another twenty minutes, but I'm excited for you to meet her."

They got dressed and walked down. "How did she know you were here?"

"I called her in case someone in the medina saw us. She's a remarkable person, and I think you'll like her." Yasmine stopped when they reached the door to the restaurant and put her arms around Levi. "I owe her so much."

"She's helped raise two incredible granddaughters."

"I love you."

"I love you too. Now, let me go make a good impression." Levi stepped through and saw Zara sitting at a table with an attractive older woman with sharp eyes and ramrod posture. She took a breath, sure this was the first step in her quest to win over Yasmine's family. Her palms were sweaty, and she almost laughed at the butterflies in her stomach.

The older woman embraced Yasmine and shook Levi's hand. They didn't talk of many things of consequence while they ate, but they did mention their upcoming trip down to the desert, and Yasmine's grandmother seemed interested. Once the dishes were cleared, she asked Levi to take her for a walk around the lavish gardens. Yasmine and Zara appeared a little apprehensive, but Levi offered her arm and Habiba Alami didn't hesitate in taking it.

"My daughter doesn't know her children are back, and it saddens me that the girls aren't close to her. Then again, she isn't close to me, which makes me wonder where she came from." Habiba laughed, and Levi joined her. "I'm not going to tell her I came here today, but I wanted to meet this person who has brought my Yasmine to life in here." She pressed her hand over Levi's heart.

"She's a special woman." She was afraid to say anything else.

"She's not a pet you're thinking of adopting." Habiba led her to a bench and yanked her down. "Yasmine is getting ready to head to the desert for you, and I'm sure Zara won't be far behind. Make sure you take care of them. If you're not back for my birthday, know I already received the best gift. Keep it that way."

"I give you my word, ma'am."

"Call me Jadda, and you're going to have to walk me back. I get so turned around in here."

It was a bizarre way to spend the morning since Yasmine had been so apprehensive about it from their first kiss, but Habiba was as open-minded as Levi's own family. It wasn't at all what she'd been expecting, and she looked forward to seeing Habiba again. Levi walked

Habiba back, then went to meet Ibrahim by the pool. The businessman spent most of his time in his store, but as a younger man, he'd been out finding the merchandise he sold. He was one of her favorite people outside her family.

"Levi," Ibrahim said, standing and hugging her.

"Hello, old friend." They talked about their families and the finds Levi had made since they last saw each other. By the time they were done, only the staff remained, and their conversation could stay private.

"We need a stop in Ait Benhaddou first. Depending on what we find, we'll take it from there."

"How long?"

"Let's count on two weeks to start and reassess from there. I'm not sure where we're going yet, so I can't be certain." She saw Yasmine walking toward them and noticed how Ibrahim was staring at her. "Stop drooling and let me introduce you."

Yasmine smiled at Ibrahim's subtle flirting, but he was harmless. "Getting to the highest point in Ait Benhaddou is going to be a problem."

"There are ways around every problem, Doctor. Leave that to me and Levi, and we'll get your answers." Ibrahim hugged Levi again and kissed Yasmine's hand before he left with a promise to call with the final plans.

"My Jadda likes you."

"I like her too, but not as much as I love her granddaughter. Let's take her to lunch if she has time, and then we have to pack to go. Our adventure awaits."

"I can't wait, but I've already found what's most valuable to me."

"I love you, and I can't wait to share this with you." Levi had loved the chase from the first time her family had included her. The excitement of hunting down clues and trekking through different terrain had been like her drug, but this time, having Yasmine with her made all her other excursions pale in comparison. Finally, she'd found the woman who shared her passion not only for life, but for what she did.

❖

Yasmine put her hair in a ponytail as Levi held their bags, waiting patiently. They'd both packed light so they could carry all the research materials they'd need. Zara had called to say she'd be ready in ten minutes, but Levi assured her she wasn't in a rush. They'd spent the day with Jadda. Levi had a talent for winning over the women who were important to Yasmine. Her mother wasn't going to be so easy, but she wasn't worried about that now.

"Did you bring something to read?" Yasmine had taken a few trips into the Sahara. It was a long journey from Marrakech because of the Atlas Mountains. "We'll be in the car for a while."

"Maybe later on we'll take the long, scenic route, but I'm not in the mood for that today." Levi dropped the bags when Yasmine put her arms around her neck and pulled her down. "Ibrahim isn't a fan of long drives either."

"Okay, I'll grill you for answers later, but Zara should be ready to go by now." A porter collected the rest of their luggage to store until they came back. Ibrahim was outside with his man, Omar. Two more guys waited in large vehicles with Ibrahim's company logo on the doors.

They drove to a small airport north of town. Ibrahim assured them there was a safe place to land twenty miles outside of Ouarzazate and that it would be a lot harder for anyone to follow them in the sky. The women took off with Ibrahim, and the others would meet them where they'd be making camp for the night.

Yasmine squeezed Levi's arm when the pilot finally circled and informed them they were getting ready to land. There was no runway, just miles of nothing below them.

"I've never done this before," she said as Levi kissed her temple.

"I promise I'll take care of you. Your grandmother will take a belt to me if something happens to either of you."

The landing was bouncy and unpleasant, and Yasmine was glad to get off the plane as quickly as possible. A man in traditional desert clothing awaited them, and he gave them time to put on their head wraps as protection against blowing sand. He drove them through Ouarzazate, the ancient city right outside Ait Benhaddou. It was a beautiful place, popular with tourists, but the wild wind had cut the usual number of visitors. The city, nestled against a hillside, was made completely of red mud bricks and surrounded by the traditional wall, which dated back to the eleventh century, though all its treasures were taken eons ago.

"We have to go to the highest point," Levi said, shouldering the backpack with all their materials in it. She motioned toward the pale stone bluff with a small building of some kind at the top that overlooked the city.

Yasmine led them through the gates. Places like this always made her feel in her heart the history she taught. Walking where people had lived and died for centuries always came with a thrill. It took the group an hour of constant weaving up the tight streets to make it to what had been a watchtower.

"The worker at the gate said he left the door unlocked," Ibrahim said.

They went in, and Levi produced a flashlight to study the space. There was nothing on the walls or ceiling, but Yasmine hadn't expected there to be. A lot of time had passed since the 1300s. Whatever clue had been there was likely now just a memory, like the people they were chasing. "It couldn't be something they left on the floor, right?" she asked.

"We're getting close to the desert, but we're not quite there," Levi said, wandering to the window. "André had to pick something that would last no matter the years, but this time I think she took a lesson from Farah."

"What do you mean?" Yasmine peered out at the vastness before them and saw only a few people and a herd of camels.

"Nothing that could be left in this space would last, but the Berbers have been traveling this area for years. You don't memorize that many miles of sameness without learning some landmarks that would last longer than even the sand." Levi gestured and Yasmine looked again. "Does anything out there seem familiar?"

"Damn," Zara said, tugging on Levi's backpack.

Yasmine stared but didn't see anything—not until Zara pulled out the picture of the stones and Levi laid it on the windowsill. Yasmine gasped. The symbols weren't some strange language but a map that would only make sense from this vantage point.

"It still doesn't fit with the rest of what they wrote, and where I think Farah was from. The rest of the description has to do with the desert, not a town where whatever they hid would've been easily found." Yasmine kept glancing from the picture to the view.

"It's not here," Levi said, taking a Sharpie from her pack. She traced on the picture everything she could find outside that matched. Zara pointed out a few more things, and between them they matched almost everything on the stones with something outside. "It's here," Levi said, pointing to the symbols she hadn't found.

"They still don't mean anything to us…" Yasmine stopped talking as something occurred to her. "Wait." She took the pen from Levi and melded some of the symbols together. "In a land divided by Muslims and Christians, you had to find something neither of them would understand easily. They hid their treasure here but left some of the clues in a new world that embraced a Christian God in an old language."

"So, as a way to keep the secret, you write it in Hebrew," Levi said, and Zara slapped the side of her head.

"Why didn't I see that? I've been staring at those forever."

"The only way to know which symbols mattered and which didn't was to stand here and line it up. What isn't part of the map is Hebrew, but you couldn't have seen it without standing in this exact spot and understanding how the constellation fit with the landscape. It's genius," Yasmine said. She was happy to finally have found something that would help.

"How's your Hebrew?" Levi asked, putting her arm around her.

"Probably as good as yours. That's what Google is for, though, so give me a minute." She accepted the burner phone from Levi and used a translation app. "We'll have to confirm, but I think these are the directions."

"What does it say, specifically?" Zara asked.

"Follow the warrior to the southeast until the road gives way to the sand and the moon is highest in the sky. Travel for two cycles of the moon in the season of winter. You will find what you seek only after you find the gates that will lead you to the branches that define life."
Yasmine finished and glanced up at Levi. "I love you," she said softly. "But I have to tell you, if all our searches have these kinds of clues, this job will be downright aggravating."

Levi laughed and squeezed her hip. "They seem cryptic, but once you figure it out like we did today, it's not that difficult. I think André and Farah didn't take into account the age of technology. It's not like they could anticipate Google."

"This also means you're the luckiest person alive," Zara said. "If you'd missed one clue along the way, we wouldn't be here."

"It's better to be lucky than good, but I'm blessed to be both." Levi blew on her nails and buffed them on her shirt.

"I'd say you were letting your ego get away from you, but that's totally true," Yasmine said and laughed when Levi blushed. "I also believe that they had to come back here once they buried whatever it was to make the map as accurate as possible. Our problem is that there are no gates anywhere in the Sahara. There are pyramids and other ruins, but no gates."

"It's time to go." Levi led them down and stopped in one of the narrow alleyways of what had to be the old souk.

"What?" Yasmine tightened her grip on Levi's hand and put her other hand on Zara's shoulder.

"I'm not sure," Levi said, looking in every direction. "Ever get the feeling someone's watching you?"

Ibrahim walked a ten-foot circle around them and shook his head. "I don't see anything," he said.

"Are we ready to go?" Levi started walking again. This time she seemed more vigilant.

"Our camp should be ready. Your guests have arrived, so the research end should be much easier." Ibrahim opened the plane door for them and flinched at the lightning that didn't look that far off.

The plane flew low enough for Yasmine to see the details of the few towns they passed, along with the Tafilalt oasis, which stretched for over thirty miles, the largest oasis in Morocco. She had good memories of playing in the palm groves as a child when her great grandmother was alive.

They landed in a small town located where the road gave way to the sand. Ibrahim's men were waiting with more four-wheel-drive SUVs. The ride to the camp took four hours, but the satellite phones in each car allowed them to get online while they traveled.

"We plotted the position of the warrior constellation back when they would've made this trip," Levi said, bringing up the map she'd started to plot. "It's only slightly off from where it is now, and it brings us to this area if you pinpoint where the shield is pointing." Levi pointed to a spot way south of them.

"The addition of the gates and the branches of the tree of life make this more difficult. I'm not a frequent visitor to the Sahara, but I can tell you there are oases in certain spots, but it's mostly sand. Nothing else." Yasmine took Zara's laptop and did a search for Sahara gates. "See, all the gates you find are for tourists to take pictures in front of, and they're in the small towns on the way out here. Once you're in the desert, it's nothing but sand."

"Ibrahim, did you bring all the boxes I asked for?" Levi asked, and he nodded. "I don't think a gate the magnitude of the pyramids is what it means, but there had to be something the nomads left behind. There's no way to be sure, but it's likely they had a winter spot and then they moved on. Wherever that was, it had to have water. For all we know those spots are still being used, but the gate is only the first part. The branches of the tree are what worry me."

"We'll have to wait and see, but I'm not sure how you narrow it down from over three million square miles." Yasmine braced herself against Levi when they hit a patch of rocky ground. The large dunes everyone thought of as the Sahara didn't come for another fifty miles or so.

"This is your first time, but I'll make a treasure hunter out of you yet," Levi said and put all her stuff away. It had been an early morning, so she put her head back and closed her eyes.

"And I might make a professor out of you," Yasmine replied, putting her head on Levi's shoulder. "We'll find a balance."

❖

Graham stared out the window of the plane following the same route Montbard and the Hassani sisters had taken. His team at the hotel had done a good job, replacing the women's pilot and gaining access to their flight plans.

"What do you think she's searching for?" Wallace Sterling asked.

Graham had spoken to Cristian again, and they'd agreed to heed Bartholomew's advice to have someone else help him. Wallace had experience with this kind of thing, and he'd come from a military background. If this turned ugly, Graham knew Wallace could handle it. Now the muscle was covered, so he had to use his wits to get them the rest of the way.

"I don't really know, but it's worrying Cardinal Chadwick. Baggio Brutos is Opus Dei and works as a fixer for Chadwick when it comes to information. From the time he took his vows, Chadwick has been on a mission to bury and destroy any antiquities that would put the Church in a negative light. At first I didn't think anything of it since the Church has done that from the beginning of time, but this is a driven narrow-mindedness that makes you think there's something off."

The sun was starting to set, and Graham wanted to be on the ground before it was dark. He'd never been to Morocco or the desert, so traveling at night was something he wanted to avoid. No matter how hard you tried not to, you missed things in the dark.

"Baggio is a bastard. I've crossed paths with him before, and he's vicious." Wallace pointed out the window and Graham saw a small strip. "Whatever Brutos's men took from the house in London, it's sent him off in a different direction."

"Chadwick's not going to give up that easily. No dead end will put him off forever."

The plane touched down smoothly, and the pilot pointed to a man waiting in the hangar. "Montbard must've found something big if Chadwick has called out all his operatives. Those guys from MI6 handle very little for him, but they come when called."

"We've been looking for proof positive of the end of the Templars, and not just what the Church has told us. The pope has always been known as the architect of their demise, but Clement V was led to what happened. Everyone accepted that the blame lay with him and the king, but Cristian and I have always thought there was more to it than that." The waiting vehicle had two men in the front and plenty of equipment in the back. "I don't want to get my hopes up, but I think Levi found something that has to do with that."

"It shouldn't matter in this day and age," Wallace said.

"It shouldn't, but people have long memories. Think of Pope Benedict. His decision to step down had nothing to do with his past, but some people never forgave him the stain the Nazis put on him. Some things carry a permanent stigma, and uncovering something that fascinates people even today will not be tolerated by some in the Church." He slipped off the new boots he'd purchased for this trip and stretched his toes.

"We'll make sure if it's there, it will come out."

"It's our sacred duty." He placed his hand over his heart and took a deep breath. "Our world flourishes when the truth comes out into the light."

CHAPTER TWENTY-TWO

"P apa," Levi said when she saw Cristobal sitting around the fire at the center of the tents they'd erected. "How was your trip?"

"Your grandmother loved it. She and your parents are back at the hotel keeping an eye on things and waiting for Percy and Jane to arrive. I'm the advance team." He hugged her, then Yasmine and Zara. "Thank God we're here, look at you." Her grandfather touched her face where the bruising was the most pronounced. "Tell me everything."

Yasmine caught him up on what she'd translated and what had happened to the group. "Today we solved another piece by figuring out the stones. All those strange symbols were actually a map, except for the last part."

"Hmm," he said when Yasmine read the message the stones held. "Our best bet is to let Jane run that. It might narrow down the places we have to search."

"I'm sending it to her tonight. There's no reason for them to come all the way out here, but they can serve as our research team in the land of internet." Levi thanked one of the men when he handed her a plate.

"If Percy misses finding anything, he'll never forgive you. Besides, we're a family, and we'll be better off together. How often do you get to have a family reunion in such lovely surroundings?"

His outlook on life always made her smile. "Okay, but let's get some sleep after we eat. Knowing that group, they'll be here at sunrise."

The tents were clustered together, but not too close to not give some privacy. Two were closer together than the others, and Ibrahim pointed in that direction. "For you and the sisters."

"Good night." Zara kissed both their cheeks and headed for the smaller tent.

Levi and Yasmine's tent had a blow-up mattress covered in

blankets on the floor, a basin for washing up, and a small folding table to sit at. This wasn't the glamping experience most tourists got on desert excursions, but it would be comfortable for as long as they had to be out here. Levi dimmed the lantern and stepped behind Yasmine. It had been a long day of travel and having to keep her hands to herself, so she was glad that was over.

Yasmine leaned back against Levi, took her hands, and placed them on her breasts. "When I was on my own and most of my friends were falling in love and marrying, I always wondered what was wrong with me. There's never been anyone I could imagine myself with and loving until the end of my life." Yasmine's breath quickened when Levi squeezed. "Having that person touch me, kiss me, and love me was a foreign concept, and I thought I'd have to settle. That filled me with dread more than anything."

"Why?" Levi asked as Yasmine unbuttoned her shirt.

"I didn't relish the thought of having someone touch me when I didn't want it. My mother always told me that was just part of being a good wife." Yasmine turned around. The white lace of her bra was sexy against her dark skin, and it made Levi crave seeing her naked. "I always felt it was so archaic."

"It is," she said, lowering her head and kissing Yasmine. "You are a desirable woman, but your body and your mind belong solely to you. Don't ever compromise that to please anyone else."

"I won't, but now I know my heart belongs to you." Yasmine's nipples puckered hard in the cold night air. The temperature in the Sahara swung from one end of the thermometer to the other, and the nights were freezing. "Take me to bed."

Levi hurriedly got undressed and slipped in beside Yasmine. She'd never loved touching anyone as much as she loved touching Yasmine, and bringing her pleasure was a clawing need. Love had softened things inside her, but in a way had made her stronger. Her vow to Yasmine was to protect her, but more importantly to be worthy of the privilege of making love to her.

"Are you tired?" Yasmine's question made Levi roll over and face her.

"No," she said, thinking it was the right answer.

"I need to talk to you."

Yasmine sounded so serious, Levi rolled onto her back and tensed. "Don't do that."

"What?" There was still that fear right under the surface that she was walking on a bed of eggshells wearing work boots. It didn't matter how she felt, losing Yasmine always seemed a conversation away.

"You always act like I'm about to hit you with something dire. I love you, and you need to start believing that." Yasmine pressed her palm against Levi's cheek. "There is no one I want more than you, and I want this to work. All I want to hear is that you're okay with everything—all of what we've become. Once I tell my family about us, I'm not going to be welcome here. At least, my mother will make it seem that way."

"If I thought you'd say yes, I'd have proposed by now."

"I fell in love with a romantic. I hope you do better than that if it comes to a proposal, so start planning. You'll be happy with the answer." Yasmine went back to the position she'd been in with her head on Levi's shoulder. "I wanted to talk to you about what happens next."

"In what context?"

"Your family will be here in the morning and we'll try and find what you've been chasing. Then what?" Yasmine didn't lift her head, and her voice was starting to fade.

"My family will be here tomorrow, and we *will* find what's out there, then it's easy." She moved again so she could see Yasmine's face. "We'll live where you want. I can do this job from any location in the world. And then, one day, after a romantic night, I'll put a ring on your finger, and then we'll make a life we'll be proud of."

"It's that easy?" Yasmine clearly needed convincing.

"Being happy isn't hard, my love. If here isn't an option, maybe you'll consider England. That way you'll be close to Zara."

"Zara needs to be set free to fly on her own. I want to try New Orleans." Yasmine pulled Levi closer.

"Home is where you are, my love."

❖

Yasmine watched Levi welcome her parents and grandparents. It was wonderful that they included her and Zara in their circle. She'd woken up too early that morning and found Levi already working, but she put it all down when she saw Yasmine open her eyes. That had made her feel like the center of Levi's world, and it almost made her cry again.

Yasmine joined the others at the fire circle, where they enjoyed an early-morning cup of tea.

"Are you feeling okay?" Madelena asked her.

"We've been through plenty lately, and I feel bad that Levi has taken the brunt of things, but I've never had so much fun."

"That's a good attitude to have when it comes to my kid. She's the best person I know, but that doesn't mean she can't drive you crazy." Madelena winked and they both laughed just as Levi called them over to one of the tents.

"I thought about all the clues we've found, and I don't think there's anything else to find. If we can't decipher what we have, it'll be lost forever. I think the clue from that window might have had two meanings, and we need to decide which one is correct." Levi put her arm around Yasmine's waist and held her tightly against her. "*Follow the warrior to the southeast* could be the constellation, or it could be André herself. This is the first time in any clue that she mentions a season."

"What does that have to do with anything?" Zara asked.

"*Travel for two cycles of the moon in the season of winter.*" Levi recited the line from memory. "Think about what she'd said when she headed into battle only to find the Vatican's troops waiting to kill them. That was followed by the death of the Templars en masse when the pope issued the order to eliminate them."

"André turned her back on the Church," Yasmine said.

"I think she did, so she used something else to hide the true location, and the warrior constellation holds the answer. Some people also refer to that constellation as Hercules. What meaning did winter have for the Greeks?"

"They worshipped Poseidon at the winter festival," Madelena said.

"Yes, but there's no constellation that honors him. He did put two people in the heavens, though. One of them, Cassiopeia, stands for the vanity of the Church. If you add her constellation to the warrior constellation in the winter in the early 1300s, it gives coordinates."

"No way," Zara said, and everyone laughed.

"When you're looking for something like this, you need to take a few liberties, and mix it with imagination," Levi said. "With today's technology, you could hide something, and even leaving clues, it'll probably never be found unless someone stumbles over it. Back then they were limited as to what clues they left, but even with those limitations, I think they did pretty good."

"So where do those coordinates take us?" Zara asked.

"If you put the constellations and general direction they mention along with the season," Levi brought them to a map unfurled on the small table, "this is the spot."

There was nothing special about it. It was the same open vastness of sand as the rest of the Sahara. "It's not far from where we are now. Good job on picking the campsite, darling."

"I figured it had to be close to water." Levi circled a spot with her finger, looking as excited as a little kid. "It's nothing but a dry, hard bed now, but it was a huge lake at one time. This would be a good location for a winter home, then they moved with the water as the summer months came along."

"So this spot would've been their winter home?" Zara asked.

"Yes, and it also protected them from any hostiles by having these bluffs behind them." The sun was over the dunes when Levi finished explaining, and the men with Ibrahim started tearing the camp down. "Let's have breakfast and move out. We've got about another five hours of travel today, but if we leave early enough, we can do a bit of exploration today."

They traveled pretty much as before, Yasmine leaning against a sleeping Levi as Zara alternately dozed and read a book. The scenery was monotonous, but even in all that sameness there was beauty. Places like this always made Yasmine think of her place in the world, and of those who had come before her. Every inch of the world was filled with history, and for once she felt a part of it.

She smiled when she felt Levi's hand going in a direction it had no business going in a crowded car. The low chuckle behind her made her warm, but she pinched the top of Levi's hand to send a message. Levi responded by threading their fingers together and not moving. They both fell asleep again until Ibrahim announced they were close.

The only sign of life was a herd of wild donkeys. They roamed free but were captured for short periods of time to move the nomads still living in the desert. Yasmine closed her eyes and tried to imagine this area much greener, full of water, surrounded by the large dunes. Their driver headed for the cliff-like rocks that lined the backdrop like red sentinels.

"Are we close to the coordinates you found?" Yasmine asked Levi.

Ibrahim held up his GPS unit and pointed to the spot where the rocks gave way to open desert. "Just over there," he said as the driver turned slightly. "We'll set up the camp away from there, but close enough to explore on foot."

"Drop us off at the end," Levi said. "We'll do a little scouting on our walk to the camp."

They put on their turbans to help with the blowing sand. Levi looked sexy in the blue a lot of the Berber men wore. They studied the area, trying to find a glimpse of what André and Farah had written about. When the rest of the family joined them, they spread out. Zara walked along the rock formations with Cristobal and Diana. Yasmine and Levi made their way around the rocks to see what was on the other side, but the damn things had to be two miles in width and there wasn't going to be enough sunlight for them to make it.

"Tomorrow, darling. Stumbling around in the dark isn't safe." Yasmine put her hands on Levi's hips and stopped her from taking another step.

Levi kept her eyes on the curve of the rock. "Tomorrow we'll take the four-wheeler and drive this. We're in the right spot, I can feel it, but ancient coordinates aren't an exact science."

After the evening meal, they said their good nights and walked to the tent they'd used the night before, only now Zara would be sharing it with them.

Yasmine enjoyed Levi holding her as they fell asleep and the way she kissed her when they heard Zara's steady breathing. "Tomorrow, my love," she said softly. "You'll finally get the answers you want. We'll know what they worked so hard to hide and why it was so important to them."

"Tomorrow means giving André and Farah what they wanted. To be remembered and to share their secret with the world."

"I love you, and I love the way you are with me." She fell asleep smiling, knowing that she was Levi's treasure.

CHAPTER TWENTY-THREE

The sunrise was beautiful as it came over the dunes, and the skin on the back of Levi's neck prickled. It was always the same when she was this close to whatever she was searching for. Adrenaline rushed through her, making her hyperaware of her surroundings. The answers she'd chased for years and had thought were unattainable were here. She just knew it.

"Where do you want to start?" her father asked. They were the only ones up, and they were having coffee while they waited for full daylight.

"I want to check the other side of this range." She pointed to the red rock wall behind them. "There's nothing on the face that makes me think it's here. We have to check, but if I'm right we'll have to move the camp about two miles that way."

"I'll take Dad and Ibrahim and check along the rock wall front while you take everyone around the side with you. We have the radios if we find something."

Levi smiled when Yasmine came out and sat close to her. "Good morning," she said.

"It is. I haven't had a chance to say how happy I am to see you both together." Renaud's words heated Yasmine's face.

"Thank you," she said softly.

"I don't want to embarrass you, but I'm happy you'll be joining our family. As a parent, all you want is for your children to be happy. My child is happy, so I'm a happy dad."

"Thank you, sir." Yasmine pressed closer to Levi and took her hand.

"Please, sir seems so formal. I'm Renaud to you and Zara. Our family doesn't stand on formality." He touched Yasmine's shoulder before heading back to his tent.

"You okay?" Levi realized the acceptance of something Yasmine had been taught was never acceptable must've been mind-boggling. "My dad is a touchy-feely kind of guy, and he has no filter."

"Your family is wonderful." Yasmine tilted her head so it rested against Levi's. "I'm a bit slow on handling all this, but I'm not going anywhere without you."

"Good, and the same goes for me." Levi kissed Yasmine's temple and squeezed her fingers. "Right now, get ready to do a bit of exploring."

They had a small breakfast and then broke up into teams with Renaud, Cristobal, Zara, and Ibrahim heading along the rocks. Everyone else rode with her and Yasmine to the end of the rock formations. Levi kept an eye on the range as they drove along slowly. They were almost to the end when she saw it—an outcropping of rock that formed a natural arch.

"The gates that lead to the branches of the tree of life." She got out of the car and walked to the rocks with Yasmine at her side.

"That's solid, love," Yasmine said. "There's no way to walk through."

"Damn, why are these things never easy?" Levi stared at it, hoping something would come to her. Two shots rang out, and chips of rock from where the bullet hit the bluff beside her cut through her cheek. She reacted by pushing Yasmine down and covering her, but she wasn't fast enough to avoid the second bullet, which slammed into her shoulder.

"Levi!"

She heard her mother scream, but the punch of pain to her shoulder made it hard to say anything. Her mom and grandmothers were hiding behind the car. She could only pray that the other group was safe too.

"Stay down," she said, as loud as she could manage. Yasmine was under Levi, crying, but she couldn't risk moving. "Are you okay?" She had to force the words out since the pain was starting to make her woozy.

"I'm fine," Yasmine said, trying to turn.

"Stay down." Levi tried to control her breathing, hoping the pain would lessen, but nothing was working. Her shirt was soaked with blood. "I don't want you hurt."

"Levi, please," Yasmine said through her tears. "I can't lose you."

Levi hoped the two short rock outcroppings would provide enough cover. "And I can't let anything happen to you."

"What do we do?" Yasmine sounded frantic. "Please, love."

Levi rolled off Yasmine and onto her back, and the pain almost made her pass out. She took more deep breaths and reached for her radio. "Dad," she said as she kept her hand on Yasmine to keep her down. "Take cover."

"We're stuck in a natural void in the rocks. Who the hell are these people?"

Yasmine took the radio from her. "Is anyone hurt?"

"No, but we can't move without exposure. Don't worry, Zara is fine."

"Levi got hit, and we need to find a way to get her out of here." Yasmine's tears were a steady stream.

"Levi, you still with us?" Jane yelled. "Yasmine, try and put pressure on that wound."

Yasmine took her headdress off and pressed it to Levi's shoulder. "Don't you dare leave me," she said, reaching for her phone and checking the screen. "One bar." Yasmine punched in a number. "Put me through to him now. I don't care who he's with or what he's doing."

"Who are you calling?" Levi had an idea but doubted Nabil Talbi would drop everything and come to their rescue. Yasmine spoke in rapid Arabic, raising both the pitch and the volume of her voice. If Levi had to guess, she'd say this was the first time in her life Yasmine had done that with anyone, let alone Nabil.

"We will be fine," Yasmine said when she hung up.

"I know I said I'd plan something romantic, but I want to ask you something," Levi said as the pain started to ebb. That probably meant she didn't have much time before everything would fade to blackness.

"What?" Yasmine wiped at her face, trying to clear the tears.

"After meeting you, I know what paradise is. Now I can't imagine living without it. Will you marry me?" Levi tried to think up a list of reasons why Yasmine should spend her life with her, but she didn't have the strength. "Will you?"

Then her world went black. Her hunt was over.

❖

Lawrence Royce looked through his binoculars trying to find the target. The priest had scored a hit with his second effort, but it was in no way a killing blow. In the end, the collar he wore meant something even when he said it didn't. The only cold-hearted bastard of the cloth who didn't put a lot of stock in life was Chadwick, who insisted that killing to get what he wanted was acceptable in the eyes of the Lord.

"We'll have to move," Royce said into the radio. His true team consisted of three other men, plenty to handle this group of civilians. "Do any of you have a shot?"

"They're all out of range. Give us forty and we'll scale down the wall. There's no chance of return fire," his agent said, and Royce settled in to wait.

"Why are you really here?" Royce asked the priest after two hours had passed. It was starting to get hot, but he figured it was part of his penance for listening to anything Chadwick said. Their families had been connected for years, and on his deathbed, Royce's father had made him promise he'd keep up their service. "Don't lie or I'll stab you through the neck and leave you here to rot."

"I want to serve the cardinal and make sure the Church is kept safe. Anything that could be dug up here serves no function to our future." The man was young and impressionable, and it was easy to see why Chadwick had picked him. "I'll be rewarded in this life and the next."

"Keep telling yourself that, kid. Aiming a gun at someone with the intent to kill is a sin that'll buy you the fires of hell no matter the reason. Some of us know that, but we're still willing to make that sacrifice." He laughed at the expression of shock, but he had very little patience for fanaticism.

"You know nothing of faith."

"True, but neither do you." He laughed again, then stopped when the sound of two shots in rapid succession cut through the wind. He brought his scope to his eye again—nothing had changed. He quickly radioed his men. "What was that?" He waited, but there was nothing. "Come in," he said loudly. "Fuck."

"What's happening?" the priest asked.

"Shut up." There was a sound on the wind that shouldn't be there. Before he could pinpoint it, the priest's head exploded. Royce had the inane thought of where the priest found himself now that death had come so quickly and violently. "Move," he said into the radio, but there was still no answer.

Before he could take better cover, a bullet ripped through his knee, and he let out a scream. He bit his lip and tried to take his mind off the pain like he'd been trained to do. As he started to crawl away, another shot stopped him cold. With his last thought, he cursed Chadwick for his selfishness.

❖

"What kind of friends are you making?" Nabil asked, looking at the bodies on the ground.

Yasmine glanced up. She was afraid to take her eyes off Levi lest she take her last breath. "You have to help her." She pressed her forehead to Levi's and kissed her lips. "Please."

Nabil motioned for his men, who ran over with a stretcher. "Go with her and I'll take care of the rest of these people. To help things along, I'll pretend you were out here on a holiday." He crouched next to Yasmine and touched her cheek. "This is the one?"

"Yes. Thank you." She watched as they carefully picked Levi up, and laid her on the stretcher, injected something into her arm, and started an IV. Nabil had even come with a doctor. "I'm sorry if that disappoints you."

"You are special to me, Yasmine, and nothing can make me disappointed in you. I'm just glad I can finally pay you back for all the things you've done for me. You still have more favors to call in whenever you need me." He helped her to her feet and pointed to the helicopter. "Go, and I promise everyone will be okay."

She hugged Nabil and kissed his cheek, and as she turned to go, saw two men hanging limply from the ropes they'd been using to scale down the cliffs. That these men had come to kill them still made no sense to her.

Levi's family, along with Zara, had gathered and now watched from a distance. As the helicopter lifted off, Renaud waved. Yasmine waved back. "Levi, don't you dare leave me," she whispered into Levi's ear and ignored the disapproving look she got from the medic monitoring Levi. The man turned his attention elsewhere when the doctor quietly spoke to him.

When they landed, the hospital staff in Marrakech transferred Levi to a gurney and ran off with her. It was like watching her heart being wheeled away.

"Come, and I'll sit with you." The doctor was a kind man with a soothing voice. "It's a serious wound, but she's going to be fine. Is there anyone I can call for you?"

"I'll do it, but thank you." She called her grandmother first and then her mother. When the first thing out of Fatima's mouth was a lecture about her and Zara being back in the city without telling her, Yasmine hung up. It wasn't long before her grandmother showed up and allowed her to cry on her shoulder. "Jadda, I can't lose her."

"I doubt Levi would give up so easily, my love. Have faith."

"What are you talking about?" Fatima said from the door. "Who is this Levi?"

"Give in now and you give in always," Habiba said softly. "I'd like to think I gave you more backbone than that."

Yasmine explained exactly who Levi was and why they were there. She hadn't planned to share her decision to leave so quickly, but like her grandmother said, this was no time to back down. Fatima's body was stiff, her face a mask of fury. A small part of Yasmine had hoped that her mother would understand and embrace her. That, though, was not Fatima Hassani's way.

"You would bring shame on your family like this?" she asked.

"Careful what you say, Fatima." Habiba's warning didn't change her daughter's expression.

"You have always put too many ideas in their heads," Fatima said to her mother. "Zara will be coming home so we can keep an eye on her."

"Zara received a scholarship to Oxford, so she'll be leaving as well. As for shame, love isn't something to be ashamed of," Yasmine said.

"Then I have no children." Fatima turned and left.

It was only then that Yasmine saw her father standing outside.

"Go, and be happy, but don't forget to come and say goodbye." He put his arms around her when she went outside. "I will keep your friend in my prayers, and no matter what, you can call me if you need me." His kindness had always been a buoy for her, and he'd pushed both her and Zara to finish university and go as far as they could in life.

"Thank you, Papa." She put her arms around him and cried until she felt better. When she let him go, she saw a doctor in the doorway removing his surgical cap.

"Miss Hassani?"

"Yes. Is Levi okay?"

"She'll be fine. It'll take a while for the bones to mend, but it could've been much worse. Levi is in recovery now. You can go in and see her in a couple of hours." The doctor smiled before going back through the double doors.

"Come on, and let's get you something to eat," Jadda said.

Yasmine forced herself to eat something to appease her grandmother, but she didn't feel like the world was right again until she entered the room where Levi slept. When she touched Levi's hand, Levi opened her eyes, and Yasmine wanted to weep from relief.

"Don't cry, love." Levi raised the hand on her uninjured side and touched Yasmine's face. "I'm going to be okay. We're going to be okay."

"You need to stop doing this," Yasmine said, sitting on the bed. "You keep scaring me."

"I didn't plan on this, but it assures me there's something there." Levi tugged Yasmine's hand, and she brought her face closer. "Are you okay?"

"I am now. We'll owe Nabil our first child for coming to our rescue, but he was the only person I could think to call." She laid her head on Levi's chest and exhaled. The weight of her fear fell away when she felt the strong body under her. "Why does this keep happening?"

"We're going to find out, I promise you that." Nabil entered without knocking. "There's a man in a secured room who's going to tell me, but I have to report it to MI6 first. Without the knowledge or consent of our government, he brought men here to do harm to tourists and to our citizens. There's nothing the British can tell me that will explain that away. The strange thing is, someone else killed them. None of you had weapons, right?" He stepped close to the bed and held his hand out. "Nabil Talbi."

"Levi Montbard, and thank you so much, sir. We owe you a debt." Levi took his hand and smiled. "And none of us were armed."

"You won't owe me anything if you promise to take care of my good friend." Nabil winked in her direction and moved to sit. "What can you tell me about this, Levi? Did you hire security? It's not often you find two men dangling from rocks with large holes in their skulls."

Levi provided all the information she could. "The only man I could identify is Baggio Brutos, and he was working for the Church, or I think he was. I don't know what's out there, but they're trying to either steal it or destroy it."

"When you go back out there, you won't be going alone. No one will impede your operation, and this won't happen again." Nabil shook Levi's hand again and kissed Yasmine's cheek. "There's one more person who wanted to stop by."

Yasmine sat up straighter, having no clue who that might be.

When Nabil opened the door, she was glad to see her cousin Ahmed. He was the son of her mother's brother, and he'd always been a good friend to her and Zara. He'd gone to work for the government and had flourished. Any antiquity or collectible found in the country was Ahmed's responsibility.

"Who knew you were this exciting?" Ahmed teased Yasmine. "And why didn't you call me? I have a security detail when it comes to things like this, though I doubt there's anything out there to secure."

"We might have to bet on that," Levi said, laughing. "How are you, Ahmed?"

"You know each other?" Yasmine glanced between them.

"Ahmed is one of my government contacts in Morocco. How do you know him?" Levi's eyelids were starting to droop.

"She's my cousin, but we'll talk about that later. Go to sleep," Ahmed said.

Levi gave in to the exhaustion and drugs they'd given her, and Yasmine never let go of her hand. "Did my mother send you to talk sense into me?" she asked in Arabic.

"My father gave me the same lecture the day I introduced him to my special friend. I don't advertise it so I'm not stoned to death, but I'm not going to live my life to make someone else happy. It makes me happy that you won't either."

Ahmed had always been a tad effeminate, so the news didn't shock her, but it was refreshing to hear that she'd have more allies within her family. "Levi changed so much for me."

He smiled before turning serious once again. "I can imagine. Nabil filled me in. When you go back out there, I and a few of my team will come with you. You'll both get credit for the find, but you know we'll have to catalog everything."

"I just want to live to see it, and I don't want anything else to happen to Levi." Keeping Levi whole was her only focus. "I need her to live so she can hear the answer to a question she asked me."

CHAPTER TWENTY-FOUR

Two days later, with her arm in a brace for the chipped bones in her shoulder, Levi convinced Yasmine she was fit to travel. "With enough pain meds we can try again."

"We're only going for a few days and that's it." Yasmine had her hands on her hips and appeared to be laying down the law.

As their group of five vehicles approached the arch in the rock cliffs, Ahmed listened as Levi explained the clues that had brought them to that particular spot. She exited the SUV and stood in the same spot where she'd been shot to study the rock formation she'd been thinking about from the moment she woke up.

"It's solid rock, Levi," Ahmed said.

"It is, but this has to be it." She turned around, looked out to the desert, and thought of the pattern of the tree of life. From the gate or circle of kingdom, the branch of victory and eternity was the first branch to the left. If she could identify the location of the crown, the six branches that remained, three on each side, could be determined by measuring between the two points. In the distance was one rock that appeared to be the beginning of the range behind them.

"Did you bring the surveying tools I asked you for?" she asked Ahmed.

They set them up, and the others volunteered to carry the flags to where the tree branches would be. Madelena held the flag that marked the answer to the clue. There was nothing out of the ordinary at that spot, but Levi wasn't ready to give up. The men began to dig.

"Wait," Levi said when one of the men dug up a rock with a small Arabic symbol carved into it. She handed it to Yasmine and hoped it wasn't too worn to make out.

"Vengeance," Yasmine said and turned it over. "And love."

It took another four feet before they hit the void in the rock that might've been visible hundreds of years before. The space was covered by wood planks that had held up well in the dry climate. Levi carefully went down the ladder they'd put in the hole, followed by Yasmine, and waited for the men to remove the cover. Her flashlight beam illuminated a large cavern filled with everything from gold to scrolls. The first trunk she opened yielded a stack of books that made her think this would be the find of her lifetime if only for the information, let alone the amount of wealth surrounding them.

"Can you believe it?" Yasmine asked.

"No," Levi said, staring at a portrait someone had painted on the inside lid of the trunk. They were much older in this depiction, but it was André and Farah. This time they were surrounded by four other people, and she couldn't wait to find out who they were. "We did it."

"You found them, love, and you'll get the credit."

"You and Zara are just as responsible, and I'll make sure and tell the king that." She kissed Yasmine where no one could see her before calling Ahmed down.

"Allah be praised," he said when he looked around the cave.

"You can start boxing this up, and we'll start going through it once it's all safe." She'd paid more physically for this search than any other, but it had been worth it. Whatever André and Farah had to teach them wouldn't be lost in history. "This will be a good addition to the national museum, but I want total access to everything first."

"Don't insult our friendship by suggesting I'd cut you out. Let's get all this packed before I get a rash from all this sand." Ahmed rolled his eyes and kept barking orders.

Levi stood in the center of the space with Yasmine and watched what she assumed was André and Farah's life's work. "You ready for this, love?" she asked Yasmine.

"With you I'm ready for anything."

"Didn't I ask you a question recently?" They'd been swept up in what had happened, and, planning to come back here, she hadn't pushed Yasmine.

"You did, and I answered. It's not my fault someone shot you and you didn't hear me. You're going to have to ask again." Yasmine left and climbed the ladder they'd lowered into the hole. "Only think romantic setting," she yelled down to her. "And this isn't it."

"I guess I have some more hunting to do."

❖

The large room that Ahmed had designated for the find was full. Levi sat at the main table and worked with him to catalogue the books and scrolls. His team was handling everything else, of which there was an incredible amount to catalogue. From the expressions on her family members' faces every time they finished another day of work, they'd found heaven on earth.

Levi and Ahmed had started with what most people considered treasure. There were plenty of mint condition Templar coins that had been stored in barrels, and an equal number of silver coins, but it was only a small percentage of the total the Templars supposedly had.

"Finding all this gives credence that there's a large stash still out there," she said to Ahmed. She glanced at her watch again and wondered what was keeping Yasmine.

"Stop worrying." Ahmed pointed to the pile of coins in front of her. "She's talking with the university today, so I hope you're serious about the promises you made her. Giving up the position she worked hard for is serious."

"Your cousin is it for me. You're welcome to come visit us whenever you like if you want to keep tabs on me."

"I doubt anyone needs to keep tabs on you, my love." Yasmine had entered from the back door, and she put her arms around Levi from behind. "Want to stop playing with the money and get to the important stuff?"

"I was waiting for you."

"You two are disgusting, but don't ever change," Ahmed said. He stopped to take a call. "Levi, you have a guest. Do you want to meet him somewhere else?"

"Who is it?"

"Someone named Graham Tomkins, he said he's a friend of Cristian Bacon."

"My old college professor?" Levi wondered how Cristian knew she was there. "Could you have him escorted back?"

When the guest arrived, Ahmed stepped out to give them some privacy. Graham Tomkins didn't look familiar, but he had a kind face. "Dr. Montbard, it's a pleasure to meet you. Cristian sends his regards."

"Do you work with him? I haven't seen Cristian since his retirement, but not for lack of trying. He's been keeping a low profile."

She picked a spot well away from the temptations in the room and waved him to sit. "What can I do for you?"

"Just this once, Cristian and Bartholomew Layton gave me permission to come out of the shadows." The young man kept his eyes on her face but glanced at Yasmine as well.

"I'm not following."

"I've been following you since you left New Orleans." Her back came off the chair as she prepared to place herself between Yasmine and whoever this guy was. He held up his hands to placate her. "I'm sorry. Cristian knew you were on to something big, but he also knew when Baggio Brutos showed up, a certain wing of the Church would try to keep it buried. All I've done is to help you along the way. The two men who were climbing down to hurt your family were dealt with by us."

"'Us,'" she said, cocking her head slightly. Brutos wore his allegiance proudly in the form of a lapel pin, but Graham took a more permanent route. A fleur-de-lis was inked proudly on his forearm. "I didn't think the Priory existed any longer."

"Our commitment to truth is our life's work. Bringing things into the light even when they are painful only serves to further our understanding of our past and future."

"I had no idea, but tell Cristian thank you for sending you. Whatever these secrets are, it must scare the hell out of someone."

"It was a pleasure to meet you both, and you're welcome. I'd appreciate it if you didn't share what I said with anyone outside your family. Spending years in a Moroccan jail isn't in my plans, though your country is beautiful." He glanced at Yasmine as he said this.

"I have so many questions," Levi said when he stood.

"When you go home, Cristian said to call him. He'll be happy to answer anything you like. Until then, we are anxious to see what you found."

"That was totally bizarre," Levi said when they were alone with Ahmed again.

"It was, but come on." Yasmine took her good hand and led her to a table with a number of journals and scrolls detailing everything from daily church life and financial accounts to the lives of Templars on the run. While Levi worked with Ahmed, Yasmine had started on the journals Farah had written. From what they could tell, Farah was the writer in the relationship, but she had also written plenty from André's point of view, probably dictated to her as they journeyed together.

"Did you find anything new?"

"Maybe I wanted you to come over here and hold my hand."
Yasmine smiled, and Levi was ready to head back to the hotel. "Hold
that thought, love, and sit. I think I found what you've been waiting to
hear." Yasmine began to read.

❖

The years have come like a rush of wind carrying
happiness into my life. We traveled as fast as we could after
leaving André's home with the archives his father had kept,
along with all the treasure we could carry, as well as the
people who followed us. Once we were back with our village
and my family, we had to stay vigilant for those who still
hunted us. As time passed, fewer of those came and we lived
our lives following the water and the people in our village.

Death came to my beloved grandmother and eventually
to my parents, but through it all André stood by me and my
siblings. When my father died, the people elected André
our new leader. With that came respect, responsibility, and
a family. Two orphaned girls who joined us came to us as a
blessing and brought us the one thing André and I thought we
would never have—a family of our own. Layla and Yasmine
have grown into strong women who love their father more
than life. Their children will be leaders one day because of
the foundation we have given them.

What brought André into my life turned out to be a
huge betrayal of all she believed. That a king and a pope
would scheme to kill good men for their gold is a story as
old as time, but there is always hope man will evolve from
such things. This time, though, greed and evil won the battle
against the army of God, as André referred to her brothers.
That part of our lives is over, and now our faith lies in each
other.

Search through the papers and scrolls André has left
behind, and you will find the map the Church and France
created to kill off the Templars. What they shared with the
world was all a lie, and their true intent was to grab power
and gold. They cannot dispute what was written by their own

hand. The truth will survive no matter how long it takes to come to light.

After the tragedies of the pope's action against the Templars, André has pledged to share the truth with all who would listen, and save it for future generations. Clement's order killed hundreds, but many Templars like André survived. The pope moved the seat of the Church to France and took André's lands as his home. His presence tainted the land André loved, but the pope's reward for all this treachery came swiftly after the last Grand Master Jacque de Molay was burned at the stake. The pope died a month later. There was never proof of the deed, but Clement's death came at the hands of someone close to him who wanted the power of the papacy.

Poison was used to usher in a new pope, who tried even harder to find the treasure that disappeared with the Templars. The small portion André had, we buried with the help of my brothers in this place that held the pages of our lives. Once both of us are dead, it will be sealed forever and buried along with so many of our secrets.

Let our lives serve as a warning to those who seek too much power. They rely on the old ways of killing and greed to take what they want. Our daughters know how to fight and will never lie down for anyone trying to take what is rightfully theirs. André has made it so. Never again will André or our children know that kind of pain.

We are bone and dust now, but my hope is that our words survive the years. Find us now in your dreams. For proof we were here, search close to where we hid our treasures, and there you will find us. Search where the sun makes its descent. We lie under the branch of serenity.

May Allah's blessing be upon you.

Farah Sonnac, 1349

"They named their daughter Yasmine," Yasmine said in awe. "I wish they'd kept up their family tree so we could find their descendants now."

"The best part of that story is the date. They had a long life together." Levi shifted in her seat and took Yasmine's hand. "That's a good sign, don't you think?"

"I have a feeling you and André would've been good friends, and I don't need long-dead people to know I'll be with you for the rest of my life."

"Do you think Ahmed will mind if I kiss you right now?" Levi asked, bringing her face closer.

"Ahmed, can you find something in the back corner of the room for me?" Yasmine asked, and Ahmed got the hint and turned around.

"I love you," Levi said before Yasmine erased the distance between them and pressed her lips to Levi's. It was nice that Yasmine had lost some of her shyness and initiated things like this. "Will you go out with me tonight?"

"She can't go anywhere with you tonight," Ahmed said without turning around. "It's Jadda's birthday, and she's not missing it. Jadda postponed it because you were hurt. You're also expected, Levi, and don't kill my aunt by proposing to Yasmine in front of the family. Tomorrow is out too since we're expected at the palace for an international news conference."

"For the find? But we haven't finished going through all this stuff yet." It was going to take more than a year to get through all of it, and Levi wasn't thrilled about having to leave it all behind.

"Stop making that sourpuss face and wait until tomorrow. If there's one person in the kingdom who will give your future wife whatever she wants, it's Nabil Talbi. He won't let you down."

They headed to Yasmine's apartment so she could change after Levi had changed into a summer suit. Levi whistled when Yasmine came out in a beautifully embroidered djellaba. "You're beautiful," she said, holding Yasmine's hand.

"You make me feel beautiful, and I'm so lucky you're my escort. You're going to be the most handsome thing there."

They took a cab to a nice-sized home in the medina. Levi could tell it was an older dwelling, but it was well maintained, and from experience, the plain exterior usually gave way to a gorgeous interior. When they stepped inside and removed their shoes, she saw she was right. The tile and woodwork were stunning. It must've been a great place to grow up with its open main courtyard.

"Welcome to my home," Yasmine's father Kareem said, holding his hand out to her.

Levi didn't hesitate to take it and complimented him on the house. Places like this didn't look this good without a lot of work.

"How are you feeling?" He pointed to the brace that kept her left arm close to her chest.

"I'm getting better by the day. I give all the credit to my excellent nurses," she said as Zara came and gave them both hugs. "Can I get a tour?"

Kareem appeared pleased she'd asked. "Yes, please. I would like it if you visited often."

Levi walked off with him, glancing back at Yasmine, who lost her smile when her mother joined her. The conversation they were having wasn't loud but it was intense, from the look of it. Levi was about to walk back when Kareem shook his head.

"That battle has waged much longer than you have been here. I find it better to let them have at it." He led her to the kitchen and poured her a glass of wine. "Do you love my daughter?"

"I think traditions are universal when it comes to some things. In the United States, I can marry her, and that's what I'd like to do because I love her that much. I'd also like your blessing."

"Are you asking me for her hand?" He smiled, which made her relax.

"Yes, sir. I am."

"I hope you know how alike she and her mother are. They are like oil and water only because they are so passionate about their beliefs. Keep that in mind if you have children."

He opened his arms to hug her, and the move surprised her more than finding André and Farah's cache in the middle of the Sahara.

"You seem shocked."

"To be honest, I am. Does that mean you approve?"

"My children are strong and independent women, so I won't stand in their way when it comes to what makes them happy. For them to truly be happy, I realize they will have to leave us and Morocco. Just remember we are here when you take her away."

"You have my promise, and my gratitude." She gave him a one-arm hug and laughed when he had to push onto his toes to kiss her cheek. "I'd also like you and Mrs. Hassani to join us tomorrow. Nabil is providing a plane to Rabat and the palace."

"Tomorrow is for you and my daughters," he said, shaking his head. "The pride I have watching them fly is boundless, but I don't want to be in the way."

"You're welcome to come, and thank you for all you said."

"He's a wise man," Yasmine's grandmother said as she joined them. "Get out there and start changing my daughter's mind about all this. Then you can help me celebrate that I am not dead yet."

The rest of the night was fun as they sat with the rest of the family and ate. Fatima didn't soften but didn't give Yasmine any more trouble. When they got back to the hotel, Levi helped Yasmine out of her dress and Yasmine returned the favor, slowing taking Levi's shirt off, her fingertips trailing over Levi's skin and making her shiver. The injury she'd sustained was going to be a pain in the ass for another couple of weeks or so, and she was grateful Yasmine seemed to enjoy taking care of her. Dressing her and undressing her was always done with a smile and plenty of touching.

"Did you have a nice time?" Yasmine asked when they got into bed.

"I like your father, and your mom will eventually come around." She lay flat on her back, trying not to move her arm too much since she'd removed the immobilizer. "I'm happy they postponed her party until I was able to go. That should mean something."

"My mother may never come around, as you say, but I can't go back." Yasmine smoothed lotion over Levi's scar with gentle fingers.

"But will you have any regrets?" That scared her more than anything.

"No," Yasmine said firmly. "I want you to—" The phone rang before Yasmine could finish, and she moved to answer it. "Yes?" She listened and finally said, "Please send him."

"Send who?" Levi asked, sitting up naked.

"Darling, please find your sleep pants and a robe. Nabil is on his way."

Yasmine closed the door to the bedroom and joined Levi on the sofa in the suite's sitting room. Meeting him in her pajamas hadn't been in her plans. Nabil, as always, appeared wide awake.

"I'm sorry to disturb you, but I've already updated His Majesty, and he wanted you informed." Nabil accepted a cup of mint tea from the attendant who'd escorted him in.

"Do we need to reschedule the press conference tomorrow?"

"No, but the Vatican has been informed of the intelligence we were able to get from their man Lawrence Royce. He finally broke when we promised not to have him executed."

"Their man? What are you talking about?" Levi asked.

"Royce and the men he brought with him were MI6 agents, and the other dead man was a priest. None of them had permission to carry out any operation on our soil. There will be no extradition now that the British have disavowed Royce and the others. We are still investigating who shot the other two men." Nabil crossed his legs and reached for one of the oranges the hotel left in the rooms every day. "You two seem to have found so much more than a treasure in the desert."

"Explain, please," Yasmine said, placing her hand on Levi's forearm.

"Levi, you mentioned a man named Baggio Brutos," Nabil said, and she nodded. "He does indeed work for the Church, or more precisely, for Cardinal Richard Chadwick. For years he's been tasked by Chadwick to find things and destroy or collect them for his own pleasure. Brutos, though, isn't the only man on Chadwick's payroll. Royce was also working for him, and his assignment was to kill everyone he deemed necessary to keep the secrets you were trying to bring to light."

"Why?" None of this made sense. The Church had been Machiavellian in its long history, but those days were long gone.

"Chadwick had ambition but also knew his family's history. Somewhere in that history was another holy man who poisoned a pope in order to take his place. Whatever you were after, so was he, but only because of what's in those archives."

Levi looked at the mounds of scrolls and books. Somewhere in there was evidence that a pope's poisoner was related to a cardinal today. It wasn't a secret anyone but Chadwick would really care about, but then, the Church didn't like proof of scandal. Whispers were one thing, facts were another, but in this case the scandal involved a serving cardinal. A man willing to kill to get what he wanted. "Did Royce mention Pope Clement V?"

"We're still questioning Royce, but he had documents that detailed Chadwick's plan to kill the current pope and persuade the other cardinals to give him the white miter, just as his ancestor did. We've sent the information to the proper authorities in Rome, so Chadwick and some man named Ransley Hastings have been taken in by the authorities. Tomorrow we want to talk about the find, but we'd like to omit anything about Royce and the other dead men."

"Did the Church talk you into that?" Levi asked.

"We're not keeping the information to ourselves forever, but we still don't know all the people working with Chadwick. He's not that close to the pope and doesn't have cause to get close to him often. If this plan is in play, there has to be someone else who's ready to kill one of the world's most prominent religious leaders. The politics of the Vatican are well known, but it's not often outsiders get to play a part in their game." Nabil smiled and placed his cup down. "This is why our great king is strict when it comes to fanatics. People like that only serve to inflame, not help."

"We'll be happy to follow Ahmed's lead tomorrow," Levi said. "All I want is access to the material."

"I wouldn't worry about that. You have someone I trust implicitly working for you."

Nabil excused himself, and Yasmine closed and locked the door. Once they were alone, she dropped her robe on a chair and stripped off her nightgown. "That's enough for one night, don't you think?"

"I do, but not for everything."

❖

"Welcome," King Driss VI said as he took Levi's hand. "And you." He offered Yasmine his hand, and she bowed before taking it like Levi had. "Yasmine, our friend Nabil tells me what an asset you are to us." He then turned to Zara. "And you, I hope, will follow your sister in service."

"Thank you, Your Majesty," Yasmine said. Her ears felt hot. She'd never been this nervous.

"Ahmed has shown me what you discovered and says there's possibly more out there. I find that amazing. I've always thought the Sahara was a treasure all its own, but I never imagined that it held something like this." Driss motioned to the table behind him. Ahmed had brought a small number of the things they'd found for His Majesty's private viewing.

"Yes, Your Majesty," Levi said. She picked up a coin and handed it to the king. For a brief moment he seemed like a small boy. "Please, sire, keep this as a token of our thanks for letting us search." Levi picked up two more coins and pressed those into his hand. "For your children. The rest of this should go to your national museum."

"May I call you Levi?"

"Please, Your Majesty." Levi bowed her head again and smiled.

"What you have done is a good thing. We shall learn much of our shared history with this find. I'm looking forward to your full report."

"Thank you, sire."

"Levi, are we ready?" She nodded, and they walked out to a grand room where a larger sampling of what they'd found was laid out. "Welcome, everyone," Driss said as he brought the crowd of journalists to attention.

Yasmine knew Ahmed and others had sold this on the scale of finding a royal tomb in Egypt. "This is incredible," she whispered to Levi.

They answered questions, and Levi spoke passionately about the long road they had traveled to find everything and the lengths Farah and André had taken to hide it. There were plenty of questions from the reporters, proving Yasmine's point that the Templars even now garnered a lot of attention. A woman from one of the major news sources asked the most questions, and from the look of her, Yasmine thought she wanted a private interview with Levi that had nothing to do with treasure. The woman wasn't blatant, but jealousy was as new an experience as finding love with Levi.

"Thank you for your answers," the king said, bringing things to a close.

"Yes, thank you, Dr. Montbard," Ahmed said in his capacity with the government. "We look forward to going through all this material before it goes into the museum. Our beloved monarch is allowing the find to leave the country until the research is done. I will accompany Dr. Montbard and Dr. Hassani to the United States as soon as we are all ready to travel, and I will bring the treasure back with me when I return."

Once they were back in the first room with King Driss, Levi took his hand when he offered it and simply held it. "Thank you so much. You have my word that you will be happy with the story this will tell."

"I'm sure I will be, and we will compensate you for your work. You have worked hard to find all this, and I can't imagine having to let it go if it was my discovery." He smiled at Yasmine and took another coin off the table. "To bring *you* luck, but I think you have more than enough."

"Yes, Your Majesty," Yasmine said, lowering her head.

He nodded and waved them off. "Good luck."

They'd been dismissed.

Their car drove through the gates of the palace, but the driver took a right and headed to another palace entrance. They stopped at a long galley walkway that seemed to head into the palace and Levi said, "Ahmed told me that there is a room in here that was built to be the sitting room for the number one wife. She would go there, wait for her love, and enjoy this garden, but her private space was more special since it was full of orchids."

"Are we supposed to be here?" Yasmine squeezed Levi's hand but followed her anyway.

A couple of staff pointed them in the right direction and they reached the room. It was tiled in royal blue, and the wood beams were masterpieces. Levi had always loved this type of architecture, but this was the most gorgeous example of it she'd ever seen.

"There are really very few pictures of this palace out in the world, but this room was reserved for romantic moments between the sovereigns. It was built years ago, so I imagine these walls have heard plenty of ways to tell someone you love them."

Levi led Yasmine to a window overlooking the garden. The arched openings that flanked the wider arch were beautifully crafted, but Yasmine couldn't take her eyes off Levi.

"So many ways and so many promises whispered here between lovers is what makes this space so special."

"I think you're right. I'm sure not every romance was perfect between the people who called this home, but I'd hope they were." Yasmine smiled at Levi, her heart nearly bursting with how happy she was.

Levi dropped to a knee and took Yasmine's hand. "History and finding it have been my obsession for as long as I can remember, but I can't say that anymore. Now I spend a lot of time thinking of what would be romantic to a woman who also loves history."

"You do?" Yasmine was having trouble hearing Levi because the blood was rushing in her ears. For most of her life she'd avoided being trapped in something she didn't want, but now she desperately needed Levi to say the words and make lifelong promises.

"Yes, but sometimes the best way to honor history is to build it with the woman I love. I want there to be a room filled with that history when we're done."

"There's one of those in our house back in New Orleans," Yasmine said, blinking rapidly.

"Yes, there is, but I want you to know how much I'm going to cherish that history and you. You're my love, and I want you to be my wife." Levi opened a box with a beautiful ring in it. "This was the most romantic place I could think of, and I wanted to add my own words of love to this place. I love you, Yasmine Hassani, and I want to spend my life with you. Will you marry me?"

"Yes," she said. "I love you so much." All her fears of marriage, of being tied to someone, the dread of giving up what she loved for the rest of her life vanished in an instant. Levi was who she wanted, and she was gaining so much more than she'd ever have to give up. It filled her with a sense of belonging and wonder she never knew existed. "This is so beautiful," she said as the ring slipped onto her finger. "How did you arrange this?"

"Ahmed did the talking for me. I don't care what he said or how he got King Driss to agree, but I wanted it to be special. I hope this was okay."

"I said yes while you were bleeding in the desert. You could have asked in the shower this morning and my answer would've still been the same." Yasmine smiled against Levi's lips before she gave in to the kiss. "I believe the American saying is *you knocked it out of the park.*"

"Thank you, honey." Levi spent a few minutes kissing her. "Are you ready? I doubt they'll let us spend the night."

Yasmine put her arms around Levi's waist and pressed the side of her head to Levi's chest. "Thank you for making this so special, and to answer your question, I am ready. I'm ready for everything."

EPILOGUE

New Orleans, six months later

The research room was open, and Levi put the last journal back on the shelf. Yasmine was still sleeping upstairs. Ahmed was living across the street where Yasmine and Zara had first stayed. Their work was almost done, and the complete story of Clement V and the man he had in common with the king of France was all in the journals.

How André had gathered so much information about the political inner workings of the Church was amazing, but it all rang true. The scrolls that contained that information had to have been started by André's father, but she'd finished them. Clement sounded like a weak man easily manipulated, and the king had taken advantage by placing a confidant with the pope. The simple village priest sounded so wise, but what he really wanted was to rise out of poverty to the Vatican.

That priest had poisoned Clement once the Templar treasure couldn't be found, no matter how much the king and Church searched. He was rewarded by being burned at the stake like the last Templar grand master. The king's only mercy was letting the priest's two sons and their mother go. They were exiled from France, and the older son, a Chadwick, tried to establish the Catholic Church in England.

He was the first of many Chadwicks who rose through the ranks of the church but never reached the promised land. That was something Cardinal Richard Chadwick was willing to gamble on in this generation by duplicating what his long-ago relative had done. Killing the pope to attain the power he craved wasn't a new idea, but it had almost worked.

The British authorities had found all the evidence they needed to prove what Chadwick had set in motion. All that scheming had ended in him being defrocked. The pope himself had issued a loss of clerical state, which was as good as a pink slip. Whatever god Chadwick believed in wouldn't save him or Ransley from spending the rest of their days in prison. While Chadwick was the planner and boss, Ransley had provided the money in exchange for recognition and a title.

Levi had to laugh at what Chadwick had in common with that long-ago ancestor. His girlfriend and three children would hopefully let the family tradition of killing religious leaders go as they went on without the Cardinal.

The paintings of Farah and André were still on the wall, and she stared at them often. "It all comes full circle, doesn't it?" She raised her coffee cup in their direction. "You didn't make it easy, but you helped me find what you shared."

She smiled as two arms circled her neck. Yasmine kissed her neck and bit her earlobe. "I don't like waking up alone."

"You looked so peaceful I didn't want to disturb you." She pulled Yasmine into her lap. "I did keep you up late last night."

"I danced more than you did." Yasmine reached into Levi's robe and pinched her nipple. Their time together had brought out the type of playmate Levi had only dreamed of. In just a couple of months they would stand before their family and friends and exchange vows, but that would change very little. She was already committed to Yasmine for life.

"You did, and you also came more than I did." That beautiful blush heated Yasmine's face, but she kissed her anyway when Levi touched her cheek.

"The things you say to me."

"That's true, I'm an infidel, but one who loves you very much."

"Do you mean it?" Yasmine combed her hair back and kissed her again.

"You know I do. I heard from Ibrahim. He said a small crew can deliver everything we want." She kissed Yasmine again and slipped her hand up her leg. "Are you sure you don't want to honeymoon somewhere else?"

"I want to find them and give them peace, even if that means leaving them where they lie."

They were leaving after their ceremony to spend a few weeks back in the Sahara. If they found the branch of serenity on the tree of life, they would also find André and Farah. It was probably only their graves, but you never knew. There might be one more secret Farah had decided to hide that would lead them to the rest of the Templar treasure.

"Will you read it to me one more time?"

Yasmine reached for the translation she'd done of Farah's account of the day she married André. The next day they set off for France, but they'd had that one night under the stars. The way Farah weaved the story of how happy they were made Yasmine wish time would speed up so she could start her life as Levi's wife.

"I can't wait to speak the words and for you to claim what belongs to you," she said. "Her prayers were answered. I have found what she did, and it isn't wrong."

"There's never going to be anyone else, love, and I can't wait to find all the treasures still out there." Levi stood with Yasmine in her arms and carried her back upstairs. "Whatever comes next, I can't wait to share it with you."

"I know exactly what comes next, my darling, and it's not the kind of thing I'll ever write about," Yasmine teased.

"Not even if I give you incentive?" Levi laid Yasmine on the bed and smiled.

"Forget the scrolls and stories and make love to me."

"That I can do."

About the Author

Ali Vali is the author of the Devil series, the Forces series, and the Call series. She's written numerous standalones, her newest being *A Woman to Treasure*.

Ali currently lives outside New Orleans, where she enjoys cheering LSU and trying new restaurants.

Books Available From Bold Strokes Books

A Woman to Treasure by Ali Vali. An ancient scroll isn't the only treasure Levi Montbard finds as she starts her hunt for the truth—all she has to do is prove to Yasmine Hassani that there's more to her than an adventurous soul. (978-1-63555-890-6)

Before. After. Always. by Morgan Lee Miller. Still reeling from her tragic past, Eliza Walsh has sworn off taking risks, until Blake Navarro turns her world right-side up, making her question if falling in love again is worth it. (978-1-63555-845-6)

Bet the Farm by Fiona Riley. Lauren Calloway's luxury real estate sale of the century comes to a screeching halt when dairy farm heiress, and one-night stand, Thea Boudreaux calls her bluff. (978-1-63555-731-2)

Cowgirl by Nance Sparks. The last thing Aren expects is to fall for Carol. Sharing her home is one thing, but sharing her heart means sharing the demons in her past and risking everything to keep Carol safe. (978-1-63555-877-7)

Give In to Me by Elle Spencer. Gabriela Talbot never expected to sleep with her favorite author—certainly not after the scathing review she'd given Whitney Ainsworth's latest book. (978-1-63555-910-1)

Hidden Dreams by Shelley Thrasher. A lethal virus and its resulting vision send Texan Barbara Allan and her lovely guide, Dara, on a journey up Cambodia's Mekong River in search of Barbara's mother's mystifying past. (978-1-63555-856-2)

In the Spotlight by Lesley Davis. For actresses Cole Calder and Eris Whyte, their chance at love runs out fast when a fan's adoration turns to obsession. (978-1-63555-926-2)

Origins by Jen Jensen. Jamis Bachman is pulled into a dangerous mystery that becomes personal when she learns the truth of her origins as a ghost hunter. (978-1-63555-837-1)

Unrivaled by Radclyffe. Zoey Cohen will never accept second place in matters of the heart, even when her rival is a career, and Declan Black has nothing left to give of herself or her heart. (978-1-63679-013-8)

A Fae Tale by Genevieve McCluer. Dovana comes to terms with her changing feelings for her lifelong best friend and fae, Roze. (978-1-63555-918-7)

Accidental Desperados by Lee Lynch. Life is clobbering Berry, Jaudon, and their long romance. The arrival of directionless baby dyke MJ doesn't help. Can they find their passion again—and keep it? (978-1-63555-482-3)

Always Believe by Aimée. Greyson Walsden is pursuing ordination as an Anglican priest. Angela Arlingham doesn't believe in God. Do they follow their vocation or their hearts? (978-1-63555-912-5)

Courage by Jesse J. Thoma. No matter how often Natasha Parsons and Tommy Finch clash on the job, an undeniable attraction simmers just beneath the surface. Can they find the courage to change so love has room to grow? (978-1-63555-802-9)

I Am Chris by R Kent. There's one saving grace to losing everything and moving away. Nobody knows her as Chrissy Taylor. Now Chris can live who he truly is. (978-1-63555-904-0)

The Princess and the Odium by Sam Ledel. Jastyn and Princess Aurelia return to Venostes and join their families in a battle against the dark force to take back their homeland for a chance at a better tomorrow. (978-1-63555-894-4)

The Queen Has a Cold by Jane Kolven. What happens when the heir to the throne isn't a prince or a princess? (978-1-63555-878-4)

The Secret Poet by Georgia Beers. Agreeing to help her brother woo Zoe Blake seemed like a good idea to Morgan Thompson at first...until she realizes she's actually wooing Zoe for herself... (978-1-63555-858-6)

You Again by Aurora Rey. For high school sweethearts Kate Cormier and Sutton Guidry, the second chance might be the only one that matters. (978-1-63555-791-6)

Love's Falling Star by B.D. Grayson. For country music megastar Lochlan Paige, can love conquer her fear of losing the one thing she's worked so hard to protect? (978-1-63555-873-9)